Take Your Partners
By Naomi K. Bembridge

Acknowledgements: I would like to very sincerely thank Mr. Toshio Tachibana, brother of the late, very gifted artist, Teruko Tachibana, for permission to use her beautiful art work for the cover picture of this book. This is just one of many of her breathtaking paintings of dancers, and I am honoured to have been allowed to use one that expresses the beauty and elegance of dancers and dancing so well.

This novel is a work of fiction. Names and characters are the product of the author's imagination and any resemblance to actual persons, living or dead, is entirely coincidental.

Copyright © By The Bay Books Ltd 2019

Chapter One
The pretty little goldfinch

Diana Wharton watched her friends weave unsteadily to their taxi, she gave them a final wave, giggled as Sheryn narrowly avoided a bush, before they all made it into the cab. It had been a good evening and, as planned, it had cheered her up. But something came into her mind as she thought back over the evening of gossip, laughter, take-away pizza and wine, now what was it?

'Ah yes, we agreed to go to dance classes.'

Well, it was more a case of the other three having agreed, and Diana being told she was coming with them.

'I do remember saying yes at one point,' she conceded, 'I shouldn't have had that last glass of wine, ' said Diana sincerely to the mirror.

The woman staring back at her was in her early forties, pretty, but looked tired, a bit on the short side, well, a lot on the short side actually. A mass of curly blond hair, a few wisps of grey, she was quite thin, the girls said too thin, so did her mother. Her glasses always seemed a bit too big for her face, but that's the style she liked. Lovely smile though, one of the girls said Diana reminded her of a goldfinch: 'You're always darting about, got a cheery song, lots of colour, full of life, small and pretty, but frantically searching.' She quite liked that analogy and it did sum her life up.

Diana was divorced, at last. That wasn't why she had needed cheering up, her son, Jacob, had gone to university and it had been this that got her down. They had been talking about it, planning for it, looking forward to it, fretting over it for years, but now he had gone the house felt empty and so did Diana.

She owned, along with the building society, a mid-terrace, Victorian house not far from the centre of the south Wales city of Newport. She was a Newport girl and liked the place, not that she had lived anywhere else, nor had she travelled that much. She had married young and had had Jacob a year after the wedding, thereafter life revolved around him and running the home, but then things seemed to go very wrong.

Her now ex-husband, Elwyn, had left her when Jacob had been six. Like a lot of Welsh lads, he was quite a 'mammy's boy' and that's who he went back to. Diana had never got on with Elwyn's mother, Phyllis, but then again:

'The old cow never wanted to get on with me,' she confided to the mirror.

At first Diana had thought Elwyn would come back after a few weeks, but no, apparently Phyllis needed him. God, what a row they had after he said that! And she and Jacob didn't need him? Looking back, it seemed every conversation with Elwyn since included at least one row, plus some door slamming.

She assumed he would want a divorce, but he made no effort to get one, and so the whole sad situation had dragged on for years. It was only when Phyllis died that Elwyn decided to find someone else. Actually, Diana was sure he would come back to her. Oh, the times she had planned what she would say when he turned up at the door, expecting to be welcomed 'home' and to pick up where they had left off, and to suddenly become a happy family again! That was going to be a brilliant row and she knew she would enjoy it. But she was shocked when he called around, not to say he wanted to come back, but that he had met a 'nice lady' (Elwyn always sounded like he would have been better off living in Edwardian times). He and the nice lady planned to marry, so he wanted a divorce.

That had broken Jacob's heart. Until then he and Elwyn had always had a strong bond, and Elwyn had always been available for his son (except when he came home from school). Elwyn made sure Jacob never wanted for anything personally. However he had been far less help to Diana in keeping a roof over Jacob's head. Though in an odd way he had been a good father, until that night when he said he wanted a divorce. He could not understand why Jacob was so upset. Given Elwyn was a lecturer at a local college he could be unbelievably thick.

It had taken Diana a few weeks to agree to the divorce, not because she still loved Elwyn, that had died after he left her, it was more because she hadn't seen it coming. She had always mentally planned how to tell Elwyn that she didn't want him back. It had never occurred to her that he would find another woman.

Mind you, there was one question she asked herself, and only herself: 'Was it my fault?'

She never heard an answer, so assumed 'no'.

She had a part time job in the Job Centre that had suited her, making sure she was there for Jacob had been all that mattered, but now he was gone. The girls told her that he would be back most weekends, but it hadn't helped. She found herself becoming depressed and hadn't known what to do about it. The girls did. The dancing classes were just part of the grand plan, but it was that item in the plan she now least liked.

She cleared everything away and got ready for bed, she still felt light-headed, but was able to think clearly about the dance classes. Part of her was really keen, but a big part of her really wasn't. She had socialised very little since Elwyn left, and what social life she had, revolved around her colleagues, her neighbours and people she had got to know through Jacob's schools, a nice crowd. Whilst Elwyn had supported her financially, most of her money seemed to go on Jacob or the house. That had never bothered her, and she certainly didn't resent it. The girls said that she had to let Jacob go and find a social life for herself, none of her excuses seemed to work, not that they had in the previous few months either.

She was only recently divorced because the whole process took far longer than either she or Elwyn expected, though most of the problems had been avoidable. Elwyn lost forms time and again. His solicitor looked more like a teenager on work experience rather than a qualified legal mind. Given the mess she had made of Elwyn's case and the fool she made of herself in court, Diana thought she may well be some kind of trainee after all. Mind you, her solicitor wasn't much better, but at least he looked and sounded like a solicitor, most of the time. When the case had been finally settled, Diana took no satisfaction, if anything, she felt empty and lost. At least the divorce proceedings had given her what came close to a hobby.

Elwyn's financial support now came to an end. She had been damn lucky that she was able to increase her hours at the Job Centre, but in the scrabble for extra hours and money, she had to take on a variety of tasks at the Centre she didn't really want or like. At least she was now fairly financially secure and independent, as long as she was very careful, but she wasn't happy.

She lay in bed thinking about how good the evening had been, but now what? As a teenager, she had lots of hobbies and interests, and quite a social life, but a good few of those vanished when she married Elwyn. He became a bore, well, perhaps it was kinder to say that he wasn't much of a socialite once married. That had surprised her at the time. Some hobbies she was looking forward to taking up again, others she no longer had any interest in, but what about learning to dance? She had never learnt to Ballroom dance, it wasn't cool when she was a girl. Yet she loved dancing, but that was in the disco, that was her world before she met Elwyn. She lay quietly staring at the ceiling, and at the crack that she planned to sort out this weekend. She remembered her cousin Andrea, how her mother endlessly talked about Andrea doing dance medals, the marks she got from examiners, the competitions Andrea had won. Diana had thought it funny and teased Andrea about her dancing when they were girls.

'God, Andrea's going to love this! Me going for dancing lessons after all the grief I gave her over it!' she told the crack in the ceiling.

Mind you, Andrea seemed to have a great time when she was a girl: she had wonderful dresses and lots of friends in dancing. She even met her husband at one of the dance classes. Strangely, they had given up dancing soon after they married, she didn't know why…perhaps she would give Andrea a ring one day for a chat.

What would these dance classes be like?

'Perhaps I'll meet Anton du Beke!' she thought out loud, now that was exciting! She was a big fan of "Strictly Come Dancing", so why didn't she fancy learning to dance herself? She didn't know, but like much in her life, this was somehow 'different'.

She reasoned with herself, made excuses, dismissed them, made up new ones and finally fell asleep after she had decided she would go dancing, though she wasn't sure why. Yes she was: she thought she'd meet Anton.

***

Sheryn, Cerys and Anita wouldn't let her get out of it. They came to collect her, there was no way they would trust her to make her own way to the dancing school. She sat in the back of Cerys's car and began to relax (in spite of Cerys's really bad driving) and enjoy a few laughs. She hadn't known what to wear and just hoped she had it right. She hadn't rung Andrea, but she wished she had, if only to ask about what kind of shoes to wear, ah well, these would have to do.

'Hmm, I'm not feeling well,' she said for the third time, it had no effect, the girls ignored her, they knew her too well, it was an excuse to get out of the dance class, it wasn't going to work. Diana decided to try and make the best of it, besides, she might meet Anton.

The dancing school was in an old part of Newport and not that easy to find, though Cerys said she knew the place, she didn't. They had to go around the back of the Victorian theatre, more recently it had been a bingo hall, but it was boarded up and had been for years. However, the entrance to the dancing school was brilliantly lit and seemed welcoming. They hurried in and joined a queue in the corridor. For some reason Diana had thought they would be the only ones. The corridor was very white, the walls were decorated with framed certificates, she idly read them, apparently they were the dance teachers' qualifications…none mentioned Anton. It was only now that Diana wondered just who it was she would dance with. Glancing up and down the queue she could see mainly couples, the only single people were woman, she pointed this out to the girls.

'Oh, there'll be plenty of men to dance with,' assured Sheryn.

'Really, they're in there already are they?' said Diana a bit sarcastically.

Sheryn glanced toward the head of the queue. 'Oh, there are a few lads up the front with no one to dance with, we'll be fine.'

'No there aren't, I may be short, but I can still see there aren't any single men up there'. In fact she was glad there were none for two reasons: firstly, if there was no one to dance with she could go home, and the second reason, she didn't fancy some bloke she'd never met before holding her.

Seconds later the double glass doors opened and everyone shuffled forward.

She knew it was stupid, but she kept expecting to hear Anton's voice. What would he be doing in a small provincial dance school? Besides, it was September and he was in 'Strictly' again. What she did find was an elegantly dressed and over made-up woman behind a red topped pub type table with an impressive cash-box. As the four 'girls' got to the table, they were almost dazzled by the woman's smile.

'Oh hello, I'm Alex! I'm *so* pleased to meet you, now let me take your names.' She picked up an expensive pen, discreetly put on spectacles, presumably hoping no one noticed, and peered at a note book. She took each name, checking spelling, she had to ask Sheryn three times how to spell her name, and yes Cerys was a Welsh name. Finally it was Diana's turn. She was surprised to find herself chatting easily to Alex, who put her at ease instantly, got her laughing, even talking about Andrea.

'Andrea, Andrea who?'

'Andrea Mooney, though she was Andrea Wing before she married.'

'She used to come here for lessons! How wonderful! How is she?' gushed Alex who then went into raptures about Andrea's dancing. 'If you're Andrea's cousin then I'm expecting great things from you!'

Diana was never one to be short of words, 'til now.

'No pressure,' whispered Anita.

They were in a lusciously decorated hall, it seemed much larger than they had expected from the outside. There was a side room with a small dance floor that had a drinks bar, which was very small, a large queue had formed around it. The only person serving was a very thin, elderly woman with ridiculously brown hair and way too much face powder and lipstick, she was almost orange. When it was their turn to be served, they could see she was in her eighties and could only just manage the work behind the busy bar.

'Ello ladies! I'm Ivy, welcome to the school, what'll you 'ave?' She was a bit hard of hearing and filling the order was a challenge for her.

As they walked away from the bar a tall, skinny man with thinning sandy colour hair came up to them.

'Evening, I'm Simon. I'll be teaching you tonight with Alex. So, have you come here as a group with your hubbies?'

He sounded as though he was struggling to be sociable and interested in them, even so, he was a nice chap. Simon was clearly a good deal younger than Alex, who seemed to be in her mid-fifties, though it was hard to tell with all her make-up and elaborately styled and very black, dyed, hair.

'Well, no, we were hoping there'd be someone to dance with tonight,' said Sheryn, glancing around the room.

'See what we can do for you. We normally have a few single gents and I'll dance with you if not. But two of you can learn the man's steps, that'll get you dancing.' And almost at once he moved off to welcome more beginners to the first night of the new season of classes.

The girls laughed at the idea of two of them being 'men', but ten minutes later the class had begun and Anita and Cerys were "the men". Diana danced with Cerys, it had been decided Diana was too short to be a man!

Perhaps Anton wasn't here, but they had a whale of a time and like everyone else, laughed a great deal. The two teachers ran the class very well, made it all fun and soon no one was bothered about going wrong or making a fool of themselves. By the end of the hour they could all make a reasonable fist out of doing basic Waltz and Cha-Cha-Cha, at least they thought so. Diana felt quite pleased with herself.

After the class, they went for a Chinese meal and did a lot more laughing and talking about the class. The girls wanted to know all about Andrea. It embarrassed Diana to realise how little she knew about her cousin these days, let alone that to Alex and Simon, Andrea was some kind of dance goddess. She really would have to give her a ring.

***

The next morning Diana couldn't remember having slept so well in months, or was it years? Hmm, years. Nor could she remember having laughed so much, she had wanted to hate last night and for her friends to have hated it, but now she was looking forward to the next class, Cerys made a good man! It had helped that she hadn't had to dance with a stranger. Simon had helped her with some steps, but once she relaxed and he had got to know them a little, he seemed a nice bloke and didn't make her feel awkward or uncomfortable. When she got up she found muscles she didn't know she had were complaining about having been taught to dance, but they shut up after a while.

On the bus to work, she thought back over the evening and also tried to remember when last she had spoken to Andrea, grimly she realised it was at her aunt's funeral a couple of years back. Mind you, Andrea had left Newport a soon after she had married because of her husband's work…what was his name? She wrote it on a Christmas card every year but she struggled to remember what he looked like. She had met him over the years at family 'do's' and most recently at Andrea's mother's funeral, but no, she couldn't remember his name, and only just thought she remembered what he looked like.

At work, the girls talked about the class and they were all definitely going again next week. Diana wasn't sure whether they really did want to go, or was it just to get her out and into a social life? It didn't matter, she did want to go, it had been fun and no where near as bad as she thought. Shame Anton hadn't been there, never mind, next week perhaps?

That evening she looked through her phone book, she didn't have Andrea's number. She looked through her address book, at least she found Andrea's husband's name neatly printed: Julian. Hmm she used to tease Andrea about being engaged to someone called Julian, not a cool name apparently. But there was a phone number too, but wasn't recognised when she dialled it. She felt guilty about having lost contact with a member of her family, not that she had ever been that close to Andrea, the fact she had been a successful dancer hadn't helped either, she hadn't been cool to know when they were teenagers. Diana cringed at the thought.

She finally got the number from her mum, though it had taken twenty minutes as she had wanted a blow by blow (or should that be step by step?) account of what had happened at the dance class and, of course, whether she had met any nice men (hmm, she never said nice *young* men anymore!). Couldn't really count Cerys as a 'nice man' could you?

Even though she had the number, she found herself making excuses to herself about why she wasn't picking up the phone to call her. Just why was she ringing Andrea anyway, guilt? Dance tips? To pass on Alex and Simon's good wishes? Perhaps a little of each, but also she felt guilty that two strangers knew more about her cousin than she did.

Finally she rang, no answer, oh good! But just as she was about to put the receiver down she heard a voice, it was a man.

'Oh is Andrea there please?'

'Well…umm, I…eh…who shall I say is calling?' The man sounded very formal, she didn't recall what Julian sounded like, was this Andrea's husband? She didn't even remember writing Julian on the Christmas cards, sending one had just become automatic during her busy and worrying years after Elwyn had left.

'Oh, is that Julian?'

'No it isn't,' said the man coldly, 'who is this please?'

'Diana, her cousin, Diana Wharton.'

'Oh, I see…I'll ask her if she can take the call,' this bloke didn't seem to believe her. And if he wasn't Julian, who was he then? She heard him cover the receiver mouth piece, he called something, presumably to Andrea. She heard him put the receiver down. Initially she could hear very distant voices, then nothing. After a few moments she began to wonder if she had been cut off, or left to hang on until she was too bored to wait any longer. Then she heard voices again, a female voice and getting nearer the phone.

'Hello?'

'Hia Andrea, it's me, Diana, Rita's daughter, Diana Wharton, your cousin,' hopefully one of these would help her remember.

There was a long pause as Andrea considered what she had been told. 'Oh, nice to hear from you…is something wrong?'

She probably thought Diana was ringing up to say someone had died!

Diana quickly explained about the dance class, Alex and Simon.

Andrea became very interested then excited. 'They remember me, after all these years?' she sounded tearful.

Within minutes they were chatting as if they had never been out of touch, she wanted to know why she had taken up the classes. 'How's Elwyn getting on learning to dance?'

Diana was shocked to think that Andrea didn't know about the separation, but Andrea didn't know and she was very embarrassed. She hadn't noticed Elwyn's name no longer appeared on her Christmas and birthday cards, they just arrived, were momentarily appreciated then thought no more of. Mind you, it probably wouldn't have hurt Diana to put a note in the card explaining would it! It seemed so long ago she and Elwyn had split, had she actually spread the news as widely as she should? Of course she had! Hmm, perhaps not.

It highlighted how much they had drifted apart, yet as kids they'd spent much of their time together, they were really good friends. But Andrea's dancing, Diana's move to a different school, and her interest in boys had then made them so distant.

'Not a problem, don't worry about it. I'm dancing with one of the girls from work, no spare blokes in the class,' said Diana cheerfully, not revealing how glad she was not to have to dance with some strange man. But she now had to know: 'So, how's Julian?' If that wasn't Julian she was speaking to earlier, then who was it? She knew Andrea had a son, he would be about fourteen, there was no way the man she had spoken to was fourteen.

Andrea didn't speak for several long seconds. 'That's Charles, Julian's brother,' there was a tension in her voice.

'Oh, I see, sorry if I caused any embarrassment…'

'No, look, I don't know how to put this, it's…well, you see…'

Oh great, thought Diana, Andrea was very embarrassed, bet she's having an affair with her brother-in-law!

'…Julian died last Saturday, Charles has come around to help me sort things out…'

Diana babbled an apology, it wasn't necessary.

'We haven't told the wider family yet, I'm still not over the shock I suppose. It was very sudden. The kids are alright, we seem to be dealing with it okay,' all the usual questions were covered like some kind of check list.

A little later, and after a lot of questions and sympathy, Diana put the receiver down, she felt so sorry for Andrea, and right now she was not really sure what to do. Did she in fact need to do anything? She rang her mum, of course, she didn't know about Julian either, apparently she was part of the 'wider family' and hadn't merited a phone call from Andrea about the bad news.

Diana rang Andrea a couple of nights later and offered her help, though didn't know what exactly she could do. The conversation was artificially cheerful, the offer appreciated, but not taken up. Diana thought no more about it. Her parents went to the funeral, but Diana couldn't get the time off work, in a way she wasn't sorry.

***

The four 'girls' carried on going to classes over the next couple of weeks and continued to learn and enjoy themselves. When Diana got home after the latest class she found a message from Andrea, could she ring please?

'Oh, Diana, thanks for ringing, I wanted to ask you about the dance classes you're going to.'

Diana was very confused and surprised.

'Well, I was wondering, what's the standard like?' checked Andrea.

'You're not thinking about coming to the beginners classes are you? That would be mad, I mean, you live in Stoke!'

'Yeah, but I'm coming home, to Newport. You see, Julian has left me quite well off. I don't really want to stay in Stoke, it's a nice enough place, but my family, my dad and sister that is, they're in Newport and I could do with their help with my kids. So when I'm home I thought, well, I'd like to get back to dancing.'

'After all these years, I thought you'd given it up?' said Diana.

'I never, mentally, gave it up, other things got in the way. After Julian and I got married we carried on dancing for a while. But with a new home and his work exams, plus work wanted him to move up here, it was difficult to fit dancing in. Once we got to Stoke Bethany, my eldest, came along, so dancing went out the window altogether. Bethany is sixteen now, nearly seventeen, and Rupert is at a stage in school that would mean it would be no big deal about moving. I thought it would be a good time to come home, and start dancing. Everything is memories up here, it's claustrophobic, and I need to get out.'

Andrea talked about her family, but curiously she nearly always included something about dancing.

'Well Andrea, knowing how good a dancer you were, I can't see these beginners classes wouldn't be any good to you.'

'But I'm very rusty, I haven't danced for nearly twenty years.'

'Even so, have a chat with Simon and Alex when you get down here.'

Andrea agreed, but asked more questions about the classes, not that Diana actually knew much about the technical stuff her cousin quizzed her about.

'I thought you'd have been sick of dancing after all the years you did it. I thought you stopped when you got married because you didn't want to dance anymore?'

'You couldn't be more wrong, I never wanted to stop. When I married Julian, we had been dancing together for a good few years, since we were kids in fact, I assumed it would just go on, but he felt he ought to give his career at the bank more attention than his dancing. I just saw it as a way for paying for dancing, but it took over after a while, and dancing was out, until now.'

For a moment it almost sounded as if Andrea was glad to be rid of Julian, surely not? Diana couldn't understand how seriously Andrea took her dancing. Andrea automatically assumed Diana understood, she was wrong, so wrong!

***

If Diana had a complaint about the school, it was that it was always very cold when she first arrived, Alex didn't like putting the heating on. It was November and she had been attending the classes with the girls every week and, even if they said so themselves, getting pretty good at dancing.

Alex welcomed them, she looked more excited than usual, but they paid no attention to this, she was a hard character to read and came over as eccentric…big time.

Just before the class began, Alex brought someone over to meet the girls.

'I want you to meet Trevor, he's joining the class from tonight and Simon and I think he would be a lovely dance partner for you Diana!'

Cerys looked surprised, who would she dance with now? But Diana was shocked.

'Trevor came to our last season of classes and you did very well didn't you Trevor? Yes he did, but he had to stop because his mother wasn't well, didn't you Trevor? Yes, that's right, but he's able to come back again now, so we thought he'd be ideal for you Diana, very good height match, so you two have a dance, see how you get on, bye!'

He stood looking at Diana, then the other three women, this was embarrassing. 'Can I get you a drink ladies?'

They all said no.

'Oh, cheap round. Sorry about all this by the way…um, fancy a Waltz then Diana? Can I call you Diana?'

He was about the same age as Diana, perhaps a little younger, it was hard to tell. He had a boyish face, a mass of very dark, wavy hair. The way it was styled, if you could call it styled, added to the boyish look. He was dressed casually, but smart, he was good looking with a ruddy faced, nice build, softly spoken, he seemed okay.

Diana agreed, they took up dance hold, it seemed odd dancing with a man. Cerys could never be mistaken for a man, Diana had only danced with Simon a few times, he didn't seem to count as a man either for some reason. They kept a respectful loose hold, it couldn't be said they danced together, no, their 'hold' was at arms length.

When the Waltz finished she went back to join the girls, Trevor trailed after her and sat with them.

'Mind if I sit with you?' checked Trevor, 'I don't know anyone here, none of the people form the last season of classes are here, so it would be nice if I could sit with you…is that alright?'

They said it was, there was an awkward silence then they all started asking Trevor about himself. To Diana, the regular references to his mother struck a sour chord, Elwyn all over again. Not that this mattered, after all, the idea was that she would just dance with him, and even that wasn't her idea. In fact he danced with each of them during the hour, even the two 'male ladies' as Alex kept calling them. It was confusing as by now they only knew men's steps, but it surprised them to find Trevor knew ladies steps.

'Oh, I love my dancing, I'm really keen,' explained Trevor. 'While I've been away from the classes, I've bought anything I can find about dancing, magazines, books (you can borrow them if you like…no? Okay then). Surprisingly the internet wasn't much good for what I wanted, anyway, when I found the steps being explained in the magazines and stuff, I learnt them both, the man and woman's steps!' He almost purred in a self-satisfied way.

Whilst Alex's idea was that Trevor dance with Diana, he actually didn't do so much at all and Diana spent more time dancing with Cerys than

Trevor. After the class she thought no more about him.

At the next class, Trevor joined them again, but tonight he asked Diana to dance far more. She noticed Alex, not so much Simon, watching them closely and guessed that Trevor had been told to make more of an effort to dance with her. Well, Trevor was alright, nice guy, hardly her type, another mummy's boy. Here he was, in his forties and never married and, apparently, no girlfriend. She had a feeling he probably never had had one either, mummy would have seen to that. As the lesson went on she thought he might be gay, this helped her relax a little with him and she actually had more fun dancing with him. He was a good dancer, well, perhaps a bit more advanced than her. Of course that didn't mean much at this stage, but he was nice to dance with, they got on well and he helped her learn the steps. He had a good sense of humour and they laughed a great deal, just what she needed.

***

She had thought little about Andrea's plan to move back to Newport and heard no more from her cousin, until that is, her mother rang.

'...oh, and Andrea is moving into a rented place next week, not far from her dad. Apparently she's sold her house in Stoke and is ready to buy a place down here as soon as she can, that was quick wasn't it?'

Yes it was, not that Diana was that bothered, mind you, it would be nice to see her again. She still felt guilty that she hardly knew anything about Andrea, her family or her circumstances. Given Andrea was dealing with the death of Julian, Diana felt it would be important to support her through what was going to be a very hard time in her life.

The next week Andrea rang, she sounded excited.

'I moved in yesterday, it's a bit small, but it'll do for now, Rupert and Bethany started at their new school, they don't like it of course, but it's the Christmas holiday soon and he's already found a girlfriend there. Typical man and he's only fourteen. Anyway, Bethany came down with us of course, but she'll be off to university before long I suppose. We're in a mess here, but I was wondering if you and Jacob would like to come over on Sunday, your mum and dad are going to come, what do you think?'

Of course Diana agreed.

'So, how's your dancing coming on?' checked Andrea.

Diana had expected Andrea to sound miserable or least stressed about all the pain of her loss, selling up the family home and moving, but she sounded positively cheerful. As they talked she guessed that perhaps Andrea's marriage had been less than perfect, was Julian's death a blessing in disguise?

Diana had been in regular contact with Andrea's mother in the years before she had died, but since then she had hardly seen her uncle, Gilbert. Her aunt often talked about her daughters and Andrea in particular, there had never been anything said about the marriage being in trouble, in fact Aunty Claire had always had a high opinion of Julian. Mind you, she was massively disappointed that they hadn't continued dancing. Diana guessed that Andrea was just glad to be home and near her father and sister again, yeah, that was it.

She explained about the weekly classes and how she had been paired off with Trevor and…

'Ooh, sounds interesting, what's he like?' interrupted Andrea.

Diana told her what little she knew about him.

'Nice change to hear about a man that's interested in dancing and has even taught himself ladies steps. I'd like to meet him!'

'Perhaps you will one day, who knows?' joked Andrea.

'Oh, I will meet him, assuming he joins the Improvers class in January, I've put my name down for it. According to Alex you've already said you'll be coming along, that's right isn't it?'

'Well, yes, she told us at the last class about the next season…'

'And Trevor's moving up into Improvers as well isn't he?'

'Yes…'

'So I will be meeting him soon. What's he like to dance with, how tall is he?'

Diana realised that Andrea intended to try out with him as a possible dance partner, this was what the phone call was about!

She made herself a coffee after the call and weighed up whether she minded what Andrea was so blatantly doing. Hmm, not really, after all she didn't fancy Trevor and if she had, then his mummy was always going to be a huge problem. Whether he'd ever admit it or not, the girls had noticed that nearly every conversation with Trevor included some anecdote about his mum. Diana had no dance ambitions, other than to keep enjoying herself. She didn't take dancing as seriously as Trevor, though now spent most of each class dancing with him, that was about it really.

Jacob came home from university for the weekend so they went over to Andrea's home for the get together. She tried to remember what her cousin had looked like at her mother's funeral, bloody awful. Aunty Claire had died suddenly, after a short and very painful illness. So when Andrea opened the door Diana had a shock, Andrea was beautiful, had an attractive figure for a middle aged mum of two. She was sensibly and prettily made up, her hair was a lush chestnut colour, probably dyed, but it was hard to tell. Okay, she was a bit chubbier than she used to be, but she didn't seem to have aged much since she got married, and was unrecognisable from the broken woman at her mother's funeral. She was genuinely delighted to see Diana and Jacob.

Jacob and Bethany spent the whole evening together, she was a stunner and Jacob was drooling. Diana's mother and father had arrived just after she and Jacob, they spent most of the evening discussing gardens with Andrea's father, Gilbert. There were a couple of other (distant) family members there too, plus Andrea's sister and Andrea's new neighbours. It could hardly be called a party, all very sober, but pleasant enough.

Andrea latched onto Diana, she seemed to talk about little else other than dancing.

The biggest surprise of the evening was when Alex and Simon arrived, they were clearly Andrea's special guests. It was as if they were really Andrea's parents and had found her after year's of separation. Andrea actually said they had been her 'dance parents' when she had been at their school. Alex even cried when she saw her.

Alex seemed to dominate everything from the moment she took her coat off, she held everyone, including the kids, spell bound as she talked about Andrea's dancing career and achievements.

'...and now she's coming back to dancing, back to our school, we can't wait can we Simon?'

He nodded, was about to speak, but didn't get a word in, Alex was off again.

'She may not have danced for many years, but I know she will make rapid progress and become the *great* dancer she was destined to be!'

Diana wondered if she should clap.

***

It was the last night of the season of beginners dance classes and the week before Christmas. The school was lavishly decorated for the season and it was more of a party than anything else. Trevor was there as usual.

Diana was a little surprised when he gave her a Christmas card, she didn't have one for him. He said it didn't matter, but she felt it did, given how small his circle of friends was, she guessed he didn't get many cards.

'Are you coming to the Christmas party?' asked Trevor hopefully.

There were signs up around the school for it and had been for weeks. Neither she nor the girls had planned to go. Christmas Day was going to be on the Friday and the party would be on Wednesday, she always found Christmas week very busy, though not socially. She didn't have any plans for that evening, but she wasn't sure she really wanted to come to the party.

'I don't know, I don't think so. Girls, are we going to the party, we're not are we?' Now that sounded bad didn't it?

'What party?' said Anita.

A poster was pointed to.

'Why, do you want to go Di?' checked Cerys.

She was about to say how busy she was that night.

'Yeah, why not, I'll go get us tickets, you can settle up with me later,' said Anita.

'Oh good,' said Trevor, 'I'll be there, can't wait.'

Diana felt awkward and embarrassed.

'What about your mother,' asked Diana, 'won't she be annoyed that you're off gallivanting?' She mentally kicked herself, she knew this sounded flippant, even rude. Trevor was devoted to his mum and Diana's words would probably be hurtful.

He looked slightly pained, his smile faltered. 'No, it's alright, she's in a home now, Alzheimer's.'

There's never a hole in the ground to vanish down when you need one is there?

Of course she apologised for being so thoughtless, he said it didn't matter, but it did. Mind you, he hadn't told anyone she was in a home, how were they supposed to know?

Diana stared at the ticket for the party at least once a day in the run up to it, each time she decided she wouldn't go, though wasn't quite sure why. This was going to be the only Christmas party she had been asked to, she didn't count the Christmas lunch at work last week. She had left soon after the meal was over, the girls had gone to a few bars and then onto a night club, but that wasn't for Diana, not these days. Besides, she had to watch the pennies.

Alright, she'd go! She wrote out a Christmas card for Trevor, something sober and unemotional, nothing that could make him think she fancied him, which of course she didn't. The girls collected her, Trevor was waiting for them at the door, somehow she guessed he would be and, well, she didn't like it. Even so, it was a great night, a lot of laughter, party dances as well as normal dancing. Some pupils did party pieces, and a professional dance couple did a Latin demonstration, it blew the beginners away, how was it possible to be such good dancers? There was a lot of talk about "Strictly Come Dancing" after the couple finally left the floor. All were certain they had seen them dance on the show, actually they hadn't.

'I want to dance like that one day,' said Trevor dreamily.

'You'll be lucky!' said Sheryn, 'they probably started dancing when they were kids, they're still only in their mid twenties now, you've left it a bit late to become a super dancer.'

'Well, you can be a senior competitor and I'd be a good age for that,' explained Trevor.

'And who's going to be your dancing partner?' asked Cerys and giggled, she had a rough idea who he might have in mind.

He was about to answer, stopped himself, but smiled at Diana. She blushed, he planned for them to become regular dance partners and start competing didn't he?

Another dance was announced and one of the other lads from their class rushed over and pulled Diana out to dance before she could ask Trevor if this was what he had in mind.

The rest of the evening went well and Diana had too much fun to bother about Trevor's ambitions. Besides, she had no intention of fitting in with them, anyway tonight was a bad time to upset him.

As the party was coming to an end, Trevor fumbled in his pocket and brought out a small package.

'Thank you for dancing with me these last few weeks, happy Christmas!' he said to Diana and thrust the parcel at her. Pointedly, she was the only one he had a present for.

This really threw her, she hadn't got anything for him, the card seemed a bit inadequate, but he had been thrilled to get it. Should she accept the present, now she knew he had grand plans for her? Diana was to be his regular dance partner and the means to him to achieving his dancing ambitions, and what else? Become his girlfriend?

'Please take it,' begged Trevor, 'it's not much really, only a little something to say thank you.'

Wordlessly she took it, stared at it, admired the wrapping paper, apologised for not having anything for him and…

'It doesn't matter, I'm just pleased you've accepted it. I've really love dancing with you and it's the least I could do after we've had so much fun together.'

They had had fun hadn't they? And she did like him, she was still feeling sorry for him about his mother, so she assured him she'd open it Christmas Day and gave him a very polite kiss on the cheek, he blushed, vividly. Cerys and Anita giggled.

After the last Waltz and lots of wishes for a good Christmas, they pulled on their coats.

'So,' said Diana, 'what are your plans for Christmas?'

Trevor shrugged, smiled his usual smile and said: 'Nothing really, the factory is closed until after New Year's Day, I'll go see my mother on Christmas morning, though that won't be for long, she doesn't know me anymore you see and she's asleep most of the time,' he looked as though he may cry. 'I don't have any family locally, I have a sister, but she lives in America, she'll ring me sometime Christmas evening I suppose, if she remembers. I thought I'd go to the pub up the road for Christmas lunch, I don't fancy cooking. I suppose most of the day I'll just watch the telly.'

Diana felt very sorry for him, also guilty again. 'Well, look, umm, why not come to my place for Christmas lunch? It'll only be me and Jacob, we've got lots of food in, more than we need, it'll be nice to have a guest and...'

'I couldn't, but you're very kind,' he said a little too formally.

'Oh please come!' Diana couldn't believe that she said that. She wasn't really sure she wanted him over for Christmas, well, actually, no she didn't. Anyway, she guessed he would say no and it made her feel better to have asked, especially as he had given her a present. 'You'd be very welcome,' she added.

'Alright then, I'll come!'

Damn! That wasn't supposed to happen!

'What time do you want me to come? I'll be away from the nursing home about 11.30.'

'Oh, right, well, any time, when ever it suits you.'

'Right-oh, I'll be at your house about 12.00, how's that?'

She agreed. What would Jacob think? Bet they won't get on!

'I'm going to my parents about four, is that alright with you?' she warned Trevor.

'Of course, I'll leave in good time for you to get away, I'm just grateful that I've been invited for lunch. Give me something to look forward to.'

In fact the plan was to go to her parents for seven, but at least this reduced some of the damage she had done to her Christmas Day.

Jacob was very surprised, but didn't seem to mind. 'He's the new man in your life is he?' Jacob smirked.

'No, he certainly isn't!' and explained about the wretched Christmas he would otherwise have.

Even so, Jacob teased her about Trevor, but Diana thought she had gotten off lightly.

On Christmas Day, Trevor arrived at twelve exactly. He brought an expensive bottle of wine and a poinsettia. Diana had got him a box of nice chocolates, she thought that was neutral. She had found he had got her a pretty costume jewellery brooch, not really her taste, but she made a point of wearing it, he noticed and was thrilled.

She assumed he wouldn't have anything to drink as he would be driving home, she was shocked to hear that he only lived a few minutes walk away. For some reason she had thought he lived the other side of town, but he was almost a neighbour, she felt guilty that she had never met him before, she didn't know why. He didn't drink much and found sherry a bit too strong for him, Diana guessed he rarely had more than a couple of pints with the lads after work, and probably not even that once he had had to spend more time looking after his mother in the years before she went into the home.

Trevor got on well with Jacob, they didn't have much in common, but Jacob taught him to play computer games, it all seemed very new to Trevor and Diana guessed that whilst he had a computer and internet access, he probably only just managed to make it all work.

She considered herself to be an adequate cook, but Trevor assured her that this meal was better than anything his mother had ever served, now that was something! She was sure Trevor would find nothing as good as his dear old mum's cooking, so was relieved, not that it mattered, after all, she wasn't really trying to make a good impression was she? No, just trying to give him a nicer Christmas than he would otherwise have, that's all.

He insisted on helping wash up. Diana didn't have a dishwasher, so it was a fairly big job, Trevor didn't mind and even seemed to enjoy it.

Diana found herself looking at the clock, it was just gone three and she had said they would be going to her parents at four, but Trevor didn't seem to show any sign of going, he kept playing computer games with Jacob.

'Coffee?' said Diana cheerily, then: 'Oh, look at the time! Ten-past-three, we'll have to start getting ready to go soon won't we Jacob? Granny and granddad are expecting us at four, aren't they?' Oh so subtle!

Jacob didn't look away form the screen, but said: 'No, it's seven isn't it?'

Diana felt herself blush.

'Oh, I've suggested Trevor come over with us, granny and granddad won't mind.'

'Great idea Jacob, wish I'd thought to ask Trevor myself,' yes, she would kill her son later.

She hurried out of the living room without finding out about coffee, now what could she do?

Trevor arrived a few moments later. 'Look, don't worry, if you don't want me to come to your parents, that's fine, I understand. I've had a lovely time and…'

'Don't be silly! Of course I want you to come, you'll probably find it boring mind…sorry about the mess up over the times…umm, better give them a ring to say you'll be coming.'

This wasn't one of her better Christmas Days.

She hoped her parents would say it wasn't convenient, but they were delighted and her mother was looking forward to meeting her new boyfriend! Diana would probably kill her mother too.

When they got there, another surprise waited for them, Andrea, her kids, her sister and Gilbert. Well, that was the last she saw of Jacob, he spent the whole evening with Bethany. Diana's father knew Trevor slightly and had been friends with his parents, they got on brilliantly. For the first part of the evening, Diana chatted to Andrea, the main topic was the children and, increasingly, dancing.

The plan was still on for Andrea to join the improvers class in January and she was obviously very excited about it. She asked about Diana's dancing, she kept referring to it as a career. Diana found it hard to call a few months in a weekly beginners class a 'career', but Andrea was obviously very serious about it. She asked a lot of questions about Trevor, glancing at him frequently. Diana realised that Andrea rather fancied him as a dance partner, apparently they were a good height match, what ever that meant. Actually, that suited Diana very well, she was concerned Trevor could see himself as her boyfriend and she wasn't ready for a new relationship, especially with Trevor, not her type at all. Actually she didn't think she had a 'type' of man in mind, she didn't have any man in mind, least of all Trevor.

It was no surprise to Diana when Andrea began talking dancing with Trevor, the two soon went into deep discussion. Not long before the sober little party broke up, Andrea seemed rather flustered.

'What's wrong,' checked Diana.

'Oh, well, no, nothing, nothing's wrong…umm, no.'

'Well it is, isn't it, I can tell, aren't you feeling well?'

'Nothing like that, it's just that Trevor doesn't seem to know much about dancing. He knows nothing about competitions, medal tests, structured practices or lessons with high-grade teachers, I thought he was a dancer.'

'He is,' protested Diana, 'he's very good, much better than any of us, he knows his stuff.'

'I thought he was more my level,' said Andrea sorrowfully.

Diana wasn't quite sure what she meant by that, but thought it sounded like an insult to Diana's dancing.

'And he didn't seem that interested in having a few dances with me at the class, he said that he usually dances with you, and I'd have to ask your permission!'

Diana didn't know whether to laugh or be touched, she certainly didn't know what to say, this was all news to her.

'Would you mind if I dance with Trevor in the classes, just a couple of dances, I don't want to wreck your partnership or cause any upset,' pleaded Andrea.

'There is *no* partnership! In fact, I'd be rather pleased if you dance with him, he's getting way too keen on me for my liking.'

'Oh, that's wonderful news! Thank you *so* much darling.' It was obvious that she considered this the best Christmas present she could have had.

It wasn't far to Diana's house from her parents home, so they walked back. Trevor went with them, though could have gone a different route and been home quicker. They chatted generally, but with Jacob there Diana couldn't really talk to Trevor about what he had told Andrea, also she wanted to find out how he saw their relationship developing. To Diana it was going to be a friendship and no more, she was damn sure lonely Trevor thought he had a girlfriend at last, well he was wrong!

At Diana's house, Jacob, annoyingly, rushed in to put the kettle on, the little monster sniggered as he left his mum with the simpering Trevor.

'I've had a wonderful day,' began Trevor.

Oh God, thought Diana, he's expecting a kiss!

He listed all that he had enjoyed, Diana could have done without this, it was fairly late, for her, and damn cold!

He finally concluded that he was looking forward to seeing her again soon, and shook hands!

Diana was both relieved and surprised as she watched him saunter down the street. Perhaps he didn't fancy her after all…was she that bad?

'No kiss then,' said Jacob.

'You were watching us?'

'Of course I was! I don't think he fancies you after all,' he moaned.

'No he doesn't, he's just a friend, I dance with him a bit, that's all!'

'I thought it would be nice for you to have a boyfriend, a bit of fun after all these years, why not?'

'Lovely idea, but not with Trevor!'

'Perhaps not then. Anyone else at the dancing school you fancy?'

Diana sighed and gave her son a mock clip around the ear.

Chapter Two
Leading and following

When it came to the first night of the improvers class, Diana went with the girls again, though Cerys didn't seem so keen anymore, but it was still a girl's night out and they did have fun. Trevor was waiting for them of course, as was Andrea, but she was in deep discussion with Simon.

The class was much the same format as it had been for the beginners. About three quarters of the dancers from the beginners classes had come back for improvers, so the girls still had a lot of their friends with them.

The first teaching session covered a new group of steps in Waltz, Diana wasn't really surprised that Simon used Andrea to help teach, she may not have danced in many years, but it was clear she was skilled and capable, it made the rest of the class's efforts seem pathetic. Most of the pupils talked about wanting to be able to dance as well as Andrea. Diana quite liked the reflected glory.

'Why don't you try dancing with Andrea?' asked Alex, she sat next to Trevor who had been enjoying a joke with the girls.

'Oh, no Alex, she's far too good a dancer for me.'

'That's silly, come on!' With that she plucked him off the bench seat and dragged him across to Andrea, a Cha-Cha-Cha was playing. Diana watched as Alex more or less pushed him at her cousin. Within seconds Trevor and Andrea were dancing remarkably well, perhaps Andrea hadn't been impressed by Trevor's knowledge of dancing, but he could dance and she was obviously enjoying every step. And Trevor was enjoying dancing with her. They continued dancing together, and learning, for the rest of the class. Diana felt a little left out, even ignored, but why? She had wanted him to be more interested in Andrea than herself, and that's what had happened, she should be happy for him, and Andrea. But she liked dancing with him and after his gentlemanly behaviour Christmas evening he didn't seem to be that much of a threat. Ah well.

In the next class Trevor split his time more evenly between Andrea and Diana, this didn't suit Andrea, nor Alex, it was clear she thought she had a new budding top-flight couple in Andrea and Trevor. Andrea tried to get him to dance to everything with her, but he put her off when she asked him, and she was lucky to get one dance in three. Diana could even see her looking enviously at her when she danced with Trevor, this was just silly.

'I thought you'd want to do all the dances with Andrea,' said Diana as they pottered rather unsteadily round the floor to a Quickstep, which didn't seem that quick.

'Oh, I like dancing with her, she's really good, but I love dancing with you and the girls, it's more fun.'

'But you're such a good dancer, so keen, surely it's better if you dance with Andrea?'

'Would you prefer I didn't dance with you?'

'No, it's not that at all. I like dancing with you, but you're ambitious, I'm not, and Andrea is. She could be your dance partner if you want to do things like competitions and medals and stuff.'

'I was hoping you'd be interested in taking your dancing further,' he said hopefully.

'Well, not really, I'm just here with the girls for a bit of fun.'

'Oh, I see. So would you be happier if I dance with Andrea then?'

Here we go, thought Diana, watch how you answer this one girl! 'Well, only from the point of view that you'd get more out of your dancing.'

'So you like dancing with me?'

Should she get a bigger shovel or was the one she was using making a big enough hole to jump into? 'Yes, I like dancing with you, you're a lovely friend.'

There! That should make him understand that she wasn't interested in a relationship with him.

'Good, I'm glad we're friends too! Want another dance?'

The ground rules seemed to have been set. She wanted him as a friend, someone to dance with in the classes, but not as a boyfriend, definitely not as a boyfriend.

'Did you know Andrea's a widow?' asked Diana as they danced. Perhaps he'd be more interested in her if he knew she was available. Yes, he did know.

When they went back to their seats, Andrea was waiting, she made sure Trevor danced with her for the rest of the class. This was a bit easier for her since Diana was happy just having a laugh with the girls.

When she got home, she had hardly taken her coat off when the phone went, it was Andrea.

'Diana…umm, this is embarrassing…would you mind if I had private dance lessons with Trevor?'

'Oh, no, of course not, why should I?'

There was quite a long silence before she answered. 'It's just that I thought you may be jealous.'

'Of course not, Trevor and I are just friends.'

There was another awkward silence. 'I see…look, it's none of my business… well I suppose it is, anyway, I suggested we have lessons together tonight, he didn't tell you?'

'No, it's up to him, besides, it makes sense, you two are brilliant together.'

'Well, he's not as good as he thinks he is, but never mind that. He said he'd have to discuss it with you because you're his girlfriend now.'

'He said what? Oh, no, I don't need this! I thought I'd made it clear to him that we can be just friends, there's nothing between us, really there isn't, he's made it up.' Diana explained what she knew about his home life and lack of a girlfriend. 'Good luck with him, but watch out, he may latch on to you and decide you're his girlfriend, I've done nothing to encourage him.'

'You had him around for Christmas lunch and you brought him to meet your parents,' pointed out Andrea.

'I only asked him round because I felt sorry for him,' she explained about the day he would otherwise have had and stressed it was Jacob that had invited him to her parents house.

'He's not some kind of stalker is he?' asked Andrea.

'Oh, I hadn't thought of that! I really hope not, for both our sakes. Listen, you dance with him all you like, suits me given the things he's been telling you.'

'Ooh, I'm so pleased! Thank you darling, I'll keep you posted.'

In fact Diana wasn't really interested.

She thought about the dance class and the call from Andrea. What if Andrea had made up the bit about Trevor saying he was her boyfriend? Andrea was very ambitious, wanted a dance partner and was frustrated that Trevor wouldn't dance with her all the time. What if this was a ploy to take Trevor off her? But so what? She didn't want him as a dance partner or a boyfriend, Andrea was welcome to him.

She read a book in bed and tried to calm down, but she kept thinking about Trevor, did he really say she was his girlfriend? He was quite capable of it. She slammed her book shut and rung Trevor. It was gone eleven, but she had to know.

'Oh hiya Diana! This is a lovely surprise!'

'Andrea rang me earlier, she said you're going to have lessons with her, is that right?'

There was an embarrassed silence: 'Yes, you don't mind do you?'

'No, I'm pleased.'

He now sounded disappointed that she wasn't arguing against it.

'Andrea was surprised you hadn't told me.'

'I was going to get round to it.'

'She was surprised because you told her I'm your girlfriend, is that true?'

'What, that you're my girlfriend?' he laughed nervously, 'you'll have to tell me,' he laughed even more nervously.

Damn it! She thought, he bloody well had told her hadn't he? 'Did you tell her I'm your girlfriend or not?' she snapped.

'Well, you are, sort of, aren't you, I mean, the only evening out either of us have is the dance class and we spend all our time together and...'

'And nothing! We are *not* dating or going out, we're *not* boy and girlfriend, get it? Do you understand?!'

'But we are friends!'

'*Were* friends, you've lied to my cousin about our relationship, you've made her think she's coming between us. If you want a girlfriend try and win her over, it may be good for your dancing!'
She slammed the phone down.

She felt better for that. She also decided she wouldn't be going back to the dance classes. She texted the girls about it right then, it helped get it out of her system. She thought she'd found a male friend to have a few laughs with and he'd turned out to be one step short of a stalker! That was more than enough for her.

***

Trevor rang back twice that night, she didn't pick up the call. He tried several more times the next day, but she still wouldn't take the call. It wasn't that she was upset about him dancing with Andrea, it was that he had lied about their relationship, made up fanciful stories, she felt used and foolish, though she wasn't really sure why.

He even sent her a card to say sorry, but she knew if she weakened now he would soon be back to describing her as his girlfriend and that could never happen.

She was surprised to find she missed her dancing classes and annoyed she was no longer going because of Trevor, he had wrecked everything. Given his track record, she guessed he would make a nuisance of himself. Perhaps turn up at the Job Centre and try to see her, become a real stalker, she was both relieved and surprised when he didn't, well not yet anyway.

A couple of Trevor-free weeks later Andrea explained why Diana wasn't hearing from him. She was dancing with him most evenings and dragging him along at break neck speed as a dancer.

'He's loving every minute,' assured Andrea.

Diana guessed that Trevor's mates at work were being assured that Andrea wasn't just a dance partner, but far more, wink, wink. And what if she was? Hmm, very unlikely, Andrea's one track mind was a dance music track.

They were at Diana's parents' house for tea. Jacob had gone back to university. Bethany and Rupert had stayed home, so it was a fairly relaxed and quiet atmosphere. Sunday afternoons at her parents had now become something of a family tradition and Diana looked forward to it, as did her parents.

'Yes, he's really coming on very well, still slower than I would like,' explained Andrea, 'I thought we'd be competing by Easter, can't see that happening until the summer now, but I'm hopeful. His shift work keeps getting in the way. I was wondering how he'd be with me, you know, after he lied about you two being an item.'

Diana nodded, she had been about to ask that exact same question.

'I've had no problem with him, we're just a dancing partnership, we get on well, mind you he's not that bright is he?'

'I found him okay, I doubt he could ever re-train as a rocket scientist, but I thought he was reasonably intelligent,' Diana felt she had to defend him a bit. She did wonder if Andrea measured his intelligence by how quickly he learned to dance rather than his actual IQ, yeah, she probably did.

'But he works in a factory, nothing very clever.'

'So? At least he's dancing with you and learning, that's all you want from him isn't it?'

She shrugged. 'Yeah I suppose so, but it would be nice to have an evening with someone you can have an intelligent conversation with.'

From what Andrea had been saying poor Trevor probably was so busy dancing he hardly ever had the puff to carry on a conversation!

'Are you going to come back to dancing?' asked Andrea.

'I doubt it. The girls have stopped so, unless they start going again, I won't.'

'You should, it'll get you out of the house a bit, great way to keep fit and get a bit of a social life back again.'

'Don't fancy meeting another Trevor.'

She laughed, stopped herself and nodded, she suddenly seemed to understand. 'There'll be another season of improvers classes starting in a few months, Trevor won't be in that, why don't you see if the girls will come with you. Alex was telling me you and the girls used to have a great time. Think about it.'

Yes, she did have a great time at the classes, and if Trevor wasn't there, well, it might be worth a go.

A few days later there was quite a bad storm, several tiles came off Diana's roof. No matter who she rang she couldn't get hold of someone to fix it. Her dad would normally have been the first number she tried, but since he'd had a heart attack her mother wouldn't let him climb a ladder. In fact Diana couldn't have agreed more, not that her dad liked doing things like fixing the roof, but he at least didn't charge for it!

In desperation she went to the newsagent and looked for the number of a handyman in the window display of local businesses and tradesmen.

'Oh hello, fancy seeing you here!'

It was Trevor.

Diana said an embarrassed hello and kept checking for a number.

'Problem?' asked Trevor.

'Umm, not really.'

'Oh, that's alright then. So what are you looking for?'

Well, it wouldn't hurt to tell him: 'A handyman, I've lost some tiles and the roof's leaking.'

'I'll fix it for you.'

'Thanks, but I think I've got the number of someone here.'

'I'll do it for free,' offered Trevor.

Five minutes later she was pointing out the missing tiles. She expected him to make an excuse and just try and cadge a cup of tea, then go, but he made a note of the colour of the tiles, how many he'd need, said he'd borrow his mate's ladders, checked his shifts, yes, he could probably get the job done the next day, was that okay?

Diana was delighted, and he didn't seem to expect to be invited in. Funny kind of stalker this guy was turning out to be.

Trevor arrived with ladders, new tiles and all he needed to fix the roof. By the time he had finished she had readily agreed to his suggestion that he also fix, paint, replace and improve a long list of things he had seen around the outside of the house. Stuff that she either had known about and hoped would go away, or was waiting for Elwyn to stump up the money for, but that was before the divorce was finalised, so fat chance he'd pay up now.

'Umm, how much is all this going to cost?'

'Not much. I'm a dab hand at DIY, I've got most of what you need in my shed, sort of a hobby DIY is to me see, so I won't charge you labour or anything, I'll be glad of something to keep me busy,' he chuckled.

'I thought Andrea was keeping you busy?'

'Oh, yeah, she is, nearly every evening when I'm not working, but I get bored when I'm not on a shift and not at the dancing school. I'm not much of a one for watching telly. Anyway, I've got a week off work coming up, I can do all this lot for you then,' and tapped a sheet of paper which had the worryingly long list of work that needed doing around Diana's house.

She was hugely relieved, she knew if he really was trying to stalk her or something, she had given him a golden opportunity, but she had to get this work done, she would deal with any problems he may cause later!

He enjoyed the work and, from what she could see, did a good job. She took tea out to him, too soon to ask him into the house, he wasn't really forgiven for telling Andrea, and probably a load of other people in the dancing school and his factory, that she was his girlfriend.

But she had to let him in to the house so he could use the toilet.

'Want me to fix the tap on the wash hand basin?' he said pointing back to the downstairs WC.

Yes she did. Before the end of the week he had a new list of jobs to do, this time all in the house, Diana couldn't believe her luck, it was luck wasn't it?

All the work had to fit around his shifts and evenings dancing with Andrea. Diana actually found herself a bit jealous of Andrea, she was dancing when ever Trevor could spare the time, though that wasn't as often as Andrea liked.

Over the next few weeks she became more comfortable with Trevor, she saw a better side to him and at least he didn't try any funny business.

One evening, Trevor rang her.

'Sorry Diana, I won't be able to get the kitchen decorated this week after all.'

'Oh, problem with your shifts, or off dancing with Andrea?' she asked cheerfully.

'Umm, no, my mother died last night, I've got a quite a lot of sorting out to do, funeral arrangements, that sort of thing.'

'Oh, I am sorry.'

'It's a release for her really.'

Yes, it was, but Diana knew Trevor didn't really mean this and his heart was broken to have lost his mum, even though mentally he had lost her years before.

'Do you know when the funeral will be?' she asked politely and sympathetically.

'In about a week or two I suppose. Would you like to come?'

Not really, but she said she would, it was the least she could do given all the work he had done for her.

That Sunday she met Andrea at her parents' house.

'... I really can't believe that Trevor isn't coming dancing at all this week and next!'

'Andrea, his mother has died you know!' protested Diana.

'I know, but you would have thought he would have wanted to get out for a dance and cheer himself up.'

Diana knew this meant cheer Andrea up rather than Trevor. She seemed to have turned into a dance machine, and a selfish one at that. Diana wanted to have a row with her about it, but her parents would be very upset if there was a barney. Gilbert was here too and she didn't want to upset him, he wasn't very well these days. So she bit her tongue and let it go, but her cousin had really gone down in her estimation.

It was a cremation, Diana arrived just before the hearse, when Trevor got out of the funeral limo' he helped out what she took to be a couple of elderly aunts, they were the only family members. They were joined by about a dozen other people shuffling into the crematorium chapel and out of the driving rain. Trevor looked back and smiled at her from the front pew, she had expected him to be tearful, but was remarkably composed. She also half expected him to ask her to join him in the front pew, thankfully he didn't, and what would she have said if had asked? Yes probably, but she wouldn't have liked it.

Andrea didn't come along.

'Thoughtless cow,' muttered Diana as she glanced around the chapel.

As these services go, this wasn't anything out of the ordinary. There was a touching eulogy from the vicar, the hymns were ones that Diana liked, the aunties cried loudly as the coffin disappeared down into what was meant to represent a grave. Trevor helped them out of the pew at the end of the service, they cried constantly and hung onto Trevor as they made their way slowly and unsteadily out of the chapel, the other mourners filed after them. Trevor smiled patiently all the time, it was a smile that said he was glad it was all over. Diana was the last of the mourners to give her sympathy to the aunties who obviously had no idea who she was, it didn't help they were hard of hearing, she tried to explain how she knew Trevor, but gave up.

As she slowly shuffled along toward Trevor she heard him ask each mourner if they would like to come back to the house as he had some refreshments. Each said they couldn't, or would call in later, or would for five minutes, each had a well prepared excuse. Diana could see Trevor didn't believe any of them, but smiled patiently, assured them he understood, all very diplomatic. Then it was Diana's turn, she couldn't bring herself to say no as with each mourners' excuse he looked a little more hurt. In fact she did have time. But she didn't want to go back to his house, what if he made something out of it?

Twenty minutes later she walked up the neat front garden path of the mid-terrace house, with an immaculate but tiny front garden. The house was incredibly well maintained. Trevor was delighted to see her. There was a very strong, sickly smell of air freshener, just the way his mother would no doubt have kept it.

'Oh, you've come! That's great, I thought you wouldn't!'

Diana felt bad about this, but glad she'd made the effort.

'Come in, Aunty Dulcie and Aunty Megan are having a lie down.'

Diana could hear impressive snoring from upstairs.

In the living room a table groaned with food.

'You like tea don't you? Help yourself while I get you a cuppa, take as much as you want, I'm not expecting anyone else. I'm going to be eating all this for days unless you help me out,' he called out cheerily as he hurried into the kitchen. In fact no one else did turn up, not even the ones that said they would call in for five minutes.

The hall and living room were immaculately decorated and maintained, he really did like his DIY. The decoration, furnishing, carpets, everything, were very feminine and colourful. Diana guessed the house was just the way his mum had wanted it, and that's the way it stayed. Even if she had been bed-ridden for many years, and mentally lost for almost as long, and finally in a nursing home. Trevor would change nothing, just in case she got better and came home, it would be the way his mum would expect to find it.

The buffet was a good quality, some interesting selections and not just plates of sandwiches and crisps, which she had expected.

'Who did the buffet, caterers?'

'No, I made it, I had to learn to cook when mum became so ill. I thought I'd have a houseful and mum would be upset if I didn't lay a good spread on.'

He was soon back with the tea, on a tray, the best china and cubed sugar, complete with tongs. She didn't take sugar, but felt she ought to if only to reward Trevor for his effort, but that would be silly.

'Thank you for coming, I really hoped you would…I was beginning to think that…well, that it would be just me and my aunties. The trouble is that mum's been ill for so many years, and we've hardly got any family left. Those that are still with us aren't fit enough to come to the funeral. Even my sister said she couldn't come, and she's rolling in money. She said she's not well, but she just couldn't be bothered…she's lived in the States for thirty years you know, since she got married. Yeah well, I did expect a few of the neighbours to come, mind you, it's cold, and mid week,' he reeled off a few more reasons why the neighbours and friends didn't come. She could tell he was trying to convince himself.

The room was comfortable and pleasantly warm, she began to relax and conversation became easy and interesting, Trevor actually was quite intelligent and articulate, it must be that Andrea didn't give him a chance to speak and prove it.

Eventually the snoring stopped and was replaced with coughing.

'Trevor, Trevor! Are you there?'

'Oh, Aunty Dulcie's awake, she'll want a cup of tea.'

'I'd better be going.'

'Please stay a bit longer, there's no need to go.'

'Trevor, Trevor, I want to go home now, Trevor?'

'Aunty Megan,' said Trevor simply and a little disappointedly.

'You've got your hands full. You see to your aunties. Call over to my place this evening if you want.'

Naturally, he jumped at the chance.

***

When he arrived, he had changed out of his best suit and black tie and was his usual smiling self, relaxed and dressed comfortably. Now he was here Diana didn't quite know what she was supposed to do or what they could talk about. It seemed ridiculous the night of his mother's funeral that they spent so much time chatting about redecorating Diana's kitchen and spare bedroom. Eventually she got him talking about himself:

'I sort of crawled through school, got a few qualifications, woodwork, metalwork, that sort of thing, but nothing special. My uncle got me a job in the factory, it suited me, and the money was good. My dad had died a few years before, so my wages were keeping the house going. Mum had a job, but it hardly brought anything in. It was only me and mum, you see, my sister is a good few years older than me, and was married by then and had gone to the U.S. It all suited me at the time. I had a good life, down the discos when I could. I had a few girlfriends, but they never lasted.'

Diana guessed his mum hadn't made them very welcome.

'Then mum had to give up work because her health was going down hill and when I wasn't at work I had to look after her, and that's what life was like for years. Then she got Alzheimer's, we were able to manage for a bit, you know a year or two, but then she got worse. I thought I'd have to give up work, my aunties helped a lot, but when mum got too much for them I changed my shifts to days. Work weren't happy about it and I got worried about losing my job. Anyway she took a turn for the worse and had to go into a home. I really felt bad about that, I thought it would only be for a while, but she got much worse and stayed that way. I used to have her home when I had a week off work and for summer holidays, Christmas and that, but even that had to stop because she was getting so frail and…and,' he began to cry.

Diana began crying too.

***

It was gone midnight when Diana realised the time, they had just chatted and had a thoroughly pleasant evening. She wondered how she ever thought Trevor could be a stalker or some kind of nut, he was actually a very nice bloke, and this wasn't just because she felt sorry for him either. He didn't try and pressure her into letting him stay the night, she would have refused anyway, he just glanced at his watch:

'Better be going! I'll be back at the weekend to start the decorating.'

'Ooh, right, yes please, thanks, that's great if you'll be feeling up to it?'

'Yes, of course I will!'

At the front door they kept chatting.

'Do you think you'll ever come back to dancing?' asked Trevor.

'I'd like to, but the girls aren't bothered, so it means I'd be going on my own and I don't fancy that.'

'Now don't take this the wrong way…' he looked embarrassed, 'why don't you start the improvers class again after Easter, I'll go with you. Don't be afraid to say no, and we're just friends, I do know that. It's a shame you're not dancing, I know you love it.'

'Andrea won't like that,' said Diana, but she was really tempted by this, dancing with Trevor and annoying Andrea.

'I don't suppose she will, but her and me and going to have a little chat very soon. D'you know she's rung me three times this week to ask when I'll be back dancing? And I've just buried my mother!'

Diana wasn't surprised, that sounded just like her dance-machine cousin these days. She toyed with reminding him it had been a cremation…nah, let it go.

'Besides, I'm not enjoying dancing with her, she's never happy, always blaming me for things going wrong and never happy with how much time I can put into dancing. She can find someone else to dance with. So, what do you say?'

Diana said yes.

***

That Sunday Andrea told Diana about Trevor breaking off their dance partnership, she was furious and couldn't understand why. Diana knew exactly why, but wasn't sure whether she should tell her, and wasn't sure how she'd respond when she found out that Trevor would be joining Diana at the improvers class, she could feel a row coming on. What about texting her later? Probably not a good idea.

'You don't think you've been pushing him too hard do you?' suggested Diana.

'Of course not! He's lapping it up, loving every minute.'

'He's told you that?'

'Yes, yes he has.' No he hadn't.

'I went to his mother's funeral.'

'What on earth for?'

Diana told her about all the work he had done about the house, that they were getting on well now and that he was a good conversationalist and intelligent. From the look on her face Diana could see she didn't believe her.

'I thought you might have come to the funeral too,' said Diana.

'No way, I've had enough of funerals!'

Well, she did have a point.

'I think Trevor would have been grateful for some sign of sympathy.'

'Suppose so, but we're just dancing partners, it's a business relationship.'

'Well, his employer sent flowers, that's a business relationship.'

'That's different!'

Diana guessed it would be.

'He told me he was upset that you rang him a few times last week about starting dancing again. He had his hands full with the funeral and clearing up his mother's estate you know.'

'Of course I rang him! He's struggling with all the routines and at this rate he'll never be ready for our first competition in a few weeks!' Diana could tell she didn't intend to let him off the hook. She was still planning to get him back and competing, probably Trevor hadn't been told this minor detail.

'He was very upset about his mother, I think you may have come over as insensitive.'

Andrea looked surprised, even confused. Then Diana recalled that very soon after Julian had died Andrea was planning to get back to dancing, she clearly assumed Trevor would have the same mental attitude as her.

Andrea went on about Trevor's dancing: 'He loves it of course and that's despite having to work so hard to keep up with me. Of course he's not as good as he thinks he is.'

Diana knew this meant that Trevor wasn't as good as Andrea wanted him to be.

Diana listened to the lecture, the bemusement. Okay, time to come clean: 'Andrea, I'd better tell you now, I'm sure Alex will. Trevor's asked me to dance with him at the next series of improvers classes, I've said yes.'

Andrea stared at her, she even looked hurt. 'But why? You're just a beginner. He's giving up dancing with me and the chance to compete, just so he can dance with you in the improvers class?' It didn't compute.

Diana tried to rationalise why Trevor didn't want to dance with her, though it stung painfully that Andrea was speaking about her as if she was some kind of sub-human, a beginner.

'So it's you've that's taken him off me and wrecked our dance partnership,' accused Andrea loudly.

'Taken him off you? No, he's stopped dancing with you because he wasn't enjoying his dancing. You've worked him too hard...'

Andrea began crying and complaining: 'I never thought my own cousin would wreck my dancing career,' she said grandly and theatrically.

Gilbert came over and comforted his 'little-girl' and ticked Diana off: 'Why can't you find your own dance partner and not take Trevor off poor Andrea?'

Diana's parents knew it had nothing to do with Diana, so an argument broke out. The pleasant Sunday afternoon tea was wrecked and within a few minutes there was a rift.

***

Trevor wasn't too surprised to hear Andrea's voice. She had rung several times trying to get him to change his mind, but he hadn't. This time her approach was different:

'I just wanted to say how sorry I was to hear your mother has…passed on.'

He guessed she was going to say died, but thought he would prefer passed on. He didn't really mind, they meant the same thing. He knew Andrea's sympathy was false and there was an agenda.

She gave obvious excuses about why she hadn't been able to come to the funeral and asked if there was a charity she could donate money to instead of flowers.

'Look, how about you and me have a coffee and discuss our partnership, see what I can do to clear up any misunderstandings?' she asked earnestly.

'I don't think so. There's no misunderstanding. I don't actually like dancing with you. You're rude to me, I can't afford all the lessons you want, my shifts make practice difficult, and you're always moaning at me. I've told you all this before. I'm sure you can find another dance partner very easily.'

No she couldn't, that was why she was ringing. She wouldn't take no for an answer.

'I'll never forgive Diana for splitting us up!' said Andrea, her voice taught with emotion.

'She didn't, you split us up, I don't like dancing with you, don't blame her,' he said remarkably placidly.

'Of course she did! There's no way she's as good a dancer as me, what's she promised you to split with me, sex?'

'What? Are you seriously suggesting that she…'

'That's it isn't it? You're sleeping with her, or she's said she will! So that's what she meant by you decorating her bedroom!'

Trevor slammed the phone down. He thought for a few moments then rang Diana, but how was he going to tell her what her cousin was accusing her of?

For a few moments he made awkward conversation about some new jobs Diana wanted done, then, haltingly, he told her.

'She said what? That evil cow!'

Within minutes she was banging on Andrea's front door. There was no answer, but it was obvious she was home. Diana had had a short fuse as a teenager, but bringing up Jacob and dealing with her dippy husband had taught her patience, but right now the lessons were all forgotten. She was clean out of patience, she was going to keep going until her cousin opened up. It took twelve minutes.

'Well, what do you want?' said Andrea sullenly.

'You know damn well what I want, an apology! Did you or did you not tell Trevor that you think I'm sleeping with him?'

'Well you are aren't you?' said Andrea sounding haughty.

Diana slapped her.

Andrea wasn't expecting that and toppled backwards, then burst into tears.

'Oh stop crying Andrea! We've got to sort this out!'

'You hit me, how could you! You hit me! I should call the police!'

'Shut up and get in the house. How dare you accuse me of sleeping with Trevor. I want an apology.'

'Why should I apologise. It's obvious the only way he would stop dancing with me is if you let him get in your knickers, look at him! Pathetic creature, probably never had it off in his life!'

They argued bitterly and viciously, but at least Diana resisted the temptation to hit her again, just.

Worn out after what seemed like hours, but was probably no more than fifteen minutes of verbal sparring and finger pointing, they sat opposite each other and glared.

'What is this all about Andrea, out with it, we're family, surely you don't really believe I'd drop my pants for Trevor. You don't believe I've lured him away from you do you, really?'

Andrea was still tearful. 'It was all going so well, I was dancing again, I was happy and you've ruined it!'

'But if it was going so well why do you think Trevor dropped you? He's not happy, it's nothing to do with me, it's to do with you. He's only a slightly more trained dancer than me, and you were expecting him to turn into a champion over night.'

'But he wants to be a champion.'

'Yes, eventually, and assuming he had the talent, but you know he hasn't.'

'But he was coming on so well.'

'You can't have it both ways, you told me he wasn't.'

Andrea began yelling abuse.

'Okay then, let's ring Alex and Simon and ask how they think Trevor is getting on, whether he's ready for that damn competition you're always on about,' she fumbled for her mobile.

'There's no need to bother them,' said Andrea sadly and very quietly.'

'And why not?'

Andrea looked uneasy.

'Cause they'll say that he's not up to your standard and not good enough for the competition, that's right isn't it?' checked Diana.

She shrugged.

'Surely you can find another dance partner Andrea?'

'Shall I make us some coffee?' she asked trying to sound cheerful.

'Andrea, couldn't you find another partner?'

She hurried into the kitchen, Diana followed and asked again.

'No, no I can't. I've been looking. There aren't many men in dancing, single men that is, and even fewer the right height and age for me. Trevor's the only chance I've got. I've even been asking in Bristol, Cardiff, Swansea, you name it.'

'What if I help you find someone else to dance with, will you leave him alone then?'

'A dancer, or just some bloke?'

Well, it was going to be some bloke, she knew no dancers, but at least she knew more men locally than Andrea did. Somehow she didn't think Cerys would do!

'Look Andrea, I'm trying to help, do you have to be so rude?'

Her cousin was embarrassed and managed a sincere, but quiet apology.

'It's just that I've missed my dancing so much since Julian got all career-minded. I thought all the good times were back when I started dancing with Trevor, he literally seemed an answer to a prayer. I've been so happy dancing with him…'

'Didn't seem like it to Trevor.'

'Well, I thought with a little encouragement he'd be up for it, but everything's a struggle for him.'

'You're a much higher standard than him, you knew that from the start.'

'I was, but nearly twenty years out of dancing sets you back, believe me! Anyway, from what you told me he was a serious dancer, learning all he could in and out of the school, just what I was looking for.'

'But he's still a beginner.'

'Yeah and not a talented one. Are you serious, do you think you could help me find someone else to dance with?' she almost begged, leaning forward, she even looked desperate.

'Well, I'll try. But first, let's get it straight, if I hear you're still putting it about that Trevor is sleeping with me I'll…' she'd what?

'I'm sorry, it's just that I was angry, frustrated and disappointed. It's the only thing I could think of that would have made Trevor dump me.'

God she was arrogant!

'Alright, but you make sure your dad knows the truth, all this has broken up the family, just when we were starting to get back together.'

Andrea nodded, she was crying very softly. 'So, who have you got in mind for me?'

Actually, no one.

Chapter Three
Improving Chances

Jacob arrived home for the Easter holiday, he had two surprises for Diana, first he had a girlfriend, Annalise Linton, and she would be coming to stay for a few days. And second, he and Annalise had joined the university dance club and had been selected to represent the university in a varsity match. He actually discussed dance steps with her over dinner.

Since her meeting with Andrea, Diana had wracked her brain about someone she could dance with, even going through her address and phone books – a waste of time. Her best bet seemed to be someone at work, but just how do you get one of your colleagues to agree to start dance classes with a complete stranger and one that's a dance machine?

Trevor had finished all the decorating, he'd breezed through the repairs around her house and even done some structural work. He seemed to be pottering around Diana's house when ever he wasn't working or at home sleeping. And it was at his own home that he slept, he never once tried to talk Diana into staying, for which she was much relieved. He had become a good friend and the house was far more comfortable and attractive since he had started helping out, all he asked for was tea and biscuits.

'Got a sweet tooth I have see,' he would assure her before helping himself to yet another ginger nut.

'Tooth? You've got a head full of sweet teeth you have!'

He kept assuring her that most of the materials he already had in store, but she increasingly thought he was paying for much of it himself. It was the least she could do to ask him to have lunch with she and Jacob on Easter Day, needless to say Trevor jumped at the chance.

Much of the time Diana was at work when Trevor was doing the DIY, he would come over when he wasn't working. To an extent this suited Diana very well, less chance that anyone could accuse her of sleeping with him. From what she could tell all he ever did when he was in the house alone was work and sing rather tunelessly to himself.

She hadn't had much chance to talk to him about the argument with Andrea. Besides she didn't want to stop him doing all the work, something she felt guilty about, but she was concerned he may stop before all the jobs were finished, he had saved her a fortune. So it was after lunch on Easter Day that they sat in her newly re-decorated living room that she told him about what she had promised Andrea, and so far she had only come up with one name and then found his wife wasn't that pleased about the idea! Diana had thought he was divorced, his marital status didn't seem to have entered any conversations over the years.

'I don't suppose you know anyone do you?' she asked as they sipped coffee.

'Oh, well, I'll have to have a think…hmm, no, don't think so.'

'Has she bothered you again since?'

'No, she did send me an Easter card and she said how sorry she was about what she had said. That was nice of her.'

Diana hadn't sent him a card, she never sent anyone Easter cards, other than her niece and come to think of it she had forgotten this year. She wondered if Trevor had expected to get one off her, she doubted it, anyway, she'd given him lunch.

'So, you still keen to come to improver's class next week?' he asked eagerly.

'Next week! That's come round fast!' Suddenly she wasn't so sure, but given how kind Trevor had been she felt she had to agree. He had even brought Easter eggs for her and Jacob, who had eaten his already whilst playing a computer game in his room. He said he was doing uni' work, yeah, right. So, with an outward show of enthusiasm, she finalised plans to come to the class.

Trevor didn't outstay his welcome, though was in no hurry to leave. Diana found the time had gone quickly and she was sorry that he was shouting goodbye to Jacob and heading for the front door.

'Now I didn't notice that before! Your radiator in the hall is leaking slightly, better have a look at that. Could do with a lick of paint too. I've got radiator paint in the shed?' said Trevor.

'Oh, is it? Yes, that'll be lovely, fixing it, painting it, thank you. Better put something under that pipe hadn't I?'

'Okay then, I'll pick you up at seven on Tuesday, that's alright isn't it?'

'Oh, you two going out on a date then?' asked Jacob as he came down to see Trevor off.

They explained about the dance class, and no, it wasn't a date. Waste of breath.

'Do you think me and Annalise could come? We could do with the practice before our competition next month.'

Neither Trevor nor Diana really knew, but said it should be alright. Jacob went to the kitchen, but kept looking back at his mum and winking.

'I'll be off then, thank you for a lovely lunch, happy Easter,' said Trevor sounding a little too formal. He hesitated, then began to walk home.

'Trevor, just a minute!'

He walked back, he looked a little confused.

She kissed him on the cheek. 'Thank you for all the work you've done and happy Easter,' said Diana and gave him a hug and a big smile.

He was embarrassed and blushed vividly, began to turn to leave, but hurried back and gave her a very rapid peck on the cheek and mumbled: 'doing the work's a pleasure, I'll fix the radiator soon, honest,' and almost ran down the street.

Diana couldn't help but giggle. He wasn't that bad a lad after all.

***

On Tuesday night Trevor was a little early, he jingled his keys nervously, he didn't get the kiss he was hoping for when he arrived.

Diana wasn't sure what to make of Annalise: nice girl, pretty, quiet, Scottish, a little chubby, but by no means fat and Jacob was besotted with her. He had been surprised when Diana had made up the spare bed for Annalise, he had expected them to sleep together.

'Not under my roof you're not! That poor girl's parents are probably worried sick about her spending a week with you, the least I can do is make sure…well, to make sure she's alright. Don't argue about it 'cause you're not going to win, understand?'

He did argue and he didn't win, nor did he understand.

Diana was surprised to see Jacob and Annalise walk to the car with dance shoes. She didn't realise they were taking it so seriously, or that he owned dance shoes, Diana didn't, but Trevor did. Perhaps she ought to get a pair?

Alex and Simon didn't mind the students joining the class and were very pleased to see both Trevor and Diana back at the school too.

Diana seemed to remember nothing, but Trevor did and worked hard with her. She couldn't believe how good Jacob and Annalise were at dancing, well, they looked good to her.

The class went well. Diana had expected to find Andrea hanging around, but thankfully she stayed away. They hadn't spoken since the row, nor had she done anything about finding her a dance partner.

She glanced around the school, all the pupils were either couples or elderly women hoping to find a man to dance with. A few men had come on their own, but had been snapped up. Besides they were either too tall, too old, or too young for Andrea, or, they weren't much good at dancing. She doubted they were really interested in learning, more likely only there to pick up woman.

She had a great time with Trevor as he was kind, patient and great fun to learn with. Jacob and Annalise seemed very serious about their dancing, huh, just like two little Andrea's! The time went very quickly. Alex loved Jacob and Annalise and before they left had booked them in for lessons and agreed that they could come to the practice sessions for competitors.

Trevor pulled up outside Diana's house.

'Coming in for a coffee Trevor?' asked Jacob.

'Oh, well, umm.'

'I'll go and put the kettle on shall I?' checked Annalise.

Diana hadn't planned to ask him and wasn't best pleased with Jacob for doing some railroading, but could hardly say no now could she? The house was in such a mess…so what? Ah well. 'Yeah, you must come in for a coffee, or do you want tea?'

'Tea please. That's very kind, could just do with one.'

Diana guessed that Jacob was trying to push her and Trevor together, and she wasn't sure she liked the idea. Trevor wasn't her type, not that she had decided what her type was, someone like Anton du Beke perhaps? Hmm, probably not. Then she had a haunting thought, had Elwyn ever been her type? What had drawn her to him anyway? D'know…long time ago.

They seemed to talk endlessly about dancing. Diana couldn't get over how deep into it Jacob was. Nor could she believe all the lessons and classes they were having with the university club dance pro', who was apparently brilliant and spoken of as if he were the leader of some kind of religious sect. They got onto the problem of Andrea and her lack of a partner.

'I don't suppose you know anyone looking for a dance partner do you?' asked Diana sarcastically as she handed Jacob more tea.

'How about dad?'

Diana laughed and helped herself to a biscuit.

'No, seriously, how about dad?'

'I think his new wife may not like the idea,' said Diana coldly.

'They never got married. Anyway, she dumped him ages ago. He's living alone in nan's place and has been going to salsa classes for the last few months, didn't you know?'

No she didn't. She asked him a few more questions about Elwyn. She didn't feel sorry for him, but was surprised, though not about the split, she doubted any woman could put up with Elwyn's mother even though she was dead. Living in Phyllis's house must have been like living in a mausoleum and shrine to the old cow. The idea of Elwyn dancing with Andrea made her laugh and she thought no more about it.

Trevor was careful not to stay too long, besides he was on 'mornings' and it meant an early start. This time it was he that made the first move and he gave her a peck on the cheek, it was Diana's turn to blush. The moment was spoilt rather when they heard Jacob giggling and Annalise go: 'Aww'.

***

Given how hard she had danced at the class, Diana couldn't understand why she couldn't get off to sleep. She kept thinking about Trevor giving her a kiss, what had that meant? That they were friends, increasingly good friends? She didn't mind him kissing her, it was hardly passionate, but it was nice to be kissed again, even if it was by Trevor. The other thing on her mind was Elwyn: she had half expected him to turn up on her doorstep when, not if, he split up with that woman, she still wouldn't have minded giving him her long practiced speech about what she thought of him. But it seemed that he was more prepared to be lonely than come back to her. Well, good! But what did that say about what he thought of her? Did it matter? Not really… And was she really that bad? Change the subject!

Would he make a dance partner for Andrea? No, never. But how could Diana know? She wasn't a dancer, as this evening had proven. There didn't seem to be anyone else around and at least it would look good if she suggested someone, even though it was only Elwyn. But all he was learning was Salsa once a week, would Andrea think of that as a 'dancing career'? Surely not? She had seen some Salsa dancing at Alex and Simon's in the Christmas dance. It didn't look that hard, or at least the couples doing it made it look easy. She found it really hard to believe Elwyn would do any dancing, let alone sexy Salsa. When they had met he had no interest in dancing, but in those days when Diana said dancing she meant disco. It never occurred to her he may like proper dancing and perhaps he'd shut up about it so as not to be embarrassed or put Diana off him?

Eventually she dropped off to sleep, but woke with a start, she had had a strange dream, it had included Elwyn dancing Salsa with Annalise, and Andrea and Phyllis both trying to lead in a Tango while she and Trevor tried to teach them and hundreds of other pupils Cha-Cha-Cha. She wasn't sure if this could be classed as a nightmare, but it must have come pretty close to it.

***

Diana thought more about dancing partners at work the next day. She considered each unattached male colleague, and even a few that were married. She even mentioned dancing to a few of them, but got no where. Jacob had mentioned Elwyn again that morning, even suggesting he have a chat with his dad.

She wasn't sure why but she said: 'No, I'll do it,' testily and not intending to make any effort to ring Elwyn.

It was whilst Jacob and Annalise were out that Diana decided to see what Andrea thought of the idea, would Elwyn do? She wasn't sure what sort of reception she'd get when she rang, but her cousin sounded relieved more than pleased to hear her voice.

'Have you got a partner for me yet? I thought you might have forgotten. I've been really hunting everywhere for a man to dance with, but no one's interested. Tell me you know someone I can dance with,' pleaded Andrea.

Diana felt guilty for not having tried harder and even more guilty for only being able to offer Elwyn, he hardly seemed much to show for several weeks of searching.

'Well, I'm not sure he'll be any good for you, but he is a dancer.'

'Wonderful, who is it, have you spoken to him about me, what's his level?'

'Do you remember my ex', Elwyn?'

'Oh, yes, yes I do, I only met him a few times.' The tone of her voice said she remembered him better than that and already wasn't impressed.

Diana explained that he was lonely, the Salsa classes, that he was in a well paid job working regular hours and was going to the classes off his own back and apparently keen to learn.

Andrea warmed to the idea.

'No, I haven't spoken to him yet Andrea, I didn't want to get his hopes up in case you weren't interested.' That was a lie.

'You've got no problem with me dancing with him have you?'

'No, I haven't,' she laughed dismissively, 'as far as I'm concerned the less I see of him the better, so just keep him away from me,' she explained that Jacob had suggested Elwyn, Diana had had no idea of what was happening in Elwyn's life these days.

'I am grateful, but let me think about it. Salsa is okay, but it's not much good for the competition dancing I want to do. He's going to have to work hard and learn a lot more.'

'Well, it's just a thought, besides, he may not be keen.'

'Ah, that's true. But Jacob thinks he'd be alright for me doesn't he?' Diana realised Jacob's view counted, he was a dancer, Diana wasn't. The classes she had been to counted for nothing in Andrea's book, but Jacob was training to compete.

Ten minutes later, Andrea rang back: 'Yes, I'd like to try-out with Elwyn, what's his phone number, or do you think it's better to text?'

'Hang on Andrea, he doesn't know about you, I think we should have a chat with him first.'

'Oh…hmm, yeah, I suppose so, but you will contact him won't you?'

She hadn't spoken to Elwyn since…since when? Probably the day of the last divorce court hearing, how long ago was that? Over a year…nearer to two. She didn't even send him birthday or Christmas cards anymore, she only had previously to keep the link before he asked for a divorce and to show willing for Jacob's sake when the divorce proceedings started, though that didn't last long, she had been so angry with him. So the idea of ringing him after all this time and suggesting he start dancing with her cousin seemed ridiculous. Yes, it was ridiculous, she didn't want to talk to him, and the only ringing he deserved was by the neck!

The phone calls they'd had over the years were bad tempered ones about access rights for Jacob, what he owed her for maintenance, though to be fair he was pretty good in keeping the payments coming. All other contact was because she needed help with the house, which he was normally very bad at shelling out for. Who could she ask about this first? Trevor perhaps? He was at work though. She tried his mobile. Initially there was no answer then she heard his voice.

'Who the hell could this be? No one ever rings me on my mobile! 'Elloo? Anyone there, who is it please?' in a high pitched voice with exaggerated local accent.

Diana laughed, very Trevor.

When she spoke he was really delighted and was more his normal self.

'Sorry to bother you at work, can you speak?'

'Yeah, go ahead, though I may have to hang up if the foreman comes round, or this machine plays up.'

She explained about Andrea and Elwyn: 'What should I do?'

Trevor was really pleased she was asking his opinion, nice to be thought of as some kind of authority.

'If he does dance with her, he'll find what he's learnt in Salsa won't help him much, she's going to want him to come up with the goods from day one. I think he won't last a month, but it's worth a try.'

'I don't know how to approach him about it,' she explained about the few times they had talked in recent years, 'besides, why should I do him a favour, why should I do Andrea a favour? They've both upset me.'

'Because you're a good and kind person, you made a promise to help Andrea, who you really do care about, and you don't like the idea of Elwyn being alone and unhappy.'

He was right about Andrea, a bit off the mark with Elwyn though.

When Jacob came home with Annalise, she talked over the problem with them. As comparative dance experts, and they could do Salsa too, they saw no problem with Elwyn becoming competent in Ballroom and other Latin dances.

'Shall I ask him?' asked Jacob.

Now that was a good idea! Mind you, all he did was text his father, not quite what Diana thought he meant, but it was a start. She didn't know Elwyn possessed a mobile phone, let alone that he could text. She thought they would hear no more about it, which when it came to replying to messages, was the norm for Elwyn.

Just as she went to bed Jacob strolled into the room, phone in hand.

'Dad wants to talk to you.'

'What's he want?' she asked sullenly.

'He wants to ask you about aunty Andrea of course.'

'She's not your aunty, I keep telling you. Look, if he's upset because you texted him about dancing with her, tell him it's not your fault, blame me if you like, but I don't want to talk to him.'

'No, he's cool, he wants to know what she's like, he can't remember her very well and wants to know what kind of dancer she is.'

'Oh, I don't know what to tell him, I'm no dancer! You tell him.'

'Yes you are. Speak to him, he's cool,' and handed her the mobile.

'Hello Elwyn, how are you?' she asked quite formally, even coolly, and she didn't care how he was anyway.

'Fine, you? Is Andrea the tall-ish girl that was one of your bridesmaids?'

Diana confirmed she was. Then he wanted to know about her dancing career, it seemed vitally important to him.

'Jacob told me you're going to Salsa classes, that's a surprise, never had you down as a dancer.'

'I've always loved dancing.'

'News to me.'

'Well, all you were ever interested in when we were courting was discos. I've got my gold medals in Ballroom and Latin,' he said casually.

'What? When did you do those?'

'When I was a kid.'

'You never told me.'

'You never asked and were never interested when I talked about dancing, unless it meant going to a disco.'

She didn't remember him talking about dancing and now didn't know what to say, how was it she knew so little about the man she had married? She did wonder if he was just saying all this to make her feel bad, he had done something similar before.

'Anyway, I wouldn't mind having a try-out with Andrea. Shall I ring her or do you want to give her my number?'

***

Andrea rang Diana first thing next morning.

'Hiya Di!' she hated being called Di, 'Elwyn's rung and we've agreed to meet at Alex and Simon's tonight! I'm so excited, and I'm grateful, thank you Di, you don't know how happy I am!'

Once she got to know Elwyn she probably wouldn't be, thought Diana.

Jacob and Annalise went back to university. Diana and Trevor settled down into a routine at the dancing school, attending the improver's class when ever his shifts permitted. He repaired everything that needed fixing in and outside the house, redecorated every room and began sorting out her garden. They became ever better friends and the kisses became longer and more tender. Though she still felt she needed to keep him at arms length emotionally, if not physically, and she had firm limits on how physical their relationship was.

She heard nothing from Andrea in the next few weeks and assumed nothing had come of the partnership with Elwyn, she hadn't heard from him again either which was fine in her book.

The dancing school had a Saturday night social dance. She and Trevor started going along. About six weeks after suggesting Elwyn to Andrea, Diana was very shocked to see them in the ballroom just before the start of the social dance.

Andrea rushed over to her.

'Oh, Diana, how wonderful to see you! We had a lesson with Simon a little earlier and decided to stay on for the social dance…you don't mind do you?'

'Of course not, why should I?' that was tactful of Andrea, she seemed to have changed for the better.

'Well, I know you and Elwyn have history.'

Hmm, a strange way to sum up the last twenty years and a broken marriage.

Elwyn tactfully stayed on the other side of the ballroom and just waved politely and smiled, it looked more as if he were in pain, mind you, he had always had a smile like broken glass.

Andrea was a changed woman, visibly happy and relaxed. She looked very fit and had lost a good few pounds since last they had met, good for her, thought Diana.

Trevor and Diana went and got themselves a drink, when they went back in the ballroom dance music was playing though it was fairly quiet and wasn't really meant to be danced to, it was meant to be mood music. The only couple dancing was Andrea and Elwyn, they were practicing and spent almost as much time discussing the steps as dancing them, but when they did dance Diana couldn't believe her eyes, they were brilliant!

Alex had a rule that the social dances were not be used for serious practice, so once the evening began properly she reminded couples not to do advanced steps.

It was fairly obvious this was aimed at Elwyn and Andrea. Each piece of music that came on Elwyn and Andrea danced to and amazed everyone watching, particularly Diana, was that really Elwyn and Andrea? Even doing basic steps they looked advanced and very competent.

'They're good aren't they?' said Trevor.

'Amazing!'

'No wonder she was never happy with me,' he said a little sorrowfully.

'I just can't get over Elwyn being able to dance!'

'Serves him right for not telling you, I bet you would have made a good dance partnership.'

She seriously doubted this, she used to make fun of anyone who danced 'old time stuff' when she was a teenager. The way she mocked Andrea in those days probably made sure Elwyn kept his mouth shut.

Diplomatically, Andrea and Elwyn stayed the other side of the ballroom, but Diana could see they were having a wonderful time, really getting on well. They were the last two people on earth she would have ever thought would get on. They had hardly talked to each other when she had first started seeing Elwyn, perhaps they wouldn't have got on in those days, but they certainly were now. My, my, how times change!

Compared to Elwyn and Andrea, she and Trevor were real beginners, but they were enjoying their dancing for all that, and in any case they had to keep everything simple and fun tonight. Elwyn and Andrea doing even the simple stuff looked great. Some of the regulars watched them admiringly, others were jealous of course, but Alex felt that they stayed within her rules so let it go.

Whilst she had a good evening, Diana was still confused, even unsettled by the change in her cousin and ex'. She hardly recognised either of them as the people she had known for so long, but increasingly realised that she knew so little about either of them. Anyway, she and Trevor had had a nice time, he even put his arm around her shoulder, she liked that.

On the way home and later at her house they discussed the evening and Elwyn and Andrea in particular.

'They're just such good dancers!' said Diana for probably the tenth time in the last half hour.

'Well you knew Andrea was good.'

'But not Elwyn, perhaps if he'd said something and I'd listened our marriage would have been in with a chance.'

'Stop the 'what-ifs', you've said before that Phyllis never really liked you and he was a mammy's boy, you were on a hiding to nothing from the start there, dancing or no dancing.'

Diana thought this was a bit rich coming from Trevor who had lived his whole life for his mother, but that didn't matter now, he was his own man.

After more tea, Trevor said: 'Why don't we have dance lessons?'

'We are, silly, every week.'

'I know, but I mean private lessons, perhaps do our bronze medals, what do you think?'

'I'll have to think about it. Though if we do it'll look like I'm jealous of Andrea and Elwyn.'

'They won't even realise and given the level they're already at it won't make any difference. They'll be dancing championships soon and we're not even good enough for our bronze medal.'

'Hmm, I suppose you're right… I'll have to think about it.'

He headed off home like a lamb, no suggesting he stay over, they were just good friends really. He did give her a nice little kiss though.

She had a text message just as she was getting ready for bed, it was from Jacob, he and Annalise had just won their first varsity competition!

Perhaps she would have a couple of lessons after all.

***

Trevor proudly showed Diana a letter, he had been promoted and with the promotion came an end to shift work.

'Do you know, I've worked shifts in that place since I was sixteen! I won't be sorry to be off them, they were beginning to be a strain at my age.'

In fact he had been allowed to change his shift pattern so he could care for his mother for about a year, but Diana knew he didn't need to be reminded of this. The death of his mother was still a painful thought, or to be more exact the years when she had existed and suffered were still painfully clear in his mind. He still cried about it sometimes when their conversation came onto anything that reminded him of her. However, this was a big day and she was very proud of him, yes, proud, her best friend had done well. It also meant that he had more time for dancing and to be with Diana, and she liked the idea of that.

She felt far less uneasy about him hanging around, now she looked forward to seeing him, and not just because the house and garden had never been in such good shape, but he made her feel safe, and they had such fun learning to dance. Of course, they argued, but it was always over nothing. Perhaps he had planted the wrong rose bush in that corner, he hadn't hung his coat up when he arrived, or he hadn't changed into his slippers when he came in. Yes, he had his own slippers at her house these days, not exactly his feet under the table, but getting closer. In the dance classes they bickered, laughed at each other, pushed and pulled, giggled then begged Alex or Simon to agree that they had been right.

They began to socialise other than at the dancing school. Trevor liked to go to the cinema, Diana could take it or leave it, but enjoyed another chance of an afternoon or evening out. She had been amazed to hear that he hadn't been to the theatre since he was a little boy and then it had only been to see the pantomime. She started taking him to concerts, plays and musicals. He wasn't that keen on most of the plays she liked, but he put up with them, she could tell, he wouldn't admit it though.

Their modest 'dancing careers' made steady if not impressive progress, they finished the improver class season and looked forward to joining the 'advanced class'. Trevor was like a dog with two tails about it. Diana found the idea a little daunting, but most of their friends from the improver's class were joining the new season, so that made it better. Alex and Simon felt they would be ready to do their bronze medals on the next test day, Diana wasn't so sure.

Jacob came home for the summer holidays. Annalise had gone home to her parents, but this time Jacob would go and spend a couple of weeks with her toward the end of the summer. They had won a couple more competitions and were seen as high-flyers in the university club. Diana was very proud, the fact he seemed to be doing well in his studies was quite nice too.

'So, when is Trevor moving in with you?' he asked casually over breakfast.

Diana laughed. 'Never.'

'Why not, he loves you doesn't he?'

'Of course he doesn't, we're just friends.'

'Really, is that so?'

She laughed again, dryly. 'Look there's nothing going on between us.'

'There is. Don't tell me you don't love him, cause you do, it's obvious.'

'No I don't! No more talk like that from you young man! How would you know about being in love anyway?'

'I love Annalise.'

'You hardly know the girl! You're still just a kid!'

He shrugged. 'Doesn't mean to say I don't know what love is. I'm about the age you were when you fell for dad.'

Damn, he was right! 'And look what happened to us!'

'Just because you and him got it wrong doesn't mean to say I will with Annalise, or you will with Trevor. He's alright, he's looking after you, he loves you, you could do a lot worse,' he explained casually.

She felt her jaw drop, she was being lectured in love by her teenage son!

Diana laughed the conversation off and went to work, but she couldn't stop thinking about what he said. Did she love Trevor? Simon had said they were like an old married couple a few times, that was because they had such a good rapport in the lessons, but that didn't mean to say she loved him, did it?

Did I ever love Elwyn? she pondered on the bus. Yes, of course I did! Right, well, do I feel the same way about Trevor as I felt for Elwyn during those early years of our romance? Romance! Is that what it was?

She concentrated again, what about Trevor? She didn't actually like the answer. Yes she did, in fact she felt she had more of a romantic attachment to Trevor even now than she ever did with Elwyn.

She discussed it with the girls at work. Sheryn was the most understanding and got least laughs out of Diana's…predicament. Anita and Cerys thought the whole thing hilarious, how could Diana ever think she was falling in love with Trevor the mammy's boy that had never had a girlfriend? Diana argued with them, at least they apologised.

She and Sheryn talked a good bit about Trevor that day. She had really begun to worry that she had fallen in love with him, that wasn't the plan. But she was so unsure, was Jacob right, was their relationship so obvious to everyone but her?

'So what's wrong with loving him? He's good to you, good company, not demanding, kind,' asked Sheryn.

'Elwyn was at first.'

'Was he really?'

'Actually, no, if he was then I can't really remember it. But I don't want Trevor moving in with me!'

'He doesn't have to, unless you want him to. Has he asked to move in?'

'No, but he's almost living in my house now, I don't think there's anything left that he hasn't repaired, painted and rebuilt! He's round at least three times a week fixing or decorating something and he's done a brilliant job of tiling the bathroom.'

'Umm, have you, umm, I mean, are you…'

'Sleeping together? No!'

'Does he want to?'

'How would I know? I'm hardly going to ask him am I?'

'So he's not suggested it?'

'No…can we change the subject please?'

'So he's not pushy, not pressuring you, he seems a good bloke.'

Perhaps he was. She had never really discussed with Trevor how he felt about her. What they had was good and she didn't want to spoil it.

***

Andrea rang. Diana had seen her and Elwyn at the school's social dance a couple of times, but that was it. She assumed the dance partnership had broken up, probably it was for the best.

'Diana! Really exciting news: Elwyn and I are doing our first competition next Saturday, do you and Trevor want to come and see us dance?'

She was expected to say yes wasn't she? 'Where is it?' She assumed it would be in Newport. But was taken aback to hear it was Port Talbot, about forty miles away. 'Well, I'm not sure, I'll check with Trevor, I'm not sure what we've got planned.'

'You're normally at the dancing school on a Saturday, couldn't you miss it this week and come to see us dance?'

Ah well, nice try. 'I'll make sure Trevor isn't working that day, but if he's free, we'd love to.' And did Andrea know that Trevor didn't work shifts anymore? Probably not, this could be a good excuse.

'You could always come on your own. You can come in the car with me, dad's coming to see us dance too!'

It didn't seem to occur to Andrea that Diana didn't actually want to be any where near her ex-husband. They had had no problems at the school when they were there at the same time, and, to be fair to Elwyn, he had gone out of his way to avoid getting into a position where they could end up arguing...shame about all the other times during the last fifteen or so years!

Diana also wondered if Andrea had told Elwyn that she was inviting she and Trevor? She had a feeling Elwyn would be none too keen to have his ex-wife in the same room for a prolonged period either. With a bit of luck he would object and then Diana wouldn't have to go.

Annoyingly, Trevor really thought going to the competition was a great idea. And apparently Elwyn raised no objections, so the last chances of getting out of it were swept away.

For the sake of avoiding embarrassment, they travelled to Port Talbot in Trevor's car rather than with Andrea, Gilbert and Elwyn. Diana enjoyed the trip, she had never learnt to drive, which hadn't been a problem, she lived close enough to work to walk if she ever missed the bus. When she had first got married, Elwyn hadn't been able to drive, so she had been surprised to hear he now could. Though apparently Andrea was driving them this afternoon. Diana couldn't visualise Elwyn driving, she guessed he wasn't very good at it.

Andrea had given Diana a leaflet about the competition. Trevor had expected to find all they needed to know on the Internet, but there wasn't anything. Andrea said the promoter, Dai Post, was an old dance teacher and this was his annual competition. At one time it was the biggest night in the Welsh dance calendar, but these days it had become rather second rate and unpopular, despite an impressive list of titles that were being contested. It didn't help that the competition was run in an old community centre in a back street, but it was an ideal opportunity for Andrea and Elwyn, a nice modest event for their first competition. Getting to Port Talbot was no real problem, apart form the road works on the M4. They drove up to the hall just as Andrea was getting out of her car very near the entrance. She waved, Elwyn got out and gave them his trademark broken-glass smile, though it looked far less negative these days. They had some trouble finding somewhere to park. When they got to the hall Andrea was waiting, a line of people were filing in.

'I'm so glad you've come, dad and Elwyn have gone in, they're going to keep us seats.'

Oh great! Thought Diana, she would spend the whole evening sitting next to Elwyn and possibly with Gilbert on her other side! After the argument at her parents' home that Sunday, she guessed that Gilbert would still be annoyed with her, but he seemed cheerful enough when they arrived. Diana never had that much to do with him when she was a girl, she spoke more with Claire, Andrea's mum. Gilbert had always seemed distant, very serious, partly because of the very neatly trimmed goatee beard.

Andrea was very excited. 'Right, I've paid for you both, my treat!' she giggled.

They protested, but she waved the idea away and pulled Diana along past the queue. Actually, Diana didn't really consider spending an evening in a tatty old hall between her ex' and an elderly relative a treat.

'Are all these people here for the competition?' checked Trevor.

'Yes they are…hello again Sheila, these are the two I told you about, we'll go on through.'

'Alright dear, lovely to see you back dancing after all these years, lovely! And you haven't changed a bit!'

'That's Dai's wife, I used to have lessons with Dai when I was a girl, brilliant teacher. Sheila was a wonderful dancer in her time, but…umm, sort of went to seed.'

'Yeah, I see what you mean, she looks as though she's been dressed by the Salvation Army,' said Diana.

'They've got pots of money, but she's partial to a little tipple,' explained Andrea sympathetically.

'She's got a glass of tipple next to her,' said Trevor, 'she honks of gin!'

'Probably to keep the cold out,' said Andrea,

'It's a hot July afternoon,' said Diana.

In the hall, they found a dance floor about twice the size of Alex and Simon's, but it was marked with tapes for various sports courts, many of the tapes were breaking up. The front part of the hall had been an old chapel hall, the back half had been added on in the 1960's, and not very sympathetically either. Normally Dai's competitions only just broke even and more often lost a lot of money, but this afternoon the turn out was quite good despite his seemingly doing just about everything to put people off. The competition was poorly advertised, the hall was unattractive and difficult to get to.

Elwyn and Gilbert had managed to find seats, not in the front row, but given how quickly the hall had filled, they were grateful to have somewhere to sit.

Much to Diana's surprise, Elwyn warmly welcomed her and gave her a polite little peck on the cheek, that was the first time he had kissed her in…actually she couldn't remember how long. He was bubbling and happy.

Andrea had competed as a Juvenile, then Junior and finally as a 'Youth' with Julian, who became her husband. Now she was entering 'Senior' events, for over thirty-five year olds, but the set up of the competition and what she and Elwyn had to do were still well known to her, despite having been out of dancing for so many years. She was more than ready for the competition, she'd filled in the registration form, sent Elwyn off to get their competitors number, he came back with a slip of white card with eighty-four printed in thick, bold, black numbers.

'Are there eighty-four couples competing?' asked Trevor rather incredulously.

'I doubt it,' said Andrea, 'Dai just uses the remaining numbers from packs of numbers he used for previous competitions. I reckon there are about forty couples so far and more arriving, not a bad turn out by the look of it.'

Next, she sent Elwyn off to get changed, made sure Gilbert, Diana and Trevor were alright, sent Trevor off to get tea, then went to get changed herself.

They sipped their tea, which had been too expensive and was far too weak, except Gilberts' which had been far too strong and stone cold. They tried to take everything in, the atmosphere was electric, everyone seemed to be having a wonderful time, dance music was playing, couples were practicing. Diana and Trevor marvelled at the elegantly dressed men and beautifully gowned women. Most of the dancers were also 'Senior', some well over thirty-five, but all seemed to be able to dance like the Strictly Come Dancing pro's, and some of the dresses looked like the ones Karen Clifton had worn...actually, they would all have looked far better on Karen than these Seniors. Diana and Trevor had discussed the possibility of whether any of the Strictly pro's would be competing today! Nah, not this time, and probably not ever.

Trevor was having a great time. Gilbert knew a lot about competition dancing, he and Trevor talked endlessly about what was going on. Soon they were like old friends, Diana felt a bit left out, but Trevor kept drawing her into the conversation, though she really wasn't that interested. Trevor soaked it up as if his life depended on it.

Diana didn't recognise him at first, but Elwyn was standing next to her, he was in a tail suit and looked a picture of elegance. Was this really her ex-husband who never cleaned his shoes, wore odd socks, never did his tie up properly and wore sports jackets until they fell apart? Yes it was, his suit fitted perfectly, his hair was immaculately styled, despite his bald spot. He wore patent leather shoes, his white bow tie was starched and neat. His white shirt was also starched, it made his rather weedy body look far more macho. She couldn't help herself: 'Elwyn! Wow, look at you!'

'Oh, oh, thanks Diana. It's second hand, but the fit is really good, we found a tailor that took it in, it didn't need much work, not bad is it?'

He even looked handsome, even his smile was nicer!

'Right, time for a little warm up I think,' it was Andrea.

'Andrea, you're gorgeous!' said Diana.

Her dress was brilliant white with peach colour under skirts, it hugged her now quite trim figure. The bodice seemed to be smothered in blue and red rhinestones, she really did look like a princess.

Gilbert began to cry. 'If only your mum could see you now,' he mumbled.

She gave him a hug, sniffed back tears: 'Can't cry now dad, it'll ruin the make up.'

A few moments later they were dancing around, rather carefully, the dance floor was quite full.

Diana couldn't believe that she was watching her ex' and her cousin, her parents would never believe this. She had to remind herself to take pictures, they would need proof!

Elwyn and Andrea didn't dance for long. They went to the side of the floor and discussed where they would start each dance and their concerns about certain groups of steps. They loosened up like athletes, stretched, took up dance hold to make sure they had it just right. They were focussed entirely on the job ahead. This wasn't anything like Trevor or Diana's dance classes, or the Saturday night social, nothing at all. It wasn't even like Strictly Come Dancing, though Elwyn's suit looked as good as Anton's, and Andrea's dress could have been one that Karen wore, but it looked better on Andrea than it would have on Karen!

They rejoined Diana, Trevor and Gilbert.

'So, you two all ready then?' checked Trevor sounding excited.

'Yep, can't wait,' said Andrea, 'back competing again, I'm so happy!'

'We're in for a long evening aren't we? All these people have got to dance, do you know when you're on?' asked Trevor.

'We won't be on the floor alone, the comp' is broken up into lots of different events, we're in four of them. Given the size of the floor I should think they'll have twelve couples dancing at the same time in each event.'

'How will you get around with so many other couples out there?' Diana pointed at the still quite busy dance floor.

'We'll manage,' said Elwyn, though he was beginning to look nervous. Andrea didn't, only excited.

'Here,' said Andrea, and held the programme in front of them, it wasn't anything more than a sheet of A4, and badly creased at that. 'There are lots of events from Beginner to Championship, some are for under thirty-five year olds, and some for over 35, that's 'Senior'. We've decided to try the Senior Intermediate, Senior Pre-championship, the Senior Championship, and the Open Basic Foxtrot, that's not just for Seniors. Alex and Simon think these events are about right for us. Though the Championship is probably too high a grade for us in our first comp,' she smiled nervously for the first time and gave Elwyn's hand a squeeze.

Diana wondered if she felt anything for Elwyn, surely not?

She went onto explain how each event would be run, the rules, the standard of dancing they could expect. In fact she wasn't really that sure as she hadn't competed in so long, though she and Elwyn had been to see a competition in Birmingham a few weeks before to get a feel for what goes on. Elwyn had no competition experience, but as a dancer was surprisingly well qualified and confident.

'Clear the floor please dancers, clear the floor!' it was Dai on the microphone.

He spoke with quite a strong local Welsh accent, but he was easy to listen to, he smiled and oozed charm. He was rather stocky, obviously in his seventies and bald as a coot. His dinner jacket didn't fit that well, plus it was very old, and they were sure they could smell moth balls even from where they were sitting. He introduced the judges, five of them, three were from south Wales, this too apparently wasn't popular with competitors, they preferred judges from a much wider area. It is also more usual to have seven or nine judges, another couple of black marks.

As the judges were introduced, cheers went up from particular parts of the room.

'That judges' pupils,' said Gilbert.

'Does that mean the judge is going to mark his own couples better than the others?' asked Trevor.

'It's possible, I hope not. It'll break Andrea's heart if she gets a bad result because of politics in her first comp.'

They didn't know any of the judges, but Gilbert said all five may remember Andrea from the old days. They had either danced against her and Julian, or been around at the same time. In fact quite a few people had come up to Andrea already to check that it was her, no one could believe it, and all seemed thrilled to have her back dancing. Two judges stared at her as they waited for the first event, maybe they recognised her too.

'Our first event of the evening is the Open Intermediate Ballroom,' said Dai with a very broad smile.

'There you go, you're in this aren't you?' said Trevor stabbing the programme with his finger excitedly.

'No, it's 'open' that's aimed at under thirty-fives, we're in the Senior Intermediate,' explained Andrea and told him a few more details and rules. He lapped it up and asked more questions.

'They're good,' said Trevor as they watched the younger dancers in the Open Intermediate.'

'But some fishes out of water too,' said Gilbert.

Really? Diana and Trevor thought they were watching some advanced dancing.

At the end of each dance there was a zipping sound. The music put on by a bespectacled man on stage. He looked to be about eighty and used a record player, he insisted on lifting the stylus up manually and not very efficiently either. Neither he nor Dai did new technology and as far as they were concerned CD's were new and fangled, another black mark. Though the music itself was good, if a bit crackly. The zipping sound amused the audience, though irritated the chairman of judges who looked fiercely at the music man each time, didn't make any difference though.

'Thank you dancers, very nicely danced. Our next event is Senior Novice…'

'Senior, ooh, that's you two isn't it, aren't you going to dance this one?' Trevor couldn't wait to see them dance, but still Andrea and Elwyn sat and showed no sign of going out to dance.

'No, we're not novices, that's the grade below us,' said Andrea.

After more dancing, all be it obviously not as good as the first event, and more zipping sounds, Dai confidently announced: 'Senior Pre-championship, numbers two to 31 in heat one, 41 to 57 heat two and all remaining couples in heat three.'

'That's us,' said Andrea, she and Elwyn both looked determined.

They watched the first two heats. The standard of dancing varied between similar to the Open Intermediate, to very good…well it looked very good to Diana and Trevor. Surely Elwyn and Andrea weren't as good as this?

Heat three was called to the floor and Elwyn led Andrea out, now they both looked confident. The Waltz was played, each heat had to dance to the same piece of music, and each consisted of about ten couples. That seemed quite a lot for the size of floor, surprising when it had seemed so big earlier.

Seconds after starting, Elwyn tripped and fell, he had caught his foot on the loose floor tapes. Almost at once, he was back up and in dance hold. Andrea had avoided falling, but both now looked nervous, the music hadn't stopped. The audience, mainly other competitors, gave them a polite round of applause. Almost instantly Elwyn and Andrea seemed to settle down.

'They're really good aren't they?' said Trevor.

'I never would have believed it, they're amazing,' said Diana.

'Hmm, nerves getting the better of them, they're struggling,' said Gilbert.

But to Diana and Trevor, they looked stunning and the best couple on the floor, but what did they know? Well, Trevor thought he knew quite a lot. Gilbert tried to be tactful, but honest about their chances.

The Waltz over, they bowed to the audience, though Elwyn seemed only just to remember to do so. Andrea curtsied elegantly and naturally, but it seemed out of place in this scruffy old community centre. He led her back to their seats. Both looked upset and apologised to each other about all the mistakes each confessed to making. What mistakes? Diana and Trevor thought they had been perfect.

This event was a four dance and the next one they had to perform was a Tango. By the time heat two had done most of their Tango, Elwyn and Andrea were back to being focussed and intense. Tango went better.

'That's more like it,' said Gilbert softly.

They were more confident when they came off the floor too, though Andrea said Elwyn had been 'too high' in one section, he apparently knew, but there was no argument, they just got ready for Foxtrot.

'That's beautiful,' said Trevor in awe as they watched Elwyn and Andrea glide by, their best dance so far.

'Foxtrot was always her best dance with Julian,' said Gilbert proudly.

The last dance in this event, the Quickstep, wasn't so good for them, even so, compared to how Diana and Trevor danced Quickstep, it looked like a really professional, and seemed to be the equal of anything the other couples dancing, but Gilbert said it wasn't.

The first round of this event over, they welcomed Elwyn and Andrea back to their seats, both were sweating and panting, though looked satisfied, but listed all the things that had gone wrong, or should have gone better. It was clear they expected to get no further in this event. As far as Diana and Trevor were concerned, they were the obvious winners. Gilbert said little about their prospects, but that seemed to mean he also felt they had blown that one.

'Shame it had to be Senior Pre-champ' for our first event,' moaned Elwyn, 'I hoped it would be the Foxtrot or Senior Intermediate, given us a chance to warm up and settle the nerves,' explained Elwyn, he looked slightly despondent.

Dai called out the heats for the next event, the Open Basic Foxtrot. Elwyn and Andrea were in this too, it made no difference that they had just danced. Though it was only a one dance event with three heats, so they had a few minutes break. They were only allowed to do basic Foxtrot steps, if they did anything more advanced they would be disqualified. When they started dancing, Diana and Trevor were certain that Elwyn and Andrea would be disqualified. What they did looked so elegant and beautiful, to them it appeared advanced and complex. But as they watched, they realised that Elwyn and Andrea were doing the same steps that Diana and Trevor did in the classes, but it was a quantum leap ahead of them in terms of interpretation and performance. Their initial nerves were gone and now used to the dance floor, they began to relax, and excel.

About a quarter hour later Senior Intermediate was called, this was only three dances in two heats, Elwyn and Andrea were in the second.

Now they brimmed with confidence and made the opposition look very inadequate. Gilbert loved this.

The competition seemed confusing to Diana and Trevor. It was broken down into grades, each grade had age classifications, so there were several similarly titled events. There was a considerable list of contests, some had numerous couples entered, some had only enough for a straight final. Some Senior couples danced 'open' events that were aimed at under thirty-fives, the rules allowed this, but obviously it didn't work the other way. Elwyn and Andrea limited themselves to their four events, even so, they seemed to be out dancing quite a lot as they were recalled to the next rounds of the Senior Pre-championship (much to their surprise), Senior Intermediate and Open Basic Foxtrot, but so far the first round of the Senior Championship hadn't been called.

Despite their reservations, they were now doing well in the Senior Pre-championship and were called into the semi-final, they were very pleased. Diana and Trevor felt sure they would make the final, Gilbert wasn't so confident and told them some of the faults he had spotted, it had looked perfect to Diana and Trevor, they thought Gilbert was making things up or just being over critical, he wasn't.

'Thank you dancers. Our next event is the 'Beginners Two Dance', all couples please all couples.'

'You two could do this,' said Andrea excitedly.

'No we couldn't!' said Diana.

'You could, you don't wear comp gear like us in this category, so you're okay to dance it as you are. You can dance Waltz and Quickstep, go on, have a go!' urged Andrea.

'I'm game,' said Trevor.

'What? Then you go out there on your own!'

'You should have a go Diana,' said Elwyn in his usual slightly superior way.

'No! Besides we haven't entered it, it's too late now,' said Diana, sitting back, arms folded.

'Could these two have a go please?' yelled Andrea to Dai and the chairman of the judges.

'Are they registered?' checked the chairman.

'No they're not, never even been to a competition before,' confirmed Andrea.

'In which case, they will be very welcome,' said Dai grandly. The chairman nodded.

'We haven't got a number!' said Diana hopefully.

'No problem,' said Dai, snatched up a numbered card and held it out.

'Any one got some safety pins,' said Trevor as he hurried off to get the card, it had a large 114 printed on it.

'Here you are!' said Gilbert fumbling in a bag.

'I'll put it on for you,' said Andrea.

'But I don't want to dance,' said Diana plaintively.

'Go on, have a go, you'll enjoy it, bit of fun, better than just sitting there just watching all night,' said Elwyn.

Trevor tugged her hand and the next thing she knew they were dancing Waltz. She was very nervous, but so were the other beginners, she also realised they were doing better than some others on the floor. No one minded if you went wrong, which Diana and Trevor did occasionally, they just laughed it off and started all over again after they had forgotten their steps. Everyone around the room cheered them and the other beginners on, she quite liked that.

The Quickstep went a bit better than Waltz, but it was still nothing like the sort of thing Elwyn and Andrea had done in terms of quality, style and performance.

There had been nine couples in this event and it had been described as a semi-final.

'There you are, something to look forward to, see if you make it to the final,' said Andrea. 'Why don't you do the Beginners in Latin too?'

They said no, but moments later said they would. Diana thought Trevor was going to faint with excitement.

'I quite enjoyed that,' said Trevor.

Diana wondered if perhaps he had this all planned, though she somehow doubted it. Had she enjoyed her first competition? Actually, yes, she felt quite pleased with herself. It had been a bit of a laugh, something to tell the girls at work.

Very soon after they got back to their seats they noticed Elwyn and Andrea preparing themselves, the first round of the Senior Championship had been called. On the stage was a huge trophy, Dai patted it and gave the full title of the event, the South West Wales Senior Ballroom Championship, it seemed as big as the trophy. There were eleven couples, including Elwyn and Andrea contesting it. Some of the opposition hadn't tried any other event that afternoon, others had been up regularly and danced against Elwyn and Andrea, so they knew what to expect from them. The others, they were different, they were high quality and accomplished competitors. They would probably wipe the floor with Elwyn and Andrea who were a new partnership in their first competition.

The ages of the couples ranged from very obviously just thirty-five to one couple that looked to be in their mid seventies. Elwyn and Andrea were one of the younger couples.

As usual the first dance was Waltz. Elwyn and Andrea powered down the floor, they were now fully prepared for this event and used to the floor. Both were fit, everything was in place, this was their best performance so far.

Diana and Trevor could tell they had pulled all the stops out and were clearly one of, if not the strongest couple on the floor.

'Hmm, hope they don't drain themselves and leave nothing in the tank for the final,' said Gilbert. Even he had confidence they would be good enough this time.

They had to do five dances: Waltz, Tango, Viennese Waltz, Foxtrot and Quickstep. This was the first time Diana and Trevor had seen them do the Viennese Waltz, however, it seemed their weakest dance, but still nice to watch. Three of the other couples had an obvious advantage over them, that was clear even to Diana and Trevor's inexperienced eyes. Gilbert said one of the couples went off time, another went wrong in what he called the Fleckerl, they took his word for it. The event wasn't broken into heats, so all eleven couples were dancing at the same time. Despite the comparatively large floor, there were still too many couples to be dancing at the same time. Some of Elwyn and Andrea's best dancing was spoilt as they found themselves blocked or crashed into, even so, they managed to look good and dance well, certainly better than some of the others.

There were only a few seconds break between dances, some of the couples struggled to get their breath, Elwyn and Andrea panted, but seemed to have that edge in fitness. Diana thought this was amazing given how unfit Elwyn was when they were married.

The Quickstep looked quite a mess as the couples struggled to get around the floor, at least two seemed to deliberately get in the way of the opposition. Gilbert said they just weren't much good, but one of the male competitors, one that Gilbert said were 'damn good', got really annoyed as a plump couple yet again stopped and did an awkward looking 'line' in front of him. If it wasn't deliberate, it looked a lot like it. Elwyn and Andrea were a little luckier, or managed to use the floor that bit more effectively and their Quickstep wasn't quite such a disappointment. Even so, when they left the floor, after bowing and curtseying to the audience, they were panting hard and moaning about other couples, opportunities lost, mistakes made, and the difficulty with tapes on the floor, the list seemed endless.

All remaining rounds were finals, some 'straight-finals' had been run earlier. Some events had attracted no entries at all, though nothing was said, it all served to confuse Trevor who followed events as best he could from the programme, Gilbert was very helpful and they had become firm friends.

Events weren't called in the order shown on the programme. Dai changed the order so that if a couple had just danced in an event, the next event, hopefully, would not be an event they were in. Though some couples just had to put up with it if Dai couldn't them a break, most dancers seemed to take this in their stride, particularly the ones that had entered as many events as the rules permitted. Diana and Trevor noticed one Senior couple in seven different events, they weren't bad and were up dancing time and again, they seemed to be remarkably fit, both looked to be in their mid-sixties and were having a wonderful time, though only made two finals.

'Final of the Beginners two dance, the judges have recalled the following five couples...'

'Here's your event, you could be in this,' said Andrea cheerfully to Trevor and Diana.

'Of course we're not!' said Diana, 'we made a right mess of the whole thing.'

'Numbers two, forty, forty-eight, seventy-five and one-hundred-and-fourteen.'

Gilbert clapped enthusiastically. 'Off you go, you danced well enough last time after all.'

'There you are, told you, you're in the final!' said Andrea and gave her cousin a hug.

Very self consciously Trevor led Diana to the floor, seconds later Waltz music began and they did their best, the nerves seemed worse this time, but they were really happy to have made it and Trevor smiled like a Cheshire cat.

'Where do you think we'll finish?' asked Trevor excitedly when it was over.

'Should be in the top three,' said Gilbert.

They thought he was being kind.

At most competitions, promoters give a running order of events so couples know how long it will be before they have to dance, or they at least warn couples which event is next part way through the previous one. This means couples can warm up and get ready, the men can put their jackets on, shoes can be scraped, drinks sipped, and muscles warmed up. But not Dai, he gave no warning and couples frequently had to scramble to be ready in time, another black mark. Elwyn was chatting to Gilbert, and Andrea to Diana when Dai announced that the final of the Senior Intermediate was next, he began reeling off the couples' numbers. Elwyn and Andrea had a strong feeling they would make this final given the way that the semi-final had felt so good, they listened hard to the numbers being called as Elwyn struggled into his jacket and Andrea checked her make-up.

'…eighty-two, eighty-four, and finally one hundred!' said Dai with a flourish.

'We're back, off we go!' said Elwyn and hurried to the floor and then presented Andrea a little theatrically as she joined him.

'Very nice,' said Gilbert as they danced.

'They've got to win this,' insisted Trevor with a new found authority.

'Don't forget some of the judges have their own couples in this final, there could be some politics.'

It was a three dance event, Waltz, Tango and Quickstep, all seemed to go very well for Elwyn and Andrea.

Just as they left the floor, both looking quite satisfied, Dai announced:

'Final of the Senior Pre-championship four dance…the judges have recalled the following six couples: thirty-one, thirty-nine, sixty-two, eighty-four, ninety-nine…'

'Oh, that's not fair! You've only just danced,' moaned Trevor, 'tell him, you can't dance again so soon, it's not fair!'

'Tough on us,' said Andrea and she dabbed away very carefully at some sweat.

They quickly checked that his suit and her dress were alright then hurried back to the floor.

As with all the other finals, there was only a few moments break between dances, but with only six couples the dancers had ample room to get about, and Elwyn and Andrea looked stunning, again they seemed the best, however, by the time they danced Foxtrot they seemed to be struggling a little. Part way through Quickstep Elwyn was breathing very heavily, but kept going and still looked happy to be dancing. Andrea appeared elegant and completely fit with no sign of fatigue.

When they came off the floor Elwyn seemed to wilt. 'That took it out of me,' he wheezed. Andrea flopped onto a chair and said nothing, despite how she looked when they danced, she now didn't have enough puff to talk.

'Final of the Open Basic Foxtrot,' said Dai happily.

'Oops,' said Elwyn, 'perhaps we're not in this final?' he added almost hopefully.

Andrea got to her feet, took a deep breath, seemed instantly fit again, smiled and listened to the numbers being called.

'…Eighty-four…' chanted Dai.

'Ask them to give you a break,' said Diana.

'No, it's only a one dance, we'll be fine,' said Elwyn, Andrea nodded and they hurried away.

'God help them if the Championship is run next,' said Gilbert.

Despite their outward appearance, they didn't look that good, they were very tired now. There had been very few under thirty-five year olds at the competition, the only young Championship grade couple was also in this final, they looked really excellent and Elwyn and Andrea didn't compare this time.

Just the one dance, but it had been almost as draining as the other two finals.

'Please don't let him call the Championship!' said Trevor toward the stage, watching Dai scrutinize a sheet of paper.

'Open Novice final...' said Dai.

'Thank heavens for that' sighed Gilbert.

Just in case, Elwyn and Andrea remained ready to dance, there was a chance the Senior Championship could be after the Novice. Soon they had their breath back and kept loosened up and warm. In fact Dai kept the Championship as the last event of the Ballroom section. They had no idea if they had made the recall and just had to assume they were in it and strained to hear their number called.

Dai asked the finalists to do a short introduction dance, a 'dance on', he would call one of the couples' number, name them and say where they were from, then they would dance a few bars of Foxtrot.

'The judges aren't marking this,' said Gilbert, 'but they are watching, so the couples have to get it right and look good, bad time to make a mistake!'

Diana and Trevor nodded sympathetically.

It seemed Elwyn and Andrea weren't in the final, six couples had been called, not Elwyn and

Andrea, but it was a seven couple final and they were the last to have their number called.

'Number eighty-four, Elwyn Wharton and Andrea Mooney from Newport! And may I say how wonderful it is to see Andrea competing again, welcome back Andrea. She was one of our pupils many years ago and we are delighted to welcome her to our competition, her first in nearly twenty years.'

Everyone applauded, Andrea cried, curtsied, even their fellow finalists applauded her. But then it was down to business. Dai's helper put a Foxtrot on and Elwyn and Andrea seemed to be carried along by the music, the few bars of the dance-on were their best performance so far.

Waltz was still the first proper dance of the final. Like everyone else, Diana, Trevor and Gilbert cheered the couples on, but particularly Elwyn and Andrea, who in fact had a lot of support from the audience. Deservedly so, they looked great. There were no weak couples and it was a real test of dancing, it was obvious Elwyn and Andrea were loving every second. Finding a winner from the seven wasn't going to be easy for the judges, but it was oh-so-simple for Diana, Trevor and Gilbert.

The final over, they welcomed Elwyn and Andrea back as if they were conquering heroes. Both panted, but were very pleased with how it had gone, they felt they had danced well and were in at least with a chance of being in the top three. Good effort for a new partnership in their first competition.

The Ballroom section was over. Most promoters give the prizes for the Ballroom events almost immediately after the last final, but not Dai. He announced the results wouldn't be until after the

Latin, yet another black mark. It didn't matter to Elwyn and Andrea, as they also planned to dance the Latin events. Elwyn loved his Latin, though Andrea wasn't such a fan. Having said that it made no difference to her, it was dancing, it was competition, and she was keen to be out on the floor giving it all she could. They went off to change.

'Well, that was amazing,' said Trevor, 'I'm really enjoying this!'

'Yeah, different sort of way to spend a Saturday!' said Diana.

'Wonder how we've done in the Beginners Ballroom?' mused an excited Trevor.

'Still want to do the Latin?' checked Diana.

'Ooh yes, you don't mind do you?'

'No, of course not, I'm looking forward to it,' no she wasn't.

A few minutes later Elwyn returned ready for the Latin. Diana felt her jaw drop. He wore a black shirt, open to show a modestly hairy chest, all be it rather pale, the shirt was decorated with black rhinestones around the collar. His outfit was completed with superbly cut black trousers. He looked confident and completely at ease in clothing that Diana knew at one time he wouldn't have worn, even for a bet! Andrea was next, she wore an amazing dress, a red bodice, fading down to deep orange that faded back to the same red on the fringed skirt. It suited her figure and showed off shapely legs, again she seemed completely at ease.

'Hmm, I wouldn't mind seeing you in a dress like that' said Trevor softly.

'What? Me, dressed like that? Never! And Trevor, wash your brain out with soap!'

'Well, I think it would suit you.'

'Yeah, right. Where's your dirty mac'?'

Andrea put the now rather crumpled number card on Elwyn's back, then they went out to practice.

Again, most of the couples were Seniors, many of the women wore dresses that would have looked better on much young dancers, but they were all clearly happy, and soon it looked normal. The entry for the Latin was considerably less than for the Ballroom, so once the events began, progress through the programme was quite rapid.

The Beginners Cha-Cha-Cha and Jive was the second event called, this time it was a straight final of just four couples. Diana felt a little more confident, but still nervous, even so she enjoyed it and the crowd got behind all the couples and made it fun. They didn't go wrong this time. She preferred the Latin dances to the Ballroom, though Alex said she was better at the Ballroom than the Latin, Diana just thought she was bad at both, but slightly less bad at Latin.

The Senior Intermediate was called as they left the floor, Elwyn and Andrea passed them on their way to dance. Trevor and Elwyn high-fived, Diana laughed, how Elwyn had changed, Mr. Stuffed shirt had apparently moved on!

Gilbert said they had danced well. They all cheered Elwyn and Andrea enthusiastically. Their Latin didn't seem as impressive as their Ballroom, but the standard seemed remarkably modest, even so, they knew Elwyn and Andrea still had a lot to prove and this was their first Latin event.

'You were so nervous!' said Andrea to Elwyn as they got back to their seats. 'I'm really glad we got that one out of the way before the other events, are you alright?'

'Yeah, I felt myself tensing up, another couple were a bit close, he even knocked me in Cha', so that affected my confidence.'

Andrea forced herself to remember that this was Elwyn's first ever competition. For her it was the first in many years, yet she had competed almost weekly from the age of…what? She actually wasn't that sure how old she was when she began dancing and then competing. She was probably about five or six when she remembered winning her first competition. Over the years she had had several dance partners, she even struggled to remember some of their names, but she had competed fairly regularly until she was twenty-two. How many competitions had she done between the ages of five and twenty-two? Probably thousands! She had no idea how Elwyn must be feeling and tried to be patient with him, after all, he had come a remarkably long way in an incredibly short time. Mustn't drag this one along too quickly! Could lose him, and she already thought Elwyn was too good to lose.

They were back on the floor to dance the Open Basic Rumba a few minutes later. That seemed a bit better, Elwyn wasn't so tense. There were enough couples to make a semi-final and the standard of dancing varied quite a lot.

Trevor watched intensely how Andrea and Elwyn danced. 'We could do better than some of the couples competing in this you know Diana!'

'I don't think so my boy!' and laughed.

He seemed a little hurt.

Like the Foxtrot, the steps had to be 'basic'. The same under thirty-five championship grade couple danced this too.

'If that's 'basic', I'll eat my hat!' said Trevor.

'Honestly, it is,' said Gilbert, 'they're just putting lots of style into it.

'They're bound to win,' said Diana.

'I agree,' said Gilbert, 'Andrea and Elwyn…hmm, we'll see.'

The atmosphere in the hall remained very good. Diana and Trevor noticed that the Ballroom only competitors remained in their dance costumes.

'Ready for the presentation,' said Gilbert, 'it's good protocol for the couples to wear their dance costumes to be presented with their prizes.'

'Does that mean Andrea and Elwyn will have to change back into their Ballroom clothes after they've finished dancing the Latin?' asked Trevor.

'No, they can stay in the Latin outfits for the Ballroom and Latin presentations.'

Diana guessed Trevor was storing all this information ready for their next competition, he was obviously bitten, she wasn't sure she was…perhaps mauled was a better word.

Andrea and Elwyn had a break before they danced the first round of the Senior Pre-championship. Again, there had only been enough couples for a semi-final as the first round. At least in this they looked more confident, and once more the standard didn't seem that high. Gilbert felt sure they would make the final of the Intermediate and the Pre-championship. The first round of the Championship had yet to be called. When they had been filling in the form and listing the events they wanted to enter, they had had quite a debate about whether they should try the Championship. Simon had felt it may not be a good idea, but Andrea thought they may as well, and Elwyn had been very keen. As they waited for the first round neither seemed to be looking forward to it.

As Gilbert predicted, they didn't make the final of the Open Basic Rumba. Elwyn was disappointed, but Andrea wasn't really surprised.

Trevor was confused: 'This may sound stupid Gilbert, but if they didn't make the *basic* Rumba final, how can they hope to make the finals of the other events? I mean, *basic* means *basic*, beginner, simple, but from what you say Intermediate and Pre-championship are more advanced standards. If they're no good in basic they can't be any good for the higher grades?'

Gilbert nodded slowly and reflectively: 'Basic Rumba is an event on its own, how they do in it won't impact on the other events. Basic Rumba can be very hard, some really good couples won't dance it in case they show themselves up. It's more than just the steps, it's the performance, the beauty of the dancing and the quality of the technique. A good few years ago, a pro couple won the World Professional Latin Championship and for their Rumba only danced basic. Of course their other four dances were amazing, but everyone felt it was the Rumba that had won it for them.

'When Andrea and Elwyn danced it they just weren't good enough. Now in the other events they had settled down a bit, they were far more impressive, but those events didn't demand as much technically from them as the Basic Rumba did, see?'

Trevor nodded unconvincingly.

Andrea and Elwyn did make the final of the Intermediate and looked very good this time. The final of the Pre-championship was announced,

Andrea hadn't bothered to get up, she doubted they had made it, but they had, this gave her a boost and they looked quite impressive.

The entry for the Championship was modest, a straight final of five couples.

There had been several others from Alex and Simon's school here, Diana and Trevor knew most to say hello to. One couple they did know well was Bryn and Siân Ace. They were Simon's couple, and Senior Latin specialists. They had arrived not long before the Latin section had begun and the only event they danced was the Championship. Compared to the other couples in the final, Bryn and Siân were a league apart, even so Andrea and Elwyn looked quite good and Diana. Trevor and Gilbert felt that they may well come second, which would be fair. Gilbert wasn't that sure things would be fair and kept warning them that politics would play quite a part in the final result.

Again, the championship was the last event and again each couple had to do an introductory dance, this time a Samba. Given it was getting quite late some people in the audience moaned audibly that Dai seemed to spinning things out, one more black mark. But he was having a wonderful time.

'Well ladies and gentlemen, dancers, we are coming to the end of what has been a very enjoyable and exciting day of competition,' he started giving his view on how well some events had been contested.

'We know, we've been here all afternoon,' came a voice from the audience, 'results please!'

'Oh, right-o, of course,' said Dai losing a little of his cool and impeccable diction. 'I would now like to invite Mrs. Sheila Post, my dear wife, to present the successful couples with their prizes.'

Sheila was already in front of the stage helping another lady to arrange the prizes, except Sheila had had more of her favourite tipple and as fast as she was setting the prizes out, the other lady took them away and put the prizes either in the right order, or replaced them with the right ones for the events. The audience quite enjoyed the show. Finally, the helper shoved Sheila to the other side of the table. Sheila was clearly tipsy and weaved around and then leaned on the table to steady herself, pushing a few prizes over in the process.

'She hasn't changed in twenty years,' moaned Gilbert.

She wore a scruffy pair of slacks smothered in cat's fur, what was probably an expensive blouse at one time though she had buttoned it up wrongly and her earrings didn't match. She smiled contentedly and waited for the first couple to come forward for their prize.

'We will start our presentation with the Beginners Ballroom Two Dance,' said Dai quite formally.

'Oh, that's you two, better get ready to go and get your prizes,' said Andrea.

'You mean we've got to go out there?' said Diana pointing toward the stage as if it were the jaws of a shark.

'Of course, to get your prize off Sheila,' said Andrea.

'First, number 114... I'm sorry I don't know your names,' said Dai.

'What's he mean?' said Diana.

'Don't be stupid love, we've won!' said Trevor and leapt to his feet.

'Wait for Diana!' said Andrea as Trevor started to hurry off toward Sheila.

'We can't have won! We were useless, we only did it for fun!' protested Diana very loudly.

Andrea tugged her out of her seat so she could run after Trevor. He stood waiting and led her the last few yards, still a bit reluctantly, to Sheila.

'Well done dears, well done,' she slurred slightly.

They were each given a small plastic plaque, they shook hands with Sheila, Trevor thought this stopped her from falling over. Then they began to walk back to the others.

'No, stay there, stand next to Sheila, you've got to congratulate the other couples!' said Andrea in a kind of stage whisper and lots of gesturing.

Uncertainly they went back and stood a bit too close to Sheila, she lolled into them. Trevor proved to be handy in stopping her flopping onto the floor.

The second placed couple were now with Sheila. Diana and Trevor shuffled a little further from Sheila as they came to greet them. They congratulated them and took their place next to Diana and Trevor.

'Stay there!' signalled Andrea and Gilbert together.

They watched the third placed couple come out, get their prizes and then join the 'presentation line'. This was repeated until all couples that had danced in the final had filed past Diana and Trevor. All the couples seemed to grin foolishly, but they were having a great time.

Gilbert and Elwyn rushed out and took their picture in the presentation line. For Diana, seeing her ex' dressed in a sexy Latin outfit, cheerfully taking her picture was surreal, was this another weird dance dream, or a nightmare? Well it felt real enough, as did the prize. At least Phyllis wasn't in this dream.

'Can we go now?' asked Trevor.

The other couples, Gilbert and Elwyn said yes.

Trevor and Diana hurried back with their plaques as if they were chests of gold, their smiles literally from ear to ear.

'Hey, I liked that!' said Trevor.

'Thought you might!' said Diana, in fact she quite liked it too.

Dai Post worked through the events methodically. Next came the Novice, then the Open Basic Foxtrot, Andrea and Elwyn came second behind the young couple. Gilbert said this was quite fair, the youngsters were very good. Diana and Trevor had expected Andrea and Elwyn to win it, so they were disappointed, perhaps this was the politics that Gilbert was on about? Andrea and Elwyn seemed very happy with second which surprised Trevor, he thought only a win would be good enough.

Next Dai called the Open Intermediate Ballroom, he seemed to be deliberately keeping Andrea and Elwyn waiting. At last he announced the Senior Intermediate. Andrea and Elwyn had won it.

There was no guarantee they would and they were just delighted to have won at their first competition, this was a welcome boost and surprise, Andrea was so thrilled. For their trouble, they also received a small plaque each.

Several more sets of results later, Dai at last got around to the Senior Pre-championship.

'First, number eighty-four, Elwyn Wharton and Andrea Mooney, from Newport!'

This time they got a nice trophy and a bottle of wine each.

'That's discrimination!' said Trevor, 'where's our bottle of wine? We just got cheap plaques!'

'You'll have to wait till next time,' said Diana.

'So we're going to do another competition are we?' he checked very hopefully.

'Well, I suppose so, I don't see why not.'

'Great! 'Ere, wait till we tell Alex and Simon about this!'

'Wonder how we've done in the Latin?' mused Diana.

'I don't want to think about it!' said Trevor a little too dramatically.

They welcomed back Andrea and Elwyn with their trophy, Andrea was so happy and Elwyn looked very proud.

Gilbert seemed close to tears. 'I wish your mum could see you now,' he kept muttering.

A few minutes later Andrea and Elwyn stood waiting to hear the results for the Senior Ballroom Championship, they had no illusions, the odds were against them this time, but they were very pleased with what they had achieved today anyway.

'Our last Ballroom result, the South West Wales Senior Ballroom Championship,' said Dai and yet again went to pat the trophy, but the lady helper was already struggling down the steps from the stage with it. She seemed only slightly bigger than the trophy. She crashed it down next to Sheila who jumped, she had dozed off.

Dai consulted his sheet of paper. Smiled broadly and turned on his microphone again: 'Winners of the South West Wales Senior Ballroom Championship, from Newport, Elwyn Wharton and Andrea Mooney! Well done Andrea, welcome back, welcome home!'

Elwyn seemed to lift off like a rocket, Diana had never seen him so happy or excited, well, perhaps when Jacob was born, but that was a different kind of excitement. He rushed to the floor and bowed dramatically, then rushed back and pulled Andrea along, she was busy hugging her father, they were both crying. When they got to the floor, many people were on their feet cheering. Andrea knew a lot of people here and it had been a big surprise for them to see her back dancing after so long and now to have done so well in their first competition, this was great.

The presentation was very emotional, Sheila hugged Andrea and gave Elwyn a kiss, he wasn't ready for that, or for the puff of gin fumes in his face either. Their win came as a surprise to the couple that came second, they had expected to win, in fact Gilbert thought they would win.

Dai began the Latin results as soon as the Championship line-up had dispersed.

Andrea and Elwyn triumphantly paraded back with their trophy and more wine. There was a lot of hugging and kissing, people came over to congratulate them, it was very exciting.

The helper from the trophy table came rushing up to them: 'Excuse me, you two are number 114 aren't you?' she said to Diana and Trevor.

Initially they didn't know what she was talking about.

'Oh, oh yes, we are,' stammered Trevor, 'what's wrong?'

'Well would you mind hurrying up please, we're waiting for you!'

'What for?'

'You've won the Beginners Latin, come and get your prizes.'

'Never!' said Diana as she chased after Trevor, who seemed to be chasing the helper.

'Oh, you two again! Here you are, well done,' said Sheila, slurring her words slightly and handed them two more plaques.

'What, no wine?' said Trevor.

'No, wine is bad for dancers,' said Sheila earnestly.

'I can see that,' said Trevor, the irony was lost on her.

Diana was going to walk straight back off the floor, but felt Trevor's hand yank her back to the presentation line to have her picture taken by Gilbert and Elwyn again, he was laughing and joking with Gilbert. Was this really the man she had learnt to hate and spent so many years in constant conflict with? Yep, apparently it was.

Their excitement over, they waited patiently to hear how Andrea and Elwyn had done in the Senior Intermediate. They won it.

Compared to the championship win, this didn't seem that significant, but it was another win and in Latin, not their strongest discipline, so they were still very pleased. The form book, and Simon, had said they shouldn't have done so well.

The next result they were interested in was the Senior Pre-championship. As before Dai worked through the various events until he came to this grade. The helper put an elaborate trophy on the table for Sheila who seemed to have dozed off again even though she was standing up, ever smiling contentedly to herself.

Dai smiled and winked at Andrea. 'Winners, number eighty-four, Elwyn Wharton and Andrea Mooney from Newport!'

'Now that *is* lucky, though given who they were up against, I did hope they would win, just shows you can't be sure can you?' said Gilbert and clapped as Elwyn and Andrea hurried off to get their trophy. Despite it looking quite impressive, it was actually made of plastic and quite light.

'Don't forget you've got to sign for all these trophies, I'll come over with the forms now,' said the helper breathlessly, she seemed to be close to the end of her tether.

'Do you think you've got enough room in the car for all these trophies, and all this wine?' said Trevor. They had received two more bottles.

'We are doing well aren't we?' said Elwyn impishly.

'So what do you think about the Latin championship?' asked Diana. She had decided they would beat Bryn and Siân.

'Second if we're lucky,' said Andrea.

She was right, second place, Bryn and Siân won it, but that didn't matter to Elwyn and Andrea, they had achieved far more than they had ever hoped for today.

As soon as they came back form the presentation line with yet more wine, they went and changed. The helper scurried across to Gilbert, Diana and Trevor.

'Here you are, you can sign for all those trophies can't you Gilbert? Nice to see you again after all these years, where's Claire tonight? They danced well tonight didn't they?'

Claire was Andrea's mum, the helper crumpled visibly when Gilbert said she had died, but he dealt with it well, after such a good evening for Andrea (Elwyn didn't get much of a mention), Gilbert was now strong enough to deal with the reminder of Claire's death. While he signed for the trophies, the helper flipped through a stack of forms.

'Right then, they won the Senior Intermediate and Senior Pre-champ' in both. That means they've qualified to dance in the "Nationwide Dance Elite" competition later this year, do you want the forms, or do you think it's not worth it given they've done so well in championship?'

'Oh, I don't know, I've never heard of that competition before.'

'I expect not, it's been going for a good few years now, but certainly not when Andrea was dancing last. Because they've won today they qualify to dance in the grand finals.'

'Sounds interesting, give me the forms and I'll have a chat with Andrea.'

'Right-o Gilbert…now then, you two,' she said turning to Diana and Trevor, 'you won the two Beginner events didn't you?' she flicked through the stack of forms, 'you've qualified for that grade in the "Nationwide Dance Elite" competition too, do you want the forms or have you qualified already?'

'You mean we've got to dance in it?' checked Diana.

'No, only if you want to, but as you've won your events, you qualify to dance in the grand finals, it's in Southampton in December.'

'What do you think love?' checked Trevor, 'I don't mind either way.' Yes he damn well did!

'Umm, well, if we've won through, we'd better look into it, okay give us the forms.' She took them apprehensively.

Trevor gave her a hug.

'Right!' said Gilbert cheerfully, 'lets go and look at the marks.'

'What marks?' said Trevor.

'Now the comp's over, the judges marks for all the events are available for the couples to check. We can see how well the judges marked you in your events and I'm really keen to see what they thought of Andrea and Elwyn!'

'But we know, they won nearly everything,' said Trevor and chuckled.

'Yes, of course, but let's see how close it was, see if any of the judges marked them to win the Latin Championship, that sort of thing.'

Diana and Trevor weren't sure they understood, or saw any point, but dutifully followed Gilbert.

He was in his element. 'Ah, very interesting, hmm, that judge didn't like them did he? Oh good, straight firsts in the Pre-championship Ballroom!' He gave a running commentary. He had his camera and photographed each page that included Andrea and Elwyn's marks. Somehow they didn't think Gilbert would be that switched on or prepared.

'Right, here are your marks…look, good, you had four judges mark you first in the Ballroom and three in the Latin, you did really well given it was your first comp and you just did it on the spur of the moment too. I'll take a picture of these marks for you, Alex and Simon will want to see them. I'll email them to you shall I? What's your address?'

They thanked him, but found it hard to believe their teachers would be interested, or that Gilbert could use email.

Soon Andrea returned, she looked at ease and happy. She was very keen to see the marks and discussed each one with her father. Elwyn wasn't familiar with the marking system, so she explained the significance. It seemed they had been easy winners in each of those they had won and encouragingly had taken some first place marks off Bryn and Siân Ace, that was a big surprise. This first competition was a big success.

The hall was emptying rapidly and Dai Post and his helpers were hard at work lugging very heavy boxes and equipment through a fire door. Sheila was no help, she was fast asleep on the stage.

'So, what happens for you two next?' asked Trevor.

'Well, we don't have much planned as such,' said Andrea, 'we wanted to see how today went before we planned our next few comps. There's another in a few months, a much bigger one than this, it's in Warwick, so we'll probably do that.'

'You'll wipe the floor with them,' assured Trevor graphically.

'That would be nice. But today was a fairly small event, though it may not have looked it, not many top flight couples here, but a good warm up. Warwick will be another matter as the standard is likely to be far higher.'

'Are you going to do this one in December in Southampton?' asked Diana.

'Don't know, I'll have to find out more about it. From what this says,' she waved the form they had been given, 'we could do the Senior Intermediate, or the Senior Pre-championship, we have to choose. But given we've already won a championship and come second in the other, I'm not sure that would be allowed, anyway, how about you two, are you going to do Southampton?'

'Oh yes!' said Trevor. 'Aren't we love?'

'Yeah, mind you, depends on how much it costs and if we can get time off work,' she was already thinking of excuses. 'Southampton in December, hmm, can't wait!' she said, grimacing.

'I'm looking forward to it!' said Trevor. Diana wasn't surprised.

She also realised he now called her 'love' quite often, yeah, she didn't mind that.

'I thought this was a big competition,' said Trevor, 'all those huge trophies, the big titles, lots of people dancing.'

'In competition terms, Dai's comps aren't big, the titles aren't that significant, the couples dancing them are mainly local and not the very top couples. The standard wasn't as high as we can expect at, say, Warwick, so today was very good, but we can't assume all comps are going to go so well for us,' explained Andrea. 'We have a lot of work to do in the next few weeks.'

Elwyn nodded sage-like at this.

Trevor and Diana knew she was just being modest.

They all helped to load the car up for Elwyn and Andrea. Diana was surprised to find she was a little sorry they weren't all going home together, yet earlier the idea of sharing a car with her ex-husband was a very bad one. This competition seemed to have changed a lot, relationships had changed, circumstances had changed, and so too had perceptions.

Trevor and Diana planned their trip to Southampton as they drove home, she would give it a go after all.

'I want to compete at Warwick!' declared Trevor.

'Now I'm not so sure about that!' but she was weakening by the time they got home.

He kissed her good night after a cup of tea. She was close to suggesting he stay the night, but she still wasn't ready for this, the look in his eyes said he was, but he would have to be patient with her. She had conceded quite enough for one day.

Chapter Four
Share and Share alike

They almost felt guilty telling Alex and Simon about having competed, but the teachers were thrilled and very impressed by the marks, just like Gilbert said they would.

'So, when are you competing next?' checked Simon.

They told him about Warwick and Southampton. He looked a bit concerned.

'Hmm, Warwick…that'll be quite a tough one compared to Dai and Sheila's comp…' he rubbed his chin thoughtfully. He grabbed a dance newspaper and energetically flicked through the pages.

'There's a nice little one in a couple of weeks in Cirencester…yeah, look, Beginners in Ballroom and Latin, they also have a social dancer's event, you could do that too if you like. You're not registered are you?'

'I don't think so, we don't know what registered means, so I guess we're not,' said Trevor.

'Oh, you have to apply to the national governing body, it's a kind of competitors licence. Beginners and social dancer competitors don't have to be registered.'

'Ah, I see, no we're not then,' concluded Trevor.

Diana sort of agreed that they would do Cirencester. 'Don't you think we're good enough for Warwick?' she checked. Should she be hurt by this?

'I don't really know, but Warwick is going to be a championship day, there'll be events for selecting the national team. None of that should make a difference to you in Beginners, but it will be a long day and because it's in the Midlands, you'll probably find the opposition much tougher and this early in your career it would be a shame if you found yourself out classed.'

There was that word again, career, they apparently now had dance careers. Diana still didn't think their sort of dancing came anywhere near to being a career.

'So we're not good enough you mean?' checked Diana.

'No it's not that, I think you could make a reasonable job, but you might find it a bit scary. You can dance it if you want, but it's after Cirencester and I'd like you to do that as your second comp', to get a bit more comp practice. It's a nice friendly one and it will help you get used to what goes on.'

This seemed reasonable and they spent their lesson working on improving their routines for Cirencester, Trevor lapped it up. Simon also confirmed that he and Alex wanted them to do their bronze medals in both Ballroom and Latin that autumn. Trevor took this very seriously. Diana found it scarier than the idea of Cirencester.

That evening Diana treated Trevor to a meal at her place. He was quiet for quite a long while.

'Something wrong?' she checked.

'Well, no, I was just thinking, when we go to Southampton…we'll have to book a hotel, or at least a B&B…for two nights…well, I'd better try and find us somewhere…got any preferences?'

'No, I've only been to Southampton once and that was when I was a kid, B&B will do me fine.'

'Umm…are we having separate rooms?'

Ah, that was it.

'Well, I'm always worried about money, you know that, I suppose we should share a room…is that alright with you?' she asked, doing a good job of pretending she thought he might be offended by the idea of sharing a room, and a bed?

Yes it was alright, very much so. She thought it might be.

***

Diana told the girls at work all about the competition, the plans for the next few weeks and the trip to Southampton, she knew it was a mistake the moment she finished telling them. Cerys and Anita thought the shared room in Southampton hilarious. Sheryn was supportive and concerned.

'Did he push you into the idea?'

'No, he was very embarrassed. And I think I'm ready to…well, move on.'

Eventually Anita and Cerys were more sensible and less giggly about the whole thing and stopped making fun. She had been upset by the way they had had such a good laugh at her expense.

***

Jacob and Annalise came to spend the weekend with Diana. Whilst he was in touch with Diana several times a week, by text at least, they only now had time to catch up on what was happening in their lives.

'Cirencester?' said Jacob and Annalise together.

'We're competing there too,' said Jacob excitedly.

Diana was shocked, she at once didn't want to do the competition and make a fool of herself in front of her son. Though she wanted to see him dance, and Annalise too of course.

'We hope to qualify for Southampton too,' said Annalise, 'there are qualifying heats at Cirencester, that's one of the reasons we're doing it.'

Now she had visions of Jacob and Annalise in the next bedroom to her and Trevor!

'Well, it's not certain we're to going Southampton,' she said trying to sound casual.

'Oh, you should, everyone says it's a brilliant weekend,' said Jacob. 'Will dad and Andrea be competing there too?'

Perhaps they would be in the room the other side of Diana and Trevor! The idea of her cousin and ex-husband sharing a bed nearly blew her mind. But why would they be sharing a bed? Nah, that was just too ridiculous and could and never would happen, hopefully, least of all in Southampton.

But as far as she was aware they had decided not to enter it, she wasn't sorry.

She actually found herself hoping Jacob and Annalise wouldn't qualify for Southampton, then told herself off for being so negative, of course she wanted them to qualify, but just not to be staying in the same hotel…in the next room to her and Trevor!

As she read in bed she thought back about what Jacob had said about Elwyn and Andrea, he viewed them as a couple, but what kind of couple? A dance partnership, or a romantically involved couple? She found the idea of her cousin having any feelings for her ex-husband, completely ridiculous, repellent even, but just what was going on?

She hadn't seen or spoken to them since the competition. The weekend was coming up, she decided to get her parents to invite her over for

Sunday tea. She had to know what was going on, this would be a good way to find out.

When she asked her parents to do this favour, they weren't that keen, they remembered well the argument that Sunday over Trevor, but Diana explained how much things had changed. It took a while for her mother to stop laughing when Diana told her that Andrea was entering dance competitions with Elwyn. She really thought Diana was having a joke and only reluctantly believed her when she saw the photos. After that her mum was very eager to invite Andrea over, but not Elwyn. Since he had left Diana she couldn't stand the man, and Diana wasn't that fussed on him either.

It worked like a charm, Diana went with Jacob and Annalise and Andrea arrived with her son, Rupert. Bethany was busy, probably just as well with Jacob and Annalise there. He had been very taken with Bethany so it may have been a bit awkward. All went well and it didn't take long for Diana to get Andrea talking about dancing and her 'relationship' with Elwyn. Diana and her parents hung on every word.

'He's a lovely dancer, of course he has had to work hard to get up to my standard, but he remembered from when he was a boy, and we get on so well, we're well matched...'

'How do you mean?' asked Diana.

'As dancers, a dancing partnership, we're a very good height and build for each other. He's a fast learner too, and so keen.'

Elwyn, a fast learner, so keen? Thought Diana, how many times had she had to show him how to turn the washing machine on?

She waxed lyrical about how they had learnt complex routines, how clever he was at perfecting the steps, she described a real paragon.

John, Diana's dad, asked: 'What do your kids think of him?' and jerked a thumb toward Rupert, who was engrossed in a school book and listening to music.

'They get on with him okay, they both seem happy that I'm dancing and that I'm happy. Bethany is hardly home these days and Rupert is always playing computer games or reading books anyway, really bound up on their own worlds, they hardly know Elwyn.'

'He's not living with you then?' checked Rita, Diana's mum.

Diana nearly fell of her chair, her mother could be tactful when she liked, but not just now.

Andrea looked a little surprised, definitely embarrassed, even hurt. 'What makes you think he's living with me?'

'It's just you sound more like a happily married couple than dancing partners,' explained Rita in a matter of fact way.

Andrea laughed, 'well, a dancing partnership can be like a marriage, but in my case without the sex,' she added emphatically and with a shiver. 'And before you ask, no, I'm not interested in him, I'm just glad to have a good dancing partner.' Then she changed the subject.

'Sorry about mum,' said Diana a little later.

'It's alright, but I'm hurt to think she believes Elwyn's in my bed…I hope you don't think that?'

'No, of course not. There's no way I could ever think of you…umm, in a… relationship with Elwyn. Having been married to him and knowing what he can be like I just find it strange you two can get on so well in dancing.' She also found it hard not to remind Andrea that she had accused her of sleeping with Trevor just to keep him as a dancing partner.

Andrea nodded reflectively. 'Well, we get on very well, we have dancing in common and that's all. He's a real gentleman with me and we respect each other.'

This still didn't sound like a description of Elwyn.

'So,' said Andrea, 'when's your next comp?'

Diana told her about Cirencester.

'Oh, Syd Gaylord's comp! I thought he'd died years ago!' She told Diana all about the old dance teacher that ran the monthly competitions in Cirencester. They were more social dances with a competition thrown in.

'You won't be dancing it yourself then?' asked Diana.

'No, we're concentrating on being ready for Warwick, I don't think there would be much for us at Cirencester, but you'll enjoy it.'

Diana really found it hard to understand Andrea, not just about her serious attitude toward dancing and competitions, but to Elwyn, Andrea obviously admired him so much. Perhaps if Diana had taken up dancing when they were married they wouldn't have divorced? Though she doubted it, Phyllis would still have seen to that.

Before they all went home, Diana satisfied herself that Andrea was only Elwyn's dance partner, they weren't sleeping together, and no, they didn't plan to dance at Southampton. This seemed to make things better in a funny sort of way.

***

Trevor drove Diana home after the dance class, it had been fun and they had laughed a lot. They discussed some work he had done on his house.

'I don't see why I'm keeping my place on, I'm seriously thinking of selling it and getting myself a flat, or a bungalow, something smaller than my old dump, and a newer place that doesn't need so much work,' he said sounding frustrated.

'But I thought you loved it? And it's not a dump, it's a beautiful home.'

'I do love it, well, I did, not so much these days. It's full of memories, all the furniture is mum's, I fancy somewhere that's more me…do you know what I mean?'

'Yes, of course I do, but after all the work you've done there, I mean, it's beautiful, you've spent a fortune on it.'

'That's true and it keeps costing me a fortune! You know I said I'd fixed the dry rot in the cellar? Well, it's back! The treatment couldn't have worked.'

'I told you that dry rot isn't something you can sort out with DIY,' cautioned Diana, not that she knew much about it.

'That's three times in the last fifteen years I've done dry rot treatment, my mate says I should get it done professionally, but it's so expensive and I really thought I did a good job last time.'

'Well, you'd better get out before you find you can't sell it.'

'Exactly…mind you, there's not much dry rot to fix and I have to say I don't fancy moving, I've never lived anywhere else, but I think it's time for a change.'

She nearly said he could move in with her, but she stopped herself, what if he was fishing for that? No, she'd try and find out a bit more about what he really had in mind. Did she actually want Trevor living with her? Hmm, one day that might be just what she wanted, but not right now. There were a lot of things to sort out first and questions to be answered.

***

They felt prepared for the competition at Cirencester. They would meet Jacob and Annalise there and Diana was really looking forward to seeing him dance…oh yeah, and Annalise too. She was a nice girl and they got on well, but Diana couldn't see the relationship lasting much longer, she had that sort of feeling about it. She wasn't prepared to believe that their relationship could last, Jacob was still so young, her little boy. She didn't want some girl taking him off her, well, not yet anyway. Hmm, had she started to sound like Phyllis? Just a bit.

The competition was in a community hall on a housing estate on the edge of Cirencester, it was quite a modest place and in need of repair. There was a good turn out of dancers, several were from Alex and Simon's. They found Jacob and Annalise in the hall already. Jacob couldn't drive, Annalise could. Diana was surprised how at home they were at the competition. They had registered and knew the set up. They recognised some judges from the varsity competitions, and were friendly with a few of the other competitors. Diana's biggest shock was when Jacob sauntered up wearing a tail suit.

'Where did you get that?'

'The uni' club loaned it to me. Doesn't fit that well, but it's okay.'

He actually looked quite smart, though the suit had a distinctly 1970's look about it. Even so, he looked very handsome and worryingly a bit like Elwyn in his tails!

Annalise came back in a dance dress, it was powder blue. It too had been loaned by the university club, but looked elderly and frequently repaired, even so, it suited her figure and she also looked very pretty.

They were so self-sufficient, there was little that they asked Diana or Trevor for, they were experienced competitors and it was Diana and Trevor that needed their help and support. Perhaps Jacob wasn't her little boy anymore after all?

The competition wasn't so well organised and run as Dai Post's, which was saying something. Syd started the competition late, and the facilities in the hall weren't so good. The floor was a better quality, but far smaller, too small. There was no programme to refer to, so they had little idea of the running order or events.

This time, they had both brought clothes they thought suitable for the competition. Trevor had a smart pair of trousers, white shirt and black bow-tie (apparently it had been his dad's, it was quite large and made of velvet). Diana wore a pretty calf length dress, plain, fairly full skirt, but just right for dancing. The changing rooms were an experience. Trevor found he had to go into a dusty storeroom under the stage. Diana went into a room off the main hall, it was lined with chairs and there was a long clothes rail which sagged worryingly in the middle under the weight of innumerable bags of dresses and competition gear. Diana avoided it and just used a chair as her 'dressing-table'. She noticed Annalise in animated conversation with several of the other women, brimming with confidence and happy amongst dancers, sharing jokes and the latest gossip.

'How are you getting on?' checked Annalise. She helped Diana with her dress. She was a nice kid really and Diana was warming to her more all the time.

There were windows that looked out onto the busy street. What could be loosely described as curtains were drawn, but they didn't meet in the middle and were so thin that you could actually see people walking by through them. No one seemed bothered about this, Diana just got on with changing and chatting to Annalise about the evening ahead.

Syd Gaylord, a legend in dancing, walked onto the stage. What Diana took to be his pupils applauded him as if he was a Shakespearean actor about to do Hamlet, and he loved it, waved and bowed. He seemed to be around eighty and wore a very ill-fitting dinner suit, the collar of the shirt was huge compared to his scrawny neck, he looked a bit like a tortoise with his head jutting out of the shell. He struggled with the microphone, even speaking into the wrong end for a while, thankfully he had help on stage. At one table there was a helper playing the music, which was actually very good, no vinyl at this competition. This music man used CD's. At the other end of the stage were two scrutineers that fed Syd with the information he needed, not that he seemed that able to deal with all the papers he was handed.

He welcomed everyone and the competition got underway. Firstly, he introduced the judges, there were only three, one of whom had been at Dai's competition.

'This is the only comp we've been to with just three,' said Jacob authoritatively, 'all other promoters use five, seven or nine, but Syd likes to keep costs down and isn't worried about what other promoters do.'

Syd introduced each judge, Jacob and Annalise said he'd got all the names wrong, but the judges didn't seem bothered. All were men and two weren't listed in the competition advertisement as being due to judge, Syd had no doubt got that wrong too.

For all his eccentricities and mishaps, it was a good and fun evening. Once the events began things went, for the most part, fairly smoothly. The chairman of the judges, the scrutineers and the music man seemed to take over from Syd. He just announced which event was next, though not always accurately.

Compared to Dai Post's competition, the entry levels were smaller. This wasn't a championship day. The events weren't for top titles, big trophies or places in the national team. This was a small, provincial competition run for the benefit of local dancers and Syd's couples in particular. He was offering qualification for the 'Nationwide Dance Elite' grand finals in Southampton too, this wasn't to find couples for the national squad, it was for couples in all the various grades and age categories. The couples had to qualify throughout a six month period in events like this. Diana and Trevor had already qualified and Jacob and Annalise were keen to. When they got to Southampton, they would dance against all the couples from their grade that had qualified in the previous six months, therefore winning it meant you would be, in Diana and Trevor's case, the best

'Beginner' couple in the country. It was a title and accolade that many dancers wanted to claim, including Trevor.

Even so, looking around the room and watching the events being contested, Diana and Trevor found it hard to believe that many of these dancers had that sort of ambition. The majority were Seniors, and this was a monthly night out, and chance to compete at a level that suited them. If they qualified for Nationwide Dance Elite they probably wouldn't bother to go. Jacob explained that if a couple was ambitious, then they may have qualified already, and if they won again here, the qualifying couple in this competition would be the second placed couple. It all seemed a bit complicated for Diana and Trevor, but they wanted to know more, just what were they letting themselves in for at Southampton?

'Think Diana,' said Trevor dreamily, 'we could be crowned the best Beginner couple in Britain!'

'I don't think so Trevor, I don't think so.'

'Oh, don't be defeatist!'

'I prefer realist!'

Trevor seemed to sulk, but not for long.

Most events were either just a semi-final through to a final, or a straight final. Jacob and Annalise were one of the few under thirty-five years of age couples dancing. They had entered everything they could, the aim was to get what Jacob referred to as 'comp practice'. The more events they could do in competition the better, he assured her that one competition was worth ten practice sessions at their club.

Diana and Trevor became bewildered by which events Jacob and Annalise were dancing and why they weren't dancing others.

'Right,' said Jacob, 'we're in the Open Novice, Intermediate, Pre-amateur…'

'Oh, is that the same as Pre-championship?' asked Trevor.

'Yes, but because there are no championships here tonight, it's called Pre-amateur, see?'

Well, actually they didn't but said they did.

'We're also doing the Open Foxtrot and the One Teacher Two Dance.'

He explained the rules about both. The Open Foxtrot was like the one Andrea and Elwyn had danced, a single dance event, however, in this case instead of being just basic steps, they could dance what ever groups they liked. The One Teacher event was open to any age or class of couple as long as they only went to one teacher.

'I don't understand,' said Trevor.

'Right, me and Annalise, we only go to one teacher for our Ballroom, so we can dance it. If we went to two or more teachers we couldn't.'

'Why would you want to have more than one dance teacher?' asked Diana.

'Some of the top couples go to several different teachers.'

Diana and Trevor found this ridiculous, but it seemed to make perfect sense to Jacob and Annalise.

'So we could dance this One Teacher' event then?'

'Well, yes, but you're not registered, so you can't.'

'Better get ourselves registered for next time then Diana,' said Trevor importantly. He seemed to be taking things very seriously, but of course, he had wanted to compete form day one, he was living the dream.

Jacob went on. 'We're doing the same events in Latin too. Plus the Open Basic Rumba, the Open Viennese Waltz, Open Samba and the Student Two Dance in both the Ballroom and Latin,' he said sounding ever more excited. There seemed to be little that he and Annalise weren't dancing in.

The student events were open only to couples in full time education at a centre of higher learning. Jacob and Annalise explained some promoters that ran competitions close to universities with dance clubs would include these events to attract the couples from the universities, but there were only two other student couples here. Apparently Syd hadn't actually told the local university clubs about his competition, let alone that there were events for students. Jacob and Annalise had only found out when they got here, that was Syd for you.

Jacob and Annalise had a busy night, they were out dancing a lot. Diana watched them intently, to her they were the best of the floor, in fact they were very good, but not always outstanding. They were still new dancers, in the lower grade events they looked efficient and competent, but when they danced in the Pre-amateur, they were up against some very good Seniors and a very smart looking young couple. Even Diana had to concede they stood little chance of winning this.

Diana and Trevor were waiting for four events, the Beginner two dance and Social dancers two dance in both Ballroom and Latin. The Beginners Ballroom was run about thirty minutes into the programme, it was a straight final of five couples, they felt it went well and quite enjoyed dancing it. The Social Dancers event wasn't run until close to the end of the Ballroom section, however, there was only one other couple in it.

'You've won that,' said Jacob with authority, 'that other couple kept stopping and were useless.'

'Wish you were judging,' said Trevor. 'I didn't think it went well for us.'

'Oh, I enjoyed it,' said Diana.

As the Ballroom section came to a close, another couple hurried over to Jacob and Annalise, they were a little older, but still kids as far as Diana and Trevor were concerned.

'Would you two mind dancing the Open Amateur Ballroom please? We're the only couple entered and the chairman's told us that Syd doesn't want to run it, just list us as winners. We've come all this way, we only dance Ballroom, it's really annoying not to be allowed to dance the event we really came for,' explained the lad.

Jacob and Annalise debated it briefly.

'Alright,' they said together.

'Thanks, I'll tell Syd!'

'Do you think that's a good idea?' said Diana.

'It's only to help out, we know those two from other comps, we don't mind, that sort of thing has happened to us too, so we'll keep them company when they dance.'

'Really?' came Syd's voice over the mike. The other couple were at the stage explaining about Jacob and Annalise being prepared to dance the

Open Amateur Four Dance, they pointed across to Jacob and Annalise. Syd stared at them as if they were naughty children. He either had forgotten the mike or didn't know it was switched on as everyone heard him moan: 'Huh! We'll run the Open Amateur next then, alright? I really don't know why! We're over-running as it is, I suppose we better had,' and sighed graphically.

After the Senior event that was on the floor now, he announced the Open Amateur, he was hard to hear because he'd turned the mike off now.

Jacob and Annalise took the floor, they looked confident, even determined. The other gentleman had a suit that was obviously made for him and fairly new, she in an elegant and expensive dress, not twenty-second hand like Annalise's. They had real presence on the floor, they were in a very different league in many ways to Jacob and Annalise. When Waltz began, Jacob and Annalise did their best, but they were very much make-weights. Diana called their number enthusiastically, but that wasn't going to be enough to make them win.

Syd also kept the prize presentation until after the Latin section, but no one seemed to mind this evening. He allowed only just enough time for couples to change for Latin. The judges were given a meal by one of the helpers, but Syd didn't allow them enough time to eat it, he was running late and didn't listen to any of the complaints.

The couples were allowed very little time for practice of Latin dances either. Diana and Trevor were going to be dancing the Cha-Cha-Cha and Rumba in the Beginners, and the Cha' and Jive in the Social Dancers event. They got one Cha', but no Rumba or Jive practice.

The Latin events began, only the Open Basic Rumba had enough couples for a semi-final, all the rest were straight finals.

Once more Jacob and Annalise were out dancing a great deal and enjoying themselves, though before long Annalise seemed to look very tired, Diana thought this odd for a fit young woman.

For Latin, Jacob had changed into a nice pair of black trousers which seemed to fit very well and a black silky shirt, Diana wasn't sure it suited him, he had it done up and virtually none of his chest showing, not like Elwyn. Annalise wore a nice Latin dress, far newer than her Ballroom one.

'Second hand', she told Diana, 'my mum bought it for me for my birthday.'

Diana wondered if she should have offered to get Jacob some dance clothes for his birthday…good idea, she normally had no idea what to get him these days.

Annalise's dress was a riot of colours, all bright and very Latin, the skirt was quite short and cut so that it flew up as they spun and turned through the various dances. They looked very happy dancing together, a real team…just like Andrea and Elwyn?

In the Latin dances Jacob and Annalise looked far more confident and competent than they had in the Ballroom, in fact they were a pleasure to watch and looked as though they would easily win most of their events, well, that's the way it looked to Diana and Trevor.

Syd worked steadily through the Latin events, or to more exact, the team around him steered the evening forward in spite of Syd.

Diana and Trevor danced the Beginners and Social Dancer events, both seemed to go quite well, better than the Ballroom. In the Social Dancer event they were up against the same couple, who seemed to make an even worse mess of it. The Beginners had mainly the same couples they had danced against earlier, but one they hadn't seen, they realised this couple were remarkably good for Beginners.

'Have we finished, was that the last final?' checked Syd.

Yes it was.

'Oh good. Are we ready to give out the prizes?' he asked a helper as she shoved a table very noisily onto the floor in front of the stage.

'No, we're not, wait five minutes!'

'Oh good, let's start then shall we?'

'No Syd, give me five minutes!'

'Thank you ladies and gentlemen, now it's time for the results!'

'I'll swing for you one day Syd, honestly I will, I'll swing for you!' hissed the helper.

Annalise stood behind Trevor and took his number off.

'What are you doing that for?' asked Trevor.

'You shouldn't go up for your prize with your number on,' she said simply as she handed the pins and number back to him.

'Why?' asked Diana.

'Don't know, but it looks nicer I think.'

'Elwyn didn't take his number off at Port Talbot,' said Trevor.

'It was their first comp, probably a bit excited and forgot,' said Annalise.

'How do you know so much about competitions?' asked Diana.

'I used to compete when I was a kid, stopped for a few years, then managed to get back to it, but when I was fourteen, my partner was sixteen and became an adult. My parents didn't want me to go into adult, or Youth competitions, at that time, so we split. I couldn't find another partner, then school work got in the way. But now I'm back!'

'Why did you stop for a few years?' asked Diana.

Annalise glanced at the floor, even looked embarrassed. 'Oh, hmm, well things were a bit complicated at home that's all.' She then searched for something in a bag that seemed to contain just about everything. It was also meant to show Diana that she wasn't about to answer any more questions about her childhood.

Now, why ever not? Thought Diana.

'Right, Social Dancers Ballroom Two Dance!' said Syd enthusiastically, 'winners, number twenty-five!'

'That's you two, off you go,' said Annalise gaily.

Diana and Trevor remembered everything they had been told about presentation protocol and went up to get their prize. They were greeted by a lady, Syd hadn't introduced her to the audience, presumably assuming everyone knew her, or he had just forgotten. Jacob and Annalise said she was the wife of one of the judges.

'Well done,' she said, then pointed to a table behind her, on which the helper was emptying bric-a-brac from a box. 'Go over and help yourself to a prize.'

'No plaque, no wine?' checked Trevor.

'No, Syd gives presents…oh, one per couple mind.'

At the table they found very random items.

'One item per couple! No more, okay?' cautioned the helper loudly.

They said they understood.

'What do you fancy love?' checked Trevor.

'Actually, none of it'.

They finally settled on a decorative plate, chipped. Even so, they had won and the win was what it was all about.

Even before they got back to their seats, Syd called out the Beginners Ballroom result, Trevor was ready to go out for first place, but they were second, he was obviously disappointed. Diana was thrilled, after all this was only their second competition and they were very inexperienced. They had beaten other couples, this still amazed her, in fact she couldn't understand how the judges thought she and Trevor were good enough to come anything other than last.

Diana really enjoyed the bulk of the rest of the Ballroom results as Jacob and Annalise had made it through to the finals of all the events they had competed in. Thrillingly, they had done very well, winning the Novice, Intermediate, One-Teacher Two Dance and the students only event, and came third in the Open Foxtrot. They seemed to be back and fore almost constantly to receive a prize. They were sixth in the Viennese Waltz, this didn't surprise them, they could only just do the dance and only did it for a bit more experience. But they won the Open Waltz. They predicted second for themselves in the Pre-amateur event, but they had a shock, they won that too.

The Open Amateur Ballroom result was the last one called, they dared to wonder if they had sneaked a win ahead of the more experienced couple. Not this time.

The Latin results were given immediately and once more the Social Dancer event was called first. Diana and Trevor won it, that felt good. But this time they were third in the Beginners, Trevor was deflated. Diana still felt elated that they were doing so well, she was having a good time.

She was burning to know how Jacob and Annalise had done in the Latin. In fact, very well. They seemed to have won nearly everything, including the Open Basic Rumba. A stack of prizes grew on the chair next to Annalise. It included a tiny vase, several packs of birthday cards, though none had enough envelopes. A pen which had obviously been a free gift with some promotion and a pack of highlighting pens, with one missing. They also got a pack of playing cards, they didn't check but guessed it wasn't a full deck (bit like Syd), a saucer, and other junk.

'Not sure I'm impressed by all this stuff,' said Diana.

'Rumour has it Syd goes around car boot sales at the end of a day and offers people a pound for anything they don't want to take home,' said Jacob. He held up a tape measure: 'Look at this, we've just got it for winning the Intermediate Latin, about half is missing.'

'But we won!' said Annalise, and hugged him.

Moments later they went out as winners of the Pre-amateur, they were very pleased, never mind the prizes, this was a good competition for them so soon in their dancing careers. Diana was so proud of them, yes, both of them.

A little later Jacob waved a couple of forms at Diana.

'We've qualified for Southampton! Which hotel did you say you two are staying in?'

Diana stared at the sheets of paper, the bad dream seemed to be coming true. Jacob and Annalise may well end up in the room next to them in Southampton after all! At least Elwyn and Andrea wouldn't be there.

***

It was a shame that Jacob and Annalise weren't coming home with Diana, they were going back to their digs in Nottingham. The university year had finished, but they had decided to stay on, amazingly as far as Diana was concerned, so they could carry on having lessons with the university club dance teacher. She discussed the competition with Trevor as they drove to Newport. He seemed to have gotten over not winning the beginners events.

'Still dreaming of being crowned best beginner in Britain?' she asked a little sarcastically.

He visibly cringed. 'We should be a lot better prepared by then.'

'Still want to go then?'

'Oh yes, can't wait. How about you?'

Pity, she'd hoped he'd changed his mind, but said she was keen. Okay, she was keen and looking forward to it, at least for the chance to get away for a couple of days if nothing else. She never went away on holiday, just stayed home: getting Jacob through university wasn't cheap, and keeping the house together even harder. Elwyn had met his legal obligations, but once Jacob had turned seventeen a lot of the money he gave Diana as maintenance stopped, though he was helping out with the cost of Jacob's university expenses. Jacob was a good lad and had got himself a part time job.

She didn't like to tell Trevor, but paying her share of the dancing was an increasing problem. The weekly classes weren't, but the private lessons were. She was quite a junior member of staff in the Job Centre and if Elwyn didn't help with Jacob's university costs, she couldn't fill the gap.

As they discussed the Southampton trip some of her financial concerns began to emerge.

'Umm, I was wondering,' said Trevor, 'going to Southampton is just before Christmas, I don't know what to get you for a present, what if I pay for all the trip, would that do you for Christmas?'

She protested, it was too generous, but she agreed, it was a load off her mind and in any case she thought it would be better than the sort of present he may have had in mind, she wasn't a costume jewellery person, not these days.

The next day, Sunday, Trevor came over to do some gardening for her. During a tea break they chatted.

'Pardon my asking, Diana, but are you finding dancing a bit too expensive?'

'No, no of course not!'

'Because if you are, we can stop, I don't mind…or I can pay for a bit more of it.' She looked embarrassed. 'Oh, umm, I'm sorry.'

'Okay, I admit it, my finances are getting tighter each month and have to be careful…I can afford the dancing, just.'

Later they went over to her parents for tea. Andrea wasn't there, she and Elwyn were competing near London. Diana envied Andrea, she just seemed to be able to live her dream and not worry about money. As in fact did Elwyn, okay, he was helping out with Jacob, but not helping Diana, why should he? That was what divorce was all about.

She found it very easy to chat with Trevor, he was a good listener and also very practical. Inevitably when they got to her house, she asked him in and they watched TV for a while, he seemed to be deep in thought. Even so, he didn't share what was on his mind, they kissed good night and he went on his way.

He picked her up for dance class the next evening. As they arrived he asked: 'Umm, do you want me to get this?'

They normally split the cost 50/50 so she was taken aback.

'No, it's alright, I'm not that hard up.'

'But don't be afraid to ask mind.'

On their way home she asked: 'thought any more about moving house?'

'Yes, yes I have, I'm going to put it on the market.'

'Oh, right! Have you got somewhere in mind to move to then?'

'No, but I'll start looking now, it'll probably take quite a while to sell my place.'

They talked about the property market and horror stories they had heard from friends that had moved house, being stuck in buying chains and what they found when they moved. She realised it probably sounded as though she was trying to put him off. There seemed to be something on his mind, but no matter how she prompted he didn't tell her and he kept changing the subject.

After the Saturday night social dance, he drove her home, it had been a particularly good night and they were both still laughing about some of the things that had gone on. Over the inevitable cup of tea, he started to look very nervous.

'Something wrong?'

'No…I've been meaning to ask you something, but don't know quite how to put it.'

She had a rough idea what, he wanted to stay the night. Well, she had been expecting this for a while and had been surprised he hadn't pressed her before, she was very grateful that he hadn't used any emotional blackmail.

'It must be an embarrassing question then,' she said, picking up a biscuit.

'Yes, yes it is…well, I was thinking…don't be cross…'

This was painful, she was prepared to say yes, he could stay the night, she felt there was more than just friendship between them now, she did love him, in a funny sort of way, and he wasn't bad looking.

'Well, umm, what if we bought somewhere together…umm, live together?' he blushed vividly and also started to sweat.

She was really surprised.

'You're not angry are you?' he checked frantically.

'No, no, not at all, I umm, well, I wasn't expecting that. Why would I want to do that? Sell my house I mean, we could just move in together.'

'Could we? You mean me move in here, or you move in with me?'

'Yeah, I suppose so, why should we get somewhere else together?'

He began to look relieved and far happier.

'Well, I don't think it would be fair you moving into my house, mum still lives there, you know what I mean don't you?'

Yes she did, all the furniture and decoration was still the same. From what she could tell he hadn't got rid of any of his mother's possessions yet.

'I do want to find somewhere that I really like and, well, I thought if you sold up and I sold up, that would make life financially easier for us both, share living costs, you know what I mean don't you?'

Her first reaction was to say no, she had worked all these years to keep this place, she wasn't inclined to let it go that easily, but he did have a point. However, did she actually want to live with Trevor?

'I'll have to think about it. I'm not saying no, but it's a big decision, I can't answer now, on the spur of the moment. Financially, you're right, it would make sense.'

'Umm, is it just that you don't really want to move in with me?'

'No Trevor, it's not that…I have to think about Jacob, I would need to discuss it with him…this is his home too.'

Trevor nodded, he hadn't thought of that. He agreed to let the matter go for now. 'Better be going then,' he said tapping his watch.

'Well, only if you want to.'

'Umm, how do you mean?'

'Oh Trevor! Do I have to paint you a picture? Do you want to stay here tonight?'

'Umm, well, umm, yes, I'd love to, if you don't mind, I haven't got pyjamas and I haven't got a toothbrush…you sure?'

She was sure. She locked the front door, he went upstairs. When she got to her bedroom Trevor wasn't there. He was in the spare room.

'Umm, it's not made up, the bed I mean, shall I do that? Or do you want me to use Jacob's room tonight?'

She went and gave him a hug. 'Neither, you're sleeping with me stupid!' and led him to her room.

Diana knew this was going to be a night like no other, mainly because Trevor was…inexperienced? That was probably putting it lightly. But after all these years of separation and divorce, so was she.

Chapter Five
Practice Makes Perfect

Andrea and Elwyn gathered up their bags and cases and struggled through the leisure centre doors, they had finished the competition and had a long journey ahead of them. This competition had been in Surrey, they had had doubts about trying it as it was such a long way for only their second 'comp', but it seemed to be worth doing. It was more significant than Dai Post's event and they were looking forward to the challenge.

By winning the Senior Ballroom Championship in Port Talbot, the top grade, they had immediately moved up through the competition structure, they could no longer dance the Senior Intermediate or Senior Pre-championship grades, though they still danced the Open Foxtrot and a 'Senior Tango' that was in the programme today. In Latin, they were luckier, in a perverse sort of way. There hadn't been six couples in the Senior Pre-championship Latin so it didn't count in terms of their ranking, and nor had they won the Championship, this meant they were still able to do all the same Latin events as they had at Port Talbot.

At today's competition, there had been a different and bigger board of judges. The floor was a good deal smaller and square, but in a far better condition, no loose tapes. They actually felt quite nervous, far more so than they had at Port Talbot, and it had shown in the Ballroom events. The early rounds hadn't gone well though they felt they gave a reasonable performance in the Open Foxtrot. The average age of competitors was much younger at this competition and they found that as the Foxtrot progressed through the rounds, they were one of only two Senior couples left in it. Andrea and Elwyn only reached the semi-final, yet they thought they had done enough to make the final, obviously not.

The Senior Tango went alright, the standard of entry didn't seem that good. Andrea and Elwyn considered themselves to be very good at Tango and they made the final, but when the results were given, they were only sixth, this had been something of a shock.

The Senior Ballroom Championship, which was what they were really interested in, had enough couples for a first round before the semi-final. Andrea and Elwyn felt the nerves, they had had to dance the first round quite early in the afternoon and it hadn't gone that well, Andrea had been pleasantly surprised to make the semi final. Elwyn didn't seem to have danced his best and he knew it. She didn't need to criticise him, he was doing that himself. The semi went a good deal better, until Elwyn went badly wrong in one group in the Waltz, he was furious with himself, and Andrea could cheerfully have hit him!

They mentally prepared themselves to not make it to the final, they did though and this time it went far better.

The results for the Ballroom section were given before the Latin and once the couples had changed for Latin.

They were fifth in the Senior Championship, this was disappointing given how well they thought they had danced. When they checked the marks they found they had been lucky, they only made it to fifth by one mark.

In Latin, they felt a lot more confident, but the bad Ballroom results played on their minds, and

Elwyn went wrong several times. Even so, they kept being recalled. The turn out for most of the Latin was quite good, so they were up dancing regularly and made the Intermediate final, but none of the one dance finals. Couples were warned that the Senior Pre-championship final was next, Andrea and Elwyn expected to be in it, but their number wasn't called, they felt quite shocked. But the lady on the microphone said she had made a mistake, they were in the final after all. That seemed to go okay.

    The Senior Latin Championship had been a semi-final through to a final. They felt the semi' went well and they enjoyed it, no mistakes. But they weren't recalled to the final. Another mistake perhaps? No mistake, no recall.

    It was a poor consolation after the success of Port Talbot to win the Senior Intermediate Latin. They were shocked to be only sixth in the Pre-championship. What had gone wrong?

    They began to explain to each other what the problem was as they trudged to the car. It was raining, they were tired, and still new to competitions. Elwyn admitted he hadn't danced his best, mind you, for such new competitors, they were still doing well. None of this seemed to help much.

    It was a long drive and a very wet night too.

    Andrea had assumed that Port Talbot was a pointer to the future, she was back with a vengeance, she, and Elwyn of course, were going to sweep all before them. Her glory days when she competed with Julian were back. But after this competition, she had to admit she might be wrong.

    There were long silences, when they talked they moved onto anything but dancing. She had become quite fond of Elwyn, as a dance partner, no more than a friend, perhaps one step up from acquaintance. She did blame him for some of the bad results, but regardless felt they should have done better, Elwyn's mistakes couldn't be blamed for all the lack of success.

They tried to be positive and kept reassuring each other.

A few days later they had a lesson with Alex. She was a very successful teacher, even spending two days a week in London teaching at her husband's studio. She specialised in the Ballroom dances, Simon was the Latin expert.

She listened intently to them, particularly Andrea, as she explained about the competition. Elwyn realised that she mentioned his mistakes quite a few times, even coming back to them, shifting the blame?

'Who were the judges?' asked Alex.

Andrea and Elwyn reeled them off between them. Alex nodded at some names, shrugged at the one she didn't know and wrinkled up her nose to three.

'Alright, who won the Championship?' she checked.

Again jointly they came up with the names of winners.

'And do you know anything about them?' asked Alex.

No, they didn't.

'They're the national number two, I teach them in London. Who was second?'

They didn't know their names for certain, but Alex recognised the description. They were able to give her four of the couples that had been in the final, Alex knew them all and their approximate national rank. Andrea and Elwyn hadn't realised it, but they had danced against a significant number of the best Senior couples in the country.

'The trouble is,' warned Alex, 'you're probably going to find them and most of the other top ten couples at Warwick. It's not that you're not good dancers, you are, but you're going to have to up your game to beat them. Some of those judges will have looked around the floor, seen these top ranked couples and simply marked them. After all, they've been at the top for many months, perhaps years, why spend time looking for someone that's better, e.g. you two. You're going to have to be so good the judges can't take their eyes off you.'

Andrea and Elwyn nodded thoughtfully. He found this something of a shock, he already thought they were dancing, or he was dancing, at the highest level they could achieve. Andrea thought back to her dancing career with Julian, had she worked harder with him, what had they achieved? They had been pretty good, but they hadn't won everything they entered. Unfortunately, Alex had a point.

Alex got them to go through each of the five Ballroom dances, then began to tweak their performance in each to make them still better.

Elwyn in particular found it physically demanding and that much of the tuition centred on him.

'That's because you're 60% of the partnership,' said Alex after he began to moan. 'If you go wrong, Andrea goes wrong. Andrea has far less scope to go wrong if you're dancing well. If you don't lead, Andrea doesn't know what to do.' The logic was simple, but meant a lot of work for Elwyn.

Simon took a similar line, except he worked far more on Andrea, she wasn't performing the steps 'competitively'.

They were soaked with sweat and worn out at the end of the two hours of lessons, both teachers had a list of things they planned to cover next time and Andrea and Elwyn had a lot they were expected to improve on at practice. At least they felt they had made progress. For Elwyn, this was something of a revelation, he thought there wasn't anything else that he had to do or learn in dancing and the top titles were his for the taking. But it seemed they now had to scramble off one mountain they had crawled up and onto a new one that that seemed a lot steeper and higher.

Andrea seemed invigorated, Alex and Simon had put many of the answers to the problems into she and Elwyn's hands, but it would take a lot more work and effort from them.

'What if we hire a hall once a week to get a bit of time when we can work on the detailed stuff? And there's a practice night run by the local club each Wednesday, I think we should go to that. I think we needed more time today in the lessons, we should book two hours with each of them each week, an hour isn't enough.' She was fired up with answers to move up to that next level.

Elwyn listened as she more or less doubled their weekly dancing commitments, it would also mean a doubling of the cost.

He liked Andrea, liked her a lot, she may think of him a friend and dancing partner, but he hoped they would be much more one day, though there was no sign of that from Andrea. He guessed he really wasn't Andrea's type, except when it came to dancing. He wanted to succeed in dancing, but his confidence was knocked, not only in the competition, but in the lessons. Was he prepared to put that extra effort, and money into the partnership? Having come this far and tasted the success and liked it, he had to say yes. But the money?

He was obviously concerned over something, even Andrea in her unreserved enthusiasm could see this.

'Is there something wrong, you do agree with me don't you?'

'Yes, yes of course I do…but, umm, well.'

'Well what?'

'I'm not sure I can afford all the extra lessons and practice.'

'Oh! I thought you were in a well paid job?'

'I am, but I'm paying some of Jacob's university costs.' He explained about some of his other domestic costs. His mother had left him a very large and old house, it was costing a fortune to maintain, but he had no intention of getting rid of it.

'Is that all? I'll pay for the lessons and extra practices, right?'

'I can't let you do that.'

'Why not, I can afford it. There, settled.'

'But you can't keep subsidising my dancing for ever.'

'But our dancing's too important to penny pinch over!' By this she meant her dancing career, it all made perfect sense to her.

'Well, alright then, but only for a few months, we should have reached a level when we can go back to a less demanding schedule by then.'

'Maybe,' she said enigmatically. 'Right, this weekend, there's a competition we can do, you can make it can't you? Good.' She didn't wait for an answer, but he nodded. Next, she rang Alex and Simon to book extra lessons. That done she drew up a list of halls they could try for private practice. Elwyn felt swept along and any concerns he had counted for nothing. But why should he complain about Andrea helping him achieve his ambition, an ambition he didn't know he had until he started dancing with her. He had thought about doing some work in the house this Sunday, but it seemed pointless telling Andrea. She was already set on the idea of competing in a small competition that a few days before they had agreed wasn't worth entering, but now she was paying the piper and calling the tune.

***

Diana and Trevor spent the night together. It had been an emotional time for both of them. He insisted on getting her breakfast in bed. She normally didn't have breakfast until later in the morning, but she let him get her some corn flakes and tea, he fussed around her like a mother hen. They spent Sunday together and he went over to her parents that afternoon. Her mother noticed that there was something new between them and tried to get Diana to tell her when ever she got the chance, but Diana found herself embarrassed and admitted nothing.

Was she really embarrassed to have fallen for with Trevor, or that she had spent the night with him? Neither really, it just didn't feel like the sort of thing she wanted to discuss with her mother. She'd had enough of parental inquisition when she had been a teenager, she really didn't feel she needed it now she was in her forties. But what about Jacob? What if she did move in with Trevor, what would he say, what would her parents say? Both weighed heavily on her mind that afternoon.

Trevor still had to be at work quite early even though he no longer worked shifts and so went home that evening. Diana found she couldn't get off to sleep, what she could say to the important people in her life about her changed circumstances, it kept playing through her mind.

Well, sleeping with Trevor was no one else's business and she hadn't decided to move in with him, though she was warming to the idea.

She arranged to meet Sheryn the next evening.

Diana explained about Trevor's suggestion to buy a house together, her worries about money, and not knowing what to tell Jacob and her parents.

'Well,' said Sheryn, 'do you really think any of them will stop you if you really want to move in?'

'I suppose not, though Jacob may not want to come to the house if I'm living with Trevor.

'But they get on okay and he's away most of the time.'

'Yeah, but I'll be selling the house that's been his home…'

'But he's more or less living with his girlfriend, and do you really think your house will be the place he actually thinks of as home much longer? Surely he'll see home as where ever you are anyway.'

She may have a point. Then they discussed her parents: 'they probably wouldn't like it.'

'Why not? They must realise you and Trevor are an item, and they know money is a struggle, they've had to help you time and again with the house.'

'Hmm,' conceded Diana with a shrug, 'well, I think mum knows there's something happening with Trevor and me.'

'Of course they know! They welcome him round on Sunday's don't they?'

'Yes, but only the last few weeks,' ignoring the fact that it was actually quite a few months and they got on very well with him. He had begun doing work around their house now.

'If they didn't like him they'd tell you.'

'Hmm,' she conceded again.

'I think you're making excuses to yourself, I bet they won't mind.'

She shrugged awkwardly.

'Don't you want to move in with Trevor?'

'Well, it's a big step, I hardly know him.'

'You've been going out with him nearly a year!'

'Oh come on Sheryn! You can't call the time at Alex's before we had a bust up 'going-out'!' I've only really been dating him since Easter. God, it sounds stupid calling us going to dance classes and the odd trip to the pictures dating! He only kissed me for the first time a couple of months back and now he's talking about us moving in together!'

'Do you love him?'

Diana looked at Sheryn as if she had been insulted, she wasn't sure why.

'Don't know,' said Diana very quietly and after a lot of thought.

'You do don't you?'

She seemed to squirm. 'Sort of.'

'Have you slept together?'

Diana nodded and blushed. 'Saturday night, for the first time.'

'Umm, was it okay?'

'If you must know, yes!'

'He didn't do anything…umm, kinky then?'

'No!' she blushed, 'I don't think he would know how!'

'Well, you must love him a bit to let him into your bed…I assume it was your bed?'

She nodded, but looked guilty.

They talked about her feelings for Trevor for some time, Diana felt increasingly confused.

'I'm worried that I might agree to move in with him to save money, not because I really love him.'

Sheryn nodded. 'So, is there anyone else?'

'How d'you mean?'

'Do you have any other boyfriends?'

'No, of course not.'

'Have you had any since the divorce, or since Elwyn left you?'

She listed a few male friends: '…but I haven't slept with any of them,' she hurriedly insisted, 'I've been so wound up with looking after Jacob, and I assumed Elwyn would eventually come back, of course he didn't so then there was the divorce.
Between all this I hardly noticed the men around me, and the male friends I've had never came to anything more than just friendships. I'm still friends with all of them…I only realised Tommy was gay recently…'

'You are joking? He's so gay he could have invented it!'

'Well, it sort of passed me by.'

Sheryn laughed hysterically.

'Anyway,' continued Diana coldly, 'I did think Kevin could turn out to be a boyfriend…'

'Bit too married isn't he?' ventured Sheryn.

Diana nodded resignedly, 'I knew that from day one, we actually went out as a three-some a few times, there wasn't anything really between me and Kevin, but I did dream for a while.'

They talked about men in general and relationships, also the latest office gossip. Finally Diana said:

'The odd thing is I feel closer to Trevor now than I was to Elwyn when I married him.'

'Perhaps you actually do love Trevor, but didn't love Elwyn?' mused Sheryn.

'Don't be ridiculous!'

'Why is it ridiculous?'

'Don't know,' admitted Diana.

They discussed her relationship with Elwyn.

Diana looked and sounded frustrated. 'D'you know, I find it hard to remember what attracted me to him! Hmm, probably because of all my boyfriends at the time he was prepared to marry me and wanted kids. None of the others did…did I really marry him because he was the only one prepared to marry me and have children and not because I loved him?' The idea troubled her a great deal and she shook her head sadly. 'No, I had to have loved him! After all, I've waited for him to come back, why else would I have done that?'

'Possibly so you could have the pleasure of telling him no? Revenge!'

'Damn me Sheryn, I think you've got a point!' she laughed, but inside it didn't seem funny, it felt like a tragedy, and of her own making.

At least the chat with Sheryn helped her put a few things in perspective. The first thing, she thought, would be to see how Jacob reacted. She felt he would be the hardest one to convince and least likely to approve of her new relationship. How would she tell him? Ring him up? No, it would have to be face to face, she would wait till he was home next. Unconsciously, she was putting off the day it had to be done, and with it the final decision about moving in with Trevor a bit longer too.

***

Elwyn and Andrea arrived at the competition venue, she was really looking forward to it. She had never danced here before, the competition was organised by a dance professional and was held in a church hall in a village in very rural Somerset. Even with sat/nav it had taken a long time to find. They had been told by other competitors that it wasn't really worth their while doing as it was so small and the facilities weren't good, though Elwyn and Andrea guessed nothing could be as bad as Port Talbot, and the other couples probably were just hoping that Elwyn and Andrea wouldn't be there to wipe the floor with them. But would they wipe the floor?

In the last few days, they had practiced a couple of times and had another hour with each of their teachers. They, particularly Elwyn, had a lot to do, and competing so soon after all the changes to their posture and style seemed a bit premature, but Andrea was so determined.

When they stood outside the hall they realised the other couples were probably not trying to put them off to avoid being beaten by Andrea and Elwyn, and they did genuinely feel this competition wasn't worth their effort – the hall looked dilapidated.

In the mid Victorian hall, which was very shabby inside and out, they found the entry for the children's events very good, far too good for what was a small dance floor. When it came to wiping the floor, they felt a mop would be more appropriate. It was obviously a mess, the surface was poor, plus it was ordinary floor boards, not a sprung dance floor. Each step across it sounded as though they were walking the deck of a sailing ship, it creaked as if in agony.

There was no where for them to sit and adult couples were arriving all the time. They wouldn't get a seat until the kids and their parents had left, and that wouldn't be for some time. Elwyn found the gents changing area, again, it was under the stage, but here it was a down flight of rickety steps. It looked as though he was going below deck on a sailing ship, a very old one. In the room, which was cluttered with props for stage shows, cobwebs hung everywhere, two naked light bulbs struggled to provide some illumination. There were no hooks to hang his suit case on, he used a very rusty nail jutting out of a rafter and that didn't seem that solid.

Andrea made her way through the mass of children and their parents to the female changing room, this she found was an area at the back of the stage curtained off form the hall. A clothes rail had been put up, but it was already too full. It wasn't well lit and the floor of the stage creaked impressively and worryingly, it sagged in various places too.

It was too early for them to change, so they met up near a refreshment counter just off the main hall, a volunteer was working full pelt to serve all the kids. The atmosphere was electric and they were all having a great time, Elwyn and Andrea weren't! The competition was run by Natalie Manston, she had worked hard to build up her business. She actually taught in Weston-Super-Mare, but this remote church hall, seemed to her to be an ideal place to run a competition, no one else thought so. Most of the children in the competition were her pupils. She also chose comparatively local judges that she thought might bring their couples along to compete, and she was right. There were seven judges, all from the neighbouring counties and all seemed to have brought coach loads of kids to dance on the far too small floor.

To try and keep the competition moving, the chairman and Natalie put too many couples on the floor in each event. The kids didn't mind, but Elwyn and Andrea guessed it would be the same in the adult events, and meant that dancing their best was going to be difficult. They seriously considered not competing and just going home, this had all the makings of a bad day.

But after some reflection, Andrea was determined and reminded Elwyn they needed the 'comp-practice', he reluctantly agreed. The fact she had paid for them both to get in also played a part in the decision. They had agreed she would pay this time, he would pay to get into the next competition. He planned that as much as possible it would be 50/50, but Andrea was more than happy to subsidise him, he wasn't so keen. Perhaps the partnership was in dancing terms 60% man and 40% woman, but in financial terms the ratio was reversed and he knew this put him in Andrea's pocket, almost literally!

Natalie ran the competition very efficiently, no time was wasted, the announcements were clear, accurate and concise, the whole afternoon was very business like. The music was played by an experienced 'music-man' and there were very few problems. Although the competition was over-running, Natalie regularly updated dancers with timings. Gradually she began to make up time, though there was very little chance the adult events would start at the advertised time. Natalie regularly announced the running order for the next few events so couples knew if they may be dancing soon, and she had the recalls to each event posted in the foyer so dancers knew if they were in the next round. Despite the scruffy hall and facilities, the day crackled with energy.

There was no sign that any seats would become available for quite a while, so Elwyn and Andrea went out to the car and waited.

They went back in good time, the hall was even more crowded now, but at least the kid's events were coming to an end. Elwyn and Andrea went and changed. Unusually, the adult Latin events were on first. The changing rooms were full of adults getting ready. Both areas were too small for the numbers of dancers and Elwyn found himself putting his arm into someone else's shirt sleeve and another man searching Elwyn's suit bag by mistake. He was glad to get out of there and register for the events.

The advert for this competition listed some impressive titles to be contested, but it was only now they realised that there were no championships, and no really significant events. These were just grandly named events that had no real importance in the wider dancing world. One of Alex and Simon's other couples, Wendy and Geraint Fulmar explained.

'This is just a small comp, Natalie runs this as a chance for her couples to have a local event, she's dreamt up the titles herself…look: the

"Somerset, Wiltshire and Gloucestershire Grand Senior Pre-amateur Four Dance Trophy", those are the counties all the judges are from. The "Southern English All Comers Open Intermediate Three Dance Trophy", these titles are just that, titles, a load of words.'

Andrea was disappointed, but it was at least a competition.

'Well,' added Geraint, 'you may not find the standard that impressive. We do this comp because it's fairly local and we're only really a modest standard, none of the quality couples come here. Mind you, don't tell him,' and pointed to a couple rushing into the hall.

'Who are they then?' said Andrea.

'Spencer Wheel and Tara Wellington. They're Seniors, so you'll be dancing against them.

'Spencer Wheel? I remember that name. I used to dance against him when I was a Junior!' said Andrea.

'Yeah and I bet he's not improved since. He only does these local and very small comps'. He won't do Warwick because he knows he stands no chance, he only comes to these comps because he thinks he can win easily against poor opposition. If you listen to him he claims he travels everywhere and wins everything, utter crap of course,' said Geraint acidly. 'Even so, he's likely to be the toughest couple you may have to take on today, though you might get some good 'Over 50's' couples…hmm, yeah. I think you've got a couple of reasonable ones, so you may have someone to dance against, no walk over.'

Elwyn wasn't sure if this was a good thing or bad. It would be nice to have some easy wins, but what if they were beaten by Spencer and Tara, or the over fifties couples, how would Andrea take that? They would soon find out.

Natalie sighed as she saw Spencer and Tara almost burst into the room, they argued about whose fault it was that they were late.

'Hia Nat'!' yelled Spencer up the floor, 'You can't start yet, we'll need time to change…you're running early aren't you?'

'Afternoon Spencer, *don't* call me Nat'!' she said over the microphone, 'no, we're running an hour late and so it would seem are you too.'

Spencer went up to the stage waving a copy of the dancers' newspaper and insisting Natalie was starting early. The chairman, Neil Kirkby, plucked the paper out of Spencer's hands, then held up the advert to him.

'Latin starts at 2.30, the Ballroom at 3.30, if you want to do Latin you're already over an hour late.'

'Oh, sorry, didn't realise,' mumbled Spencer,

'I don't see why,' said Natalie, 'it's the same timing and running order in all my comps, and you're at them all…' still using the microphone, '…worst luck,' she added, though had turned the mike off.

'You going to change or what?' said Kirkby.

'Will you shut up and go change?' said Tara to Spencer and stormed off.

'I don't remember her, but I remember him alright,' said Andrea.

'And he's going to be like this all afternoon,' said Wendy sullenly.

Natalie knew which events Spencer and Tara usually danced. She started the Latin section and ran grades and age classes that would be of no interest to Spencer. Even so the competition had to be stopped for about a quarter hour whilst they waited for Spencer to finish changing, he took far longer than Tara.

There were quite a few events in the Latin section that Elwyn and Andrea were able to dance, the first of which was an Open Rumba. As they had feared there were too many couples on the floor, but they managed.

Spencer and Tara also danced in every event they could, so Elwyn and Andrea were up against them quite a lot. Spencer was actually not a good dancer. His poor, long suffering and long time girlfriend, Tara, was actually quite skilled, but this counted for nothing because of Spencer.

Elwyn found Spencer's hand clop him across the back of the head several times, he guessed it wasn't malicious, just incompetence. Though he did begin to wonder if Spencer was trying to get in their way, it started to feel like it.

The Latin section proceeded well, if frantically. Elwyn and Andrea were pleased to find they were recalled in everything they danced, but also realised the standard wasn't that high and even though the floor was very full, they still outshone most of the opposition.

They reached the finals of all their events, great, except several were run back-to-back with no breaks between. At least they were a bit fitter than they had been in Port Talbot, even so, it was draining.

The events they were most interested in were the Senior Pre-amateur and Open Senior Latin Four Dance Trophy, the latter being the equivalent to championship grade. They danced both the significant finals and gave each dance all they could. Spencer and Tara also made these two finals, though they hadn't done as well as Elwyn and Andrea. Spencer seemed to be increasingly rattled to see a couple he didn't recognise out dance him. The effort he put into each dance became more exaggerated as the afternoon went on.

Elwyn and Andrea quite enjoyed themselves, but Spencer started to make a nuisance of himself. In the Samba he managed to dance between Elwyn and Andrea as they danced apart, it looked deliberate and an attempt to put them off, it didn't work. Elwyn wasn't experienced enough to just ignore it, Andrea helped him get back on track and the rest of the dance went quite well. During a Rumba, Elwyn and Andrea noticed Spencer dancing quite close. Seconds later he led Tara into a step that required her to rondē her leg impressively. Elwyn had just gone into what's called a 'press-line', in other words he was stationary while Andrea did an elaborate step. All of his weight was pressed onto his right leg. He could see Tara's Kung-Fu like rondē was coming his way, it all happened in just a few seconds, she cracked him across the knee squarely. Elwyn went down like a sack of spuds.

The chairman, Neil Kirkby, stopped the music and checked with Elwyn to see if he was alright. Initially it seemed he wouldn't be able to get up, let alone dance. Andrea too had fallen, but wasn't hurt, just worried about Elwyn.

'You did that on purpose!' she accused Spencer.

They argued whilst Elwyn recovered. Tara was full of apologies and helped him up. He guessed, as did Kirkby, that Spencer couldn't really have planned to make that happen. He was unlikely to know they would do a press-line just as Tara did her rondé, but they felt Spencer had hoped he could do damage, the kick across the knee had been a bonus.

'Do you think you can dance?' checked Kirby.

'Not sure, let me try and put weight on it… Okay, I'll give it a go, it's not too bad.'

'Good man!' Kirby hurried off and gave the thumbs up to the music man and Natalie.

Andrea and Spencer were still arguing.

'You were just the same when you were a Junior!' she blurted.

'What d'you mean?'

'Don't remember me? I'm Andrea Wing, my surname's Mooney now. I used to dance against you with Julian Mooney.'

'Good God! I do remember you! How are you? Hey, dumped old Julian have you? He couldn't dance on time to save his life he couldn't!' Spencer grinned foolishly.

Andrea was shocked and the hurt immediately showed, but she was soon ready for Spencer: 'Julian, my husband, died nearly a year ago.'

'Oh, oh, I'm sorry.'

'I bet you are! He was a better dancer than you and you know it!'

'Umm, now, excuse me,' said Kirkby, 'time to start dancing again. Finished insulting people have we Spencer? And Andrea, nice to see you back dancing, love, I was very sorry to hear about Julian. I was shocked to hear of his…passing.' He was quite sincere.

'Thanks Neil, didn't think you'd remember me after all these years.'

'How could I forget you Andrea, you and Julian always beat me and Bryony.'

Spencer squirmed as he heard the conversation. He and Tara were up against Elwyn and Andrea time and again throughout the remaining finals. They tried to keep well away from Spencer, neither thought Tara was that much of a problem.

It was only when he went to change for the Ballroom section that Elwyn was able to look at his knee, then he knew there was something seriously wrong, dancing had become almost impossible. It was bruised, swollen and very painful.

'That'll be fun to dance on in the Ballroom section,' he said to Geraint with a bit of gallows humour.

'Wow, nasty! Do you think you can dance?'

'I can give it a try, hope the adrenaline works.'

In the ladies changing area, Tara cautiously came over to Andrea.

'I'm sorry about what happened,' she said nervously.

'Don't worry, I know it wasn't your fault, it was Spencer, he's always been like it.'

Tara was clearly going to protest, but knew it wasn't appropriate.

'I'm sorry to hear about your husband, I didn't know him, but it must have been terrible.'

At least she was trying to be nice and make amends, they began chatting. Andrea soon found she quite liked Tara, which was more than she could say for Spencer.

When she got back to their seats, she found Elwyn pulling on a support bandage, she could see his knee was bruised. They discussed whether he could dance, she doubted it, so did Elwyn, but said they should give it a go.

'I want to dance if only to get the better of Spencer,' said Elwyn.

Spencer was on the other side of the hall holding court with anyone who would listen. To many of them he was a wonderful dancer and something of a dance hero.

The competition was still running late, but Natalie had begun to claw back time during the Latin section. She continued to run it efficiently and with very little wasted or lost time. The biggest controlling factor was the inadequate size of the floor.

Elwyn and Andrea were only able to dance the Open Foxtrot, Open Viennese Waltz and the Open Senior Four Dance Trophy in the Ballroom section, thankfully the first time they were called to the floor was for the Foxtrot and that was the fourth event in this section, it gave Elwyn time to check his knee and how much strain it could take, he didn't feel confident.

The entry was quite good and they were in heat four of five, not because of the numbers of dancers. It was just that the dance floor could only take at most six couples for the Ballroom events, and really that was too many. Spencer and Tara were in this too, but heat five.

Having had some time to rest his knee, Elwyn felt a little more confident, especially as he watched Spencer and Tara. He led her off time to the music within seconds of beginning the dance, a cardinal sin in Foxtrot.

Wendy and Geraint had been right, there were two very good over fifties couples also dancing the Foxtrot, and they were far more impressive than Spencer and Tara. It was these that Elwyn and Andrea were dancing against rather than Spencer and Tara.

The competition programme included an over fifties championship, Elwyn and Andrea were too young for it. It had attracted two good quality couples, though they seemed to be the only ones. Over fifties events are for couples that are both over the age of fifty. Most of these contests are to championship level and the competitive nature of the competition is often as high as amongst the younger couples.

The Foxtrot was uncomfortable for Elwyn and he hesitated to put too much effort into the dance. At this stage they both guessed he could get away with it.

The Open Senior Four Dance seemed to be a long time in being called, Elwyn and Andrea were very glad. The Open Foxtrot recalls came regularly, then they had the first round of the Viennese Waltz. It was not their best dance, but it went fairly well, his knee was very painful throughout, but he just about managed to get through.

They had a discussion, should they withdraw form the two one-dance events and save themselves for the Open Senior Four Dance? No, they would risk it, but both knew their answer should have been yes.

Elwyn knew he was being stupid, but he felt he had a lot to prove to Andrea, and she very much wanted to dance. In fact, she felt great to dance with, which was making his job so much easier.

The short length of the floor wasn't helping. In Viennese Waltz it hadn't mattered too much as they were able to do this as a circuit of the floor. Foxtrot was more of a problem, but Elwyn and Andrea were able to cut out groups of steps when they ran out of space and improvise. In the early rounds they knew that it was more important to look good, the accuracy of the footwork would count in the semi-finals and final, assuming they made it.

It was surprising to find that they were recalled to dance the final of the two one dance events before they had danced the Open Senior Four', was there a problem, why wasn't Natalie running it? Both one-dance finals pitted them against the two good over fifties couples. Spencer and Tara hadn't got very far in the Foxtrot. No surprise there, but remarkably, were in the Viennese final. Though the entry for the Viennese had been far smaller, and most couples that danced it seemed to have little idea of the dance. The judges presumably felt charitable to Spencer and Tara.

As they danced against him and Tara, Elwyn and Andrea were able to see them careering ridiculously fast around the floor, off time. They launched into a step called the Fleckerl in the centre of the floor, it went wrong and Tara found her legs knocked out from underneath her by Spencer. He yanked her up and charged her back into the dance like a battering ram, at least it felt like it to a young couple they collided with.

The last final of the day was the Open Senior Four Dance Trophy, a straight final, which was why there had been no initial rounds. Elwyn and Andrea weren't sorry as the two one dance finals had been painful for him. Natalie kept up the illusion of a high status event by getting each of the five couples in the straight final to an introductory dance.

'Now for our last final, the Somerset and Devon All Comers Open Senior Ballroom Trophy! I would like to invite our finalists to dance on to a little Foxtrot, and our first finalists, number four, Ernie and Doris Westram!

They proudly took the floor. The portly couple looked to be in their late seventies, normally Ernie and Doris danced any event they could and would not expect to make a final. As they danced Foxtrot for the dance on it was fairly obvious they were no real challenge to the rest of the finalists, even to Spencer and Tara. Ernie and Doris had only entered it because the rules said they could, and it made the competition a bit more worthwhile coming to. They were having a grand time.

'Thank you Ernie and Doris. Our next finalists, number eleven, John and Alice Southcott!'

This was one of the two good over fifties couples. Elwyn and Andrea watched them intently as they swept up the floor, they were good all right. They were also comparatively fresh. They hadn't danced Latin, but hey had of course done the over fifties event, but that had been completed much earlier.

Elwyn and Andrea were next on the floor, the Foxtrot was painful for him, and with no one else on the floor their attempts to crop their routine must have seemed more obvious, and not well rehearsed.

'Our fourth couple in what promises to be a lovely final is number sixteen, Ian and Jeanette Cheshire!'

The other over fifties couple, they looked about the same standard as John and Alice.

'And completing this beautiful final, Spencer Wheel and Tara Wellington!'

Again Spencer led Tara off time just seconds into the dance. He struggled with the length of the floor, but instead of adapting his routine he just went to the end of the floor, stopped and bowed exaggeratedly, which his fans loved.

The final got underway. At the far end of the floor from the stage, there were two aisles between the rows of chairs leading out of the hall. Elwyn and Andrea used them to give them more space on the long sides of their routines, it felt silly, but it helped. The other couples also seemed to struggle. Elwyn and Andrea felt each step jarred his injured knee, but he struggled on.

After the Tango, the second dance, Natalie introduced the couples again, this time also telling the audience where the dancers were from. She was just doing this to give the finalists a breather, though the over fifties couples didn't seem to need it. Spencer did, though Tara clearly didn't. Ernie and Doris were having a whale of a time, and what dancing they did, apparently didn't tire them. Elwyn was very glad of a break because of his knee. Andrea hadn't needed the breather, but realised Elwyn was struggling. She felt sorry for him, was she pushing too hard? No, he was up for it and so keen. It had been his idea to stay in the two one-dance events, she wouldn't let him down. Well, actually it may have been more her idea.

The Foxtrot was the third dance and for Elwyn and Andrea, and the hardest to fit onto the small floor. This time they whooshed down it along the aisle and out of the door at the far end. This hadn't been the plan, and getting back into the hall and still dance their routine wasn't that easy. It got a big laugh from the audience, which they didn't want, and what did the judges think? Well, none of them were laughing, Neil Kirkby seemed to give a wry smile though.

Then there was the Quickstep. Elwyn and Andrea found that the first side of their routine, if curved round the floor, actually took them about two thirds of the way around the room, and that was with dancing as 'small' as they could. There was no pleasure in dancing like this, and what did they look like to the audience, or the judges? It didn't help that Ernie and Doris kept getting in the way, Elwyn and Andrea kept lapping them! They would come out of a corner and there was Ernie and Doris tootling along. Elwyn could have cried with the pain as he varied the groups of steps to take them around the couple. Doris and Ernie never seemed bothered, though it must have looked to them like a boulder coming down a mountain, as Elwyn and Andrea loomed up at speed.

Elwyn and Andrea were aware that Spencer and Tara seemed to stop a lot. The other two couples danced smoothly, this was a very strange day at the office.

Gratefully, Elwyn and Andrea heard the last chords of the Quickstep fade. Just as well, the pain was now so bad he wasn't sure he could carry on. They bowed to the audience, there was a cheer from behind them, Spencer was bowing elaborately to a group of their enthusiastic supporters. Tara curtsied delicately, and appropriately, then left Spencer lapping up what seemed to be mock applause.

At last off the floor, Andrea took Elwyn's number off while he put a freeze pack on his knee.

She brought enough first aid equipment to each competition to equip a small A&E department, but the expensive compress didn't seem to help.

'I'm not going to be able to dance for days, my knee's wrecked,' he said miserably.

'Well I think you did very well. I'm proud of you, well done,' she even gave him a peck on the cheek.

'Oh, thanks,' he had expected her to dismiss the injury and order him to turn up to practice. Had he missed something, was she up to something?

As couples had been knocked out of the various events, they had changed and left, so the hall was becoming increasingly empty. Just the couples that were waiting for the presentation of prizes remained, helpers and a very few spectators.

Spencer and Tara came over.

'How's the knee old man?' checked Spencer. He looked so superior and the sounded insincere, in fact that's just what he was.

As Andrea had watched them approach, she had guessed what Spencer would say almost word for word, he hadn't changed much since he was a kid!

'It's alright, painful though,' conceded Elwyn, he really didn't like Spencer.

'Well, I thought you danced quite nicely today, good effort.'

'Thanks. And did you have a good comp?' asked Elwyn. Tara had edged Andrea to one side, she knew Andrea would go off like a gun if she heard some of Spencer's condescending remarks.

'Oh, brilliant, all to plan, it was an easy day with no competition really. Our experience tells on occasions like this.' Spencer was grinning and self-satisfied.

Elwyn started to wonder if he was serious, yes, he was!

Andrea heard most of what was being said and laughed, Spencer didn't seem to notice.

'To present the prizes, please welcome…' said Natalie, and asked the wife of one of the judges onto the floor.

The format was the same as the other competitions they had been to. The lowest grade was called first and then Natalie worked up to the higher grades. The non-graded events, such as the one-dance competitions came about half way through the list. The Latin results were the first discipline given. Elwyn and Andrea's first result was the Senior Intermediate, Spencer and Tara hadn't been in this. Elwyn and Andrea won it, the form book said they should.

'Well done, worthy winners,' called out Spencer and clapped his hands above his head, nodding condescendingly from the other side of the hall.

'I think I'm going to slap him before we finish today,' said Andrea as they walked up to get their plaques.

'Ladies first when it comes to slapping, then me second,' smiled Elwyn. He limped up to the lady presenting the prizes. Now he'd stopped dancing and the adrenaline had dried up the pain was over powering. Though at least he kept his sense of humour, Diana hadn't known he had one.

Geraint and Wendy were still under thirty-five, they danced the 'Open' events and had a good day too winning or coming second in the several events. They cheered enthusiastically as Elwyn and Andrea went for their prizes and then was cheered by Elwyn and Andrea when they went up for their prizes.

Almost embarrassingly, Elwyn and Andrea won the two Latin one-dance events. They wondered if it might look as though they had been 'slumming-it'. The dancing was well below their standard. Though actually this wasn't what they had intended, they really thought they wouldn't do so well. Then it came to the Senior Pre-amateur Latin. Spencer stepped onto the floor and beckoned Tara to join him, he knew they had won.

'First, from Newport, number twelve, Elwyn Wharton and Andrea Mooney!'

Spencer looked shocked, and then furious. 'That's your fault!' he yelled at Tara, she just rolled her eyes and told him to shut up. In fact they were an embarrassing third.

A little later the result to the Open Senior Four Dance Latin Trophy was announced. It also had a very long and impressive title, but by now to Elwyn and Andrea that wasn't important, where they came in the final was.

'First, from Newport, number twelve, Elwyn Wharton and Andrea Mooney!' Natalie said with slightly artificial enthusiasm, but that didn't matter, it was her competition and she was clearly now worn out.

Spencer looked very shocked and stood with his hands on his hips as he watched Elwyn and Andrea go up to receive a very large, plastic trophy. Spencer turned away and seemed about to leave the hall in disgust.

'And into second place...' began Natalie.

Spencer stopped, realising he and Tara would be called out now.

But she didn't call them out to take second, they came sixth, Spencer was obviously seething.

From the presentation line, Elwyn and Andrea could see all Spencer's antics. Including Tara having to tug him back into the hall and up to get the plaques for sixth place. When he received them he was all smiles, though the first couple he had to congratulate was Elwyn and Andrea.

'Very well done, I'm *so* pleased for you! Quite an achievement for you two eh?'

'Shuddup Spencer, come on,' hissed Tara.

Elwyn and Andrea had expected something like that from Spencer. Everyone else in the hall congratulated them. By now they found Spencer rather funny and didn't actually care what he thought. They had won all the events in Latin they had danced. They had had more of a challenge from the dance floor than the other couples.

The Ballroom results were then given, again starting with Beginners.

Elwyn and Andrea didn't expect these results to be good, after all, Elwyn had struggled to dance injured. Andrea told Elwyn not to expect much and he fully understood why.

Again, Geraint and Wendy had some good results.

'Open Foxtrot,' said Natalie.

Geraint said, 'this one's yours,' to Elwyn and Andrea

'Hopefully we should get fourth, though I wouldn't be surprised if it's sixth,' said Andrea.

'I think you may be in for a nice surprise.'

They were surprised, they won it.

'Told you,' said Geraint as they got back to their seats.

'But we danced that appallingly!' said Andrea.

'You should have seen the others!' winked Wendy.

'Open Viennese Waltz!' said Natalie, 'first, from Newport, number twelve, Elwyn Wharton and Andrea Mooney!'

'I can't believe that!' said Elwyn.

'Neither can I,' said Andrea, let's go get the prize before for they change their mind!'

Of course, Spencer had been confident of winning that too.

As Elwyn and Andrea went up the floor to get their prize they heard:

'Well that's a fix!' Spencer wasn't taking it very well and no amount of shushing form Tara could shut him up.

'You two are having a good day,' said Wendy, and gave Andrea a hug.

'Yeah, much better than we expected given the floor and all the changes we've made to our dancing this week,' said Elwyn, 'not to mention my bloody knee!' and rubbed it carefully.

More results were given, then Natalie said: 'Now for our last presentation of the competition. The Somerset and Devon All Comers Open Senior Ballroom Four Dance Trophy! And into first place…'

'Huh don't tell me, I've guessed!' said Spencer, loud enough to be sure Elwyn and Andrea could hear.

'Will you shut up,' snapped Tara.

'From Newport, number twelve, Elwyn Wharton and Andrea Mooney!'

'Well I'm going to complain,' said Spencer.

As Spencer moaned, Neil Kirkby was leaving the hall, his job for the day finished. He heard Spencer. Andrea and Elwyn clearly head him say: 'I've had enough of him!' and almost marched across the floor to the moaning dancer just as Elwyn and Andrea went out to get another very large plastic trophy.

From the presentation line, Elwyn and Andrea could see Kirkby prodding Spencer in the chest, he looked taken back and protested half-heartedly.

'Second,' said Natalie, from Bristol, number eleven, John and Alice Southcott!'

Spencer had been edging away from Kirkby's finger and pointing to the stage, clearly he expected they would be second. But gave up when he heard Natalie say who actually had taken second.

'Not having a good day is he?' said John smiling as he and Alice joined Elwyn and Andrea in the presentation line having congratulated them.

'Well, I think this is far more entertaining than his dancing,' said Elwyn as they watched Kirkby giving Spencer a piece of his mind.

'Third…' began Natalie.

Spencer again started moving away from Kirkby and pointing at the stage.

'…from Birmingham, number sixteen, Ian and Jeanette Cheshire…'

Spencer seemed to crumple.

'…fourth…'

'Hmm, don't think Spencer will be joining us yet,' said John. 'At this rate he could well be behind Ernie and Doris.'

'Surely not,' said Elwyn, 'he's not that bad.'

'He can be, besides, there's not a judge he hasn't upset either today, or in the past, and that's not a good idea when they're judging you!'

Spencer had given up now and just stood listening to Kirkby who seemed in no hurry to go or finish ticking the moaning dancer off.

'...from Bath...'

'Oh dear, oh dear, oh dear,' said John.

'...Ernie and Doris Westram!'

'Tara's going to have a long trip home tonight don't you think?' mused John.

Elwyn and Andrea smiled as if they were embarrassed, but couldn't help enjoying a snigger.

'And into fifth place, from Reading, number forty-three, Spencer...'

Tara strode up to Spencer and tugged him out onto the floor even though Kirkby hadn't finished with him.

Spencer mumbled congratulations to the other couples, posed for a photograph, but couldn't smile.

As Elwyn and Andrea made their way back to their seats, they noticed Neil Kirkby waiting for them. Perhaps it was their turn to get a lecture from the chairman?

Neil smiled warmly and gave Andrea a polite kiss.

'Good to see you again after all these years love. God, seeing you takes me back. Remember that team match in Austria we went on when we were Juniors? Happy days eh? Happy days!'

They had a chat, but Andrea and Elwyn kept wondering what this was all about, he had been on his way home a few minutes before.

Finally, he glanced around to check no one was near and said: 'You two are bloody good, lovely dancing. I just had to tell you, and also make it clear that you should ignore Spencer. He's a bloody idiot and I've just told him so.'

'Oh, thanks, but we really weren't much cop today, my knee's in a hell of a state, that floor is far too small for us,' Elwyn listed more problems.

'Really, well it didn't show.'

'That's very kind,' said Elwyn, not really believing Kirkby.

'Nah, not kind, Andrea, Elwyn mate, listen, you two wiped the floor with everyone here, you're a league apart.'

They had no idea what to say and just mumbled their thanks.

'Listen to me, ignore Spencer, I'm going to complain to his amateur governing body about him. I won't have him insulting the judges when I'm chairman, thinks he's God's gift to dancing he does.'

'The standard here wasn't that good though,' said Andrea.

'Come on, you know the Southcotts and Cheshires are damn good, they do very well in the over forty-fives and over fifties events. They've been dancing together for years and they have national rankings. They've even represented the country in the over forty-fives European championship and reached the semi-final. You did well to beat them, don't write them off. You won against some good opposition, really.'

They shifted uncomfortably in their seats, after the disappointment of the other day they were quite prepared to dismiss this competition result as not relevant and achieved against no real opposition.

'We're doing Warwick soon...' started Elwyn.

Kirkby interrupted: 'Are you doing Southampton in December?'

'Well, we've qualified, but didn't think we'd bother,' admitted Andrea.

'Why not? What grade did you qualify at?'

'Senior Pre-champ' in Ballroom and Latin,' said Andrea.

'If I were you, I'd dance it. Dancing the way you two are, then you stand a good chance of winning, that'll get you known. Think about it. You shone on that floor, you need something to get you recognised as quality dancers. Dance at Southampton.'

'But we lost our Senior Pre-champ' status at Port Talbot...'

'Read the rules, you qualified as Pre-champs, you're still able to dance that grade at Southampton. Think about it, don't throw away that opportunity. Nice big floor too,' said Kirkby.

He gave Elwyn a handshake and Andrea another kiss, then hurried off.

A little later, Andrea was driving them home as Elwyn's knee was too painful for him to drive.

He chatted away about the competition, excited, but confused. Competitions were still new to him, he had come a remarkably long way in a short time but wasn't so stupid as to think it was all thanks to his skill. Andrea was a great partner and, as he had just found out, she was known, liked, and very good. But Andrea was saying very little. He wondered if there was something wrong, had he said something out of turn?

She had been thinking about Southampton, Kirkby's advice was good, but right now that wasn't what was on her mind. She thought back to that team match he had talked about, she had been dancing with Julian in those days. They had had so many good times together and now here she was dancing with another man, Diana's ex' for God's sake! Neil Kirkby…huh, he had been a flighty and naughty little boy as a Junior. He drove the various parents on that trip mad, always getting lost or into trouble. He and Julian had been best friends, there had been so much laughter, yeah, happy days.

Julian had been a great dancer, but Andrea had never really understood why after they married he seemed to lose interest, and become a career man at the bank. Of course, they still danced, but only until they moved to Stoke. He had talked a lot about dancing again after they had settled down, but they never did. Partly because she had become pregnant with Bethany, from then on, all ideas about dancing stopped.

She had wanted Bethany to learn to dance, but Julian didn't seem that keen. For the first time she wondered why. At the time she had just let it ride, besides Bethany was a good swimmer and they were happy to let her achieve what she wanted in that. Then Rupert came along, she had wanted him to learn to dance too, but still Julian seemed not to be interested in either of his children taking up the sport that he, apparently, had loved all his life. She then suddenly wondered, what if Julian hadn't really loved dancing? What if he only danced because his parents pushed him into it and only carried on to make Andrea happy? Now she would never know, and that hurt her.

And what about Bethany and Rupert? Andrea was so wound up with her dancing she hardly seemed to have had any time for them since she had partnered up with Elwyn, what did they think of this, of him, of her?

'So, Andrea, what do you think, should we dance Southampton?'

'What, oh, umm, sorry, well, I'm keen, yes, but it'll mean a couple of days away. I better discuss it with the kids.'

'Of course, how are they?'

Andrea didn't actually know. Was she becoming just like Julian's parents, not really aware of what he actually wanted? Surely not, but she had better find out.

Chapter Six
Guess Who's Coming to Dinner!

Diana and Trevor spent more and more time together, and Diana was enjoying life, she laughed so much more these days. That was such a tonic after all the years of struggle. But she was torn about Trevor's idea, did she actually want to live with him? Was it such a bad idea? She just wasn't sure.

She had started dropping hints to her parents, but they hadn't seemed to pick up the meaning, though what little response she got suggested they didn't see much wrong with the idea. Did she actually want them to object? Hmm, possibly.

Jacob had been busy and not been home for several weeks. Of course they had been in touch regularly, but she didn't want to sound him out about selling the family home and moving in with Trevor over the phone, or in an email, or a text, she wanted to have a face to face chat. Though she realised she was delaying deciding about moving in with Trevor until Jacob came home, was this an excuse? Yes it was.

At least Trevor wasn't pressurising her over it, though it came into conversation regularly. His house was on the market and he had begun viewing properties, and he wanted her to come with him. So far she had made excuses which he accepted, though did look a little hurt. This was an annoying, but effective trait he had. He could look like a scolded puppy, complete with big brown eyes, and say he understood and that it was okay, but actually meant that you had hurt and injured him deeply. Thankfully he soon bounced back and she was beginning to get used to his version of emotional blackmail.

She was delighted when Jacob said he would be coming home for the weekend, but also a bit worried. Now she'd have to tell him about Trevor's plan, what would he say? He was bringing Annalise too, so Diana would have less time to talk to Jacob on his own. Well, one part of her said that wasn't such a bad thing, it might mean she could put off making a decision a bit longer. Then again, did she want to put the decision off? Umm, yes.

The night they arrived, Diana prepared them a nice meal. She decided not to tell Jacob about Trevor's idea this evening, tomorrow perhaps. But it was Diana that had news broken to her.

'Did I tell you we've booked into the same hotel as you and Trevor in Southampton?'

'Oh, umm, no you didn't,' she felt very uneasy. She and Trevor were going to be sharing a room, and she had sort of forgotten to mention this to Jacob, and she knew he wouldn't approve. Did he know that she would be sharing with Trevor in Southampton? So far he had said nothing about it. Nah, of course he wouldn't know that!

He and Annalise talked about how they had sorted the booking out for their room. *Their room*, they would be sharing a room!

'Yeah, that's right, of course we are,' said Jacob, 'what's wrong with that?'

'Well nothing, of course, it's up to you, you're adults now.' Though she didn't see Jacob or Annalise as adults, and the idea of these 'children' sleeping together, seemed wrong. She told herself not to be stupid. She thought back to when she had been Jacob's age…hmm, if only her parents had known eh?

The meal went well and conversation flowed easily. Diana really enjoyed hearing how their courses were going, university life and of course their dancing. They mainly competed for the university club and were to doing well. As the evening progressed Diana heard more about her son's new life, it only slowly dawned on her that they were living together, Annalise had moved in with Jacob after the summer holiday. This hit Diana like a brick. She was no prude, but the idea of her little boy now living with some girl she hardly knew was difficult to accept. She worked hard not to show shock or annoyance, if she did neither Jacob or Annalise seemed to realise.

'So,' said Jacob, 'how's Trevor?'

'Oh he's fine,' she told them that he was planning to move.

'That's great, good luck to him, I don't know why you two don't get somewhere together,' mused Jacob.

Diana nearly choked on her coffee. 'Oh, I don't know about that, that's ridiculous, don't be silly, we're just friends.'

'Really? Just good friends?', he smirked.

'Jacob! What a thing to say!' Oh no, Diana felt herself blush!

'Is it, why? He obviously adores you and I think you're…umm, yeah, in love with him.'

'That's rubbish!' and hurried off to the kitchen with some dishes. Annalise joined her.

'I'm sorry about that,' said Diana.

'It's alright, I'm sorry he embarrassed you,' it seemed odd for Annalise to make apologies for Jacob.

'I didn't think Jacob would say such things in company,' admitted Diana.

'Well, you and Trevor do seem to get on well. Jake does worry about you in this house on your own. He was so pleased Trevor did so much work for you. He was considering giving up uni' so he could get a job and help you pay for the repairs.'

'I'd never let him do that!'

'Perhaps not, but that's what he was prepared to do. He's very pleased you've found Trevor, they get on well too.'

'They hardly know each other, they've only met a few times.'

Annalise looked a little taken aback. 'Didn't you know that Jake and Trevor keep in touch all the time through "Facebook", we've heard all about your dancing, nights out, work he's doing on the house...'

'No, I didn't know that! He never said!'

'Well, I think he didn't want you to think that by his keeping in touch with Jake that he was trying to find out more about you, sort of stalking, know what I mean?'

Diana nodded, but wasn't sure she did understand, there would be words with Trevor when she saw him.

'So, Jacob already knew that Trevor is selling up,' checked Diana, 'and has he said that…umm…we might be…umm…'

'That he's suggested you set up home together? Yes.'

Diana had to sit down. 'What does Jacob think?'

'I think it's a great idea,' he was standing in the doorway.

Diana felt dreadful, she didn't know what to say and couldn't look at Jacob, yet she felt relieved in a strange sort of way.

'Oh mum! Don't feel bad about it. I'm so pleased you're in a relationship, Trevor is great for you. It's high time you got rid of this place, make a life for yourself, enjoy life.'

For some reason none of this seemed to help. She laughed nervously as she listened to Jacob lecture her on what a good bloke Trevor was and how she should move in with him. But she began to feel angry. She had sacrificed so much to keep this house, and put Jacob at the centre of her world, but now he was urging her to sell up and even not to consider him. She couldn't help crying. Jacob, who had started helping with the washing up, didn't notice, but Annalise did. She sent him to get something up stairs. As soon as he was out of the room, she gave Diana a hug.

Diana was surprised, but welcomed it. Annalise comforted her as if she was a child, reassured and tried to help. Incredibly she understood exactly how Diana felt, but how?

It was some time later that Diana and Annalise were able to find time together to talk away from Jacob.

'Thank you for earlier,' said Diana simply.

'Glad I could help.'

'It's just that I found it really hard that Jacob doesn't seem to think it's worth keeping the house…I've sweated blood to keep it going, and all for him.'

'He loves you, you know that. All he wants is for you to be happy, and he knows how much pain you've gone through to meet the bills and keep the house.'

'But I thought he'd want it to be his home when he finishes uni'.'

She shrugged. 'I don't think he's considered that.'

'The way I saw it is that he could have the house when he graduates and I'll rent somewhere. I haven't got much to give him. I thought this would give him the best start in his adult life.'

'But why? When he graduates he's going to be snapped up by some big firm, he's already had talent scouts asking about his plans after uni', he could get a job in America and the drop of a hat.'

Diana gasped, she had never considered this for a minute.

They talked about Jacob, the house and the possibility of her moving in with Trevor. Annalise was far easier to talk to than any of the girls at work.

'Diana, it's none on my business, but I think you should get a house with Trevor, if his house is full of memories, then so is this place for you. I know many will be happy ones because of Jake, but probably just as many are bad ones over your divorce and struggling to make ends meet. Why not live a bit?'

Diana thought for a long while. 'Okay, but I still need more time.'

'Not too much I hope Diana?'

Diana changed the subject. Over a coffee she got Annalise talking about herself.

'Well, I'm one of three girls, my parents are brilliant,' she talked about her childhood. Almost as if it wasn't anything she mentioned leukaemia. Diana thought she had misheard, but she hadn't, Annalise had had leukaemia as a child. But she was still only a child now as far as Diana was concerned.

'That's history, I'm fine,' insisted Annalise. 'I was ten, I didn't know much about what was wrong with me for quite a while. My parents didn't explain what it was, I just didn't feel well and wanted someone to make me better.'

Annalise calmly, though quietly and a little sadly talked about it. Not that she wanted to, but she knew Diana was interested, and it was as if she owed her an explanation. She told Diana about the treatment, how ill she was, her parents growing fear that nothing seemed to work. Then finally a new treatment did work, the cure seemed a miracle. But it had all dragged on for years.

She had lost a great deal of schooling, so her parents were hugely proud of her for making up the lost time and getting into university, though hadn't been so keen that she was so far from home:

'I was ready to live life and to be independent…mum and dad eventually understood and are now happy for me. Well, so they say… And in case you're wondering it was the leukaemia that had caused me to give up dancing…and that was worse than feeling ill.'

What ever reservations Diana had had about Annalise before, they were now gone and they were firm friends. She was very glad Jacob had found her.

The next evening, Saturday, Trevor arrived ready to take them all over to the social dance, but first he found himself towed from the passage into the kitchen.

'Wow, what's the matter now, what have I done, what's wrong?'

'Facebook, that's what's wrong! Jake knows more about us two than I do!' She read him the riot act. He mumbled apologies every so often and looked at the floor.

'Oh, yes, and another thing... I *am* going to move in with you, right?'

'Okay, yeah, sorry, it won't...eh?'

'I've decided, I'd like to move in with you, set up home. Is the offer still open?'

'Oh, yes, yes it is! Umm...'

'Good, found anywhere you like yet?'

'I'm quite keen on...'

'Right-o, make an appointment and we'll go and see it together.'

Trevor rubbed his hands in delight. He was like a dog with two tails at the dance that evening. Alex noticed.

'So lovely to see you having such a good time,' gushed Alex toothily.

Diana hastily whispered to him not to mention their moving in together. She knew Trevor probably was burning to tell someone, but Diana didn't really fancy Alex being the first to know. She guessed it would be well broadcasted by the end of the night if Alex had anything to do with it. Diana wasn't ready to make her business that public.

A few moments later Alex casually said: 'did I tell you the medal test is the first Sunday of next month?'

No she hadn't, that was three weeks away. Alex said she was sure she had, Trevor and Diana were equally sure she hadn't.

'Oh, never mind! I've entered you to dance your bronze Ballroom and bronze Latin medals, that's right isn't it?'

'Is it?' said Diana.

'Well, if you think we're good enough,' said Trevor, trying to sound as though he wasn't that bothered, which he was, very bothered and very excited. He had been really looking forward to this. Diana wasn't so keen on this either. She was getting used to the idea of competing, they had another competition planned soon, but the medal test, hmm, there was that word again, test.

'Alex, is this going to be hard or embarrassing?' Most things in her life that included the word 'test' had been embarrassing and hard.

'No of course not! On the day, you'll dance with Trevor and do the routines you've been learning these last few months, nothing you haven't done in competition, Ballroom and Latin...'

'What dances will we have to do?'

'In the Ballroom: Waltz, Quickstep and Slow Rhythm, and in the Latin Cha-Cha and Rumba.'

Diana and Trevor listened intently.

'We're not going to have to do a written test are we?' checked Trevor. Diana hadn't thought of this, if Alex said yes, then they weren't going to do it!

'No, all you do is dance your routines.'

'How long will it last?'

'As long as it takes you to do the five dances.'

'What if we forget our steps?' asked Diana.

'I doubt you will, but if you do, stop and start again, the examiner will understand.'

Trevor and Diana weren't so sure. Hmm, not fussed on the word examiner either!

Alex was full of reassurance and very soon they felt far more at ease, well, Trevor did.

Despite finding they had a new dance challenge ahead of them, they had a good evening. Annalise and Jacob danced almost constantly, had a wonderful time, and made lots of friends. They looked like brilliant dancers to Diana. By the end of the evening, Diana had almost forgotten the medal test, but Trevor hadn't and seemed to talk about little else on the way home.

Diana realised that they hadn't seen Elwyn and Andrea at the social dances for some weeks. Though she had heard from her cousin that they were working harder than ever, and the partnership was working out well. Diana wondered if Elwyn thought that too.

Normally after a Saturday night social dance, Trevor stayed the night with Diana, but she made it clear that wasn't going to happen whilst Jacob was home. She still wouldn't let Jacob and Annalise share a bed in her house. She could hardly then invite Trevor to stay when she was ruling that out for her son and his girlfriend. Trevor fully agreed, Jacob thought this very funny, Annalise didn't seem to mind either way. Diana guessed that when she was asleep Jacob crept into Annalise's room, though she preferred not think about it.

***

Andrea tried to get Rupert and Bethany chatting, it was hard work. Rupert was now a typical teenager, very much into his computer, though thankfully he was doing fairly well at school. Bethany planned to go to university and was doing her A Levels, her marks were very good. Andrea was pleased, but rather surprised, up until now Bethany had said she didn't want to go to university. Andrea was embarrassed, no, upset to find she had to admit that she hadn't really made much effort this last year to find out just what was happening in her children's lives. They still lived with her, yet they seemed to be far more resident in the house than she was. Andrea was out dancing all the time. Her father had been more of a parent to Rupert and Bethany than Andrea had. In a way that was just as well, it had given him something to live for, and he clearly loved it.

'Do you mind me going dancing?' she asked Bethany one evening.

'No, of course not, we're both glad you've got an interest,' she kept staring at the TV.

Andrea plied her with questions about school, what was it she wanted to do at university? Her guilt at not knowing began to be painful, why didn't she know?

'French and Spanish,' said Bethany.

'But I thought you hated languages?'

'Well, I didn't used to like them, but I do now. The teacher here is great, much better than the one in my last school.'

That was nice. What else didn't she know about her daughter?

She began fishing about boyfriends.

'Haven't got one,' she said absently, still not looking away from the TV.

Somehow Andrea doubted that. Bethany was strikingly beautiful and she had attracted boys from the first day she went to comprehensive school. Andrea and Julian had found themselves opening the front door to a long succession of blushing adolescents trying to think of an excuse as to why they were calling to see Bethany. She had had quite a few boyfriends, some seemed quite nice lads, though the relationships had only lasted a few months. There was never anything serious or enduring. But Andrea realised she had seen no sign of any boys calling around since they had moved…should she be worried, was this a bad thing?

As they talked Andrea spotted something showing through Bethany's sleeve, near the shoulder, a mole perhaps? She looked closer.

'A tattoo! You've got a tattoo!'

'Yeah, had it for months,' she said casually.

Andrea was furious, not only with Bethany, but with herself, why hadn't she known, why hadn't she noticed? Andrea hated tattoos and considered them scars.

They had a row, Bethany went to her room. Andrea cried. She began to wonder what else she didn't know about, and was there anything she didn't know about Rupert? Yet she was terrified of finding out. How had she let this happen? The trouble was she knew the answer. She had been more of a dancer than a mother this last year, a year when her children were still getting over the death of their father. What the hell had she been thinking?

***

Andrea asked if she could meet with Rupert and Bethany's teachers. Getting interviews outside parents' evenings wasn't easy, but once she explained that they had lost their father so recently and she had noticed changes in them, the school agreed.

Firstly, she met Rupert's head of year.

'A bright boy, Mrs. Mooney, a bright boy, he's really working hard, particularly this last term. He's settled in well and is a pleasure to teach.'

She was pleased of course, but hadn't really expected to hear this. Julian had always had to push Rupert and he seemed to struggle with everything in school, including sports which he said he wasn't interested in, yet watched it endlessly on TV. Not so much these days though.

'Well, he's very good at sciences, he really applies himself. He appears to have a good circle of friends here. He's quiet in class, certainly not disruptive, not quick to ask questions though, but knows the answer when asked. I think he should do well and achieve his ambition.'

What ambition? Thought Andrea. She didn't want to admit she didn't know, so asked any question she could that might help her to work out what Rupert had in mind. 'Is he taking the right subjects?'

The teacher looked confused. 'Surely you helped him decide on what to take?'

'Yes of course…' no she hadn't, 'but I want to be sure.'

He nodded sympathetically and explained what subjects he needed to do well in.

Finally she realised, Rupert wanted to be a doctor! She was so proud, but then again, confused. He had always talked about being an engineer, not that he seemed to be good enough at maths or any other relevant subject. Why would he want to suddenly be a doctor, and more to the point, to have begun working toward it so fervently? Why didn't she know, why?

Her meeting with Bethany's languages teacher was also confusing and embarrassing. More trying not to admit that she had little idea about her daughter's ambitions, if in fact she had any.

'Well, actually, I'm glad of this chance to talk to you about Bethany,' said the teacher, Marcus Brampton. 'I take her for both French and Spanish.

Bethany is an excellent pupil, but…umm, I'm not sure she's taking the languages because she's interested in them…you see, well. I think she's got a crush on me.'

Andrea was surprised, confused, upset, worried, she had just about every bad feeling. For long seconds she said nothing, but finally apologised, she wasn't entirely sure why.

Mr. Brampton said that she was doing well and should get the necessary grades for a university place. He was in his late thirties, only a few years younger than Andrea. He was tall, looked fit, dressed smartly, but was hardly handsome. He had a mass of wavy brown, greasy hair, though with a good few strands of grey. He didn't seem to be the sort of man a seventeen year old would fall for. Brampton had to be exaggerating, imagining the infatuation.

'She's always first into class and last to leave, she sits at the front and as near to me as possible, she rarely completes a piece of work without asking for my advice or help…'

'Well, there's nothing wrong with that!'

'No,' said Brampton, 'very true. I wish more of my pupils took their work so seriously, but there's a difference between an enthusiastic student and a girl that spends every second with me that she can, and I mean every second. She'll stay in the class until I either leave or the next class arrives, even though I tell her she ought to be on her way. When I leave the room at the end of a class, she'll come with me for as long as she can. One of her lessons with me is right after a break, she'll spend the break in the classroom, but only if I'm there, she says she wants to use the break to get work done…'

'That's good isn't it?'

Brampton seemed to sigh. 'Yes, but I can tell, she stares at me all the time. She hardly does any work at all in those breaks, and the way she looks at me is also…' he looked troubled. No matter how he tried he couldn't complete the sentence and was obviously worried how Andrea would respond.

She nodded nervously. 'I'll have a word with her.'

He was relieved and moved on to her school work. What he said hardly registered with Andrea.

When she got home she cried, what was she to do? She went to see her father and told him how the meetings had gone.

'Why didn't you ask me first?' said Gilbert.

She didn't know. Yes, she did, she was too embarrassed to ask him, to admit that she was struggling as a mother.

'Rupert wants to be a doctor so he can find out why Julian died,' he said casually.

Andrea stared at him, she even gulped. 'But he knows why he died, he had a heart attack.'

'Yes, yes, of course, but Rupert wants to know *why* Julian had the heart attack. I've discussed it with him quite a bit. He's a clever lad you know?'

She nodded absently. 'Does he see himself becoming some kind of medical researcher, tracing Julian's family medical history?'

Gilbert shrugged. 'I suppose he might think that. It upset him a great deal that your mother died comparatively young too.'

'I hadn't realised…well, I hadn't realised all this had hit him so hard.'

'He's bottled it up, that's probably why he's so quiet.'

'If I get more than a two word answer out of him to anything I ask I think I'm doing well.'

Gilbert smiled knowingly. 'He's a bit more chatty with me.'

Andrea felt hurt, why did her father get more out of Rupert than she did?

'I don't know what to do about Bethany,' she explained, and for the tenth time told him about the tattoo and Brampton's opinion.

'As regards the crush,' said Gilbert, 'I not surprised, probably sees Mr. Brampton as something of a father figure.'

'But surely you fill that role?'

'It would be nice, but I doubt it, I'm her grandad, always have been. I'm not a dad. As regards the tattoo, well, it's only a tiny butterfly, and I thought it was very pretty.'

'You knew about it!'

He squirmed slightly. 'Well, yes I did…'

'And you didn't tell me?'

'No, because Bethany asked me to keep it to myself, she knew you'd go mad.'

'Damn right!'

'All her friends have got one…'

'It doesn't mean to say she has to have one!'

'No, of course not, but it is pretty, and it is covered most of the time.'

They argued then she stormed off home.

She tried discussing with Rupert his ambition, all he would say was that he wanted to be a doctor and what was wrong with that? He wouldn't admit why. She praised him for it and promised to support him all she could. At least he seemed pleased with this and got a little more talkative as a result.

Bethany had kept out of Andrea's way since their row, but they were on speaking terms now, just.

She knocked softly on Bethany's door. After what seemed quite a long pause, Bethany asked her to come in.

Andrea felt she was intruding, not wanted, until she realised Bethany was listening to music with earpieces in and hadn't heard her knock first time.

'I'm sorry I lost my temper about the tattoo,' said Andrea.

Bethany didn't really look convinced. 'I suppose I should have told you, but you would have only said no.'

Damn right she would! Andrea gave her a hug and said what she hoped was all the right things. Her dad was right, it was a pretty tattoo.

'Actually, it's one of those that fades in a few years,' explained Bethany.

'Oh that's good!' Damn, she shouldn't have said that!

Bethany looked irritated. 'I did tell you the night you noticed it.'

Andrea was sure she hadn't, but let it go.

She decided to try and use the tattoo as a kind of lever: 'What does your boyfriend think of it, did you have it done for him?'

'I haven't got a boyfriend, I told you.' she looked away, she was embarrassed, and it wasn't embarrassment about not having a boyfriend either. It was because she did, or at least in her mind she did.

'Go on, you must do! You always used to have loads of boys following you around in Stoke. Surely you've got a boyfriend, someone in school perhaps?'

'Well, yeah, there's a…boy, a lad, I like, but I don't think he fancies me.' she changed the subject.

Andrea changed it back and asked her about the 'lad', what was his name. She got nowhere.

She couldn't sleep that night, she was too worried.

***

Diana stood outside the house that Trevor was interested in. It would never do, but he liked it. In fact he raved about it, discussed the possibilities with the estate agent even before they went in, but Diana was looking at the very busy 'A' road that went straight past the front gate. Trevor didn't seem to notice that he had to raise his voice to be heard over the roar of traffic. The estate agent showed them around, Diana guessed he had told the owners not to be present. This place needed all his skills as a salesman, he didn't want the family around if there were any awkward questions. The inside was badly decorated and maintained, and it smelt of cats. Diana liked cats, but this was a dirty smell, yet she could see a lot of cleaning had gone on, not enough though. There was a large stain on the ceiling too. The floor sagged in one room. The bath was royal blue, the wash hand basin light green, the toilet purple and the walls pink. Trevor could see nothing wrong with anything, it wouldn't have surprised Diana if he had offered the agent a deposit there and then.

Over a cup of tea in a café, Diana tried to get Trevor to see the faults. All he could see were simple challenges he could fix easily and reasons to knock down the already modest asking price. The house was very handy for his work, but not so much for Diana's.

At last she got him to see sense and they reviewed the property news, this time Diana listed the ones she, not Trevor, felt they ought to see.

'Any luck with your house, anyone interested in it yet?' checked Trevor.

'Far too soon, it won't be advertised for about another week.'

'Someone's looking at my place tomorrow. What if they want to buy it, I haven't got anywhere to live!'

'It depends if they're stuck in a chain doesn't it?'

This was the first time Trevor had moved house and he knew little about buying chains and how quickly, or slowly, the property market worked.

'Anyway, if they do buy it and want to move in right away, you can always put your stuff in storage and move in with me.'

'Can I?'

'Of course, why not? You spend most of your time with me anyway.'

'I don't know, I just thought you wouldn't like me there permanently.'

She giggled. 'You can be very funny sometimes. Why do you think that?'

He shrugged. 'Don't know really. It's just that it's your house, your home, where you brought up Jake. Where you lived from the time you got married, the house you've worked so long to keep, that sort of thing.'

She was touched, he could be so sensitive and thoughtful. But she really didn't mind if Trevor came to live with her. The house was only that, a house, not a home anymore. Since she had made up her mind, or Jacob had made it up for her, the house had become nothing more than a place to sleep in, not a home. She was looking forward to a new life with Trevor now.

It was Saturday, so they went to the school social night. They found themselves thinking more about their steps, and working to get them right, not just having a fun and relaxing evening. They wanted everything ready for the medal test. Diana still felt they weren't good enough and not ready, but Trevor was brimming with confidence.

He stayed over that night. The next day they went to the competition in Cirencester, they had become regulars at Syd's monthly events and had made a good few friends.

Trevor had 'registered' them with the national governing body, this meant they were able to do more events, but not compete in the 'beginner' grade.

By now, they had become quite experienced dancers and normally won, or at least came second, in the beginner grade in both Ballroom and Latin. Alex and Simon had advised them that it was perhaps time for them to give up the lowest grade, though Trevor was disappointed, he liked winning.

Even so, he was ambitious and the idea of moving up a grade, to Novice, and even higher, appealed to him a great deal.

Since injuring his knee at the competition, Elwyn and Andrea hadn't competed and in any case they felt the Cirencester competitions were too small for them. They didn't like the dance floor, but for Trevor and Diana, Cirencester suited them perfectly. In some ways it was almost like Alex's Saturday night social dance.

At the scrutineers table, Trevor proudly handed over his entry slip and their registration cards.

'Thanks! Number fourteen,' said the chap behind the table and pushed a white card with the number printed thickly on it. He paid no attention to the registration cards and got on with jotting down which events Trevor and Diana planned to enter onto his sheets.

Trevor felt a little disappointed, surely they were going to check the cards thoroughly, or at least admire them. Ah well, back to Diana.

This time, they were entered not only in the Novice, but also the One Teacher Two Dance, the Intermediate in Ballroom and Latin, and the Open Basic Foxtrot plus the Open Basic Rumba. As they were 'Seniors', they were able to do both the 'Open Novice' and 'Senior Novice'. Diana wasn't so sure she wanted to be dancing against couples much younger than her. Though Trevor pointed out, nearly every couple here was a Senior, and danced everything they could, 'Open' and or 'Senior'. So she agreed. She was far less convinced about entering both the 'Open' and 'Senior' Intermediate events. Intermediate was the next grade up from Novice and in the Latin that meant, Cha-Cha, Samba and Jive. She didn't feel she was any good at Samba, though Trevor thought they (he) were naturals at it. Diana knew they would be up against much better standard dancers, only reluctantly had she allowed herself to be talked into it.

The competition began about twenty minutes late, it wasn't clear why, probably Syd forgot what time it was. Trevor and Diana were up to dance in the first event, the Senior Intermediate Ballroom. They did their usual routines, the ones they would do for the medal test. The floor seemed quite full, and some of the couples looked very good. Diana felt they were out of place, but Trevor kept her mood light and besides, it was all a bit of fun.

It helped that, as they were in so many events, they were out dancing regularly. Diana guessed they didn't dance this much at either the school practices or the Saturday social dances. Trevor made her laugh, and with all their friends it meant that the atmosphere and mood was positive, she was having a good time. She relaxed as they danced, probably helped by Trevor singing along to some of the music, in fact he didn't have a bad voice.

In the Ballroom section, they found themselves being recalled through the rounds to the final of both the Novice events. Trevor was very proud. They were very pleased to get a recall in the Senior Intermediate, though got none in the Open. Diana wasn't really surprised and, if she was honest, she was not sorry. In the One Teacher Two Dance Ballroom, they felt more at home. Though there were some good couples in it, the event was open to any grade of dancer as long as they only had lessons with just one teacher in that discipline. The dances were Waltz and Foxtrot. Diana enjoyed Foxtrot, but knew she was no expert, and in lessons Alex spent more time working on this dance with her than she did with Trevor. Normally it was the other way around.

As the afternoon progressed and they took stock of how the competition had gone so far, they felt pleased with themselves. They had danced in the two Novice finals, and were now waiting to hear if they had made the final of the One Teacher Two Dance and the Open Basic Foxtrot. Though they really didn't feel they had been good enough for that. They weren't concerned about the Intermediate results, they knew they weren't really up to it. It had been good experience though and Trevor was looking forward to more competitions and getting further in this grade, and to dancing in Southampton in December.

The entries for all events had been okay, the standard though didn't seem that impressive. They were pleased to be doing so well and winning through against more experienced couples though. Particularly in the Ballroom dances, which they felt they weren't so good at, well, Diana didn't think she was so good at. Trevor never admitted that he wasn't anything less than an expert.

They weren't surprised to miss the final for the Open Basic Foxtrot, the standard was comparatively high. But what about the One Teacher Two Dance? Syd ran the competition in his own rather haphazard way. It at least worked, mainly thanks to his army of helpers, all of whom watched him carefully and ran up to him to deal with the latest problem he had created. He seemed to be keeping the One Teacher' final until last, he wasn't, but Trevor and Diana were getting excited, and nervous, about it.

At last Syd announced it, but when he called out the numbers, they didn't include Trevor and Diana, but no one else came to the floor either, people began to look confused. Someone yelled:

'We didn't dance this event Syd!'

'Oh yes you did! Your number is on this sheet of paper,' and pointed to it fiercely.

'We didn't dance it either,' said another man.

The scrutineer strode across the stage, checked the paper, tutted, snatched it out of Syd's hand, scrabbled for another sheet on the table next to Syd, and then thrust that at Syd.

Syd looked slightly hurt, though nothing had been said. He looked hard at the sheet.

'Right then, as I was saying, final of the One Teacher Two Dance Ballroom, the judges have recalled the following six couples: two, twelve, fourteen…'

'That's us!' said Trevor, clapped excitedly and sprang to his feet.

Diana was pleased too and took Trevor's hand, they hurried out and waited for Waltz.

Both dances seemed to go well, though Diana could see they were the only Novice couple to have made the final. The rest were at least Intermediate or higher, she guessed they had scrapped in, but they had made the final, great news. At least they received a lot of support from around the room.

As usual, Syd insisted on leaving all the results until the very end of the competition. Once they had finished the One Teacher Two Dance, Trevor and Diana hurried off to change for Latin, they knew Syd wouldn't allow much time between the two disciplines. Diana was really looking forward to the Latin, she felt she could relax in it.

The Latin entries were unusually poor, far worse than they had seen here before, several events weren't run at all, and the rest were just straight finals. Syd looked disappointed. Trevor crowed to some of their friends that they were in the final of every event they had entered in the Latin, conveniently forgetting they were all straight finals. But he was having a lovely time and Diana enjoyed seeing him happy. It surprised her to find that she had a feeling for him that could only be love, she had never felt like this about Elwyn, though she told herself she had. Increasingly she didn't believe that though.

They were second in the Senior Novice Ballroom, fourth in the Open Novice. Trevor thought they might have won both, but he still had a lot to learn about competitions. Their only other final in the Ballroom was the One Teacher Two Dance, after hearing the Novice results they doubted they would win this, and of course they were right, but third against some good opposition was very encouraging.

Trevor had a feeling they had swept the board in Latin, after all, they had made all the finals.

'Excuse me,' said Diana, 'they were all straight finals!'

'Oh, I forgot that.'

'I bet you did!'

But it seemed Trevor might just be right! They won both Novice Latin events. Trevor waited eagerly for the Open Intermediate, Diana almost had to hold him in his chair. They were an impressive third, and second in Senior Intermediate, they could be proud of that. Diana thought Trevor was going to burst into tears when they only came fifth in the Open Basic Rumba, but it was actually a fair result.

Trevor began speculating: 'Where d'you think we'll finish in the One Teacher Two Dance! My guess is fifth,' he said reflectively.

'Well, there were only five couples in the final! So I expect you're about right.'

They didn't really listen closely to Syd as he announced the winner of the Two Dance, as it wasn't going to be them. But it was. They had to be called a second time. They had done very well, small entry or not, this was a good set of results, as Trevor kept telling Diana all the way home.

***

Andrea didn't know what to do for the best. She was worried about her kids, but had just pushed Elwyn into agreeing to far more dancing. Though she knew she should be spending more time with them, would that in fact help, is that what they needed? Both seemed to be firmly on the rails, were proving to be intelligent and doing well in school, but the reason they were doing well was the problem. Rupert wallowing in a morbid obsession, and Bethany besotted with her teacher!

She had a feeling Bethany wasn't that interested in Marcus Brampton. He had to be imagining it, a mid-life crisis or something, that was it…unfortunately she didn't really believe that either.

Perhaps if she tried to get the kids more interested in her dancing? She doubted that would work, worth a try though. But how?

They had met Elwyn many times. After all, they were related by marriage, all be it a broken one. Though neither had remembered him when she told them she planned to start dancing with him. It had been so long since he'd been in their family circle. He called at her house a few times a week and one or other of the kids normally answered the door to him. They were polite and pleasant to him, they didn't show any resentment about his taking their mother away from them. That bothered her too, shouldn't they resent her being out of the house so much? But she had to remember they were of an age when she was no longer the centre of their universe. Andrea cried that night as she realised she had lost something magic between herself and her children.

Elwyn's knee injury meant they weren't able to dance for a couple of weeks after their last competition, even then he struggled at practices, and particularly the lessons. His college work was demanding at this time too.

Then she had a brilliant idea. 'He's a college lecturer or something, he deals with adolescents all the time! He's qualified in working with them, or trained in it or something!' Elwyn could give her advice she told herself.

The next evening as she drove them to the dance school, she explained about her worries. Elwyn had never had any adolescent girls fixated on him. He knew colleagues that had had pupils following them. It had always been very bad for the teacher, not to mention the child, and there was always the fear a resentful child would make something up about a teacher to get their own back. He knew a few lecturers that this had happened to.

'She'll get bored of him soon, especially as he's ignoring her. She'll find a boyfriend any day now,' he assured her. This was what normally happed with his colleagues…except for the one that found the girl's father waiting for him. She had told her dad that the teacher was pestering her, even though it was she that was pestering him! Elwyn thought it not a good idea to tell Andrea about this.

He was far less able to give any advice about Rupert.

'At least he's motivated, it's a good career, and what's so wrong with wanting to help other people by being a doctor?' asked Elwyn.

'But, well, yes, but Rupert's still very young and its obvious his decision was made through grief. That can't be a good basis for his studies and career choice?'

Elwyn nodded thoughtfully.

'Umm, Elwyn…would you come to dinner one evening, get to know them, get them talking. I'm sure you could get more out of them than I can.' she sounded slightly nervous and very hopeful.

He really only heard 'come to dinner'. He didn't like cooking and most of his meals came out of a tin, so he at once said yes. But began to regret it as the old adage about 'no such thing as a free lunch'. He was expected to get Rupert and Bethany talking with Andrea, and, and what? He was a history teacher, not a psychologist.

As for Andrea, all she heard was the 'I'd love to' from Elwyn and not the comments about his doubting he could help that much.

***

Initially, Bethany said she would go to her friends that evening and Rupert said he had a lot of coursework to do. She more or less had to insist they had to be part of the dinner party. In any case, Andrea very much wanted Bethany's help in the kitchen. Andrea was an adequate cook, but not very organised, Bethany was. Rupert said he would help with laying the table and entertaining Elwyn.

Andrea knew neither was going to work very well, ah well, at least he was prepared to help.

On the day of the dinner, Rupert arrived home from school and went straight to his room, apparently things hadn't gone well and he had a lot of work to do. Andrea guessed this just meant he didn't want to be in the dinner party.

Bethany project managed her mother, in fact they had a good time together, even if the menu Andrea had chosen for the evening wasn't quite going to plan. She was struggling to get everything ready, and nothing she prepared was co-operating.

Elwyn struggled to know what to wear. Should he be formal because he was a college lecturer (well more of an administrator these days)? Or informal as he had to get to know the kids, or be semi-formal and dress for comfort? He decided to dress for comfort and to be at least a bit smart, he was in for a long night in one way or another!

In the last few days he had discussed Bethany and Rupert with colleagues, though didn't let on who they actually were. The advice he had received was contradictory. He talked to a couple of colleagues he knew had been the subject of student fixation. One didn't want to talk about it, the other laughed it off. None of his colleagues seemed to have come across a situation like Rupert's, but they all wished they had students that were committed and applied themselves to their studies. Elwyn had read some old text books on child psychology, checked the internet, between it all he at least felt he had some knowledge of the subjects he had to deal with. However, he was no longer looking forward to dinner this evening.

Andrea hadn't seemed to realise that Elwyn taught post school age students and adults, rather than school children.

Rupert let him in, led him to the living room, offered him a drink. Rupert seemed like a typical kid of his age.

Andrea quickly greeted Elwyn, made sure Bethany came to speak to him, then vanished into the kitchen, swiftly followed by Bethany.

He sat in awkward silence, as did Rupert.

'Your mum says you want to be a doctor.'

'Yeah.'

'Good for you. I wanted to be a doctor, but wasn't really good enough at the subjects you need. How are you getting on with them?'

Rupert seemed to relax a little and discussed his studies, Elwyn only asked about his school work and where he was having problems. He meant it when he said he hadn't been good at the subjects that were necessary for getting into medical school, though he had never actually wanted to be a doctor. At least he had broken down a barrier. Rupert even brought some course work down and discussed it. Elwyn wasn't sure whether he should, or how he could raise the subject of Rupert's motivation. Elwyn wasn't sure that it was that bad a thing that Rupert had found such strong motivation to be a doctor. After all, he had met one young doctor that said he had chosen medicine because of the money he could make when he qualified as a plastic surgeon. At least Rupert seemed to be more in touch with the principles of the Hippocratic Oath than some medical students and even doctors he had met over the years.

Where Elwyn came into his own was that he could tell Rupert about university and medical school options. The boy was keen, what was wrong with that?

Over dinner, Andrea had to force herself not to talk dancing with Elwyn and to remember just what the dinner party was about.

Elwyn had an 'A' Level in French, but that was long ago, he had to make a major effort to remember any French to talk to Bethany in the language. But at least they did manage a short conversation in French. She was a bright girl, intelligent and able to talk sensibly about the various subjects that came up during the meal. Her light brown eyes and beautifully styled honey-blond hair seemed to melt Elwyn's emotions.

She told him about some recent translation she had done, how she had been hard pressed to get through it. She had been home each evening for a week and worked well into the night at least twice.

'The translation was that hard?'

'Well, it felt hard to me,' she conceded.

'Is your teacher pushing you too hard?'

'No, of course not, he's brilliant and really inspirational.'

Elwyn nodded. 'And what does your boyfriend think about you having your nose in a book all the time?' He knew Bethany said she knew a *boy* in school.

Did he detect any hesitation, any embarrassment? No.

'I don't have a boyfriend. I've got a few boys that are friends.'

'I would have thought you'd be fighting them off!'

'Nah, not me, there are lots of boys hitting on me, but I don't fancy any of them. I find them all so immature.'

Elwyn kept on about boyfriends. Bethany's answers did seem to become more evasive. He asked about the teachers what they were like, she only mentioned Brampton in terms of what he was like as a teacher, and how much work he gave her. She didn't give anything away about her relationship with him, if in fact there was one. Elwyn doubted it.

After the meal, they all sat chatting, he was relieved to find the kids seemed to like him and were able to chat and share stories. It turned into a pleasant evening, he even quite enjoyed it, though Andrea had served salmon, which he didn't like, she hadn't thought to ask. He had forced it down in case the kids hated him for not eating something their mother had prepared.

He thought he might have learnt more if he had been able to spend more time talking to them on their own, but that didn't really happen. When ever one or other of them was alone with Elwyn, Andrea seemed to burst in. Of course, she wanted to know what they said, to hear it for herself. But so far there wasn't much to hear.

As the evening went on, there was a certain awkwardness. Bethany seemed to usher Rupert up to his room, then she found jobs to do in the kitchen.

Elwyn and Andrea realised that she was trying to give them time on their own!

'She thinks we're an item,' said Andrea, she looked and sounded embarrassed.

Elwyn wondered that as well, he didn't know what to say, so just shrugged.

'Well, what do you think?' hissed Andrea.

'What, about us being an item?' stammered Elwyn.

'No stupid! About the kids!'

'Let's discuss it next time we meet...away from the kids.'

Andrea nodded, though looked impatient. Not that it mattered for long, she was soon talking about dancing.

Bethany softly knocked on the door. 'Coffee?'

'She was worried she was disturbing something' said Elwyn once he was sure Bethany was out of earshot.

'I suppose she thinks I've asked you round so she can get to know you,' she giggled.

'I hope you're going to tell them there is nothing between us?'

'Of course!'

Oh, that sounded more emphatic than he expected, than he had hoped. He did quite fancy Andrea. Ah well.

***

It was the morning of the medal test, a Sunday. Trevor had spent the night at Diana's, but he had tossed and turned. This morning he was stressed, Diana wasn't. She was quite looking forward to it now, the competitions had given her some confidence, but Trevor thought the other way. As they hadn't been winners of everything they entered in competitions, he was sure they wouldn't do well in the test. Alex and Simon kept telling Trevor that he would do just fine and not to worry, waste of breath!

Diana wasn't so sure about Trevor's mental state given how he drove that morning! At least he didn't crash.

At the school, they found that two other couples were in the corridor waiting to go in for their test, music was playing inside the ballroom. Diana and Trevor joined the others and quickly changed into their dance shoes. They all talked in hushed voices, though weren't really sure why as with the music playing it was doubtful anyone could hear them. They were all here for the bronze medal test. The couple in the ballroom now were the second to go before the examiner that morning.

'They started a bit late,' said Dale.

'Yeah, about a quarter hour, said his wife, Becky.

They were, to Diana, an unlikely couple to be in Ballroom Dancing classes. They had started having lessons a few months before they got married ready for the wedding dance, but had become hooked and were now regulars at all the classes and other events in the school. Both were in their mid twenties, though seemed younger. They were an attractive pair, not particularly gifted dancers, but loved everything they did and were looking forward to the medal test. If they were nervous, they didn't show it, well, not much.

'I'll have to have a word with Alex about this,' said Warren, 'I was nervous enough before I got here, now this waiting is killing me!'

'Chill out Warren,' giggled his wife, Bridget.

Warren and Bridget were in their sixties, he always looked like a worried businessman, probably because he was. His wife had never quite gotten over being a hippy she looked and sounded laid back. They were another unlikely couple to be in dance classes. In the early days they had looked like two donkeys trying to negotiate cobble stones when they 'danced', but had now turned into one of the better couples in the class. Simon wanted them to compete, but Warren wouldn't even consider it, though Bridget was keen. Doing the medal test seemed to be something of a compromise.

Moments later, Simon popped his head around the double glass doors, smiled at the three couples in an impish way, he welcomed Diana and Trevor, then pointed at Dale and Becky.

'You're next, Drew and Liz are nearly finished.'

They hadn't realised the music had stopped, Simon held the door open for Drew and Liz, they came out grinning, he even gave a thumbs up. Liz gave Becky a hug and wished them luck. Moments later Warren and Bridget had moved to the seats next to the door, like parachutists getting nearer the aircraft exit. Drew and Liz told the waiting dancers how their test had gone.

He didn't look like a 'Drew', more like an Arthur. He and his wife, or what they assumed was his wife (didn't wear a wedding ring), were in their seventies and had began dancing to keep fit. They had joined the classes at much the same time as Diana, they weren't natural dancers, but loved the classes and lessons. They liked the social life in the school and really wanted to dance well. They glowed with pride at having completed their first dance medal and felt it had gone well, though listed all the things that they had done wrong. How could they have passed the test then? At least they were happy.

The music began again, so Dale and Becky's test had begun.

The three couples chatted away quietly and laughed a great deal, Drew and Liz only left after Becky and Dale came out from their test.

'How did it go?' asked Trevor.

'Oh, it seemed okay, didn't it love?' said Dale in his usual slow drawl.

Becky nodded enthusiastically.

More couples had arrived, the atmosphere was slightly tense, but pleasant all the same, lots of giggling.

It came as something of a surprise when Simon appeared at the glass doors with his now habitual impish smile and warned Trevor and Diana to be ready, Warren and Bridget were nearly finished.

When it was at last their turn, they almost tumbled into the Ballroom. Alex was behind a wooden structure that she grandly called a console, Simon called it the wooden thing. On the top of it, apart from dusty plastic tulips, was a music deck. She waved enthusiastically to Diana and Trevor. At a table the other side of the ballroom from the console sat a very thin lady in a very colourful floral dress.

'Who've got here then?' she said smiling broadly at Trevor and Diana, it had the desired effect they felt far more at ease.

Alex carefully read out their names, 'they are doing Bronze Ballroom and Latin, Alison.'

Alison Woodford was the examiner, a dance teacher from another part of south Wales, she sounded down to earth and devoid of any airs and graces. She had no intention of making the test anything other than as pleasant an experience as possible.

'Right you are Trevor and Diana, ready when you are!' she beamed at them through a pair of glasses that seemed a bit too small.

Alex put her own, very discreet, glasses on, she hoped no one would notice.

Trevor and Diana realised a Waltz would come on very shortly, so they hurried to the corner they usually began Waltz in and waited for the music, it started almost at once.

Given how many competitions they had danced, the test seemed more demanding and intense, probably because they were the only couple on the floor and being watched carefully by Alison. The Waltz lasted until they had completed one circuit of the floor, Trevor noticed Alison give Alex a nod to signal she had seen enough. She had been watching them throughout the dance, but now she began writing enthusiastically.

'Quickstep next,' reminded Alex.

Trevor and Diana hurried over to their preferred corner, though this time they had to wait a few moments before Alison was ready. She then looked at them and smiled encouragingly before giving Alex a thumbs up.

Quickstep music filled the room, Trevor counted the time, he didn't need to for Diana's sake, but he always had and probably didn't know he was still doing it, in any case, he stopped once they got into the dance.

This time they completed just over a circuit of the floor. Diana could see that Alison was watching them with her head slightly inclined, as if she was trying to make sense of what they were doing. It didn't seem a good sign.

They gradually worked through the five dances of the test. Alison encouraged them, chatted to Alex briefly, always cheerfully, even having a few laughs. She was in her late thirties, her hair was a mass of mouse-blond curls, she seemed a bit too thin, but looked fit and strong.

Diana and Trevor enjoyed the Slow Rhythm dance in the classes, now it seemed a bit like hard work, but at least it went well enough. The Latin dances they had to do were Rumba and Cha-Cha-Cha. Diana didn't really like the Rumba, she had always struggled with the timing and found Trevor's efforts to make it 'sexy' funny, which he obviously thought he was doing very well. Even so, they managed the bronze syllabus steps competently and as far as they could tell, they didn't go wrong. They both loved Cha-Cha-Cha and within seconds of the music starting were really into it and even enjoying it. This dance seemed to finish very quickly, though Diana guessed it just seemed this way.

'That was lovely, thank you!' said Alison sounding quite genuine.

'Well done Diana and Trevor, you can go now,' said Alex softly, as if talking to small children.

Simon was waiting for them at the double glass doors, he smiled knowingly.

'Have we passed?' said Trevor as they got to the doors.

'You danced well, you should have passed, we won't know 'til later. Come up to the school tonight about seven, we're having a medal test party,' then he called the next couple in.

As the others had done, they hung back and chatted to their friends and new arrivals. Trevor, the seasoned campaigner, told them how easy and fun it had all been. Diana wasn't sure she thought it had been fun, but no where near as bad as she expected. But yes, she'd do that again.

When they finally did leave, they decided to go for a coffee. The weather was dismal and they were glad of something to warm them up.

As they drove Trevor said: 'how about that place?' and pointed to a house with a for sale sign. He pulled up and they looked at the façade, it was a semi-detached property away from the main roads, though not that far from the city centre and an easy walk to work for Diana. Plus it wasn't too far from the factory for Trevor. It seemed to be in a reasonable condition, but the front garden looked untended. It was a nice neighbourhood too. As they considered it, the property seemed more and more suitable.

'I think it's empty,' said Diana squinting through the rain.

'Let's have a look around then,' and Trevor hurried across. Diana wasn't so sure, partly because it was raining.

She was right, the house was empty, no furniture.

'Can I help you?' asked a chap from the front door of the neighbouring house. They quickly explained they were interested to know something about the empty house.

The neighbour invited them into his house.

'It's been empty for about four years, since the lady that owned it moved into a home, but she's since died. Her family haven't been able to agree over selling the house, so a lot of time's been wasted while they wrangled. The for-sale board's only been up a few days, but I can tell you we're very keen to see someone move in. It's been empty too long and we're worried about kids hanging around, or squatters.'

He showed them around his house so they could get an idea of what next door was like inside.

'I should think you'd get a good deal on it,' said the neighbour, 'from what we hear, the old girl's son is keen to sell before his brother and sister change their mind again.'

They looked at the outside of the empty house. It was dowdy and dirty, it should have been uninviting, but it wasn't, it actually felt welcoming, even standing outside it felt good. They looked at each other, smiled excitedly, just gave a nod and hugged.

Mentally, they felt they had already bought the house and on the way home began planning what they would do with each room. Every so often they seemed to take turns to say how silly this was and they might find they didn't like it when they got inside. But secretly thought they were certain to love it and find it perfect. What if they found they couldn't afford it, or there would be some other problem that would stop them buying it? Not that they believed that.

They spent the day discussing the house, the medal test and how quickly they might be able to sell their own properties. Trevor was waiting to hear from a couple that had viewed his house. He talked himself into believing they would put a bid in. Diana thought he was being over optimistic.

That evening they went back to the school, by now feeling nervous, it was only after they got home they had remembered all the things in the test that hadn't gone that well, or that they actually did wrong...or thought they'd done wrong.

Many medallists arrived at the same time, they were all excited and laughed a lot. Simon was at the double glass doors.

'Evening! Well done, you've passed!' he said as they went in.

'Are you just saying that?' checked Diana.

'No, you've passed, everyone's passed, Alison confirmed it before she left.'

'No one failed at all?'

'No, all passed.'

'That's amazing! But we went wrong all the time,' protested Trevor.

'All examiners make allowances for nerves, they don't expect you to be perfect, anyway. I was watching you, you actually danced pretty well, you didn't make any mistakes that I noticed, honestly.'

'I bet no one ever fails a dance medal test!' said Diana.

'They do, but we don't put anyone in for a test unless we're sure they're good enough. You two are good enough, be proud, well done,' said Simon.

A few minutes later they were having a great time and, yes, they did feel proud.

In bed that night they looked back over a remarkable day, but also planned how they would put a bid in for the house. They had to force themselves back one step, first they needed to have a look around it:

'Four years empty could mean big problems,' said Trevor gravely.

Diana struggled not to doze off, she could still hear Trevor listing the things he already could see he would need to do to the house before they moved in. She was aware that he was still talking as she drifted into sleep, she didn't register about what.

She had a funny, or odd, dream that night, something to do with weddings, it didn't seem much of a dream though…at least it didn't include Phyllis!

Chapter Seven
Family Matters

Andrea spent much of the practice session asking Elwyn what he thought about her children, was she right to be concerned?

'No, Andrea, they're fine, well adjusted, really lovely kids, you should be proud of them.'

'I am, it's just that I don't think Rupert is going into medicine for the right reason and I'm worried about Bethany throwing herself at her teacher.'

Elwyn reassured her, but it seemed to have no effect. While she once more told him her worries, he thought through the problem, it was obvious he was expected to *do* something.

'Okay, what if I arrange for Rupert to meet a friend of mine, he teaches at 'The Heath' in Cardiff, the teaching hospital. I'll tell him what's worrying you, Dennis can ask him searching questions about his motivation.'

Andrea thought this a stroke of genius. 'But what about Bethany?'

Elwyn had no bright ideas there and still thought if in fact she was infatuated with Brampton, Brampton and the school were in the best position to end the problem.

'But you're a teacher, why not have a word with him, one professional to another?'

'I don't think it would be wise. I think you're going about this the wrong way. Why not have a chat to Bethany's friends? They're bound to know far better what she's thinking than either you or certainly me, or even Brampton'

'Oh…hmm, alright, I will.'

But how could she broach this subject? She knew Bethany had four close girlfriends. Elwyn was probably right, if anything was going on, they would be the first to know. But how to approach them without Bethany thinking she was spying?

Until this was settled, she couldn't think about her dancing, she and Elwyn practiced, but she couldn't concentrate and planning for competitions seemed ridiculous. In one way Elwyn wasn't sorry, he felt under less pressure. She had said she didn't feel mentally prepared for the Warwick competition and only made vague promises about the others. She only remembered they had applied for places in the 'Nationwide Dance Elite' in Southampton when the confirmation came through. Unconsciously she booked rooms for herself and Elwyn, the same hotel as Diana and Trevor, Jacob and Annalise. It never dawned on her to mention it to Diana, or that this might bother her, why should it?

Andrea manufactured a meeting with Shelley Harries, one and Bethany's best friends. Shelley had a Saturday job which finished at lunch time. Andrea hung around near the shop until Shelley came out and pretended she had been just passing and was going the same way. They chatted fairly easily, Andrea did all she could not to immediately start asking about Bethany's love life, lack of it, or who she seemed to be hooked on. She had little time to play with during this limited window of opportunity.

'I'm sure Bethany has a new boyfriend,' she more or less blurted out, 'but if she does, she doesn't bring him round, doesn't talk about him, but the way she's behaving...well, she's just like I was when I was her age,' she laughed nervously and falsely. 'Have you met him?' her words were rushed and tense.

Shelley laughed, she sounded embarrassed. 'Umm, yes, sort of.'

Andrea was shocked, there was a boy, a boy? Really a boy, or a man?

'Thought so,' said Andrea trying not to sound or look perturbed, 'I hope he's a nice lad, I can't see why she doesn't mention him to me…he is a nice lad isn't he?'

'Oh, very, very nice. Very respectable,' she looked flustered.

'That's alright then. Just as long as he hasn't got two heads or anything… he's not into drugs or anything is he?'

'No, definitely not,' she giggled.

'Sorry, I'm embarrassing you. But one of our neighbours said she'd seen a real low life following Bethany home the other evening. I was terrified it was him.' The neighbours had said no such thing, but it sounded good, didn't it?

'No, he's nice, really. Well, nice speaking to you Andrea, got to go now.' As she hurried off, Shelley got her phone out. Andrea guessed a text would be on its way to Bethany within seconds.

'Bloody hell, what have I done?' moaned Andrea as Shelley vanished into the crowd.

She had been right. Bethany almost flew at her as she came through the door.

'You're spying on me!'

Andrea wasn't surprised, she had seen Bethany like this before over other things, generally no where near so significant. Most had been since her father died. As usual, she let her rant for a few moments, even gave the impression she wasn't listening or concerned. She knew the worst thing she could do was argue back, anyway, Bethany was right, she was spying on her. As she listened to the tirade, she amazed herself at how calm she remained, because she really didn't feel it.

When Bethany's initial anger was spent, Andrea said quietly and simply, 'I've met with Mr. Brampton.' She was taken aback by the reaction, because there initially wasn't one.

Bethany stared at her, said nothing, she stopped crying, looked confused, then pleased, embarrassed, worried, seemingly every emotion.

'Spying on me at school as well?' she asked hoarsely, it was meant to sound accusative, sarcastic, but it didn't really come over that way, more resigned.

'Spying? No, I wanted to discuss your schooling. I met with Rupert's form tutor as well. I know I haven't paid enough attention to you two in the last year, I was feeling guilty. I wanted to know if the school thought there was anything I could do to help.'

Bethany didn't look convinced and said nothing, though did roll her eyes dismissively. This hurt Andrea a great deal.

'I'm really pleased with how well Rupert and you are doing at school…'

'What else did Mr. Brampton have to say?' she looked very tense.

Suddenly Andrea felt entirely in control, though trembled in side, she already knew from Bethany's reaction that what Brampton had said was probably true.

'What do you think he told me?'

She shrugged and glanced nervously at the floor.

It was so hard to say what she wanted to, so she just talked about how pleased he was with her academically, then forced herself to say: '...and you've got a crush on him, is that true?' A crush? Did she really call what her daughter no doubt thought was true love a *crush*, something trivial?

Bethany burst into tears. 'You don't understand! I hate you!' and ran off.

'Oh dear, I could see that coming,' said Andrea to herself, worn out now, and followed Bethany up to her room.

The door was slammed shut as she approached, she paid no attention and just went in, Bethany was sprawled on the bed, face down, her head under the pillow, pleading for her mother to leave her alone.

She sat on the bed, apologised, spoke to her as if she were a little girl, comforted her. This was the most important conversation she had ever had with her daughter, her little girl, so she let Bethany choose the time. After what felt like hours, but was probably about fifteen minutes, Bethany pushed the pillow to one side, sat up and hugged her mother, crying pitifully. Andrea hated herself for what she had done, she had hurt her daughter, but knew what she had done was right. She just had to sort this out now.

More long minutes passed while Bethany sobbed, but said nothing. Finally Bethany said: 'I do love him, I know he doesn't love me. I just want him to love me.'

Andrea wanted to tell her that he was too old for her, that he was old enough to be her father, anything that would make Bethany understand that there was no future in offering her love to her teacher…but would that really work right now? No.

She let Bethany talk for a while about how she felt about Brampton, why she felt she loved him. Bethany's explanation was touching, beautiful, but so very sad. Andrea did feel that she saw a father figure in Brampton, though probably that was furthest thing from Bethany's mind. What she felt for Brampton was to her a natural and normal love.

When she was sure Bethany had finished and when she felt the time was right, she said: 'Mr. Brampton knows you love him, but you have to know you're far too young for him, and you're a pupil, if he did have a relationship with you he'd lose his job, you wouldn't want that would you?'

Bethany nodded or shook her head almost imperceptibly to each fact. Andrea guessed she had gone through all these arguments and dismissed each one, she loved Brampton and that was all that mattered, to her anyway.

'If you carry on…' what could Andrea describe Bethany's one sided relationship as?, 'trying to win Mr. Brampton's love,' she thought she sounded like a social worker, 'he told me that he was going to have to ask that you be transferred to at least another class, or possibly another school. He said he planned to raise the matter with the head teacher, that would mean the school psychologist would get involved. If I hadn't met with Mr. Brampton when I did, then I would have been told very soon by the head teacher.'

Bethany looked startled by this, she really had no idea that what she thought was her offer of love could escalate into something so bureaucratic and threatening. She again protested that all she wanted was for Brampton to love her as she loved him.

How to put this? 'Darling, I'm sure he's fond of you, but to him you're a little girl, a pupil, do you know if he has a girlfriend, or a wife?'

She shook her head, for some reason she assumed he didn't, or decided to dismiss the possibility.

'When I met him he explained that he's a divorcee, has two children and is now in a new relationship, he lives with her…she's pregnant. He's not looking for another relationship.'

Bethany looked surprised, a divorcee with kids! And a pregnant girlfriend! She thought that somehow he had never had any relationship and that he had been waiting all these years for her to turn up. Why was he divorced? There was another woman, a pregnant one! Suddenly he didn't seem the ideal man she had thought he was. She loved him, he knew it, he really owed it to her to tell her about his love life…didn't he? She began to feel foolish and also angry with herself, with Brampton. The tears kept coming.

But then she screamed: 'Lies, it's all lies! You're just saying that!'

Patiently Andrea said: 'No I'm not, and I think you know I'm not.'

It became a long and painful afternoon for them both. Wisely Rupert kept out of the way, though Andrea had told him Bethany had had some bad news, she left it at that. He didn't seem that interested after he found out the problem was emotional rather than physical, if it had been he, as a budding doctor, might have been able to help. He made them coffee every so often, very little of which they drank, but it kept coming.

Andrea wanted to ask Bethany an important question, was she throwing herself at Brampton to get back at her for being out dancing so much? Or was it to find a father figure like Gilbert had said. Now seemed a bad time to ask. She felt she had to distract Bethany, fill her mind with something else.

'Would you like to come to London to look at new dance dresses?'

She agreed with mock enthusiasm, it was a start anyway.

Suddenly it dawned on Andrea that whilst she had probably made her daughter see sense about Brampton, what about her studies, the A Levels, her university ambitions?

Perhaps best leave that 'til the morning as now seemed a very bad time to discuss if she would stay in Brampton's language classes.

***

The estate agent let Diana and Trevor into the house. At once they noticed that there was a smell of damp, no surprise there. Every room seemed to be decorated with green wall paper, the darker the better, it made the place seem very small. The kitchen was probably just as it was when the house had been built in the 1950's, there were no appliances either. The house had been cleaned, but it still seemed rather dirty. After the first burst of enthusiasm, they now felt disappointed, Diana heard Trevor mutter 'dump' several times.

Over a cup of coffee they discussed the pro's and cons. It was the right size, they could get it for a reasonable price, it was structurally sound, and so on. But it was gloomy, even depressing. The view at the front of the house was only a street scape, mind you, it was better than the one from either of their current homes.

They would have to think about it. In fact Diana was doing a lot of thinking lately. There was that strange dream she had the night of the medal test, something about marriage, but she couldn't remember anything else. Trevor seemed to be in an odd mood lately, miserable even, he said everything was fine, but he wasn't himself.

'So, what's the matter?' she asked.

'Nothing.'

'Really? Really nothing?'

'That's right, nothing, I'm fine, what makes you think there's something wrong?'

She explained.

After a long silence, he seemed to be about to tell her, but he didn't, he even looked a bit annoyed.

'Is it to do with the house? Selling your place, what?'

'No, it's not that…'

'What then?'

'Nothing.'

She got irritated, that made no difference. Even so, a little later they arrived at the school and soon the tension was gone and they were laughing and joking, but something was definitely wrong, or different between them.

***

Elwyn took Rupert to see his friend Dennis Nicholson, a lecturer at the medical school in Cardiff's vast Heath Hospital, he was a surgeon. The aim was to try and make Rupert see that becoming a doctor was hard, long, often distressing work. Dennis was doing Elwyn a big favour, he really didn't have time for this sort of thing, but liked the idea of helping Rupert make up his mind. Elwyn knew that Dennis was likely to give Rupert a hard time, he had a reputation for being blunt and short-tempered. This meeting should make Rupert really see sense, if in fact he needed to. Elwyn had doubts as to whether he did, but he had promised Andrea to 'do something', and this was the something.

Dennis had a bushy grey beard and lush moustache, was in his early fifties, yet seemed much older. He was portly and if he didn't look so bad tempered would have passed for Father Christmas, this look was definitely deceiving. He shook hands with Rupert and was quite formal, but pleasant. There was no beating about the bush, welcoming him to the hospital, no subtly, no invitation for tea, Dennis simply plied Rupert with questions about why he wanted to be a doctor. Elwyn heard nothing about Julian or the grand mother's death, the reasons he gave were all good, too good.

Elwyn hadn't primed Dennis about Rupert's real reason, he wanted to see what the boy said, right now is sounded more like a statement written on an application form for a job than a reason born from a deep-seated, even morbid conviction.

Dennis showed them around, though Elwyn, never that happy to be in a hospital, eventually left them to it and said he would meet them in the café.

Dennis treated Rupert like one of his young student doctors and even began speaking to him like it, but Rupert was full of questions and apparently having a great time.

When Dennis brought Rupert to find Elwyn they were both smiling and chatting like best friends, the meeting was over. That evening Elwyn rang Dennis.

'What a wonderful young man, I think he'll make an ideal student and an excellent doctor,' assured Dennis.

Elwyn was taken aback and asked why. Dennis explained how adult the boy seemed, how well informed and clearly sincere and ready for the profession.

'But we think he might be aiming at becoming a doctor for the wrong reason.'

'Rubbish, I think he's got the best of reasons,' insisted Dennis.

'Well, it didn't sound that convincing to me.'

'You mean the stuff he came out with when we first met?'

'Yes, trite and unconvincing.'

'That was, but when we talked candidly, when you left us, he explained about his father dying last year, and his grandmother and how this has motivated him.'

'But don't you think that's a bit morbid?'

There was a long silence, an almost physically assaulting sigh. 'I became a doctor because I wanted to understand why my mother died of cancer and because I wasn't able to help my sister after she had an accident, so I think Rupert's reasons are excellent.'

Elwyn winced. Ah well, now to tell Andrea.

***

Bethany and Andrea seemed to be on good terms since their heart-to-heart, though Andrea found it hard to think that her daughter had bounced back so quickly and easily. As planned, they went to London so Andrea could order a new dance dress. In fact she didn't plan to get one so soon, but it was a chance to spend a girly day with Bethany, away from Newport and Rupert. Hopefully she could get her interested in the world of dancing, maybe even learning to dance.

Andrea drove them to Reading, then they took the train, she didn't consider herself to be a particularly good or confident driver, and certainly not confident enough to drive in London. The car journey gave them a chance to talk. Bethany wasn't that stupid, she knew that her mother would ask about Brampton, also what she planned to do now about studying languages at university. She was actually quite open about how she now felt about him. 'I just assumed he was available and would be attracted to me,' said Bethany with a dismissive laugh, too dismissive.

'And if he wasn't?' checked Andrea.

'Then that he would eventually choose me instead of anyone else.'

Bethany said it so sincerely, so coldly, it made it hard for Andrea to concentrate on her driving. 'I had a crush on a few of my teachers when I was your age,' no she hadn't, and she knew that calling Bethany's 'love' for Brampton a crush was going to annoy her. As it was she could almost feel Bethany become tense and fight to stay calm. She ignored what her mother said and carried on talking about him, then about her school work. Yes, she would carry on with languages and studying them at university, it seemed stupid to change subjects now. She would stay in Brampton's class, but no longer hang back or follow him around.

'Won't that be very hard for you…and him?' said Andrea cautiously.

Bethany didn't answer at once. When she did, Andrea barely heard: 'Yes.'

By the time they had reached London they had cleared the air and conversation was more normal, they began to laugh and joke. But what Bethany hadn't given was any clues about was what had attracted her to Brampton…did she see him as a father figure? Nothing she had said suggested it.

They went to several dancewear shops. Bethany loved the dresses and sighed delightedly over nearly every design. They talked endlessly about which was Andrea's best colour for her Ballroom and Latin dresses, about decoration, how they would 'dance' when she wore them.

Dancing had played virtually no part in Bethany's life, there had been a couple of framed photographs around the house of her parents in dance costume, but once they moved to Newport Andrea hadn't put them on display. Bethany had never had dance lessons and had shown little interest in her mother's dancing. The fabulous colours, decoration and designs she saw now excited her immensely and, for the first time she began asking her mother about dancing:

'Could I come to watch you at a competition?'

Andrea couldn't have been happier. If only Bethany would take up dancing, with a nice lad of her own age, that would solve the problem wouldn't it? Wouldn't it? Yes, of course it would.

Chapter Eight
Love is in the Air

'I've sold my house!' said Trevor hoarsely down the phone. He explained that he had accepted an offer and that the couple buying his house wanted to move in as soon as was practical.

Diana was very pleased for him, but...

'We need to make a decision about the old lady's house then.'

It had been a couple of weeks since they had been to see it and had said and done nothing more. Trevor seemed to have lost interest. Diana had her doubts about it, but couldn't get Trevor to look at any other properties. Something had definitely changed, he wasn't himself and she still couldn't get to the bottom of it.

'Hmm,' was all that he said.

'You'd better move in with me until we've sorted out where we'll live.'

'Hmm.'

'Don't you want to move in?'

'Well yes, if I'm welcome?'

She laughed, 'of course you are!'

'That's alright then, we'll sort out the details and everything when I see you tonight.'

Diana talked to Sheryn about Trevor, what was the matter with him?

'Have you had a row?'

'No, we have the usual banter. I moan at him, he moans at me, but no rows, we're really good mates.'

'Not in love then?'

Diana laughed and looked embarrassed.

'Come on, this is important, you're about to have him move in with you and then buy a house with him?'

Diana gawped for a few moments. 'Listen, this is going to sound stupid…'

'I doubt it,' said Sheryn patiently.

'Well, I do love him and realised that some time ago, but I find it hard to admit it…admit to myself as much as to anyone else.'

Sheryn nodded reflectively.

'Does he know you love him?'

'Of course he does!'

'You've told him?'

'Yes, yes I have…lots of times.'

'Would you like to reconsider that answer? You haven't have you?'

Diana thought back over the last few months…hmm, no she couldn't actually remember telling him. So she shook her head. 'This is very embarrassing, Sher', can we leave it now?'

'Up to you, but do you think this is why Trevor may be a bit reticent about moving in, perhaps he doesn't know how you feel. Has he told you he loves you?'

'Yeah, he has.'

'Was it sincere?'

She shrugged. 'I suppose it was.'

'You two need a chat don't you? I think he's not sure how he stands with you.'

***

Sheryn had to be wrong. Trevor must have realised there was something strong between them, they slept together, went dancing together, everything!

Trevor arrived as planned, he seemed excited and they quickly made arrangements for him to move in until they found a suitable house.

After about a half hour of plans and tea, Diana felt she was brave enough to ask: 'How do you feel about me Trevor?'

He looked confused. 'How do you mean?' he blushed.

'Do you love me?'

He didn't answer for quite a while. She asked him again.

'Would it spoil things if I said I do?' he said, glancing at the floor.

'No, of course not, you've said you it before, I know that, I just wanted to be sure you meant it.'

He smiled, relieved, but still thoughtful.

'Yes,' she said.

'Yes what?' he looked confused.

'The answer to your question is yes!'

'I haven't asked you a question!'

'No you haven't, but you want to, but you're too nervous to ask it. Yes, I love you.'

'Seriously?'

'Very, I do love you Trev', I really thought you realised. I'm sorry if didn't make it clear.'

There, that should do it.

Trevor looked happy, but then confused, he gave her a hug and a kiss and fussed around, clearly flustered.

'It's just that after the other night I thought you just wanted to be friends…or something like that.'

'No!' she said cheerfully and gave him another hug and a kiss.

'Oh good, good…right…how do I go about putting my stuff in storage then?'

The conversation went deep into practical issues and Diana felt they were back on an even keel, he did seem more his usual self.

On the bus the next morning, she reflected on what had been one of the oddest conversations in her life. She found herself smirking at how Trevor took the news. Yes, she did love him, more so than she had ever loved Elwyn.

Then she recalled one particular thing he said: "It's just that after the other night I thought you just wanted to be friends." What did he mean, what 'other night'? She went over their conversations, but she could think of nothing that he might mean by that. It was a tough, even bad day at work and she thought no more about what Trevor might have meant.

***

A couple of days later they were looking around the old lady's house again. Trevor was making a list of things he could fix and what would need professional attention, both columns on the sheet of paper seemed very long, and expensive.

'Well, what do you think?' said Trevor as they trudged back to his car.

'It's got a lovely feel to it.'

'Probably the damp.'

She sniggered. 'Oh come on now, there's no damp to speak of, it just needs airing.'

'That's about the only thing not wrong with it!'

'So you don't want to buy the place?'

'There's no where else we like.'

'We can keep looking,' said Diana patiently.

He gave one of his very eloquent shrugs. 'What do you think, do you want to live there?'

'Yes, well, yes, I think I do. I like the place, the neighbours seem lovely.'

'Alright, we'll buy it!'

'Are you sure?'

'If you like it, that's all that matters.'

She was taken aback. 'But is it what you want?'

'I'm not sure what I want. Tell you what, I'll see if I can get a bit more off the price. If I can, then I'll be really happy about it. But yeah, I think it'll do us nicely.'

They hugged, and kissed, and went back to her place.

As they relaxed and watched TV, she remembered that odd remark Trevor had made: *It's just that after the other night I thought you just wanted to be friends.*

'Trevor, have I missed something lately, have I misheard you, or not heard something at all?'

'Now what are you on about?'

She reminded him about what he said. He looked very uneasy.

'Oh, well…it doesn't matter, forget it.'

'No, something's still bothering you.'

'No it's not, I'm fine, I'm happy, really.'

The phone rang, it was Jacob, so she had to let Trevor go on this, for now anyway.

***

Andrea was back to training hard with Elwyn, but now was far more mindful of what the kids thought, even though they said they supported her dancing. Bethany still wanted to come and see a competition, so Warwick seemed to be the best one for her, it would be a big day and no doubt full of top couples.

The only problem was, if Andrea and Elwyn did badly, they may be out of the competition early, would that put Bethany off? It was also likely to be a long day, but if all went well, it would be a great showcase for dancing.

They left Newport early. Initially Elwyn and Andrea discussed the competition, strategy, who might be there, the judges, and…then Andrea realised that Bethany was sitting rather left out in the back. She worked to include her. Elwyn tried too and before long the three of them were chatting fairly easily. Bethany asked Elwyn a lot about his work.

Having lived in the Midlands, Andrea had a fairly good idea of where she had to go in Warwick to find the competition venue. Elwyn didn't and was relieved that he wasn't expected to map read, he was no good at it. Andrea had sat/nav, but insisted she didn't need it, so left it at home…big mistake.

Andrea became more and more stressed as she headed up the Motorway, and away from the junction they wanted. She told Elwyn it was two junctions further on, but Bethany had Googled it. Andrea only now realised she was right after some bickering and a few miles driving. All being well they would still be on time, but there was less time to get ready at the venue, which was a comparatively modern hotel near the centre of Warwick. Elwyn was confident they would get there in ample time. This didn't seem to help Andrea. Nor did Bethany help ease her mother's troubled mind when she kept telling her how far it was to the hotel, and the time dear old Google estimated it would take to get there. Too long.

Every traffic light was on red, then there were the road works, Sunday drivers, you name it.

When they got to the hotel, they found there was no room in the car park, one of the reasons they had wanted to get there early was parking. They had to park several streets away, and it was raining. Andrea was almost more worried about all this putting Bethany off competitions as she was about being late. Elwyn tried to calm her, in fact they were still in good time for the first round of the competition. But she wished Elwyn would shut up about how the competition was probably already running late anyway! But Bethany seemed quite happy with everything and genuinely interested.

Elwyn had been right, the chap at the table outside the ballroom said they were about an hour behind. Andrea was relieved as this gave her time to get ready without rushing. Bethany helped her with her dress and make up, she loved this, though Andrea found it odd to have her daughter acting as her dresser. It was rather too much like the sort of thing her mother had done when Andrea was a girl. Just as she had guessed, her daughter loved the dresses and kept pointing out ones she liked. The Junior and Juvenile events were still being run and Bethany thought all the kids were wonderful, so far so good, thought Andrea.

The one hour delay turned to two, Elwyn was bored, but so far Bethany was revelling in everything. Because the turn out for the kids' events had been so good, there were few seats for the adults as they arrived, this didn't bother Bethany, she stood at the side of the floor admiring the kids dancing and the dresses. Elwyn sat on the floor, Andrea didn't want to do this given what her dress cost, she managed to perch on the edge of a table. If Andrea had hoped Bethany would be blown away and absorbed by the glamour of the competition, then to day was only going partly to plan. The ballroom was very full, crowded and noisy, most competitions are. Andrea watched Bethany as much as she could. As the afternoon went on she noticed that a young man was standing next to Bethany. They were chatting, he was in a tail suit, she recognised him as quite a good middle to top grade dancer, hmm, they were getting on well, or was it she just she wanted to believe that?

The kid's events finished and the hall began to empty, only to fill again with adult dancers. Andrea, Elwyn and Bethany got seats with a fairly good view of the dance floor and within minutes Bethany's new friend, Dan Alcorn, happened to find a seat right behind Bethany, what a bit of luck!

Elwyn noticed Andrea become agitated as she tried to see and hear what was going on between Bethany and Dan.

'Andrea, leave her alone. He's a nice lad, they're getting on, he's a dancer. What's more…he's about the same age as Bethany!'

'What do you mean?'

'Well, what would you prefer, she carries on moping over Marcus Brampton, or that she fancies a handsome young man her own age?'

She nodded nervously, but today was becoming more stressful by the moment.

The adult events started at last. The organisers were efficient and wasted little time. As expected the standard of dancing was high and the numbers of couples entered quite high. So this was going to be a hard competition for Andrea and Elwyn, more so for Andrea for different reasons. At least once events began being called, Dan rejoined his dancing partner, his sister, and only came over to chat to Bethany for a few minutes at a time, but did Bethany like him?

She didn't seem to show that much interest, though clearly enjoyed chatting to him, she asked him lots of questions about dancing, his dancing.

Andrea decided this was all good. The Senior Ballroom Championship was called about twenty minutes into the adult section. They had had ample notice and were warmed up and ready. The ballroom floor was a good size, but that bit too small for the numbers entered. It took four heats of eight couples for all the Seniors to complete the first dance, a Waltz. Even then there seemed to be too many couples on the floor for comfort. Elwyn and Andrea found it hard work to get around without hitting anyone, or being hit. After each dance they moaned about how it had gone and how badly things seemed to be going, but Bethany was raving about how beautifully her mum danced, how great she looked. Bethany had little idea of what was happening, at least she seemed to be having a good time.

In Viennese Waltz, the third dance, Andrea noticed that Dan was sitting next to Bethany, obviously explaining what was going on in the competition. They were both cheering Andrea and Elwyn on, Bethany looked very happy, so Andrea felt happy, but not with the Viennese Waltz, it was still their weakest dance and had felt even worse on a crowded floor.

Their only other Ballroom event that afternoon was the Open Basic Foxtrot. This time the chairman of judges decided the floor was big enough to take twelve couples, even then it took three heats to get through all the dancers. The couples groaned as they realised the floor was going to be so full. Elwyn groaned as another couple crashed into them, thankfully doing no damage, not intentional either, but very frustrating.

Andrea wasn't sure what to make of it all. As Dan danced by them with his sister, Miranda, Bethany cheered them on loudly. Had she fallen for Dan already? Surely not? And if she had, was that a bad thing? Nah, she'd just made a new friend that happened to be a good looking boy.

'Senior Championship couples stand by please!' said the chap on the mike.

Andrea had now to think of something else.

Their event was down to three heats, though the floor still seemed too full. At least some of the less able couples hadn't been recalled so Elwyn and Andrea could dance better.

One of the judges was Neil Kirkby, not the chairman this time, but an ordinary judge.

As Elwyn and Andrea danced a 'line' in front of him, Andrea saw Kirkby wink and smile broadly, did this mean he thought they were dancing well? Possibly. Knowing Andrea's luck it might only mean that he fancied her.

Much to their surprise, Andrea and Elwyn found they kept being recalled and their dancing became easier and better. They had thought their efforts in the Open Basic Foxtrot to be rubbish, the judges disagreed and they made the final, so they gave it all they could…too much perhaps?

It was a big relief to make the semi-final of the Championship. Looking at the couples they were up against, this was probably as far as they could reasonably expect to get. Andrea had to admit, she was pre-occupied with Bethany, hoping she was enjoying herself and not bored. Hoping this boy wasn't coming on too strong, hoping that Bethany wasn't falling for him too easily, on the rebound?

Andrea discussed the competition, what was happening, what Bethany was watching, some of the rules, and her experiences as a girl in competitions throughout the afternoon. Bethany seemed genuinely interested. Andrea wasn't too surprised that even more questions flew when Dan danced by, was he a good dancer. Bethany wanted to know what were his chances of winning, what did Andrea know about him? Not much.

Dan and Miranda didn't make the final of the Open Amateur Championship, but they did make it to the Open Pre-championship final. Given the opposition in the Championship, that was actually not a surprise. Andrea felt they were in with a chance of winning the Pre-champ' though. Bethany was excited. Hmm, she had fallen for this lad already hadn't she? Andrea kept asking herself if this was good or bad? Well, at least he was her age, and in any case, she probably wouldn't see him again after today.

Elwyn and Andrea knew they stood no chance of making the Senior Championship final. If they were in it, they would have displaced several couples that were in the top ten in the country in this grade. Even so, they got ready, just in case. Couples were warned they would have to do an introductory dance. They listened impassively as the numbers of the successful couples was called and the dancers 'danced-on' to a Foxtrot. They appreciated the couples' skill, Elwyn mused that he had better go and change for Latin, Andrea was feeling hungry and she might just have a…

Bethany began cheering. 'Well done mum!'

'What, we're in the final?'

'I think she's right!' said Elwyn.

The chap on the mike read out their number and called their names out again!

There introductory dance was a mess! Despite having prepared themselves physically to dance, they actually weren't ready mentally!

The final two couples completed their foxtrot, they looked great. This at least gave Andrea and Elwyn time to compose themselves and to properly consider how they would dance. They also noticed a very grumpy couple at the side of the floor that clearly had expected to make the final, but hadn't. Elwyn realised the disappointed couple were No. 5 in the country, he felt really excited.

This was no fairy story final for them, they felt outclassed, there had been an element of fluke in their making it. More a question of the other couples in the semi-final not having been good enough rather than Elwyn and Andrea being one of the best, but they were in the final. They had danced well in the semi and clearly the judges, at least some of them anyway, felt they deserved to be there. Perhaps that was what Neil Kirkby was smiling about?

Both thought they didn't dance their best, it wasn't anything to do with the other couples. Elwyn went wrong at least once, thankfully not spectacularly, Andrea realised her posture was wrong in Tango. They began to flag quite a lot in Viennese Waltz, unfortunately it was a long one. Foxtrot went okay, but Quickstep was too fast and too long. But at least they had made the final. Bethany cheered them on until she was hoarse.

There was little time for debate about how the final had gone, Andrea and Elwyn went off to change, Bethany helped her mum again.

'Well, umm, are you enjoying yourself, you know, enjoying the comp'?' asked Andrea nervously.

'Oh yes, this is brilliant, this is the best day I can remember in years, really cool.'

Phew! That was a relief, or was she just saying that, did it have anything to do with Dan? She nervously said: 'Dan's a nice lad…I think he fancies you!' Not sure this was the right thing to have said, but…

Bethany blushed and sniggered. 'Yeah, he does doesn't he,' she changed the subject, but Andrea guessed the feeling was mutual. Wasn't this a bit too quick?

The Ballroom results weren't given until the first round of the Latin events had been run. Bethany loved to see her mum dancing Latin, though thought it odd to see her dressed in what she called a "sexy way". Andrea was shocked, she didn't think her dress sexy, it was a Latin dress, that's all.

Dan and Miranda also danced Latin, which meant he continued to spend all the time he could with Bethany, they got on very well and it soon looked as though they had known each other for years.

The first result that interested Elwyn and Andrea was the Open Basic Foxtrot, they came third, they had expected forth or fifth given whom they were dancing against. They had been the only Seniors to make the final, so this was a good result. The Senior Championship was almost the last Ballroom result given. They were fifth, now that was very good! Another scalp taken, but Bethany was disappointed, she had been sure they had won. It took a lot of explaining as to why this was actually a good result and just how good the couples were in first to fourth places.

Andrea enjoyed Latin, though Elwyn felt he was no good at it these days, he was certainly better in the Ballroom dances. Even so they had a good time. They were in the Senior Latin Championship, Senior Latin Pre-championship and Open Basic Rumba, so were out dancing quite regularly. They were fairly confident of making the final of the Rumba, but didn't, this seemed a bad sign and unsettled them, Bethany was disappointed, more explanations followed. They did make the final of the Senior Pre-championship, it seemed to go well. The big question was the Championship final, the semi' seemed to go okay, they weren't so familiar with the couples they had danced against, plus they knew Latin wasn't their best discipline and guessed they wouldn't be lucky this time. But they were. As they danced they realised the opposition wasn't as strong as they at first thought, all the other finalists were still damn good though.

Bethany was really pleased, Dan and Miranda made their finals.

By now it was well into the evening, the organisers had managed to get through the Ballroom programme quite quickly and efficiently. The Latin events had begun about an hour later than advertised, so Elwyn, Andrea and Bethany would be home very late. No time was wasted during the presenting of prizes for Latin. Dan and Miranda won the Pre-championship for their age group and came second in the Championship, they were thrilled…so was Bethany.

Elwyn and Andrea were delighted to win the Senior Pre-championship, on form they felt they might, it had felt good. About ten minutes later they listened, tense and even nervous, as the man on stage announced the Senior Championship result. As usual the places were given from first to sixth. Elwyn and Andrea weren't first, hmm, disappointing, they had had a feeling they might just…

They were second! That was good.

When Andrea got back to their seats with Bethany from changing, Elwyn was sitting chatting to Neil Kirkby, he had changed into casual clothes. He wore an anorak and a ridiculous flat cap, he gave Andrea a hug as she walked up. Now the competition was over, he felt no qualms about showing recognition or familiarity with competitors. Besides they were old friends, hmm, she hadn't really liked him when they were Juniors.

'There, see! Told you, you two were brilliant! Well done today, looked good. When's your next comp?'

They reeled off three they thought they would try before Christmas.

'And what about Southampton, you're doing that aren't you?'

'Oh yeah, forgot that,' said Elwyn, 'we weren't sure about it,' he was thinking about the cost.

'Well, I think you'd be mad not to…and…oh, yeah, I'm going to be there!'

'To judge?' checked Elwyn.

'No, to watch, support my couples, help out if I'm needed, you know.'

'We've booked a hotel, we've entered, but it's right before Christmas, it's an expensive weekend, and it's a long way away…'. Andrea listed more reasons, in fact she did want to do it, but the idea of such a big event was daunting, she remembered similar events when she had been a Junior. Julian had always been scared stiff in them, though she generally felt okay, she doubted Elwyn would.

'Besides,' added Elwyn, 'we'd have to dance Senior Pre-champ' and we're doing well in Championships,' he pointed at their prizes, 'surely it would look like we're slumming it, or trophy hunting to dance down a grade?'

'It's a big comp', quite a few of the couples you danced against today will dance it, so it'll be a demanding comp with demanding standards, no one will think you're dancing down. Think about it, I really think you should dance it.'

They nodded reflectively, as did Bethany.

When Neil left them, Andrea realised Bethany was now chatting to Dan. Aww, they did look nice together, and he was a dancer, that was a huge plus, but Bethany wasn't a dancer and that was bound to put Dan off, wouldn't it?

Chapter Nine
Safe as Houses

That was that then, Trevor and Diana had signed all the paperwork they had bought the house. As it was empty, they could move in when they liked. Trevor had sold his house, so there was enough money to complete the purchase without Diana's house sale, which was just as well, there had been little interest in it so far.

It had surprised Diana that Trevor now seemed eager to move out of his old home, especially as he had had so many reservations about buying the old lady's place. He often said he had been born in his old home, though Diana guessed he was actually born at the local hospital and that saying 'born there' was a figure of speech. But she also knew that the place held far too many memories for Trevor, perhaps his own personal ghosts, and he was eager to be rid of them?

In late November, Trevor moved into the old lady's place, as they still kept calling it. This was only so he could work on it and make sure the builders did what they had to, Diana wouldn't move in until the house was at least a good deal more habitable. Each evening and weekend they spent hours working and decorating. Inevitably, each job was more complex, and costly, than anticipated. Despite this they had a good time, laughed a lot, and bickered a lot, but that was just how they were, there wasn't anything wrong with their relationship. Diana was looking forward to moving in with him, this would be a very happy home.

It was only when they sat in a couple of garden chairs in an echoing living room, at last decorated if not furnished or carpeted, that Trevor realised:

'We haven't been dancing for weeks!'
'No time really.'
'Yes, but it's Southampton soon, are we still going?'

Diana had literally forgotten all about it. 'I don't see that it's worth it, we haven't practiced, we've got too much to do in the house, it's costing a lot more than we expected...'

'But I want to go!' Trevor whined. 'Besides, we're entered, it's all paid for...'

'Yes, but we haven't got the time!'

'We have. You haven't sold your house, so you aren't under pressure to move out. This house is coming on nicely now, and in any case, there's no rush to finish it, no deadline. Us going away for a weekend won't make any difference. The tickets and everything in Southampton, it's all paid for, we've paid a deposit to the hotel, we'll lose it if we don't go,' Trevor cajoled and even begged a little. Diana gave in.

The next evening they went to dance class again and booked some lessons. Diana thought it would be a break for her to go to Southampton, a bit of a laugh, besides, Jake and Annalise would be dancing there, she wanted to see them.
After the class they didn't think competing in Southampton was a good idea, it hadn't gone well and they found they could remember little of their steps. Alex and Simon weren't bothered and reminded them that they only had to do Waltz and Quickstep in the Ballroom and Cha-Cha-Cha and Jive in the Latin. So they would concentrate on these dances, they were still eligible to dance in the

Senior Beginner grade, so the steps would be comparatively simple.

They didn't seem simple tonight.

***

Dan rang Bethany regularly. Andrea also realised, based on the big smile, that he sent her texts several times a day and quite a few emails. They were becoming very close (if only electronically) and Bethany seemed very happy. Andrea liked to see her happy, but hoped this wasn't some kind of infatuation on the re-bound after Brompton.

It came as something of a surprise, even a shock, when Bethany said a couple of days after the Warwick competition that she would like to learn to dance. Of course Andrea was delighted, but was she learning because she wanted to, or because Dan was a dancer and it was another chance to have contact with him? Yeah, it probably was more to do with Dan.

'Who would you dance with?' asked Andrea.

'I'll just go to Alex's dance classes,' explained Bethany so simply, 'see if I can dance with any available boys there.'

Andrea had expected her to say Dan.

Andrea and Elwyn also had a lot on their mind, about dancing, should they do Southampton? Almost reluctantly, they agreed they may as well do it, though for some reason it felt more as though they were being forced into it, but they weren't. Alex and Simon both said it was up to them, yes it would be good for their dancing careers and if they did well, it would get them noticed. But if they did badly, what would that do to their reputations? This was normally answered with a dismissive, slightly forced laugh from Alex and a toothy grin from Simon.

Ah well, they may as well give it a go, their results were good, Neil Kirkby thought it a good idea, as did Alex and Simon, and Bethany…Dan and his sister would be there, so she decided she wanted to come too. They also wanted to support Diana, Trevor, Jake and Annalise, it would be something of a family weekend. Even Gilbert said he would be coming, and all staying in the same hotel. Was this a good idea? Probably not. At least Dan wasn't in the same hotel, though Andrea wouldn't have put it past him to try and get a room there too. She also guessed that whilst he might not actually be booked into the hotel, Dan would probably spend all his time there to see Bethany.

To add to the expense and planning, because Bethany and Gilbert were coming, Rupert too had to come too, otherwise there was no one to look after him and, despite his assurances, there was no way Andrea was prepared to leave him to look after himself for a few days. Unfortunately, he wasn't really that interested and moaned. Tough!

Life seemed very complicated these days.

***

Andrea pulled up outside Alex and Simon's dancing school, she was dropping Bethany off for private dance lessons with the two teachers. This late in the year, the season of beginners classes was nearly over and the next series wasn't due to start until January. Bethany had had two private lessons so far, dancing with the teachers and she still seemed very keen and to enjoy learning.

Andrea didn't notice at first, then she did a double-take, Dan was strolling over from his car!

Dan lived in Bristol, it wasn't that far from Newport, but he had dance lessons with a teacher in the Midlands, not Alex or Simon, what was he doing here? This was a silly question wasn't it?

Andrea stalled the car when Bethany hurried over to him and kissed him! It wasn't passionate, only a friendly peck, but now they were going into the school, and holding hands!

Andrea parked, badly, and dashed after them. The evil purple painted outer door of the school crashed shut as she got to it, it had never liked her. Andrea knew it had a mind of its own, probably possessed or something. She shoved the door open, it seemed to realise it wasn't going to win and let her in.

In the school she saw Bethany and Dan, hand-in-hand, listening to Alex as she explained what they would be covering in the lesson.

'Umm, Bethany, could I have a word please! Sorry Alex…umm, now please Bethany!'

'What's up mum?'

'What's Dan doing here?' hissed Andrea.

'He's partnering me.'

'When did he become your dance partner?'

'Today.'

Andrea laughed nervously.

Dan came and joined them.

'I did tell you,' assured Bethany.

Andrea went over in her mind what Bethany had said to her during the day, she was damn sure mention of Dan would have entered on her consciousness, particularly if it included that he was now her dancing partner! Andrea protested that she hadn't told her.

'I texted you this afternoon.'

Andrea had had her phone off and had been too busy to check, she quickly looked at her messages, yes, there was one from Bethany and yes, she did say Dan had asked if he could dance with her.

'Is something wrong?' asked Dan.

'This is sudden, Bethany is only starting to learn to dance. You're a skilled and experienced dancer, you've been dancing since you were a little boy, what about Miranda?' she listed sounding flustered.

Dan seemed very adult, he was eighteen, but remarkably mature, or at least he seemed so this evening. 'Miranda's dumped me. She's got a boyfriend and doesn't want to dance anymore, my parents are really upset.'

'I'm sure they are, but you could have your pick of really good girls to dance with, all your standard in dancing.'

He sat next to Bethany, they were still holding hands. He nodded, Andrea was right, young men are always in short supply in dancing, several girls had said they would love to dance with him, but…

'I really like Bethany and she's a perfect height for me, we get on so well, she's so keen to learn,' he went on, all good reasons. At least he didn't say he loved her, Andrea guessed that was one reason he left out. But Dan was an ambitious dancer. He could with a trained dance partner probably proceed rapidly and win top titles. It could be many months before Bethany would be ready to compete, even then she might actually not make it as a dancer. For Dan to partner Bethany was a huge gamble, but Andrea guessed that his dancing career was the least important consideration, being with Bethany was.

Andrea had quite a lot of things to do, but stayed to watch part of the lesson. Dan was wonderful with Bethany. Alex was patient and constructive with her new beginner. Bethany learnt well, though it was all very new and she had to work hard. But Bethany and Dan did look good together. Andrea didn't know whether to be proud or worried, right now she was both. But why was she worried? Her daughter wanted to be a dancer, which was what Andrea had always wanted, she had met a lovely young man and her own age, and a dancer. Bethany was clearly happy. Was that so bad? Actually no, but things were happening that bit too fast for her liking.

***

To add to their complications, Diana found herself escorting an eager looking young couple around her house, they raved about everything. They're being sarcastic aren't they? Thought Diana.

'Bet they're time wasters,' said Trevor as they discussed the viewing later. They were both busy decorating. 'Hmm, going to need another coat is this wall, shame that. Anybody else asked to view your place?'

'No…I expect you're right, they were probably just winding me up. Besides, I don't fancy moving this close to us going away and to Christmas.'

Trevor nodded sagely. 'If they do make you an offer, they might be stuck in a chain, it could be months before they could move anyway.'

Whilst they were having a break, Trevor said: 'The builder and roofer have finished now and we've only got the front bedroom to decorate, then the carpet can be laid. I reckon I can get my stuff out of storage then! Do you want to move in as soon as the house is finished?'

Diana was pleased, at one point it seemed there was so much to do that the house probably wouldn't be finished for quite a few more months. She also knew that Trevor was glossing over more than just the skirting board. There were scores of minor jobs he planned to do, but none that meant the house wasn't habitable.

'Like I said Trevor, I'd be happier moving after Christmas, the house should really be finished by then. Pointless bringing more stuff into the house before that.'

'Hmm, suppose so,' he didn't seem convinced.

After some hard work when the only discussion was on how to solve a new problem in this room, Trevor said:

'I'm really looking forward to us moving in together to our own house.'

'Me too. Mind you, we've been more or less living together at my house for the last few months.'

'Yeah, but you know what I mean.'

She nodded, and she too was looking forward to life together with Trevor, he was a good man.

He looked pensive.

'Anything wrong?' she checked.

Now he looked a little worried. 'No, nothing.'

'Really?'

'Really.'

Here we go again, thought Diana. 'You look like something's wrong.'

'No, nothing's *wrong*…umm, I was just wondering, which is your favourite room in the house?'

'What? Well, I don't know, all of them, I love the place, why?'

'Oh, just wondering… Umm, my favourite room is the bathroom, I'm really pleased with how that's turned out…even though the shower was a…horrible job to put in.' He was going to use more colourful language, but knew Diana didn't approve.

'The bathroom? I thought you'd say it's our bedroom,' she giggled.

Trevor blushed, smiled, embarrassed, it sounded odd, but wonderful to hear her talk about 'our bedroom'.

'It's not finished yet,' he reminded her.

'No, but it's going to be great, it's already looking just the way I hoped it would.'

'Let's go have a look at it now!' and off he rushed.

'What for? We're busy here!'

'Come on!'

She rushed after him moaning as they went.

It was fully decorated, no carpet, in fact there was no carpet anywhere in the house. Trevor planned to install the wardrobes that weekend, so the room seemed very large and it echoed.

'Right, here we are, our bedroom,' said Diana testily. She noticed the wallpaper hadn't stuck properly in one corner.

'Umm, Diana…I…'

'Do you want to fix that tonight, I've got some paste down stairs.'

'Oh, yes, yes I will…Diana, I, umm…'

'I'll go get it,' she hurried away, she heard him sigh noisily, but thought no more about it, only the wallpaper.

It was only when she got home she thought back to Trevor and the bedroom, he had been about to ask her something. I wonder what, probably something about putting a new bay window in, but the old one would do for now. He knew that, it was pointless his bleating on about it. Actually, he seemed remarkably uneasy about discussing a bay window. Ah well, it didn't matter did it? It couldn't have, he hadn't raised the matter again.

At work the next morning she had a phone call, it was the estate agent:

'That couple have made an offer, do you want to accept it?' said the agent calmly.

'What? How much?'

'£10,000 less than you're asking.'

'No, I'm not prepared to drop that much.' She was having a stressful and busy day at work, so resented the agent ringing that afternoon again. Until…

'They've made a fresh offer, this time it's only three grand below your asking price, what do you think?'

While she considered this, he added:

'No one else is interested, this is a bad time of year to sell properties… I know they've been to see several other places…'

'I'll have to think about it, I can't talk now. I'll ring you later.'

Only when she was on the way home did she really have a chance to think about the offer, let alone calling the agent back. The new offer seemed just about good enough. She rang Trevor.

'That's great! Do you want to accept it?'

'Well, they're keen, nice people, I'm happy enough with the offer. Yeah, I suppose I'm okay with it.'

'Great! When do they want to move in?'

'Don't know.'

'Probably not until they've got a buyer for their place, are they in a chain?'

'I don't know, suppose so, the agent hasn't said and I don't remember them saying anything about it when they visited.'

'They won't want to move this side of Christmas, that's for certain.'

'No, and I don't want to move out yet,' said Diana, visualising getting the decorations down from the loft and having Jacob home for Christmas.

The agent had closed when she rang back, it could wait till tomorrow.

It was a bad morning at work and it was lunch time before she could spare the time to ring the agent, but she guessed there was no urgency.

'Thank goodness you've rung! I didn't want to risk ringing you at work again, but I've been really desperate for your decision!'

'Oh really? Anyway, I'll accept the offer.'

'Great, I'll tell them. By the way, they want to move in as soon as possible.'

'They've got a buyer for their house have they?'

'No, they rent and their tenancy is up on New Year's Eve, they want to be in as soon as contracts are signed. Ideally in the next couple of weeks.'

'What? That's impossible!'

'Why? I thought you were going to move into a house with your partner? It's not as if you're in a chain or anything.'

'Yes, that's true…I know…but it's so close to Christmas, and we're going away soon.'

'Anywhere nice? How long for?'

'Southampton for a long weekend,' that didn't sound that impressive really did it?

'Nice,' said the agent.

Diana felt foolish. 'Oh well, I suppose if the money's on the table and they're keen, I'll have to agree,' she said resignedly.

The call over, she rang Trevor, he was surprised, but also very pleased.

'Ooh! We'll have Christmas together in our new home!' he bubbled.

'Trust you to see it that way and not to realise the work and disruption involved! Anyway, I can't see all the conveyancing, the paperwork, being done before Christmas.'

'True, so we're still alright to go to Southampton then?'

She began to hope that the conveyancing might just get done quickly after all, it would probably get her out of going to Southampton.

***

Andrea and Elwyn had one competition planned before they went to Southampton, in fact it was the Sunday before and it was quite a big one near Bristol. Bethany was really eager to come, Andrea was delighted, but then realised it was probably only because Dan would be there.

In terms of significance, it was much the same as Warwick had been, though this time it was in a huge sports hall. The weather was very wet, Elwyn dropped Andrea and Bethany near the entrance, but by the time they had unloaded her dress bag and case and hurried in, they were soaked, her beautifully styled hair was a mess. The car park was huge, but the sports and leisure centre was a very big complex and busy, Elwyn had to park well away from the entrance, he too got drenched.

The children's events were poorly supported. A committee official moaned to Andrea that there were two other competitions on that day, one in the Midlands and the othrt near London, both with important Junior and Juvenile titles, so no one seemed to want to come here. It meant that the adult events would start on time, pity, Andrea needed all the time she could have to fix her hair and dry off. At least most other couples seemed to be suffering the same problem.

The hall was more like an aircraft hanger and draughty, also cold.

As expected, Dan was here, so were his parents. Dan was very keen for them to meet not only Bethany, but Andrea and Elwyn too. Andrea wasn't sure if she should sympathise with them about their daughter stopping dancing. Dan had several times said how upset they were about the break up of the partnership. It was not helped by the new boyfriend being an evil looking piece of work. He was rude to Miranda's parents, talked to the Miranda as if he really didn't like her in front of her parents, yet Miranda doted on him. Andrea thought how Bethany had been besotted with Brampton, was that worse than her falling for a punk-rocker with an already long criminal record? Suddenly she felt very lucky that Bethany had found Dan, or had he found Bethany?

Andrea had never met Dan's parents, they seemed very nice, she had heard that they were actually quite wealthy, perhaps that's what attracted Miranda's boyfriend! Andrea in the run up to the start of the adult events had little time to socialise or chat to Mr. & Mrs. Alcorn, but they knew all about competitions. Michelle Alcorn even gave Andrea a hand with her hair and dress. Bethany was too busy with Dan to be much help. Michelle was actually better to have helping than Bethany, not surprisingly she was good sorting out everything having spent years helping Miranda and Dan at competitions.

As Andrea stood patiently while Michelle finished off her hair, she watched Dan and Bethany dance by, music was playing for couples to practice and warm up to. They looked very happy, but they also looked to be dancing fairly well, all be it quite basic steps, Bethany was learning fast and well. Russell Alcorn watched them intently. Andrea knew they were concerned as to whether Bethany would be any good as a dance partner for their son. They were ambitious, so was Dan. She wondered what their verdict would be, based on what she saw right now, Bethany was shaping up nicely, but it would be no quick fix to get her up to competition standard. This wasn't "Dirty Dancing" or "High School Musical" where dancers suddenly became expert over night. Even though Andrea loved her daughter and was impressed by how quickly she was learning, she knew what it would take for her to become a real 'dancer', and the Alcorn's saw that too.

The competition went badly for Elwyn and Andrea. The floor whilst wonderfully big, was very hard to dance on, it was also slippery in patches and they didn't feel any dance went that well. They had entered their now usual range of events. Helpfully, the organisers had a notice board on which the recalls to each round were posted as soon as the marks became ready. They didn't make the final of the Open Foxtrot. They were disappointed, but not really surprised as they had been dancing against some very good young couples and, of course, it hadn't gone very well.

It was a pleasant surprise to make the semi-final of the Ballroom Senior Championship. The entry had been quite large and the standard similar to Warwick. Elwyn had slipped and fallen in the last round during the Waltz, he had recovered quickly and didn't hurt himself, but Andrea knew he had become tense and wasn't dancing that well. Yet they were in the semi', a great relief. That only went slightly better, at least they didn't fall.

Bethany was having a wonderful time, she danced with Dan whenever 'general dancing' was put on. She seemed to be getting on very well with Michelle and Russell too. She cheered her mum and Elwyn on and even discussed what kind of competition dress she should have with Michelle. But something wasn't quite right, Andrea wasn't sure what though.

Elwyn went to check the recall to the Championship final when it was posted on the board. He stared at the board for some time. When he came back he shook his head, that was all Andrea needed to know. Right, off to change for Latin.

At least the Latin went far better, well, they thought so. The entry was more modest, though they felt the standard was quite high. They didn't make the final of the Open Rumba, but did make the finals of the Senior Pre-championship and Senior Championship. As they felt they were under scrutiny by the Alcorn's (particularly Andrea), they were relieved to have made it this far. At least they felt they danced well in the finals.

Despite some initial tension, Andrea seemed to get on with Michelle and Russell. While they all waited for the results to be given, Bethany and Dan went out to dance a very basic Jive.

'Daniel said Bethany is doing very well in her dancing lessons,' said Michelle, unintentionally it sounded patronizing.

'Well, yes, but she's only been dancing a few weeks…'

'Yes, we thought so…she's got a lot to learn hasn't she?' said Russell.

'Oh yes, but they're having fun,' concluded Andrea.

There was a thick silence from the Alcorn's.

'Daniel gave us the impression that Bethany would be up to comp standard within a few months,' explained Michelle.

Andrea was taken aback, but it was obvious the Alcorn's were very disappointed with Bethany. She wanted to defend her, but their opinion was based on Dan's view, not Andrea's. She considered what she could say, could she say anything? She had to say something, anything.

'I was very surprised when Dan turned up for a lesson with Bethany, she didn't discuss it with me,' she explained.

The Alcorn's looked uneasy. Andrea guessed they didn't believe her.

'So far Bethany hasn't said anything about when she hopes to start competing, but I know she's talking about it as an aim. Though she's also finding learning to dance harder than she expected, but she's not been put off.'

'Oh,' began Russell, 'we thought this new partnership was your idea.'

Ah, so that was it! The cards had now appeared on the table. Andrea thought for a moment and decided to be honest with the Alcorn's about the problems of the last year or so and the affect that it had on Bethany. They listened carefully, they were very sympathetic and not a little surprised, but did this help? Andrea didn't mention Bethany's obsession with Brampton, God knows what the Alcorn's would make of that!

'I take it you don't want Bethany to partner Dan? Don't worry, I do understand, I would be thinking just the same as you.' said Andrea, sounding remarkably considerate, she even surprised herself.

'It's not that, it's just…it's just that, umm,' hesitated Michelle.

'She's a beginner?' added Andrea.

'Yes, but that's not really what we mean…is it dear?' Russell seemed to be scrabbling about in an effort not to cause hurt, he was only partially successful.

'You see there are several other girls that would love to dance with Daniel…'

'I realise that. The partnership is their idea, not mine. And I think they believe they're in love.'

The Alcorn's both looked as though they had been physically pushed backward when Andrea said this.

'Don't you think so?' she asked them.

They squirmed.

'I suppose so,' conceded Michelle.

'Even if he did agree to dance with someone else, he's going to be trying to spend all the time he can with Bethany. I hope you're not going to try and get me to split them up?'

'No, no of course not!' said Michelle, Russell muttered much the same thing. Oh yes they did! And they were probably up for it themselves!

'Let them dance together for a while. Bethany's far more likely to get bored with dancing, than Dan is likely to lose interest in her. He's not going to give up his dancing that easily, that's obvious. I doubt this relationship will last more than a few months, so let's see if they break up naturally. Because if you try and engineer it you'll probably drive them closer together. Give them a chance. If she gets through these early days of learning, I think she'll make a damn good dancer. She'll be an ideal partner for Dan, give them a chance.'

The Alcorn's said nothing, though nodded patiently, they clearly weren't that convinced. Andrea knew this wasn't the end of the matter.

Bethany and Dan returned, very happy and discussing dancing, the Alcorn's were suddenly very supportive and kind to Bethany. Andrea knew it was an act, but they did at least seem to be prepared to give the new partnership a chance. Good, because increasingly Andrea felt these two kids actually were in love and would make a good dance partnership.

The Latin results for Elwyn and Andrea were a big disappointment. Second in the Senior Pre-championship, sixth in the Senior Championship, they thought they might have won both. Clearly they weren't on form.

'But we're still a new partnership, we're doing better than we expected so soon after beginning to compete,' reassured Elwyn.

Of course, he was right, but it didn't really feel like that as they trudged, wet, to the car. It didn't seem to help either that Dan gave Bethany a more than friendly kiss when she said good bye. She could have done without Elwyn chirruping on about Southampton next weekend either. Given how much it was costing her, the added expense of taking the kids, plus the worry about Bethany, life didn't seem that much fun and Southampton was becoming a bad idea. Today's results didn't suggest that it would be a worthwhile trip either.

'Oh mum! I've seen the dress I want for when I start competing! Will you help me buy it? Can I have it as part of my Christmas present?'

'It wouldn't be that pink one on sale this afternoon would it?'

'Yeah! Wasn't it cool?'

'Freezing! I saw how much it was, I'll have to think about it.'

Bethany took this as meaning yes. She was the only one who did.

***

'Everyone at work says it takes months for house sales to go through, how come these two get it all sorted out in a few days?' moaned Diana.

'I dunno love, but they have. You'll have to move out next Friday at the latest.'

'But we're supposed to go to Southampton on that Friday!'

'Oh yeah…is that alright?'

'No it's not! We'll have to scrap going to Southampton, it's all too much!'

Trevor looked very disappointed, though he was obviously thinking it over and probably agreed. He wasn't going to admit that though was he?

Then, quietly, he said: 'I don't see why. We can move the stuff in here right away, we don't have to wait until the Friday. The carpets are down now, all the rooms are just about finished...'

'But we'll be in such a mess!'

'How?'

Yeah, how? She reluctantly agreed, for now, that they could still go to Southampton.

Within minutes, Trevor had arranged with a mate to borrow his van, another mate agreed to help move Diana's house contents to their new home. Diana agreed to take the week off to pack and suddenly it all seemed remarkably simple. Of course, it wasn't.

Each evening Trevor and his mate loaded the van up several times and moved Diana's furniture and possessions. Diana had carefully marked each box and item of furniture, inevitably they ended up in the wrong room, but they still managed to laugh it off. Diana's parents helped her no end. Even so, Diana was stressed and resented the rush, though it was going better than she expected...well, in some ways. And all the time Trevor quietly made sure everything was ready for them to go to Southampton. Diana didn't expect they would actually go, but he did.

By Wednesday afternoon Diana's house was clear and she slept, deeply, that night in her and Trevor's new home. The next morning the final details and handover were completed. She and Trevor hugged.

'I should have carried you over the threshold last night,' said Trevor. 'Yeah, I'll carry you over when we get home!'

'No you won't! I don't want you putting your back out with the competition coming up!'

'I wouldn't put my back out, there's nothing of you!'

'Still, not worth the risk, anyway, that's for newly weds. Hmm, Elwyn did that…said I weighed a ton! Cheek.'

Trevor's driving became erratic for a few moments.

'What's the matter?' she asked.

'Nothing, nothing, just thinking.' he smiled knowingly and changed the subject. Soon they would leave for Southampton, but Diana didn't need reminding and now was sorry she had let herself be talked into it.

'Oh come on,' urged Trevor, 'it'll be fun! Take your mind off all the house moving and everything!'

'Yeah, but it'll put my mind on competing! House moving seems far less stressful than dancing right now!'

He thought she was joking. She wasn't.

***

Elwyn packed ready to leave for Southampton, he was tired, it had been a long week. After the competition the previous Sunday, they had practiced all they could, and it had been a hard time at work too. He was looking forward to a couple of days away, it would be a nice change. He couldn't remember the last time he had been away that wasn't to do with work, and it was a good few years since he had had a holiday. Any time off work he spent at home, generally working on the house.

He looked around the place that had been his home for most of his life, apart from the few years he lived with Diana. His mother had loved this house, and so had he at one time, but these days it had taken on all the qualities of the Forth Bridge.

No sooner had he finished one job than he had to fix or decorate something else. Seemingly each time he came up the garden path he noticed something that needed doing. It was far too big for him, five bedrooms for goodness sake! He had taken in lodgers for a while, but some he didn't get on with, and some had done a 'moon-light'. A couple of them he had to order out because they were so noisy, or did damage. What he made out of the rent seemed to be spent on fixing damage caused by the tenants or trying to keep the house up to a standard that it needed to be for lodgers.

Elwyn really needed to spend a lot of money on the place. He thought that after he finished paying Diana maintenance money he would have a lot more. But he still didn't seem to have much money to spend on the house, or himself.

What money he did have now went on dancing. That he had no objection to, but if Andrea wasn't meeting the lion's share of the cost of their intense training, he couldn't afford to, and he resented that. It didn't seem right, besides, he felt obliged to do all the dancing Andrea wanted, seeing she was paying for it. It was lucky he enjoyed the dancing, but still that wasn't the point. As for the rest of his money, it went on this damn house. He knew that it was going to have to cost a lot more soon. The roof was leaking, again, it really needed a new roof, and some of the window frames were rotting. There seemed never to be a week when he didn't have a builder or some kind of tradesman working in or outside the house. If he didn't spend so much on the house, he could meet his share of dancing costs quite easily.

He had kept the house on because it seemed like a good idea when his mother died, he even thought he owed it to his mother's memory. He also knew she would have hated many of the improvements and changes he had made, but most were necessary. As he finished putting the last of his luggage in the hall, something caught his eye. The passage floorboards were sloping slightly towards the wall, one of the joists must have dropped! He rushed to check, yes it had, the timber was rotten.

'That does it, I'm selling the place!' he yelled at the sagging joist. Suddenly he felt very happy, relieved. It was too late to get hold of an estate agent now, but he got a number ready, it would be the first thing he would do in the morning, before he left for Southampton.

'But where will I move to?' he asked his luggage in the hall. Unfortunately, the cases weren't forthcoming with any suggestions.

***

Andrea's home the night before they left for Southampton was utter chaos. Apart from packing her competition dresses, make-up and the incredible range of things that always seemed essential, she was packing also for Rupert and, for some reason, Gilbert. Rupert still insisted that he didn't want to go. Though Andrea could tell he was actually looking forward to it, but being a teenage boy, there was a principal at stake. Gilbert was more excited about going than the rest of the family put together. Bethany did her own packing, but Andrea made her unpack most of it. Her cases for the two night trip nearly filled the hall: '...and if you mention Dan one more time I'm going to ban you from coming!' No she wouldn't and Bethany knew it!

A new complication was that Dan would be at the competition, the Alcorn's had booked to stay the weekend when Dan and Miranda had qualified to dance in the Grand Finals, but a lot had changed since then. Dan decided he may as well go and watch. Bethany assured Andrea it would be a great chance for her to practice her dancing with him during the periods of general dancing, yeah right! And the rest!

Andrea had a bad feeling about the weekend, after the dip in form lately it wasn't impossible that she and Elwyn wouldn't get past the first round, what would they do then? Well, she thought she would cry for a start.

But with her family down there, plus Diana and Trevor, Jake and Annalise, not to mention Dan, it seemed to be inviting an anti-climax and a big opportunity for embarrassment. At least being so busy packing gave her less time to think, and to worry, though she still did.

Even rationalising the luggage, Andrea could see she couldn't fit it all into her car, plus her family. The original plan had been that only she and Elwyn would go in her car, he didn't have a car as he couldn't afford it. Her dad could drive, but his car was very small and not reliable enough for a long journey. She rang Diana and Trevor. Problem solved, they would take Bethany and Gilbert plus some of the luggage. Andrea would fit Elwyn, Rupert and, hopefully, the rest of the luggage in her car. Jacob and Annalise would drive themselves down from Nottingham. Dan was driving himself down from Bristol.

On Friday morning the chaos picked up where it left off the night before. She had to go and get her father. She returned to find Bethany and Rupert arguing, it was over nothing as usual. Trevor and Diana arrived a little early. Andrea was stressed and wishing she had never qualified to go to Southampton, she was seriously thinking of cancelling the whole thing. She tried to calm herself and decided she was being silly, actually she wasn't.

Trevor helped load her car, then she packed Bethany and Gilbert off with Trevor and Diana. As soon as she was ready she set off with Rupert to get Elwyn, she really hoped he didn't have much luggage, though knew he was bound to, he normally did for competitions.

He was ready and waiting when she arrived, and yes, he had loads of luggage, there was only just enough room in the back for Rupert.

The plan was for them to all meet up a Chieveley services just off the M4, here too they would be joined by Jacob and Annalise, but not Dan. Andrea guessed if he had joined them Bethany would have insisted in travelling down with him. Was that such a bad thing? Probably not, but Andrea knew she would worry about her, and she had enough on her plate right now without that.

Rupert sat quietly in the back listening to music and reading text books on chemistry. He still planned to be a doctor and seemed even more single minded, plus academically able to achieve it. Andrea's stress levels reduced and she began chatting generally with Elwyn. She had thought about putting him in with Diana and Trevor, but realised that this might not be a good idea, given their history. Most of the discussion was about dancing and dancers, he rarely talked about his work or home and she knew little of the problems, only that it cost him a lot of money to keep the house in a good state. She had seen it many times, but had never been inside, she assumed it was very comfortable and attractive.

After about a half hour Elwyn became thoughtful.

'Alright, comfortable?' checked Andrea. 'Not too warm or cold?'

'What, oh, yeah, fine thanks…umm, it's just that…doesn't matter.'

'It might help to talk about it… Rupert isn't listening.'

He shrugged. 'Okay then, I put my house on the market this morning.'

'Oh, is that a good idea? Why did you do that? I mean, have you got somewhere in mind to move to?'

'No, I'll have to start looking when we get back from Southampton.'

He told her about the rambling house, all the work that needed doing, the expense, the history of the place, that it was depressing him these days. It didn't feel like a home anymore and…and he felt lonely in there. He felt surprised that he had admitted it, he hadn't admitted it to himself, why tell Andrea? But it was true.

They discussed the sort of place that would suit him, probably a flat near his college, the likely cost, how easy it would be to sell the house and so on. Elwyn found the discussion helped. At least he cheered up a bit.

At Chieveley they found the others, Andrea, Elwyn and Rupert were the last to arrive. They had a break, discussed the route, Trevor was determined to use his sat/nav even though it seemed a simple trip south. The only complication being finding the hotel. At least now they seemed to be having a good time and getting on well.

Diana found it hard to believe that she could share a joke and a laugh with Elwyn. It was as if they had never been married and had always been good friends, there was no animosity. Diana was very happy these days, she had a new and good life with Trevor. She did love him and all the worry of the past seemed to be nothing more than bad memories that could be stored away. She didn't depend on Elwyn financially any more, and certainly not emotionally. She didn't have to deal with him over money for Jacob, that was more or less dealt with between them rather than including Diana. And now she had sold her house she would have more money to help Jacob out when he needed it.

She saw a different side of Elwyn, a good dance partner for her cousin, he had a sense of humour she didn't know about, he seemed happier these days, she even admired him as a dancer. It was hard to believe how times had changed and for the better, far better.

Elwyn drove the next stage with Andrea and Rupert. Rupert chatted away to Elwyn about his school work, Elwyn tried to give him help and study tips. Some of the subjects Rupert were studying Elwyn could help quite a lot with, but not the science ones, he was out of his depth there. They got on well and it was obvious Rupert trusted and liked Elwyn. Andrea dozed off, she hadn't slept well last night.

Not surprisingly for December, the weather was poor, thankfully only wet, though Elwyn gloomily said he thought there was sleet coming down as well. Even so, apart from being unpleasant driving conditions, they weren't delayed and made good progress.

The little convoy had managed to stay together fairly well and now edged into Southampton, Trevor, proudly, led the way with his sat/nav. In fact the modest hotel not far from the Guildhall was comparatively easy to find.

It wasn't much of a place, it boasted two stars, Trevor said the owners had probably painted one on themselves. But it would do, it was only for two nights and it was very handy for the Guildhall, the venue for the competition.

Diana's dread was that they would all be in adjoining rooms. As keys were handed out she felt relieved that they weren't.

Much to his disgust, Rupert had to share a room with Gilbert. Bethany shared a room with Andrea, Elwyn had a room to himself, Jacob and Annalise shared a room, they could almost hear Diana tutting mentally. Diana and Trevor of course had their own room, though he was disappointed to find it was twin beds, Diana told him to shut up and start shifting the cases. Andrea was relieved to hear Dan was in another hotel, but what d'you know, he arrived in reception just as they began heading for their rooms. What luck, he was able to carry Bethany's cases up for her.

Diana only now realised that their room was actually between Andrea and Bethany and Jacob and Annalise's, how embarrassing!

'Why?' asked Trevor.

'Well, they'll know we're...' yeah, why was it embarrassing?

When they had booked she was worried they would find out she was sleeping with Trevor, but she was living with him now. She had for some reason assumed that Elwyn and Andrea would share a room, that of course was ridiculous, wasn't it?

She had even been surprised when they checked in to see Elwyn being handed keys to his single room.

But it niggled at her that Jacob and Annalise were next door, though again, so what? They had been living together for months even if Diana wouldn't let them sleep together when they came to visit her. The rest of their party were on different floors. It didn't matter, but it just didn't seem right!

It was mid afternoon by the time they had unpacked. They gathered in the rather threadbare lounge of the hotel, it was still raining outside, and a bit in the lounge too, the roof of the bay window leaked.

'Huh,' moaned Elwyn, 'makes me feel right at home!'

They decided to go over to the Guildhall to see if they could have a look around and to check how long it would take to get there, the answer was just a couple of minutes. The doors were firmly closed and there was no chance to get in. There seemed no point in wondering around the city centre when it was so wet and cold, so they went back to the hotel. In the lounge they all sat and chatted easily, in fact Diana really enjoyed herself. Before Elwyn had started dancing with Andrea, if you had told her she would spend an afternoon in the same room as Elwyn, and actually that she would enjoy it, there was no chance at all she would have believed you. Times had changed.

Andrea was amazed, Elwyn and Rupert chatted happily. She hadn't seen her son look so relaxed and at ease since before Julian died. Then there was Trevor and Diana, they were clearly in love. Her cousin, Annalise, Jacob, Dan and, remarkably, Bethany, all in deep discussion about dancing!

'Funny how it's all turned out,' mused Gilbert.

Andrea couldn't have agreed more.

'Are you happy?' checked Gilbert.

'Yes, of course I am!'

'That's alright then.'

'How do you mean dad?'

'Well, with your dancing, about dancing tomorrow, your relationship with Elwyn…'

'Relationship! He's my dancing partner, just my dancing partner dad!'

'Yes, I know, that's what I mean, what did you think I meant?'

'Umm, I don't know, I just thought you might have the wrong idea.'

'Now why would I have the wrong idea?' Damn it! He's smirking!

'Dad, you're confusing me!'

'Elwyn told me that he's put his house on the market and doesn't have anywhere in mind to move to yet.'

'And you thought I might suggest he move in with us?'

He shrugged, but smiled.

'No thanks! He's a nice chap, but he's a dancing partner, *nothing* else. Besides, I don't have a spare room for him.'

Gilbert giggled.

'What's the matter with you?' she checked.

'Why would you want a spare room for him?'

'What? You don't think I'm sleeping with him do you?'

'Aren't you?'

'No, I never have and never will!' she almost hissed. And to think how he had been when she married Julian! Julian had been fine for her as a dancing partner, but he was dead set against him as a husband. He wasn't good enough for his little girl, even on the way to the church Gilbert had asked Andrea if she wanted to change her mind. After they had married Gilbert took well to Julian the son-in-law and they had been quite good friends. But listen to him now! He seemed to be encouraging her to shack up with Elwyn, Diana's ex'!

'But he's a nice chap, the kids think the world of him. He's a great dance partner for you, you spend all your time with him anyway...'

Andrea stared at him, he couldn't be serious, but the more he spoke the more she realised he was. She refused to discuss it further and changed the subject.

Dan said there was a dancing school in town that had a social dance that evening, they could all go and have a practice. Jacob and Annalise thought this was great, Bethany of course couldn't wait. Elwyn was keen so Andrea thought they may as well, in fact she was more interested to keep an eye on Bethany and Dan. Initially Diana wasn't keen, but Trevor was really excited about it and she finally agreed. Gilbert and Rupert stayed at the hotel.

The dance was in a local community centre and organised by a dance teacher, they found quite a few other competitive couples also planning to get a little extra practice. The regulars found themselves rather swamped as the competitive dancers practiced their steps.

Bethany and Dan danced almost continually. Andrea was impressed with how Dan helped her with steps, coached her, taught her simple dance groups. She was equally impressed how quickly and well Bethany was learning, but look who her mother was! Definitely in her genes.

Trevor and Diana concentrated on the dances they would have to do tomorrow. The steps were far more simple than they had been learning for Novice and Intermediate grades, or their medal test, but they hadn't practiced much lately and Diana struggled to remember anything. At least by the end of the evening they seemed to be able to do the routines, hardly inspiring though.

Jacob and Annalise looked very competent, though not happy given the frequent pauses during which they discussed what had gone wrong, which was nothing as far as Diana could tell.

Elwyn found Andrea distracted, too busy watching Bethany and Dan. At least she was dancing adequately, if not impressively.

Toward the end of the evening, it became more of a party night and they all relaxed at least a bit.

It wasn't a late finish. Andrea watched Dan with Bethany as they did the last dance, they did look good together, and she too looked happier than she had seen her for far too long. They came over to her. She guessed they were going to ask something she wouldn't like.

'I'll drive Bethany back to the hotel,' said Dan.

'That's kind of you…and?'

'Um, nothing. I'll drive her back to the hotel, that's all, that's alright isn't it?' he explained, confused.

'Oh, yes, yes of course.' She expected him to suggest they go clubbing, well he could forget that!

'What's the matter mum?'

'Nothing, nothing at all…you're coming straight back to the hotel aren't you?'

'Yeah, why shouldn't we?'

Andrea said it didn't matter.

They all followed Dan's car as he knew his way around Southampton. Andrea peered at his car but there wasn't anything to see, just the two of them chatting casually.

'You'll have to learn to trust her,' said Elwyn quietly.

She glanced at him uneasily. Of course he was right, but after all that had happened in the last year or so, it was really hard. Besides, she had promised herself to be there for both Rupert and Bethany, but they didn't actually seem to need her as much as she thought. Was that a good thing? Was it right?

'He's a nice boy, trust him and trust her, you sounded…' he thought hard for a few moments, 'you sounded a bit neurotic at the dance when they came over to you.'

'I did not!'

'You did, and I think you know it too.'

A few moments later they arrived at the hotel, she hadn't been able to think of a suitable reply by then. She made a conscious effort to go straight in and not hang around to keep an eye on Bethany, not easy.

'Good girl,' said Elwyn, 'trust her, she'll be fine, really.'

Andrea gave a rather jerky nod.

Dan kissed Bethany goodnight, it was beautiful, it made her happy. Andrea need not have worried, he was, in fact, a nice lad, a gentleman even.

Bethany lay in her bed and dreamily stared up at the ceiling, Andrea was trying to read, but not doing very well as her bed, a single, wasn't comfy. The bedside light was poor and in any case Bethany didn't stop talking.

'Mum, I definitely want to go to uni' next autumn.'

'Good, still doing languages?'

'I'm not so sure now. I want to do English and I thought history would be good, Elwyn's really inspired me.'

'He has? Oh, well, that's great anyway. Have you thought where you'd like to study?'

'Yes, yes I have, I think Bristol would be good.'

'Hmm, I somehow thought it might be!'

Bethany didn't seem to notice the sarcasm. 'And they've got an excellent Ballroom dance club!'

'Would Dan be planning to go to Bristol uni' next year?'

'He's already studying there.'

'What a coincidence, and how convenient!'

Chapter Ten
Southampton – City of Dreams?

At least it was a dry morning, but bitterly cold. They all met over breakfast, Diana wasn't hungry, Trevor was, so were the rest of the men. Andrea only had toast, she was more concerned about fitting in her dresses.

The doors were due to open at nine, the first round of the first event was due at 9.30. They left in good time, but found a queue outside the still closed Guildhall had formed already. Everyone was cheerful and there was a lot of laughter as well as catching up with friends. Dan seemed to appear from no where, Bethany contentedly waited in the queue with him, arms linked. The doors opened exactly on time. After the cold outside, the hall seemed far too warm.

It was a busy time. The Senior Pre-championship Ballroom was the first event to be contested, Jacob and Annalise were dancing in the under 35's Intermediate Ballroom, and would be dancing about a half hour after Elwyn and Andrea. Trevor and Diana were dancing the Senior Beginners, they would be on right after Jacob and Annalise. Later they would dance the same grades in Latin. Apart from the adult contests, there were also numerous events for children, so it was a very full programme. No couple was allowed to enter more than one event in each discipline. The highest grade was Pre-championship and all couples had had to win through to qualify to dance here. Therefore they were already accomplished dancers in their grade and, like Andrea and Elwyn, since qualifying, most had progressed still further. This was going to be a challenging day of dancing.

They bought glossy programme, this caused Diana to want to withdraw.

'There are ninety-five couples in our event!' she shrieked.

'Ninety-four, only ninety-five if you include us,' corrected Trevor.

'Oh, that's alright then! Only ninety-four! Can't see what I was worrying about! It doesn't matter anyway Trevor, we're not dancing!'

The rest of the group talked her around, just.

Andrea wore her new dress, chosen for her by Bethany, for the Ballroom. She found her hands shaking when she applied her make-up. Diana and Bethany helped her. Elwyn looked very smart, elegant and sophisticated, he seemed very ready for the day. This was going to be a tough event, 122 couples in their Senior Pre-championship, far more than they had anticipated.

Jacob and Annalise had it comparatively easy. Only thirty-six couples, but as they pointed out, most couples they were dancing against would be dancing down at least one grade, so they felt they would be lucky to be recalled to the second round.

Looking closer at the names in the programme, Andrea and Elwyn recognised quite a few. They too would be up against good couples dancing down, truth be told, perhaps they were as well.

The dance floor in the Guildhall was very big, only Andrea had danced on such a big floor before. Diana was ready to quit, again. Trevor wasn't, more cajoling followed, but talking her around was getting harder.

It seemed to take a long time before the lady on the stage introduced the judges, nine of them and a different panel of nine for the Latin events. Most they knew from the 'circuit comps', but at least two on each panel were top names in the profession and rarely judged. Unfortunately, Neil Kirkby wasn't one of them, though he was in the audience, he was ever cheerful and encouraging.

The woman on stage told the Senior Pre-championship couples to standby, Andrea and Elwyn were now ready, and nervous. Their first round was split into five heats of twenty and the rest in the last heat. Andrea and Elwyn were in the second heat, their number was twenty-two. They were used to dancing with about twelve couples at a time, twenty seemed a huge number, even on such a big floor. It didn't help that some couples were, surprisingly, not very good and seemed to get in their way throughout most of each dance, this was a disappointing round. They had to dance Waltz, Tango, Foxtrot and Quickstep. They had ample time having danced Waltz to recover ready for the Tango, too long it seemed. The other heats did their Waltz, then heat one did Tango, they all looked so good in the other heats.

There had been no pleasure dancing the first round, they were tense and unsure of what to expect. Their family and friends thought they danced beautifully, well, they would say that wouldn't they?

Andrea and Elwyn had nearly an hour to wait before they heard if they had been recalled, at least they had a lot going on to distract them.

As planned, the under 35's Intermediate Ballroom event was called soon after Andrea and Elwyn had finished their last dance. Everyone watched Jacob and Annalise intensely, cheered them on loudly and called out their number, just how were they doing?

Well, they looked out classed, but were dancing well enough for Intermediates. The trouble was they were up against couples that danced regularly in higher grades. They only had to do three dances and were up against just thirty-five other couples. The number seemed remarkably modest after all the couples in the Senior Pre-championship.

'They should get a recall, concluded Andrea.'

'I thought they were brilliant,' said Trevor.

'Yeah, they were,' insisted Diana.

'They were, but it's a tough comp, they looked a bit over awed,' warned Andrea.

Annalise flopped onto a chair as soon as she was off the floor, she looked drained, yet had only done three dances…it must be the nervous tension.

As they discussed how Annalise and Jacob danced, the first round of the Senior Beginner event was being called. Diana and Trevor were due to dance, but not until the second heat, they were number forty-three. The organisers had put twenty-five couples in each heat, the beginners weren't expected to find this a problem and for the most part they were right.

As they watched the first heat, Diana and Trevor felt they too were going to be out-classed. All these dancers seemed to be so good, well, quite a few did.

'Don't think like that!' said Gilbert. 'Go out there and dance your best, you know you're already better than a beginner, you're accomplished dancers!'

That sounded a remarkably grand way to describe Diana's dancing, or so she thought, but Trevor looked inspired by it.

As they stepped onto the floor, Diana took a deep breath. She consciously relaxed herself and decided she was going to have fun, and so she did, though wasn't really sure how that happened.

They hadn't competed recently and the last occasion had been good. It was hard to view today as just another competition. They both thought they danced well. Andrea and Elwyn thought they made a mess of it, but said nothing.

Now the first rounds were over, all the dancers relaxed slightly, chatted, had fun. Bethany and Dan danced when there were breaks in the programme. The competition was well and efficiently run and the times were almost exactly kept to. The atmosphere was excellent and there was a lot of laughter.

Eventually, the recall for the Senior Pre-championship was given. Andrea was actually surprised to get in the next round. Of the 122, eighty had been recalled. Most of the less able couples hadn't made it, so this time dancing was easier, though the floor still seemed very full. There were of course fewer heats, but the numbers on the floor at the same time remained twenty.

Andrea quietly got ready to comfort Diana, she didn't expect Jacob and Annalise to be recalled, remarkably though, they did! This time they seemed more confident and competent, but so did the other couples and they still looked out-classed.

But what about Diana and Trevor?

By now Diana was having a great time, supporting Jacob, and Annalise of course. She wasn't the only one surprised to find they had been recalled, so she went out and had fun again.

This was the biggest dancing event most of them had been to. Andrea had competed in major events when she had danced with Julian, in fact this competition was far smaller than she had been used to in those days, but it was certainly the biggest event she had danced with Elwyn. He was soaking it all up. Though she could tell he was still nervous and finding the numbers they were dancing against, and the size of the floor, and the significance of the competition was all quite a challenge. So far he seemed to be rising to it, at least he wasn't letting himself be pushed around on the floor as she had feared may happen. In the second round he seemed far more confident. She hoped he would stay that way, it was going to get tougher from now on, if in fact they got any further.

Gilbert thought Diana and Trevor were doing well. Out of all of them, he knew dancing, dancers and competitions the best. He had been almost a business manager for Andrea when she had been a little girl and progressing through grades. As she learnt to dance, he learnt too. He learnt what good dancing was and what made a good dancer. What results were important and which to be dismissed. He watched all of them as they worked through their dances. None could expect to dance as well as they normally did today, it was too much, too demanding, it saturated the senses. But if they could get through the rounds, make it to the finals, then that would lift them, then their dancing would become something else.

Annalise and Jacob had a long wait to see if they had made it to the next round, the last twelve. Jacob thought they might be in with a chance, no one disagreed with him, but mentally they did. It was a tense few minutes before the recall, it would be the semi-final, but there was a delay. The organisers said that another event would be run instead.

While they waited, Neil Kirkby strolled up, smiling from ear to ear as usual. He hugged and kissed all the girls, even Bethany who had never met him before. He gave Gilbert a hug, he had known him when he had danced against Andrea and Julian, it was quite a reunion. Then he went into a huddle with Jacob and Annalise.

'Right, listen, you didn't make the semi', right? But one of the couples has had to withdraw, the girl's injured or something. You two were the next couple back, so the chairman's put you in the semi', you're lucky! Give it everything you can give, okay?'

They nodded mutely and wide-eyed.

As predicted, the recall to the semi-final of the under 35's Intermediate Ballroom was called next, Annalise and Jacob's number, eight, was called. The lady on the microphone casually mentioned that a couple had had to withdraw, nothing else was said, Waltz music began, so did Annalise and Jacob.

'That's better!' said Gilbert and rubbed his hands.

It was a good day, so far, for them all, Andrea and Elwyn, Trevor and Diana all kept being recalled. Diana seemed to laugh her way through each dance, Trevor smiled confidently, but with each recall they became more confident. As did Elwyn, his nerves were easing, he knew he wasn't dancing his best, but he tried to relax and dance the way he knew he could. Andrea was enjoying it all, it was so good to be back, she was pleased with Elwyn, he was a good partner and working hard. She wanted to make the final, but knew the chances were against them.

They listened carefully to the recall to the semi-final of their event. The numbers were called out slowly and precisely, but with no ceremony. On form, they knew they should at least make the semi-final, but this was a big day, the dynamics were very different from their other competitions.

'… Number twenty-two…' said the woman on stage.

'That's us!' said Elwyn triumphantly, punched the air, grabbed Andrea's hand and led her to the floor.

As they stood a few feet apart waiting for the music. Elwyn looked very happy, then he stepped forward and gave Andrea a hug.

'Well done, well danced!' he said, and kissed her.

She hadn't been expecting that, just smiled, and thanked him and got ready to dance.

'Interesting,' said Gilbert smiling slyly.

'Did you see that,' squealed Diana, 'he kissed her!'

'Aww, wasn't it nice,' said Trevor.

'But that's Elwyn!'

'So? They make a nice couple,' protested Trevor.

'But that's Elwyn!' insisted Diana.

'It was only a little peck on the cheek,' said Bethany.

'I'm surprised she wasn't sick!' said Diana.

'He's changed love, he's a nice bloke,' explained Trevor.

'Not in my book he isn't.'

'Well I like him,' said Rupert.

'Me too,' added Bethany, 'mum could do a lot worse.'

'Am I missing something here?' begged Diana.

The music started and they got on with cheering them on.

'Very nice dancing,' said Gilbert.

'They're the best on the floor,' ruled Trevor authoritatively.

'Hmm, not really, but they've upped their game,' clarified Gilbert.

'Yeah, in more ways than one,' said Diana, 'and I *don't* mean dancing!'

***

The Ballroom section of the programme was now moving onto the children's finals.

Andrea was torn, should she change into another dance dress for the final?

'Could change your luck,' said Gilbert.

'There's nothing wrong with that one,' said Elwyn, it's beautiful, suits you very well, it dances well.'

'Yeah mum, keep that one on for the final, it's a lucky dress,' appealed Bethany, still arm in arm with Dan.

'That assumes we're in the final,' said Andrea. 'I'll stay in this dress, we probably haven't made the final anyway.'

'Well I'm going to keep this dress on too!' said Diana laughing, it was the only one she had brought to dance the Ballroom events in and she was confident they hadn't made the final anyway.

In fact she was wrong, they had.

She wouldn't believe it and refused to go on until their number was called for a second time.

Trevor was almost in tears, he was so proud.

Their family and friends watched them intently as they danced by.

'Well, they're in with a chance,' said Gilbert.

'Yeah dad, they're looking quite good. I'd put them in the top three.'

Gilbert shrugged. 'Third or fourth I'd say, but very nice.'

There was no hiding the disappointment on Jacob and Annalise's faces when they didn't make their final, even so, they became more determined to do better in the Latin.

And what about Andrea and Elwyn, were they in the final? Theirs was the last final of that section of the programme, not helpful!

Elwyn was shaking. Andrea was fairly sure they hadn't made it. There were too many damn good couples out there as far as she was concerned. No, not this time, they wouldn't be lucky.

Gilbert thought they just might make it, he was right.

Elwyn whooped and cheered, hugged Andrea and this time kissed her, properly.

Andrea hugged and kissed him back, this was really a great result. Hugging and kissing each other right now seemed perfectly natural, it was because of dancing, nothing else.

'He never kissed me like that, I've never seen him like that before!' said Diana.

'Nice to see them happy,' said Trevor.

'Yeah, it is, but he's kissing my cousin, doesn't seem right.'

'They're a couple, they're happy, they're doing well, deal with it!' said Trevor.

She sighed impressively and shook her head. 'But it's Elwyn!'

Only just in time for the start of the Waltz, Andrea and Elwyn rushed to the floor. This time they looked relaxed and confident, perhaps they wouldn't win, but they were going to have a very good try.

All four dances seemed quite long, in fact they weren't. There were six couples on the floor, so space was no problem, even so they had to work hard to avoid collisions. They were, in terms of experience and achievement, the weakest couple, but worked to move up a level. In any case, reaching the final was a remarkable achievement for such a new partnership.

When they came off after the last dance, their friends and family welcomed them like heroes, and they were. They were hot and exhausted, but the day wasn't over.

The children's Ballroom results were about to be given, then there would be an interval. Late afternoon the children's Latin events would commence, it would be a good while before the adults would dance their Latin contests. Andrea and Diana both looked excited and giggled a lot. Andrea shivered,

'Ooh, I'm getting cold!'

'Let's get changed and comfy, get something to eat, then come back in ready for the Latin,' said Diana.

Everyone agreed. Jacob and Annalise had already changed into ordinary clothes. It was only now that Andrea realised that Elwyn had had his arm around her waist since they had finished dancing in the final. She didn't mind, in fact she quite liked it. Elwyn was a funny old stick, but she really quite liked him and he had danced well today. Yeah, she quite liked him.

***

All the restaurants in the neighbouring streets were very busy with dancers, eventually they found a pizza place that could give them a table together. They were all in very good spirits and cheerful. It seemed almost an anti-climax to go back to the Guildhall and dress up to dance again, though Jacob and Annalise couldn't wait, they were determined to do better in Latin, but were very pleased with making the semi-final, all be it by the skin of their teeth.

Diana watched Andrea and Elwyn, increasingly they were a real couple, not just a dance partnership, she still couldn't get her head around that. Nor could she really reconcile herself to the fact that, after all she had gone through thanks to Elwyn, she was sitting opposite him listening to him cracking jokes! She didn't know he knew any, and had never thought that he had a sense of humour. But there he was, the jokes were good and his arm went around Andrea's shoulder when ever he got the chance, and, remarkably, she was enjoying it.

Diana was having a good time, a good weekend, she was relaxed and happy. The past seemed that, past and a long time past, they had all moved on.

They all glanced at their watches regularly, there was no chance they would get back late.

Bethany and Dan went back early, there was general dancing and they didn't want to miss it. She just might make a dancer after all, mused Andrea as she watched Bethany leave hand in hand with Dan.

When the rest of the party arrived back in the ballroom, Andrea was relieved, and pleased, to see Bethany dancing prettily with Dan, he was coaching and helping her and she was trying hard. She felt proud.

Oh yes, Andrea found she was holding hands with Elwyn, she hadn't noticed until now. Rupert was in deep discussion with Elwyn about his school work. Elwyn seemed to be really good with him, as he should be given his job. But she too remembered Elwyn as Diana's husband, a sour-puss and hard to talk to, but that was then, certainly not now. She decided to help him find somewhere to live and would help him move house, it was the least she could do.

'Right, better get changed,' said Trevor earnestly.

'That's not going to take you long,' said Diana.

'No, I know, but you know what I mean!' He was so excited, he seemed to bring every conversation over dinner back to the final of the Senior Beginners Ballroom. Diana hoped he wouldn't get too disappointed when they didn't win. There was no way they were going to be the winners. She really felt there had been some mistake, probably they should not have been in the final and the organisers didn't like to tell them to get off. It doesn't happen like that, they had in fact earned their place.

Diana had a nice top and pretty skirt to dance the Latin, her parents had treated her to it when she qualified for Southampton. She hadn't expected to actually wear it to the competition as she hadn't really planned to go. She helped Andrea into her beautiful Latin dress, and she looked stunning, a deep blue and white with a comparatively long skirt. Annalise was with them, her Latin dress was second hand, but good quality, beautifully decorated in shades of orange and yellow, thousands of rhinestones, it was a rather snug fit, she looked good.

When they got back to their seats, Diana noticed that Annalise looked very tired.

'Are you okay love?'

'Bit tired thanks Diana, long day yesterday and a real emotional roller-coaster today. I've danced a lot, worked hard, it's taken it out of me.'

She didn't say anything as to why an apparently fit and young woman was feeling the strain, it wasn't that many years ago she had beaten leukaemia. Was she completely recovered? A few moments later she was enjoying the general dancing with Jacob, he didn't seem to notice that Annalise was very tired and now they were dancing she looked alright again, but was she?

A top professional dance couple gave a demonstration, the five Ballroom dances, Trevor was in his element and gave his expert opinion throughout.

Elwyn and Andrea watched the professionals intently. They were looking critically, yet admiringly, but also trying to learn from them.

Dan sat close to Bethany and pointed out steps the professionals were doing, she seemed riveted. Andrea found it hard to believe her daughter had become a committed dancer in just a few weeks. It certainly looked like it, apart from anything else she was genuinely happy and that was very good.

The entries for the Latin events wasn't as big as for the Ballroom, even so, Andrea and Elwyn were dancing against eighty-one other couples. All the couples had a new number for the Latin events, Andrea and Elwyn this time were number fifty.

Senior Beginners had sixty-three couples including Trevor and Diana, they were number thirty-six.

Jacob and Annalise had it comparatively easy, just twenty-five couples, they were number twenty-four.

Andrea and Elwyn's event was called first. It was split into four heats, three of twenty and one of twenty-two. On this big floor, and for Latin, that was no great problem. Again it was a four dance, Cha-Cha-Cha, Rumba, Samba and Jive. They were glad not to be dancing Paso Doble, they never thought they were any good at it, and neither did Simon. For a first round, it seemed to go reasonably well, though Elwyn found himself distracted by some of the other couples. In Samba they danced apart for a few bars of music and another couple steamed between them, just like the time Spencer and Tara had. This really threw Elwyn, thankfully only momentarily. In Rumba, Andrea found another woman's hand waving in her face, they had got a little bit too close, no damage done, just off putting. Over all, it went fairly well for a first round, they had danced worse, and endured worse in other competitions, hopefully they would get a recall.

Trevor and Diana went out to dance about a quarter hour after Andrea and Elwyn. By now Diana was in a great mood, she had no nerves and was having a wonderful time, a real laugh. Trevor took it more seriously, danced his heart out and smiled lavishly. Their event was in three heats of twenty-one, Diana felt they had vast amounts of space to dance in, their steps were quite simple and they moved very little in either their Cha-Cha-Cha or Jive.

Everyone in their party cheered them on, they were really becoming quite a happy family.

Gilbert welcomed them off the floor, told them how well they had danced, gave them a pep-talk. Trevor said Gilbert sounded like a boxing trainer and began calling their group of seats the blue corner. But Gilbert was serious and really having a good time, he wanted to be part of the world of dancing and his knowledge was literally invaluable. He knew all the judges personally, though Andrea hardly remembered any of them from her years dancing with Julian. She didn't like to say it, but she guessed none of the judges would remember Gilbert. Even so, the now ever-present Neil Kirkby spent a lot of time swapping stories about 'the old days' with Gilbert, Andrea had no idea that her dad had such a dirty laugh.

She realised she hadn't seen Rupert for a while, but she found him chatting to lads his own age that had stayed on after the children's events. He was happy, laughing joking, listening to their dance stories, but not bored like he said he would be. Though each time one of their party danced he was at the side of the floor bellowing their number out.

The weekend was going better than she had dared hope. Surely something had to go wrong? Like the results perhaps?

***

Eventually, Jacob and Annalise went out to dance their first round, Cha-Cha-Cha, Rumba and Jive.

All twenty-five couples were in one heat, that seemed a few too many, but it worked.

They watched Jacob and Annalise dance and cheered them on. Gilbert gazed at them like an art critic viewing a new artist's work, he looked unimpressed, but muttered regularly that he thought they were doing well.

Diana stopped cheering them on during the Rumba, it suddenly didn't seem appropriate: 'My God, that's beautiful, they're so good!' Quiet admiration seemed far more in line with a performance like this.

'Hmm, yeah, very nice,' conceded Gilbert.

'They're looking great Di', said Andrea, he's a lovely little dancer and that's a stunning girl he's got. Their Latin's much better than their Ballroom.'

'I never thought Jacob could be so…so…earthy!' Their Rumba really seemed to characterise the *dance of love* a little too well.

Trevor yelled their number then chuckled. 'Bit saucy aren't they?'

'That's what Rumba's supposed to be,' said Elwyn, watching his son proudly.

'There's obviously good chemistry between them,' said Gilbert.

'Hope they don't form an explosive mixture,' said Trevor.

'Well they're smouldering as it is!' said Diana.

Jive seemed to be Jacob and Annalise's weakest dance, part of the problem was that Annalise was starting to struggle. She was looking tired, but completed the dance.

They came off looking triumphant, everyone hugged them and talked about their dancing, but Annalise flopped onto a seat and lolled forward, her head between her knees. The rest of the party didn't seem to notice, Diana did.

'Something's wrong isn't it love?'

Annalise nodded.

'You don't feel well, is it…are you, umm, are you alright, I mean…'

'Don't know, might just be flu coming on or something.'

'You don't think it's flu do you, really?'

Annalise said nothing, but after a few moments just shook her head.

'Are you alright to carry on, do you think you ought to withdraw?'

She shook her head again. 'I'll be fine, just overdid it in that Jive.'

'Going to see the doctor when you get home?'

She didn't answer for quite a while. 'We'll see.'

'You mean no? I think you should, promise me you will.'

Annalise at last sat up, she was crying. 'I'm frightened.'

Diana hugged her and cried too. Eventually she said: 'I don't think it's leukaemia. I don't know much about it, but from what I've seen I don't think it would suddenly hit you tonight, out of the blue and like this, do you? Do you feel like you did…umm, back then?'

'It's a long time ago, I can't remember. I've spent years trying to forget it.'

'Well, I don't think it's that, I think you're just run down. I think you don't have anything to worry about, go to the doctor, but I think you'll be fine, honestly.'

Diana hoped to God she was right.

***

Some of the other events were comparatively small and the competition went quickly and smoothly. Andrea and Elwyn and Diana and Trevor were recalled to the next rounds, these seemed to go well enough. Diana was still having a great time, helped by Annalise bouncing back, thankfully she and Jacob's next round wasn't for some time. Diana did suspect that Annalise might just be working at being okay for the sake of Jacob and Diana. She'd make damn sure that girl went to the doctor though.

It was a busy evening and there was a lot of laughter. It was a relief, and to Diana, but not to Trevor, a surprise that they kept being recalled. Their first recall was to the last forty couples, then the last twenty-four. Trevor became nervous as the recall to the last twelve, the semi-final, was called. Diana wasn't that bothered, she was having fun and to her the competition didn't really matter, any success was a bonus, besides, they had made the Ballroom final and that she still couldn't believe.

But they were recalled and danced wonderfully, well Trevor thought so. Diana found Elwyn cheering her on from the side of the floor both funny and disconcerting, this was something she never ever thought would or could possibly happen, when did he turn into such a nice guy?

Andrea and Elwyn weren't so confident in Latin. The first round had been alright, but it was their weakest discipline and the standard was high again, too high. As expected, they were recalled to the second round, the last sixty couples. On form they guessed they should make it at least one more round, but most couples in this event were of a fairly equal standard and more experienced than

Andrea and Elwyn. Gilbert said they were dancing well, though Andrea guessed he wasn't likely to tell them they weren't. When she had been a kid he used to do just that, but that was a different world, a different time, she wasn't a little girl anymore. Oddly, Gilbert seemed to think it was alright to tell her she wasn't dancing well as a little girl, but not now.

They listened intently as the man on the microphone read out the numbers for the next round, the last thirty-six, thankfully they made it. Andrea personally didn't think they would be lucky. Once they had danced, they agreed that this was about as far as their luck would stretch. They had about a half hour wait to see if they had made it to the next round, the last eighteen…a long wait.

According to the programme, the semi final of the under 35's Intermediate Latin was due to be called in the next few minutes. Given how well they had danced in the first round, Annalise and Jacob felt they deserved to be in the semi', so did the rest of the party. In fact Diana knew they deserved to win, they were the best on the floor, the proud mum's view though, unfortunately, might not be the same as the judges. Neil Kirkby had made one of his regular calls and guardedly said he thought they would get back, even so, no one was going to take it for granted.

Diana took Annalise to one side in the moments before the recall.

'How are you feeling now love?'
'Much better!'
'Honestly?'
'Honestly,' said Annalise breezily and with a big smile.

'Because earlier you looked dead on you feet. Do you really feel you're going to be able to dance your best, to dance at all?'

'Yeah, of course, I'm fine! Ooh, listen, they're calling the numbers!' she hurried off to stand next to Jacob.

Seconds later they walked proudly and confidently onto the floor, they had made it, the semi-final.

They all watched them carefully, cheered and yelled. Their Cha-Cha-Cha looked very good, lively and well danced. The Rumba, if anything, looked even more intense, but beautiful…Trevor put it more graphically. He seemed almost moved to tears. 'I wish I could do Rumba like that,' he lamented.

'If you danced it like that with me I'd slap your face,' jeered Diana.

The Jive was again weak, too weak, Annalise's energy and spark seemed to ebb away with each beat of music, but then she fought back, got a second wind.

As soon as they left the floor, arm in arm, Annalise's knees buckled and Jacob had to hold her up.

'I think I'm anaemic,' she said weakly.

'Could be,' said Diana, 'but doctor's Monday, right?'

'I've got a lot to do Monday, I'll try and get an appointment…'

'I've got a better idea,' interrupted Diana, 'you and me go to A&E tonight, now!'

At least this made Annalise laugh, but Diana was serious.

'I'll go to the doctor Monday, honestly, I'm not that ill, it's just a virus.'

'All the more reason to sort it out now.'

'Perhaps it's best if you withdraw from the comp,' said Andrea sympathetically.

'No point,' said Annalise, 'we won't be in the final.'

'And what if you are?'

Annalise laughed, 'then we dance it of course!'

Neil Kirkby strolled up grinning impressively, but looked shocked when he saw Annalise stretched out on some chairs and looking pale and sick.

Diana grabbed him by the lapel of his suit.

'Is there anyway you can find out if they've made it into the final?' she said, pointing at Annalise and a worried Jacob.

He shrugged, 'I doubt it. I'll see if I can talk the chairman round. What's wrong with her?'

Diana looked at him critically. Dare she tell him what she really thought, that the leukaemia may be back? No, not Neil, she had the feeling that if she told him it would get around the hall very quickly.

'She's got some kind of virus, she's feeling very ill. I think she should go to…' should she say hospital? No. '…back to the hotel and rest.'

Neil peered over Diana's shoulder at Annalise, she seemed to be asleep.

'Well, if she's that ill she should withdraw and leave,' he said breezily, almost chuckling. 'Mind you, she does look bad doesn't she?'

'She's worked damn hard today, she wants to know if she's made the final, if she has…' And what if she had, would she dance it, could she dance it? 'She deserves to know, if she's not then it'll be easier for us to get her to agree to go now.'

Neil shrugged. 'See what I can do,' and hurried off.

Diana had a feeling that would be the last she saw of him.

Everyone was concerned about Annalise, so much so, someone had to come and get Elwyn and Andrea, they had been recalled to the last eighteen.

Annalise seemed to recover, though slowly, and was well enough to sit up and watch Elwyn and Andrea. This time they danced well, relaxed into it and enjoyed it.

It was a good while before any of them had to think about recalls. All the finals were at the end of the programme. Elwyn and Andrea had about twenty minutes to wait to see if they had made it into their semi-final. Diana sat with Annalise, she looked weak. Diana felt so helpless.

She had a chat to Jacob about her. Of course he was as worried as everyone else, but seemed less apprehensive.

'But she's always like this mum.'

'How do you mean,' checked Diana.

'For the last few months, she gets really washed out by the end of practice or lessons, or competitions, she'll be fine, she always is,' he explained cheerfully.

'But she isn't well, look at her! I thought she was going to pass out!'

'Well, yeah, she's bad today, but she's nearly back to normal now,' he said hopefully.

'I've got her to agree to go to the doctor on Monday.'

'She won't go.'

'She will!'

'I've been pushing her to go for the last couple of months, since she started to get so weak after dancing, she never does though, always makes an excuse.'

Diana thought for a moment, did Jacob know Annalise had had leukaemia? So she asked.

His jaw nearly hit the ground, he looked frightened. The question was answered.

'I think you should withdraw now and we'll get her to A&E,' said Diana almost with no emotion.

Jacob nodded thoughtfully. 'I've got to speak to Annalise,' he said and hurried off.

Diana hoped she hadn't gone too far by telling Jacob, but he clearly had no idea how bad things could actually be. Perhaps it was just a virus, one that most people could shrug off, but not Annalise. And what if it was the leukaemia back, it could happen, couldn't it? She had no real idea.

Jacob and Annalise were deep in discussion, she seemed to be laughing it all off.

This time Andrea and Elwyn were listening to hear if they had made the semi-final, but talked more about Annalise than they did about their chances of being recalled. Despite being pre-occupied and worried for her, they heard their number being called, for the moment Annalise was put to the back of their minds.

They danced well in each dance and it felt good, not perfect, and they knew they could have danced better, but they were pleased to make the semi'. On form they felt this was a good result and probably about 'it' for the night as far as they were concerned.

Now all three couples were waiting to hear if they had made the final. Annalise and Jacob didn't have to wait for the tense experience of listening to the man on stage reading out the finalists numbers, Kirkby came up, grinning.

'Hia love!' he said cheerfully to Annalise, 'how you're feeling now, better?'

She lied.

'That's good, 'cause you're in the final, better get ready.' He winked and slapped Jacob on the back. 'Best keep that to your selves, right?' Kirkby laughed, gave Andrea a kiss on the cheek, shook hands with all the men in the party, then went to Diana and held her hands, he looked earnestly at her.

'She's going to be able to dance isn't she?'

Diana was going to say no. She glanced across to Annalise and Jacob, they were excited, very excited, they obviously couldn't wait to dance, though she looked unsteady on her feet. Diana knew there was no chance of getting them to withdraw now, perhaps it was what she needed?

Diana looked at Neil, she really didn't feel she could tell him just how bad Annalise might be.

'She's going to have to be alright isn't she?' said Diana acidly, though of course it wasn't Neil's fault.

He looked over at her and asked 'What's wrong with her then, she looks alr…'

Annalise staggered backward and flopped onto a seat as he watched, but sprung back up again, Jacob hadn't noticed.

'She was very ill as a girl. She…she, umm, well… Look, it's not for me to be telling you, but she had a tough time. She was very ill, that's all you need to know, and we're worried…worried that a health problem, might be…back.'

Neil looked confused, but nodded, putting two and two together, but probably not really coming up with the right answer.

'Ah, I see, well, I'm sure she'll be fine, good luck to you two in your final too,' he said and giggled.

'Thanks,' said Diana without emotion, then it stuck her as she watched Neil stride away just what he had said. 'Hey, what do you mean?' she called after him.

He came back glancing around conspiratorially as he approached. He winked. 'I had a quick look to see if you and Trevor were back, you are! Don't tell anyone will you?'

'What about Andrea and Elwyn?' she hissed, this should all be secret.

'Their marks weren't in when I checked, so I don't know,' he then rushed off, waving as he went, but only until he saw someone else he knew, then there was more kissing and handshakes.

Now Diana had time to think about it, she was shocked, they were in the final! She wanted to tell Trevor, but thought better of it. He would never be able to keep it to himself and he would get so nervous and excited he probably wouldn't be able to dance. But what about Annalise? She looked across to her and Jacob, she had sat down and stayed seated, but seemed to be alright…of course she wasn't.

***

It was now nearly ten o'clock, but none of them felt tired, not even Annalise, so she said, but she looked pale.

Diana and Trevor's final was about to be called. Trevor still didn't know they had made it, he stood at the side of the floor looking nervous, excited and hopeful. Diana pretended she didn't know. She thought he would explode when their number was called, he was so proud and happy. He rushed out onto the floor, yanking Diana after him, they received a good round of applause from the large audience, but it wasn't anything compared to the loud and enthusiastic cheers from their own party.

When the music began Diana had to concentrate on dancing, thankfully Trevor's enthusiasm was infectious and once more she had a great time. They weren't on the floor that long, but it had seemed to her that they were dancing for hours, in fact it was roughly two minutes of music for each dance. Two minutes was more than planned as the couples were so evenly matched, the judges needed more time to sort out the placings. The couples had nearly a full track of music. Diana just relaxed and had a good time.

Later, the Intermediate final was called. Only Jacob and Annalise amongst the finalists knew they were in it. They still felt that they would only believe it when they heard their number, and it still came as a surprise when their number and names were called out. They hugged and sniffed back tears, then tried to look relaxed and strolled onto the floor hand in hand, just like the very top couples did.

Diana felt so proud of Jacob, and of Annalise. She glanced at Elwyn, it was often hard to remember that he was Jacob's dad, now he was full of pride too and cheered his son even before the music began.

They danced the Cha' easily and looked good, Annalise seemed to manage it with no trouble, they looked confident and the dance went well. Next came Rumba, as in the earlier rounds, they danced this very well, almost too well. It was earthy, far more so than the other couples managed…good! Finally, the Jive. The music began, they started well, she was smiling, but that quickly faded, she looked troubled, but kept dancing. Even from the side of the floor, they could see her breathing heavily, but smiling. Two minutes of Jive, it doesn't sound much. For Jacob and Annalise it wasn't normally a problem, but she was ill and weakening visibly.

She struggled to keep going, to breathe, let alone to dance. Finally she stopped and crumpled down onto her knees. A few seconds later the music stopped, there was a great deal of applause, the other couples left the floor, but Annalise was still on her hands and knees, and crying.

Diana, Andrea and Bethany rushed to help. One of the judges came over too.

With care, they helped her off the floor. First aiders arrived, but there was little they could do, she was conscious and seemed to be recovering.

'That was a long one,' she said barely audibly, 'I'll be fine in a minute.'

'We're taking you to A&E right now love, Trevor, go get the car.'

'No, I'm getting better, it's nothing to do with…with the leukaemia.' there seemed to be a painful silence after she said it. Only Jacob and Diana had known, so the others were shocked. 'I've been thinking about it, I didn't feel then like I do now, honestly, it's just a virus. I Googled it,' she waved her phone at Diana, 'I'm *not* going to A&E. I'm fine. I'm not missing the next dem' and I'm not missing being in the presentation line-up!'

'What d'you think love, still want me to get the car?' checked Trevor.

Diana looked at Annalise critically. Her instincts told her that she should go to hospital, but she looked defiantly at Diana, the girl wasn't ready to go. She sighed noisily.

'Alright, but you've got to promise me you'll go to the doctor on Monday, there's something wrong with you, we're worried sick.'

'I'll take her myself,' said Jacob.

'And don't let her talk you out of it, right? If you don't take her I'll give you hell!'

There was nervous laughter, though no one really felt what had happened was anything to laugh at.

Annalise smiled beguilingly, sat back, clapped excitedly, then said: 'So, how do you think we danced?' She looked pale and sick, but she was recovering and wouldn't have to dance again tonight. Diana guessed if she did, then Annalise would probably end up in A&E whether she liked it or not, there would be no arguing with paramedics.

***

The last but one final of the evening was the Senior Pre-championship Latin. Elwyn and Andrea's final, well, they hoped it was their final, they didn't know if they were in it, all they could do was hope. It was a good while since Annalise and Jacob had danced, they were all more relaxed and the mood had lightened. Annalise remained seated, partly because, despite what she said, she could hardly stand, her legs simply buckled. Of course, she would be fine when the presentation was made, nothing was going to stop her getting her prize.

Andrea and Elwyn stood well back from the side of the dance floor. If they didn't get a recall, they didn't want their disappointment to be obvious to everyone. Bethany stood next to Andrea, she was excited and chattered away. Dan, Rupert and Jacob were all talking to some dancers near by. Diana and Trevor sat with Annalise.

'Look at that dress mum! I want something like that, what do you think? But I want it in a shade of green…bit like that colour, see it? Over there…' she explained, browsing through pamphlets from dance wear suppliers, of which she seemed to have quite a stack. She had changed her mind about her first dance dress colour and style roughly every half hour throughout the day.

Andrea simply nodded or threw in the odd yes or no, her attention was on the recall to the final. She shifted from mentally going over how they should dance it, to calming herself, to assuring herself that they wouldn't be in.

She wanted to dance it, she felt they had danced well enough, but, but…what?

They were still a new partnership, inexperienced, their Latin results weren't as good as their Ballroom. Elwyn was learning fast and well, but he had only been competing a few months, they had made meteoric progress, yet his dancing was wracked with weaknesses. Statistically, realistically, they wouldn't be in the final. That's what she told herself…but what if, what if they had just managed to make it? She forced herself to think of something else.

Damn, this man on stage was stringing out the announcements, putting off the recall needlessly. She thought about it logically, no he wasn't.

At last he picked up a piece of paper, *the* piece of paper, the list of couples re-called to the final, her final? Their final? Her hands were shaking.

Bethany was excited and held up crossed fingers.

The first number was called, was it higher or lower than their number, they were number fifty, but fifteen had been called, so there was still a chance, she began to doubt that they were number fifty, yes they were. Another number:

'…twenty…'

Still a chance, but forget it, they hadn't made the final, she knew that, how could they have?

'Twenty-four...'

How many was that, how many spaces were left in the final?

'Number thirty-one…'

The man on stage read each number out clearly and allowed time for the cheering and applause to die down.

'Fifty…'

Bethany screamed. Initially Andrea was frightened, what was wrong with her, was she alright?

Suddenly everyone was standing around them, kissing and hugging, cheering, laughing, what for, why?

Elwyn was running around in circles whooping.

Then she realised, fifty was them, they were in the final!

She rushed over, stopped Elwyn, gave him a hug and a kiss, then dragged him to the side of the floor, with difficulty they calmed themselves and went out to dance.

Just as the music for the Cha-Cha-Cha was about to start, Andrea noticed Neil Kirkby with Diana and the others, he was grinning and had his thumbs up.

Instantly, they concentrated on their dancing, they had no expectations of winning, so relaxed at least a little and enjoyed each dance, but they worked hard and well. They had ample space, the music was good, no crashes with other couples, no real problems, this time it didn't feel like a gala night, but an ordinary competition.

Elwyn looked relaxed, he seemed to be having a great time, he smiled at Andrea throughout the final. In Rumba, one of the groups brought them face to face, he kissed her. Only a little one, but on the lips, he had never done that before, it wasn't part of the dance, he just kissed her, and she liked it.

Diana saw the kiss, Elwyn had just kissed her cousin while they were dancing! She wasn't jealous, just confused. Did Andrea feel anything for Elwyn? Surely not, but it was beginning to look like it, there was a chemistry between them. Diana actually felt happy for them. She actually felt happy for Elwyn! It just didn't seem right.

When they had finished their last dance, a Jive, they left the floor beaming, almost at once they hugged and kissed, but this time it was longer, it was a tender kiss. Andrea stared at Elwyn when the kiss stopped, she had to accept it, she had fallen in love with him and she could tell he loved her. She glanced around and saw Gilbert, Rupert and Bethany giggling. Andrea blushed.

***

After the last final of the evening, there was a Latin dance demonstration by another professional couple, it was very good and again everyone watched the dancers intently. Gilbert said he had seen better, Trevor couldn't believe that and said their dancing was so good he almost cried, again. Andrea remembered dancing against these dance pro's parents! Diana sat next to Annalise who could only stand with difficulty. Even through her make-up she looked pale, but insisted she was feeling better all the time, her hands were cold and clammy, at least she looked happy. Jacob sat on the other side of her, his arm around her shoulder. Diana could see he was devoted to her, she could understand why, but they were still so young, and…and how ill was she?

After the dance demonstration, there was only a few minutes before the presentation of prizes, the time was filled with general dancing. Bethany and Dan hurried out and enjoyed the music.

Andrea watched her daughter. Hmm, nice posture already and very good sense of timing. It was hard to believe Bethany would be off to university before too long, and would she move in with Dan? Andrea felt a little shocked as she considered this, but the answer was probably yes. Though Dan lived with his parents, so with a bit of luck... Andrea quite liked Dan, a nice lad. She had got to know him fairly well over the weekend, and a dancer too, but was he good enough for her little girl? Probably not, he had a lot to prove.

But Bethany wasn't a little girl any more. She was taller than Andrea, stunningly attractive, elegant, intelligent. Andrea was very proud of her. Of course, she was relieved she had a boyfriend her own age, only a few months before it was so different, so frighteningly different.

The prize presentation ceremony was quite business like. The managing director of the firm that sponsored the competition was brought onto the dance floor, he looked nervous, but cheerful. The first prizes were for the Ballroom events, starting with Beginners. The under 35's Beginners event was called first, Trevor was very excited and didn't seem to know what to do, Diana hung on to him and tried to keep him calm, waste of time! He couldn't wait for their result. She hoped he wouldn't be too disappointed with sixth, which she felt was what they would get.

Now it was the Senior Beginner result. It didn't help that the results were given in reverse order. Sixth place was called, it wasn't Trevor and Diana, she was surprised. Then fifth, still they weren't called, by now Trevor was a nervous wreck. Fourth, then third, they realised they must be either second, or…

Now Diana was excited, she couldn't speak.

'Second place, from Worcester…' said the man on stage.

'Oh my God!' said Diana, 'that means we must have won!'

Yes, they had. Everyone went wild, Trevor began to cry, again. 'We're the best Beginners in Britain! If only mum could see this!' he blubbed.

They were called out for their prize, but it took some time for them to compose themselves.

Diana was very happy, she too was crying, as much for Trevor as for the joy of the moment. As they took their place in the line up, she realised that everyone in their party, even Gilbert, was now on the floor taking their picture, so was Elwyn. Had she really been married to him? She even quite liked him now! Diana was sure she would wake up in a moment and this would all have been the longest and best dream she'd ever had, and the crack in the bedroom ceiling would still be there. But she didn't wake up, it was real, she was holding the trophy with Trevor.

The next result they were all interested in was the Senior Pre-championship Ballroom, it was the very last result in the Ballroom section, by which time Elwyn and Andrea were tense. Gilbert stood next to Andrea, held her hand, Bethany stood just behind her with Dan, hand-in-hand of course. Rupert was next to Elwyn, they were chatting, but Elwyn was really not in the mood to talk, Rupert didn't notice.

Again, the results were in reverse order. Elwyn and Andrea felt considerable relief not to be called for sixth place, so it would be fifth, that was fair, it still meant they had beaten a very good couple and…another couple was called out for fifth.

'You two alright then?' said Neil Kirkby breezily, grinning as ever, he had suddenly turned up alongside them.

They nodded dumbly.

Forth place was called, but not Andrea and Elwyn, it had to be third, that was a brilliant result, far more than they hoped they would achieve and…

'You two danced really well today, I knew you would, well done, told you it was the right thing to dance here didn't I?' said Neil, jerking a thumb toward the dance floor.

'Into third place…' said the man on stage.

Andrea, still in her Latin dance dress, began to move toward the floor.

'From Brighton…'

Must be second then, she thought. What a fabulous night they were having! She hadn't dared hope they could be placed as high as second.

Neil was talking to her and Elwyn, but she couldn't hear what he was saying. He gave her a kiss, shook Elwyn's hand and stood to one side.

Long seconds later, the announcer said: 'Into second place…'

'Got to be us,' said Elwyn. Andrea nodded. No one dared speak.

'… from Edinburgh…'

Everyone around them screamed and cheered, there was a lot of kissing and hugging again, Neil rushed up and joined in, did he ever stop grinning?

They hushed everyone so they could listen to the man on stage call out their names, just in case there had been some mistake.

'And the winners, from Newport, number *fifty…*'

No mistake. There were more tears.

Diana actually felt proud of Elwyn and especially of Andrea.

'Oh, if only her mother could see her now,' cried Gilbert.

'That'll be us next year!' said Bethany to Dan.

'I hope not,' said Dan, 'they're Seniors! Is going out with you going to age me that fast?'

'You know what I mean! Oh, this is so cool, I've got to get their picture,' and rushed off with her phone.

Andrea and Elwyn strode out to get their trophy, it seemed very large, they shook hands with the dignitary. He gave Andrea a peck on the cheek, probably not a nice experience for him given that she was still crying and sweaty. They were directed by the cheerful official photographer to stand either side of the dignitary. Andrea found she had a bouquet of flowers, she didn't remember being given it, Elwyn had the trophy. It was their turn to see all the flashing lights of cameras from the official photographer and their friends and family. Finally they went along the presentation line to congratulate and be congratulated. More photographs.

Back at the side of the floor, it all seemed so magical, unreal. They talked to everyone, laughed and described how they felt.

Someone said: 'Shh!' They had all forgotten the Latin results, soon Diana and Trevor would hear how they got on in their other final, it was bound to be an anti-climax.

They all laughed and joked, still discussing Elwyn and Andrea's win as the Senior Beginner's Latin result was announced. Despite being hushed, they were chatty and divorced from the rest of the evening. Diana and Trevor realised that the man on stage had already called out couples into sixth to forth places, so they were at least third. Diana didn't believe this and insisted that they had missed their names being called, they had to have been sixth, but there were three couples out there already, obviously a mistake.

'Into third place…'

'Trevor, go and ask if there's been a mistake,' insisted Diana.

'No love, don't be silly…'

'…from Hull…'

'Ooh, we're not third either!' said Trevor, rubbing his hands.

They were second, it was still a wonderful result and no anti-climax.

A little later they all gathered around Jacob and Annalise. She was able to stand now, all be it rather unsteadily, her colour was better. Diana was still worried. Jacob had his arm around her, it was more to support and steady her than affection.

'In sixth place...' said the man on stage.

Jacob and Annalise looked nervous, no one spoke.

'...from Leeds...'

He steadily worked through the places.

They began to dare to hope, to hope that they might have...

'...into second place, from...'

From where, Newport?

'...from Newport...'

'Aww! I thought they'd won!' said Trevor.

Diana was very disappointed and went to sympathise with Jacob and Annalise, but they were hugging and crying, delighted.

'Never mind love, second is really brilliant.'

'No mum! We've won it, we've won!'

'But he just said...'

'We're not listed as coming from Newport, we're down as being from Nottingham, where we're at uni', we've won!'

Diana stared at the dance floor, a couple she knew slightly that went to another dancing school in Newport walked confidently up to be presented with their prize for coming second.

'That Rumba won it for you!' said Trevor.

'And winners of the under 35's Intermediate Latin, from Nottingham...'

Jacob led Annalise to the dance floor, but she stumbled and sprawled forward. He grabbed and saved her. Unsteadily, she made it to the dignitary, but Jacob held her up. At least they looked very happy. Diana was so proud, so happy.

There wasn't too long to wait for the Senior Pre-championship Latin result, oddly, to Andrea, it didn't seem to matter, they had won the Ballroom event, nothing could top that. She was worn out, her senses were in overload.

The usual tense silence filled the ballroom as the man on the mike began to read out who had taken sixth place, not Andrea and Elwyn.

It seemed to take a long time for him to get to third, the place that Andrea and Elwyn agreed was probably theirs. The man on stage didn't agree. Instead he called them out for second place. But that didn't matter, it was still considerably better than they had dared hope for.

'We'll have to have a party!' said Trevor.

'Not tonight we won't, not in our hotel, we'll get kicked out, besides, have you seen the time? And what about poor Annalise?' moaned Diana.

'Mum, I'm starving,' Rupert rubbed his stomach.

'Good point,' said Trevor, 'so am I, we haven't eaten anything all day!'

'Yes we have, tea time, pizza, and you've been stuffing biscuits as if they're going out of fashion,' insisted Diana as she packed up.

'How about a curry?' said Jacob.
'Great idea!' said Elwyn.
'You don't like curry!' said Diana.
'Yes I do, always have.'
'Not when we were married you didn't.'

'I did, but you never liked them, so that was that. Anyway, there's a place near by, let's go there,' said Elwyn.

Diana realised yet again that she didn't actually know that much about Elwyn, but she was learning fast.

'What about the party?' asked Trevor. 'Why don't we make it a combined house-warming, Christmas, winning all these prizes and…and…' said Trevor.

'And what?' asked Diana.

'Oh, I'll think of something.'

Everyone thought it was a great idea and as they went to change plans took shape very quickly.

When they got outside, they found it literally freezing. Elwyn and Trevor were sent to the hotel to get the cars, before long they were packed in uncomfortably and searching for an Indian restaurant. The one Elwyn had spotted was full, but they found a Chinese one instead. They had a happy time, other dancers arrived, it began to feel like a party. Having eaten something Annalise seemed a little stronger. Diana was relieved. Annalise refused to let the 'virus' ruin the evening.

When they got back to the hotel it was another matter, Annalise started to climb the stairs, but stumbled, thankfully there was a lift, it worked, reluctantly. Diana was still minded to insist Annalise go to A&E, but she lost the 'discussion'.

Noisily, too noisily, they giggled and chattered their way to their rooms. Bethany went into the room and left her mum to say goodnight with Elwyn.

They had been arm in arm almost constantly since they had returned from the Latin presentation line. Bethany had noticed and thought it was cool.

Andrea hadn't really noticed, she was just so happy. Even as they talked about dancing, the competition, the win, the Latin result, everything, Elwyn held Andrea's hand.

'Elwyn, thank you for today,' said Andrea earnestly.

'No thank you! We're quite a team aren't we?'

She agreed. 'What time is it, I haven't got my watch?'

'Oh, it's half past one!'

'Better get to bed then! Long drive tomorrow and the weather's likely to be bad.'

Even so, neither seemed keen to say a final goodnight.

Eventually the bedroom door opened, Bethany peeked out and said quietly: 'Elwyn, will you kiss her good night and let her get to bed! I'm trying to get to sleep and there's no chance with you two making your minds up about having a kiss!'

Andrea was fairly sure she had never been so shocked, Elwyn laughed nervously. The door shut. He looked at Andrea, he was blushing.

'May I kiss you?'

She nodded, they kissed. It was beautiful, very beautiful.

Long seconds after the kiss ended, Elwyn whispered goodnight, kissed her hand and began climbing the creaking stairs to his room.

'He kissed you then?' said Bethany, she was lying on her side, snuggled up in the single bed.

'Umm, no, umm, well, sort of, yeah, he did, you know, friendly kiss, umm.'

'I'm really glad you've fallen in love again mum, night.'

'Don't be silly! Love Elwyn? That's silly.'
'Hmm, it's not though is it? Night.'
Perhaps it wasn't after all, something she pondered as she took her make up off.

Chapter Eleven
Celebrate!

They were noisy at breakfast, laughed a lot, swapped stories about what had happened the day before. It seemed a great shame that they had to go home, to reality. No one really noticed, except Bethany, that Elwyn, who sat with Andrea, held hands with her under the table.

Annalise looked very much better, though Jacob said she had slept so deeply that he had had trouble waking her. It was more like that she had passed out rather than just being asleep, but it had at least done her good. Diana was relieved that they had agreed to come back to Newport, at least she could see that Annalise would go to a doctor. She made an excuse that she wanted their help preparing for the party.

Dan turned up at the hotel as they were loading the cars. Bethany said a cheerful, then tearful good bye.

'You're going to spend the whole trip home texting him and you've got a lesson with him tomorrow evening,' moaned Andrea, 'he's not going off to join the Foreign Legion!'

'What's the Foreign Legion, Elwyn?' asked Rupert.

Gilbert smiled. 'He's bonded very nicely with Elwyn hasn't he?'

'What? Oh, yeah, I think he has…pass me your case dad.'

'He needs a father figure in the house.'

'He's got you.'

'I mean in your house, someone to be his dad, he's at an awkward age.'

'Every teenage year is awkward! Okay, pass me that case now please dad…no, that one.'

'True, but it's nice that you've found Elwyn, it'll be good for Rupert.'

'He's my dancing partner dad, he hardly ever comes round the house, hardly a role model for the boy!'

'Oh, I think he will be.'

'How d'you mean dad? Damn, broken a nail.'

Gilbert laughed dryly. 'You're in love with him aren't you, he's certainly in love with you, that's obvious.'

Andrea blushed, again. She found herself lost for words and stood opening and closing her mouth like a gold fish.

'He's selling his house isn't he? Well, why don't you suggest he moves in with you?'

'Dad! That's ridiculous!'

'Really? I don't see why.'

Elwyn drove the first half of the journey, Andrea fell asleep, though she was aware that Rupert and Elwyn were chatting quietly. She didn't register much of it, but it did include his history assignment, what he thought of one of his teachers, his present list for Christmas and something about a computer game.

Trevor had to do all the driving. Diana was wide awake and chatted happily to Gilbert and Bethany about the competition and the party, plans for which seemed to be getting more elaborate all the time.

They stopped for coffee, it was snowing slightly. Diana watched Annalise walk across the car park, she was more steady today, though clung onto Jacob firmly.

Andrea drove the next leg. Elwyn and Rupert were in deep discussion about just about everything. The latest topic was his house and how he had put it on the market.

'Where are you going to live?' checked Rupert.

'Don't know yet. I'll start looking seriously next week, there's no rush, it'll probably take months to sell my place. This is a bad time of year to sell houses, especially when they need a lot of work doing on them like mine.'

Rupert pondered this for a while.

'What if you had someone that wanted to buy your house, like, now, what would you do then?'

'Umm, probably rent somewhere, or just buy one that seemed suitable and available, but it won't happen.'

'It could though couldn't it? It happened with aunty Diana's house, she had to move very quickly.'

Elwyn had to agree.

'Well, you could always move in with us,' said Rupert casually.

Andrea nearly crashed the car. 'Rupert! You're very rude! You've embarrassed Elwyn! Sorry about that.'

Elwyn didn't really know what to say. He shrugged and said he didn't mind. In fact it sounded like a rather nice idea, particularly after that kiss last night, of course, he didn't say that.

***

After the magic of the weekend, reality, and the weather, was cold and hard. Annalise was taken to the doctor by Diana. The doctor agreed with Annalise, it was a virus. It had hit her harder because her immune system was weaker, and of course student life didn't help. Jacob and Diana were relieved, it wasn't…it wasn't as bad as it could have been. Though they would have to wait for the result of tests. Even so the doctor was fairly confident that Annalise didn't have anything really to worry about.

The party was planned for the following Saturday, not much time to prepare, but they didn't want to leave it too long after the wins. Each evening Trevor worked around the house, finishing decorating and repair jobs that suddenly needed doing. They thought they had just about finished, but no, something else needed doing. Besides, Diana wanted the place looking perfect for the party. Jacob said he would help, but was no use as a handyman. Annalise happily painted what ever needed it. She helped in the kitchen and went shopping with Diana, the food for the party began to take over the house.

'Bloody hell Diana, since when did this become a Tesco warehouse? Look at all this stuff! How many have you got coming to this party?'

'You know how many, but some of it'll be for Christmas too, and we've got the kids staying with us.'

'Kids? Annie and Jake? She hardly eats enough to keep a fly alive and Jake's not exactly at risk of becoming obese. Well, he will be if he eats all this!'

'Don't call her Annie, you know she hates it!'

'She doesn't hate it, you do! Anyway, I got the party poppers, and I asked the neighbours either side to come in for the party…'

'There, told you, just as well I've got enough food in isn't it?'

'There'll be three of them love, not the whole street!' Trevor sighed. 'Umm, want the Christmas deckies up?' he asked hopefully

'Ooh yes, it'll make it really special. I was thinking, well, umm, shall we get a real tree? I scrapped mine, it was a tiny, ancient artificial thing and would be lost in this place.'

'Awww, that would be great! Mum never liked decorating the house for Christmas, we never had a real tree. The one we did have was pathetic and I had to leave putting it up until Christmas Eve too. Let's go pick one now!'

Like two kids, they ran off to get their coats, then the next stop was somewhere that sold Christmas trees!

***

Andrea found herself thinking a lot about Elwyn and not just as a dancing partner, had she fallen in love with him? It seemed everyone thought so, of course they were wrong, but she did like him…good kisser too.

She hadn't seen much of him in the couple of days since getting home. He was busy at work and was trying to get the house respectable in case anyone did come to see it, plus he had started house hunting. They had planned to compete the following weekend near London, but decided the party was a better idea. Their next competition would now not be until early January. They could afford to let up on training, besides, they felt they deserved a rest after winning in Southampton.

The trophy had pride of place in Andrea's living room, she couldn't stop herself admiring it every time she passed. They did go to practice at

Alex and Simon's school the Wednesday after they got back from Southampton. As usual Andrea picked Elwyn up from his house, he seemed flustered.

'What's wrong?'

'Oh, just had a phone call from the estate agent, someone wants to look around the house tomorrow evening!'

'That's quick, I never thought you'd get a buyer this side of Christmas.'

'He's only going to have a look around. I can't see it turning into a sale. Anyway, when he sees it I bet he'll turn his nose up, it's such a wreck.'

'It's not that bad, you've done a lot of good work on it. It looks lovely from the outside.'

Elwyn grudgingly agreed, though listed all the things he knew either needed doing now, or would need fixing in the near future.

'Well, I wouldn't be too negative and I certainly wouldn't tell this bloke all you know is wrong with it. That's his problem, let him find it, don't put him off!'

Practice turned into a relaxing evening chatting to the other dancers, Alex and Simon about how Southampton had gone. It was what they both needed, when they did dance it was for fun.

Alex smiled approvingly as they gracefully danced a Foxtrot, not an intense competition standard performance, but relaxed, full of dancing jokes.

'Oh, look at them Simon, they're in love!'

He squinted at them, pondered what he saw for a moment, then said: 'I think you're right! That should improve their Latin dancing!'

***

The party seemed to start early at Trevor and Diana's, the guests began arriving from late afternoon. Diana had asked the girls from work, they were amongst the first to arrive and, despite being 'glammed-up' they helped in the kitchen.

Andrea, her sister, Elwyn, Rupert, Gilbert and Bethany came in a taxi. Dan was invited and duly arrived to become inseparable form Bethany for the rest of the evening.

Andrea realised Elwyn was pre-occupied. 'Something wrong?'

'Well, no, but at the same time, yes! You know that chap that came to see the house the other night? He wants to buy it!'

'See, told you! Are you accepting the offer?'

'No, it's too low, but the agent seems to think he'll make a reasonable one.'

'Better start trying to find you somewhere to live then!'

Elwyn nodded reflectively. 'He's a property developer, the agent says he won't expect me out immediately even if he does buy it, so there's probably no rush.'

'Seen anywhere you like yet?'

'Not really, I haven't even had a chance to go and look at the ones I have thought worth a visit. Mind you, I went past one on the way home the other night, the house is fine, but the area is vile, so that's now off my list.'

They carried on discussing dancing and the house.

Before long the party was going well, Diana was laughing a lot, they had a few party games, but a lot of the time they all just seemed to chat, eat and relax. Annalise played Classical guitar beautifully, it seemed almost immoral to play charades after that. They all sang carols, though as the evening went on and the wine flowed, the tunefulness and accuracy of the singing reduced.

Bethany and Dan came over to Andrea, they looked excited.

'Ooh mum, you two holding hands again I see! You make a lovely couple.'

Andrea hadn't actually noticed she was holding hands with Elwyn, in fact she was snuggled up against him. She gave Bethany a withering look, but just got a giggle back.

'So what are you two up to?' asked Andrea, trying to sound normal.

'We've got some really great news for you!' said Bethany.

Oh God, she's going to say she's engaged isn't she? thought Andrea.

'Dan's applied to the amateur governing body to come down a competition grade next year so he can do comps with me, and we've decided to do our first one next month. We thought we'd come with you and Elwyn when you go to Bath to compete, what do you think?'

Compared to what she thought she was going to say, this sounded just fine. She said she was delighted, though now thought it was far too soon for Bethany to start competing and tried to put it tactfully to them. Of course it had no effect, so she just discussed dance dresses, again.

Gilbert got to his feet and tapped his wine glass until he had everyone's attention.

'Right everyone, I'd like to propose a toast! To Diana and Trevor, good luck in their new home!'

'You should have proposed that,' said Diana's mother to Diana's father.

'And I'd like to propose a toast too!' said Trevor, 'to Andrea and Elwyn, congratulations on your results in Southampton!'

For the next few minutes toasts were proposed in quick succession, firstly to Trevor and Diana for their results, for Annalise and Jacob for their win, to everyone for Christmas, and so it went on until they were all giggling too much to carry on.

Trevor had been very happy all evening, too happy it seemed to Diana, but she was busy, having a good time and guessed this was the first time Trevor had had a party since he was a kid. But he also seemed nervous. Time and again he came up to her, obviously wanting to ask her something, but then changing his mind, or getting distracted.

Andrea had sat next to Elwyn all evening. She could tell he was worried about the house sale and the more he talked about it, the more it was obvious he was worried about finding somewhere to live. He had no real idea about the sort of place he wanted.

'Well, why not move in with me?' she said casually.

Elwyn nearly dropped his wine. 'That's really kind, but you don't have that much room in your place. You haven't got a spare room, where would I sleep?'

Andrea laughed. 'Actually, I was thinking you could sleep with me.'

Now Elwyn did drop his wine, thankfully it wasn't red.

After the initial shock, they decided on a plan. They would look for a house big enough for them and the kids, but also for Gilbert. He had started talking about wanting to move into a retirement home. This had shocked and worried Andrea and her sister. Andrea had no intention of letting him feel he wasn't important to her or wanted.

'Umm,' began Elwyn sounding embarrassed, 'and does this mean you, umm, that you, sort of like me?'

She laughed. 'Of course I do, and do you sort of like me?'

He nodded enthusiastically and they hugged.

Bethany was watching and giggled.

They didn't hear Rupert say: 'Gross!'

A little later, some of the guests began to talk about the time and that they would have to go soon.

Trevor looked worried, went over to Diana: 'Have you got a minute love?'

'Oh, yeah, no problem, what's the matter?'

'Nothing, I just want to show you something.'

'What?'

'Come and see!' Now he seemed remarkably calm.

He led her to the Christmas tree, it was too big, but they hadn't cared and it was smothered with decorations.

In front of the tree he called out for everyone's attention.

'Thank you everyone. Thank you for coming…Happy Christmas!' now he looked very nervous. Diana stared at him, she knew she shouldn't have let him have that last glass of port.

With everyone looking at him, he fumbled in his pocket. 'Umm, I had it all planned about what I was going to say tonight, you'd have loved it. But I can't think of any of it now!'

Everyone laughed politely.

'Anyway, you are all very important people to me and to Diana and I wanted you here at this special time.'

'What special time?' asked Diana.

He turned to her, smiled, then opened his hand, there was a ring. Trevor went down on one knee.

'Diana love, will you marry me?'

She stared at the ring. Some people in the room cheered, some gasped, someone clapped.

'About time too!' yelled her mother.

Diana took the ring from Trevor's shaking hand.

'Yes love, yes I will!'

Then everyone cheered, then gathered around the happy couple, congratulating them, no one wanted to leave now. Neither Trevor nor Diana knew where it came from, but champagne appeared and was handed around liberally.

***

The last of the guests had gone, the cleaning up would wait until tomorrow.

In bed, Trevor and Diana couldn't sleep, so they discussed the party and, of course, the engagement and what sort of wedding they would have.

'You're a sly dog Trevor, I didn't see that coming!'

He smirked, then gave her a kiss. 'I was terrified you'd say no in front of all those people.'

'And what if I had?'

'I really don't know. I just knew deep down you'd say yes.'

'Reckon you know me that well do you?'
'I think I do.'
'Well, you're going to have a life time to find out!'

Eventually they settled down. Diana was drifting off to sleep when she thought of something.

'You asked me before didn't you? Asked me to marry you, didn't you?'

He said nothing.

'It was that night a few months ago. You were really odd the next day, you asked me to marry you didn't you?'

'Yeah, but you didn't say anything, so I thought you weren't keen.'

'I'd fallen asleep stupid! I remember dreaming something that included weddings.'

He laughed. 'Well, I thought I was dreaming tonight when you said yes!'

They hugged again.

Just as it seemed they were going to drift off to sleep, Diana heard Trevor say:

'Medal test presentation and Christmas party at Alex's next week! Mustn't forget that. And there's a competition I thought we could do in January at Cirencester, so we'd better book some lessons and get to practice!'

'You and your dancing!'

'No, *our* dancing, from no on it's our dancing! '

'You want to carry on then?'

'Oh yes, particularly now we're national champions,' he said grandly.

'Well, we won a beginners event and second in the other one. I wouldn't call that national champions.'

Trevor would have none of it. 'After all, it's dancing that's brought us together,' he concluded.

He did have a point. She thought back to the night when her mates pushed her into having dancing lessons. She never did get to meet Anton, and Trevor seemed a rather strange consolation prize! Though she was now rather glad she had let herself be talked into going dancing.

'I'll get us breakfast in bed tomorrow,' said Trevor excitedly, 'what would you like?'

Diana had a feeling that that was one offer Anton was never likely to make her. She touched her engagement ring. It didn't fit that well, but it was still there and she was so happy. And to think she had tried to get out of going to that first dance class, if only she had known how it would turn out.

'Just toast love…and a kiss from you would be fine.'

The End

Printed in Great Britain
by Amazon